i

DEFENDING INFINITY

Ken Janjigian

Pocol Press

POCOL PRESS
Published in the United States of America
by Pocol Press
6023 Pocol Drive
Clifton, VA 20124
www.pocolpress.com

Publisher's Cataloguing-in-Publication

Janjigian, Ken.

    Defending infinity / Ken Janjigian. – 1st ed. – Clifton, VA : Pocol Press, 2008.

        p. ; cm.

        ISBN: 978-1-929763-34-4

        1. Artists--Fiction. 2. Midlife crisis in literature. 3. Self-actualization (Psychology)--Fiction. I. Title.

    PS3610.A545 D44 2008
    813.6–dc22   0804

This is a work of fiction. All the characters and events of the story are the result of the imagination.

Cover René Magritte, "Decalcomanie," 1966.
© 2008 C. Herscovici Brussels / Artists Rights Society (ARS), New York.

Author photo on cover taken by SGJ.

ACKNOWLEDGEMENTS

I would like to thank Aram Arkun (editor) and *Ararat* for publishing an excerpt of this novel (Fall, 2005 issue). I am very grateful to the following people who were supportive and generous early readers: Jeff Tinkham, Soo Choi, Michael Oudyn, and Thomas Pickette. Thank you to singer-songwriter, Brian Webb, for the use of the lyrics to his song, *Shame* (from the album, *Broken Folk*).

I am also thankful for the constant support of my mother, Alice Janjigian, and my parents in India, Satya Ranjan and Purnima Ghosh.

Most of all, I want to thank my wife, Sharmistha, who makes everything possible.

The title of the book was inspired by the unpublished novel, *La Défense de l'infini*, by the French Surrealist Louis Aragon. Only fragments of the once enormous novel exist today.

This book is in memory of my grandfather, Kegam Manasian (1902-2005), one of the last Armenian Genocide survivors.

There's no money in poetry, but then there's no poetry in money, either.

- Robert Graves

It is living and ceasing to live that are imaginary solutions. Existence is elsewhere.

- Andre Breton

PART I
THE BISHOP

I parked the car in front of our house. Unfastening the seatbelt, I noticed that the strap traversing my torso was frayed and cut as if someone had randomly run a razor blade across it. There were drops of blood on the steering wheel, the odometer, and on top of the dashboard. I put my head down onto folded arms resting on top of the steering wheel, closed my eyes and tried to relax. Think of something peaceful. My thoughts quickly digressed into the secret pile of pages locked in a safe in the house. I visualized the growing mountain of words. A few moments of peace undulated in my mind until the throbbing wave of pain in my hands and face rid its presence. I couldn't believe what had just happened. I lifted my head and looked down to the end of our street. I saw some students from the nearby high school walking in a group laughing and cavorting. I noticed one student lagging behind uninvolved in the fun. I wasn't sure if he was with them or separate until someone ahead turned and waved trying to get him to keep up with the group. In moments the group and the laggard were gone, disappearing behind the last house on the street. Everything was now quiet on Church Street. I got out of the car.

I saw Shaillie's car in the driveway. I was glad she was home. I unsteadily walked up the four steps that led to the front porch and put the house key between my thumb and index finger. My hand was trembling as I attempted to slide the key into the keyhole. I couldn't seem to get it in. I moved my eyes closer to the key and concentrated on the path to the hole. I started again, but failed. A drop of blood fell onto the doorknob, quickly disintegrating my focus. I watched the blood-drop slide down the left side of the doorknob and curve underneath. It left a streak in its wake. The color was a dark and foreboding crimson, so unlike the blood in movies. I ran my fingers across my forehead. I could feel cuts and open skin. I put my finger into what seemed to be the largest lesion and felt the subcutaneous flesh. It was spongy and moist with life, making the epidermis seem withered and spurious.

My mind whispered to let go of the macabre digression. I steadied my hand and aimed the key at the hole. It was still quivering despite the attempted focus. I couldn't get the damn thing in, reminding me of my early carnal daze. I sighed and then threw the keys down in anger. I think I was more piqued by failing to put the key in the hole than from the attack I had just endured. As the keys rattled off the wooden slats of our front porch, I banged on the door. The door opened seconds later.

I watched Shaillie's countenance revolt from a smile to see me to eye stretching and jaw dropping shock at my damaged face. She was frozen for a moment, speechless.

"I was attacked," I said.

"You're kidding me. My God!" Shaillie shouted. She seemed like she was going to say more, but stopped herself. She guided me inside our house, leading me to the couch in the living room. She didn't ask any questions. Instead, she transformed into a nurse with Zen focus. She told me to wait one second while she got some supplies and then I could tell her what happened. She returned from the kitchen with a wet washcloth and some first aid materials. After cleaning the cuts and scratches with warm water and gently dabbing them dry, Nurse Shaillie prepared a cotton swab with some antiseptic.

"It's going to sting a bit, sweetheart."

"Go ahead." I would let her do anything to me. She had my trust, complete and pure.

She gently ran the swab along the cuts. In addition to my forehead, there were cuts and abrasions on the bridge of my nose and my cheeks.

"My hands, too," I said.

Shaillie repeated the process. She didn't ask anything while cleaning me up. She just stuck to the task at hand. She'll be a great wife, I thought.

After finishing, she brought me a tall glass of water. "You want something stronger, too?"

"Yes."

Shaillie went to back to the kitchen, got a snifter, and poured a healthy shot of scotch.

"Here, my dear. It's the good stuff."

"Macallan 18?"

"Yes."

I ignored the water and took a healthy blast of my favorite liquor. This was no time to savor it properly, just gulp it down to accelerate the calm.

"Have some water, too, honey. Now, tell me what happened. Who the hell did this to you?" She had revenge in her eyes.

"You're not going to believe it."

"Who did it, Van?"

Shaillie was kneeling beside me, holding my left hand gently between hers. It had stopped shaking. I had a vision of myself on one knee, ring in hand, another trembling yet seemingly perfect, eternal moment, just a few months ago.

I looked Shaillie in the eye briefly in this very imperfect moment. My eyes darted away and latched onto her engagement ring. I didn't say anything. I didn't want to tell her. I wish something else had happened.

"It's ridiculous," I said, diffidently.

"Go ahead, honey. I'm dying to know who did this to you. I'll kill him."

I smiled. "I don't know if it was a *him*."

"What? What do you mean? It was a woman?"

"I don't know. Could have been female."

"Van, what the hell is going on?"

"It wasn't a person."

Shaillie closed her eyes for a moment as if it would help her understand. When she opened her eyes, she said, "So, it was an alien? An animal? Van, out with the truth. Stop playing games."

"A crow." I smiled with embarrassment. I wished it had been some thug who I had wrestled to the ground, but it wasn't it. It was a damn bird and I was no hero.

"You're kidding." Shaillie was now smiling with an appearance of relief.

"No, I'm serious. A fucking crow, Shaillie. Can you believe it? What the hell did I do to the crows?"

She was laughing. I just nodded my head, absorbing the derision. What else could one do when you lose a fight with something that weighs about two pounds? I took another gulp of scotch. I pictured myself in a boxing ring with the crow standing on its skinny legs on a stool between rounds staring at me and readying to fly at me once the bell sounded; ready to dismantle its opponent that outweighed it by nearly two hundred pounds.

"Yeah, I guess it's funny," I conceded.

"Have some water, Van," Shaillie said between giggles. I took a drink of water and then a final beer-like gulp of the high end Macallan 18.

"I'm sorry, honey." She got control of herself, temporarily. "So, how did the fight happen? Who started it?" She asked, as more laughter broke through her attempt to be sober.

I waited a bit. It was comical, but painful comedy. "Are you done, yet?" I asked.

She took a deep breath. "Yes, yeah, I'm sorry. I know it's not funny, just look at you."

3

"No, it is funny. It's absurd. Theatre of the absurd, starring an Armenian and a crow. Beckett would be having a laugh right now if there were an afterlife."

"So, tell me exactly how you got into this absurdity. What happened?"

"I was at a red light down by the library on Concord Ave. I notice a crow fly off a telephone wire heading directly at the car. As if he'd been waiting for me to arrive and we had an appointment. I keep telling myself that he's going to veer off. Birds don't fly into cars. Except for this one! He flies right through the open passenger window and careens into my closed window."

"I have never heard of such a thing."

"Damn crow must have been anti-Armenian," I said.

"Yes, Van, it had to be a Turkish crow," Shaillie wryly played along.

"Of course. I never thought of that. Probably flew in from Istanbul just to get me. A descendent of Ottoman ravens and probably..."

Shaillie interrupted me before I could digress into my grandfather and the long, tragic plight of Armenians. She knew where I was headed. "So, what happened next, Van?"

"Probably not Istanbul. Their crows might be urbane and cosmopolitan. This must have been from Southern Turkey. Armenian land that..."

"Van!"

"Ok, ok. So, the damn bird falls into my lap. I don't know what the hell to do. He was knocked out, or so it seemed. I didn't want to touch the thing. You know how birds kind of frazzle me. But I have no choice. The damn thing is huge for a bird, black and scary looking. Big, pointy beak, sharp as a Bowie knife. Deep, dark, cold eyes like a shark. My heart's pounding, but I reach down to pick him up and he comes back to life in a wild and furious reincarnation. He's flapping his wings trying to fly and keeps going into my face, claws first. I'm swiping at him and he just keeps coming at me like he's Joe Frazier in his prime. I try to push and slap him away, but he's poking at me with his beak. The damn thing hurts like hell. The beak is shredding my skin like a scalpel, and the claws are slicing and puncturing anything they can grip. A couple times he got my fingers inside his mouth. Look at them."

I showed Shaillie my right hand again. My index and middle fingers looked as if they had been gnawed. They were puffy, bloody and turning black and blue. I could feel my pulse beating in my fingers.

"Van, maybe we should go to the hospital."

4

"No, no. I'll be fine. Nothing is too deep. It looks worse than it is."

"Are you sure?" Shaillie asked skeptically.

"Absolutely. You're better than any half-ass, emergency room resident. Doctors are a joke these days. We'll be there for hours anyway waiting for machines to tell the doctors what to do. You and Mr. Macallan will do just fine. Old school and much more bedside manner."

"And then? How'd you get him off you?"

"I realize I'm not going to swat him away. I try covering up with one hand and reaching for the door with the other, but I can't find the handle. Then, suddenly, the door opens. The guy behind me at the light had come over. As soon as he opened the door, the crow flew away."

"My God! Van, that's horrible. It's like the Hitchcock film."

"That's the first thing the guy said to me. I was thinking Edgar Allan Poe."

Shaillie was shaking her head and wasn't laughing anymore.

I picked up the empty snifter and took a sip of fumes. "I'll be fine, honey. Nothing's too deep. Superficial cuts. I'm more shaken up and embarrassed than hurt."

"Unbelievable, Van."

"What luck! Damn crow is a poster child for bad luck," I said.

"Maybe not." Shaillie took the snifter and poured me a refill. I shut my eyes and tried to allow the alcohol to soothe my pinball nerves. I could feel the pacifying warmth of good scotch, images of the rolling green hills of the Scottish highlands with bagpipes blowing in the distance danced momentarily in my internal vision. I wished we were in Europe. Every situation for me lately was a call to go elsewhere, to go to Europe. Imagining Europe in a romanticized, mythical way relaxed me. My heart was slowing down. Scotch, Shaillie, and escapism were a potent and magical amalgam.

"Who's Joe Frazier? Shaillie asked, handing me the glass of scotch,a half-pour. I took a proper sip this time.

"A boxer from the Ali days," I said. "Smokin' Joe. Ali gets all the credit, but Joe was damn good. Just not as pretty or poetic."

She nodded, uninterested.

"So why not? Why isn't the crow bad luck?" I asked.

"It's just kind of ironic. Ironic that it was a crow."

Of course it was, I thought. Shaillie loved irony. There was irony in everything for her. It seemed like everyone these days was looking for ironies upon ironies within further ironies as if direct and straightforward communication had been rendered anachronistic. We were the ironic generation.

Shaillie leaned over and kissed my forehead and then lips. "Take a rest sweetheart. We can postpone the irony. When you wake up, I'll have a special dinner waiting for you."

I nodded and finished the second snifter of Macallan at a more dignified pace. I didn't want to get drunk, just relieve the pain and anxiety, while diluting the humiliation. The adrenalin was fading and fatigue quickly replaced it. I was suddenly exhausted. Sparring with a crow was tough work.

When I woke up, the TV was on, the volume down. I recognized the ivy of Wrigley Field. Nomar Garciaparra was outside the batter's box beginning his ritual. He tapped his cleats several times trying to get his toes to the end of the shoes. He adjusted his sweatbands up and down his forearms until they were right back to their original position. Nomar then went to work on his batting gloves. He had to get his fingers to the end. He pulled hard on the base of the gloves while pushing his hand inside the glove as if he were trying to burst his fingertips through the leather. Push and pull. Extremities to the extremes. He wiped under his terrifically Roman nose with the back of his index finger then ran the back of his hand along his chin. He took a few practice swings before putting his right foot into the batter's box, gingerly as if he were testing the cold waters of Cape Cod in late spring. His left foot eventually followed, the tip of his shoe used like a pick to dig a hole, heel settling down. Nomar was finally ready to hit. He stared at the enemy, bat cocked and ready. After all the methodical and meticulous preparation, he swung instantly at the first pitch, flying out routinely to centerfield.

"He always does that," I said, shaking my head. "First damn pitch. All that build up for nothing. Why won't he take a few pitches, Shaillie? He refuses to evolve. Stuck in the same damn routine. Change can be a good thing Nomar," I said as if he could hear me.

"I'm more concerned about you than Nomar's routine. How you feeling, honey?" Shaillie asked.

"Just 'cause he won those batting titles doesn't mean he can't change things. The pitchers are adapting and he's stuck in the same swing-at-the-first-pitch mentality. Life is about change. Baseball's no different."

"How are you feeling, Van?" She asked a little more loudly this time.

I sat up. "I'm ok. Scotch helped and so did you. You're my Clara Barton, except you're a hell of lot better looking."

Shaillie smiled while checking the cuts on my hand.

6

"I'll tell you, Shaillie, Nomar killed me with the Sox, now he's killing me with the Cubs."

"So, you seem better. Are you hungry?"

"Yeah, I can eat."

"Let me take a look at your facial wounds, soldier."

"Soldier," I sighed, "in an avian war."

"It must have been scary, bird or no bird. I was imagining it while you were sleeping. I shouldn't have laughed at you. I'm sorry, Van. If that had happened to me, I would have freaked out. You were pretty calm, all things considered."

"I guess so. It was and wasn't funny."

I noticed the score of the game. The Cubs were losing 4-2 to the Cardinals. All birds have it in for me today. I had become a Cubs fan this year after a life long commitment to the Red Sox. One of many changes in my life.

"I'll clean and dress them again after dinner. I think you'll be all right. No hospital needed."

We sat down at the table. Shaillie had cooked my favorite dinner—steak smothered in a sauce of olive oil, red wine, black olives, and mushrooms. White rice and black beans on the side. There was an open bottle of red wine on the table. I looked at the label. A Portuguese red from the Dao region. Another favorite. I poured each of us a glass.

"To the mighty and mad crow and Edgar Allan Poe." We toasted.

Shaillie put the Cubs game on the small kitchen TV.

"Sweetheart, this is great," I said.

"Is it cooked right? I'm not used to grilling. I never do it. It's your area."

I cut into the steak. It was a bit overcooked. Pink in the middle. I liked it rare. "Perfect," I said.

"You're being kind, but it's pretty close."

We ate and made small talk. She told me about her day at work and one of her co-workers who was sleeping with a married man. We took pauses when something happened in the Cubs game. Shaillie was also a baseball fan. Her father had gotten her into it many years ago. She was still a Red Sox fan and thought I was ridiculous for jumping ship after the Sox finally broke the curse and won the World Series. "Armenians should be Cubs fans," I had told her.

"What if the Cubs win?"

"Short-term pleasure and then what? However, I'm not too concerned about that reality."

After dinner we moved into the living room. We sipped the last parts of the Portuguese red as I waited for Shaillie to venture into the inevitable irony. I knew a heavy conversation was looming. It was hovering in the air as quietly and subtly as a helicopter. Couples could sense their next moves, their next words. Layered patterns tamped indelibly in concrete over many years. All prior chatting had merely been filibuster. Small talk just bought time while silent conversations galvanized strength for exposure. The crow had given me a temporary reprieve, but eventually it would be utilized as a catalyst for some things on Shaillie's mind. Some things on our collective mind. We had a lot going on and the crow wouldn't be a random event for Shaillie. Nothing was arbitrary for her. She dutifully subscribed to chaos theory—a squirrel kicking up dirt on the run from a predator causes an avalanche in Siberia. Everything random is really deeply rooted and widely connected according to my fiancée. One enormous nexus intertwining everything ironically so.

Shaillie was also an avid bird watcher, an amateur ornithologist. She knew her birds. I knew the random attack by a crow would be great fodder for her philosophy. I was doomed.

Once the workplace adultery story was exhausted, she made her way into crow chaos theories. "Van, you know the fact that you were attacked by a crow is quite remarkable." The filibuster was officially over.

"Yes, ironic, you will say. How so?" I asked.

"Don't be so immediately resistant and harsh. Hear me out."

I nodded.

"Because even though crows have a stigma in literature and movies, they're actually very sweet and big-hearted. Dark and foreboding on the outside, but not inside. It's symbolic racism. Crows are monogamous birds, Van. Loyal to their mates for life."

My eyes opened wide. "I see. So because you think I'm getting cold feet about the wedding, therein lies the irony. The monogamous bird attacks the trepid groom. It's perfect, right Shaillie?"

"Don't be so smug and derisive to my ideas, Van."

I took a deep breath, wondering why I was getting so angry, so instantly. "But there's one problem. I'm *not* getting cold feet. You are projecting. Projecting cold onto my feet and they are offended. They're as warm blooded as any other feet in the engagement world."

I lifted my left foot into the air. "Touch it."

"Van, it's not funny."

"Touch it. Feel the warmth. It's ready to shout I do to my beautiful bride. You can put the wedding band on my ring toe if you'd like."

"Enough with the foot," Shaillie said, head slowly shaking in obvious impatience.

8

"Just touch it and feel the blood flow, honey. Please. It's not cold at all."

"You are such a pain in the ass! Put your foot down!"

"That's what I'm trying to do by raising my foot."

"Van, enough."

With my foot still hanging in the air I went on, "No, I'm tired of irony, sarcasm, allegories, metaphors. All of the indirect and all the analytical analysis. Instinct is not analytical. I'm sick of it. With us and everyone. How 'bout just direct, literal communication. Stop connecting the dots and looking for celestial coincidences. My feet aren't cold. It's that simple."

Shaillie swatted my foot away.

"You're such a hypocrite. What nonsense. You're writing the most cryptic, mystical, indirect communiqué there is."

"That's different. Individual communication is entirely different. Operates on a different geometrical plane."

"Look Van, we don't have to get into it, especially if you are going to mock me and raise your voice. My fears are legitimate. Surely, you can literally see that. Your behavior hasn't been normal lately. Of course, I'll connect that to the wedding. Who wouldn't? I'm human."

"I'm just kidding about the foot. Don't take it seriously."

"I don't think you are."

"Well, we might as well get into it. It's inevitable. I'll say how much I want to marry you and you'll doubt me and bring up the symptoms—the insomnia and its accompanying journal, the change in jobs, my father. The four horsemen of my alleged cold feet. Then I'll defend each of them and you'll tell me why I need to go to therapy and…"

"Are you going to have this conversation by yourself?" Shaillie asked.

I shrugged and thought for a moment. "Schizophrenia is easier. Whole lot of friends and you don't have to go anywhere. Less loneliness and…"

"Look, do you want to talk about it or play games? Talk about indirect communication, Van. It's all jokes to you and so damn hypocritical."

I could feel the tension in my body and I wanted it to stop. I wanted to have a peaceful conversation, but I wasn't sure about my capacity to talk calmly. These conversations always rattled my core.

Shaillie continued, "Those four things are interrelated. Don't you see it, Van? Don't you see how you're overreacting right now?"

I was going to answer, but Shaillie smartly cut me off at the rhetorical pass.

9

"But your father, Van. That's the root of it all, I think. You're not handling it too well. I mean, the problem is you're actually handling it too well. I just think you're hurting a lot more inside than you're letting anyone know. Even yourself. Most importantly yourself. Your emotions are misdirecting your actions."

I shook my head. "Of course, denial. Everyone's favorite word since the entire country has become psychologists. So, I need to create big drama and cry every night."

"No, just once would have been something though."

I thought back to the one time I cried after the funeral was over. After all the social pomp and circumstance of death ended. I never told Shaillie about it. I should have because it would have cut me some slack with her, but I kept it to myself. I wanted it to be private.

"Do you want some Port?" I asked to break the silence.

Shaillie nodded, unenthusiastically.

I poured two glasses of Port that we had gotten at the source in Oporto, Portugal. We'd had a three-week vacation in Portugal a few months before my father passed away. It was the best trip we'd been on since our backpacking trek through Europe at the age of twenty-two, the age of glorious possibilities. Possibilities that I wanted to recover. The Portugal trip, though, had been mesmerizing despite its brevity. An intensely spiritual moment for my godless mind. During the trip, we'd decided to return for our honeymoon, maybe hit Spain and the South of France, too. But I wanted more than a superficial honeymoon trip. I wanted to live abroad with no real plan being the plan. I wanted this conversation to be different. I didn't want to talk about the recent upheavals in my life; quitting a *real* job to go back to bartending; sleeplessness turned into obsessive, middle-of-the-night journal writing—a virtually spontaneous novel of sorts; the loss of my father. I didn't want to talk about any of it. Not at this moment. But I could talk about Portugal. I could talk about escaping to Europe.

"Shaillie, let's go." I said, knowing she wouldn't.

"Huh?"

"Let's go. Let's get out of town and truly travel. No let's sojourn and stay there. Live in Lisbon then Paris. Then we can go to Africa. We have friends in Nairobi and Cape Town. Then, we'll go to Asia and..." I stopped myself as the speed of Shaillie's shaking head increased with each new destination. I should have just focused on Europe. Asking for the world was too much, stick to a continent. I backtracked and told her we'd just go to Europe and do it bourgeois-style like good middle- class travelers. We find a place over there before going, even look for some English teaching jobs. We'd make reservations, get maps, research, buy *Frommers* and all the safe trimmings. The only difference being that we wouldn't come back. Not for a while. I reminded her about how romantic and enchanting Costa do Sol and Lisbon were, how they were still a affordable gems hidden behind Paris, Rome, and London. I brought up how we were never happier traipsing across Europe after college and we caught some of that elusive vibe on the last trip. I wanted to go on and on, but it was turning into a monologue.

"Too much to think about, Van. Too much right now," Shaillie said.

"Think about it, honey. Just consider it. You conceded how magical Lisbon was."

"It won't be magical if we live there. It's only magical in your mind. It will all disappear once it actually appears. "

"You're too cynical. Dream a little. A honeymoon that doesn't end. What's better than that?"

Shaillie laughed. "My Armenian romantic."

"So?" I saw a chink in the armor. Her artist side wasn't fully buried.

"Van, moving to Europe the day after the wedding is too much to plan. Plus, your mother would die if you left."

"She'll be fine."

"She just lost her husband. Her brother had a heart attack that's reduced him to a shadow of himself. And you want her to deal with a son living abroad? You want her to lose three men in her life in one year."

"My brother is here and I won't be lost. I'll be across the pond."

"It's an ocean, Van. A big ocean."

"Look, the world is tiny now. Going to Europe is no big deal. People are booking trips to Mars these days. Europe's nothing. Besides, how long do we have to mourn? Is there some protocol I'm missing?"

"Van, don't be so selfish and cold."

"Like my feet, right? Shaillie, I'm not selfish. I'm just not following some bullshit Dr. Phil book on the steps of grieving. My old man wouldn't have wanted me to do that. He would've voted to live, right? His whole life was about living. Flawed, but passionate living. He was Walt Whitman disguised as a salesman. Willy Loman and Walt Whitman all wrapped up in one convoluted song of himself. How's that Shaillie? Isn't that self-awareness of my father?"

"I don't think he'd advocate you running recklessly overseas."

"I think I'd be doing the same thing with him dead or alive. The insomnia has underpinnings that are wholly disconnected from my father. You refuse to see that. You reduce and over-simplify everything to him. Too damn Freudian. I'm at peace. Why can't you see that?"

Shaillie shook her head, eyes rolling.

11

"Ok, ok, I'm not at peace," I admitted, "not even close, but who the hell is? This little anarchy in my mind is intoxicating and is going to lead somewhere better. Somewhere enlightening — great secular enlightenment — the real kind. I can't explain it, but I feel it."

"You're right. You're not at peace."

"Peace is for death. It's very overrated, Shaillie. Right up there with happiness. But I am at peace with losing my dad. That's what I meant. He's at peace. So, why should I make a big ballyhoo about it? Besides, the eulogy…"

Shaillie pounced. "Because you delivered a eulogy at the funeral? That gave you peace? I know that was immensely powerful, Van, and you were beautiful up there reading Dylan Thomas and eulogizing your dad. I've never been more proud of you than that moment and I'll never forget it, but that moment does not encompass the entirety of grieving. It was five minutes."

"It did for me. You weren't up there."

"I know, but …"

"Shaillie, don't tell me how to grieve. Don't make me feel sad if I am not. Death doesn't have to be sad. It's peaceful. I've let go. He's gone. What am I supposed to fucking do? Feel sorry for myself for twelve months because some cheesy self-help book or afternoon talk show demands a year for the grieving cycle. I prefer a New Orleans funeral. Let's celebrate. It's bad enough I've been a lemming in life. I'm not going to toe the line with death."

"Grieving doesn't mean feeling sorry for yourself. You are so far off-base, Van."

I wanted to say "whatever," but bit my tongue. Words were flying out of my mouth and I wasn't sure what I was saying anymore. Some of it made sense in the moment, but I knew later, upon reflection, it would all strike me as odd and strange, not quite me. It seemed that I hadn't been able to say exactly what I wanted to express in a long time. Speech hadn't mirrored thought in far too long. I couldn't remember the last time.

"Van, whether you admit it or not, there are loose ends with you and your dad that death and eulogies didn't tie up. And this constant invoking of lemmings has got to cease. Everything's lemmings lately."

"Actually, I think the crows have taken over."

"Good, I'll take the crows any day."

We continued on in various directions and digressions. I told Shaillie that there weren't any loose ends. Death is clear without any fraying of the edges. She told me I needed closure on some things, that I'd grieved only intellectually rather than emotionally. I thought I understood what she had meant, but I didn't want to go down the

12

therapy path. It seemed so childish for adults to need a therapist. So pathetic and narcissistic.

I detoured to my preferred path of narcissism.

"What about Portugal? Let's focus on one topic, honey."

"I'm not living in Portugal. I'm not even going to talk about Portugal. You've turned that place into some mystical oz. You are mythologizing it, creating some fantasyland out of a three-week vacation. We will never recapture that vacation. It was special, Van. Let it stay that way. Let it rest in peaceful memory. Moving is the wrong thing to do. In our thirties, we need to do the right thing. We don't have time to screw up anymore."

I hated when she invoked age-related pressure. "We've never screwed up. We have choices, honey, and we can follow instinct for once instead of a plan. This isn't about right and wrong."

"Of course, it is. Every decision is. We analyze instincts rather than chase them. That's what adults do."

I sighed. "You've changed so much, Shaillie."

"You know, I was hoping that the bird would've pecked some sense into you. Instead, it appears to have pecked you further into madness."

"Our plan is what's mad. It's maddeningly boring. Goddamn life of a lemming. It's a pretend life we're heading for, Shaillie. Listen to Picasso's maxim—have only a vague plan of the future. Let's be displaced cosmonauts for a while. An alternate orbit for us. You can paint like you used to, instead of giving tours and all that uncreative curator stuff that you do. People should be looking at your work. I'll pursue some form of creativity. Turn all those sleepless words into something. We're becoming so mediocre. This is about spiritual dystrophy, not my father, Shaillie."

"We're speaking different languages, Van."

I nodded in complete agreement. Everything was coming out tonight. Things we'd only skimmed in other spats were coagulating tonight and I was the catalyst. I couldn't restrain myself. Something within sought to break the fragile levees at our borders. I could feel our own personal Katrina coming. "And your pursuit of a suburban starter house. God, it sounds so fatal. It should be called an end house. Once the mortgage gets us, we're doomed. Living a disinterested life of interest rates."

"What the hell did that crow do to you? It's really accelerated your deviation. I think you've got paramnesia."

"So be it. Reality is constantly a day late and a dollar short. I've unsubscribed from it and I salute all paramnesiacs."

"Van, maybe you just need some sleep. Real deep sleep. Or maybe serving drinks to those foolish hipsters has infected you. Or both."

"They're not foolish. Maybe foolhardy, but not foolish."

"Whatever, the point is that the bartending job has changed you. You're getting caught up in Bishop and Derek's own wayward neurosis. That Bishop is really a mess. An atheist who calls himself a Bishop? God help me! Why don't you see him for what he is?"

"Which is?"

"A drunk."

"He's more than that, but this isn't about Derek or Bishop. Not directly," I said. Shaillie was too damn smart. I both hated and revered how she saw through me. I urged myself to calm down and withdraw, but I wanted some resolution. I wanted to straighten the eternal orbit we were revolving in.

"Sweetheart, listen. Let's just live our own little *La Boheme* for a while. Puccini would be proud."

"I don't give a shit about Puccini or Picasso or any other dead artist."

I continued, "We'll walk the streets of Lisbon and listen to the waves crash along Costa do Sol. Go to Setubal and wake at dawn to see the fishermen head out. Paint and write while the sun rises. Jesus, sweetheart, that's life. Bring it down to its real essences. I can't live in a 401K cubicle anymore. Blame it on Bishop if you want, but it's how I feel. I need to divest."

"Van, you're not even in the cubicle anymore. You quit. Why are you still complaining about that? You're not there. You're behind a damn bar. Now *I* carry the insurance and retirement burden."

"By choice, Shaillie. Let it go. Retirement? Let's not get lulled and lured by that bait. We don't need it now. We're still young. In Portugal we'll get national healthcare. No worries. It's a government that actually gives a shit. Life will be about existence, not accumulation. That's all we have here. Piling up things. Riding the conveyor belt up money mountain. It's time to jump before it's too late."

Shaillie inhaled deeply and exhaled slowly. She was about to say something and then stopped herself.

"You've been co-opted honey," I said, finishing my Port and then pouring a bit more for both of us.

"Really. By whom? *The combine?*" Shaillie snickered, knowing that I loved Ken Kesey's *Cuckoo's Nest* metaphor for the consumptive mainstream.

"Precisely," I said, nary a trace of abashed sarcasm.

14

We were silent for a bit. Time for a pause. I turned my attention back to the Cubs. They had men in scoring position, down a run. Shaillie finished her Port, got up, and started doing the dishes. Nomar was the last chance. After his endless routine, he swung at the first pitch again and he hit a long fly ball. It was caught in front of the centerfield wall, four hundred feet away.

"Jesus, it's tough being a Cubs fan. Nomar still doing his first pitch, impatient bullshit."

"Come back to the Sox. Enjoy the victory," Shaillie said over the sound of running water.

"Can't do that. What's the point?"

I went into the kitchen and rubbed her shoulders as she did the dishes. I didn't want things to come completely apart. Maybe just expand our frontiers. I kissed the back of her neck, slowly going down to her shoulder with my lips and tongue gliding along her soft skin. Her neck arched, goose bumps rose on her skin. I felt guilty for overwhelming her, guilty for the things racing in my head.

"I love when you do that," she said softly.

"Don't worry, honey. I'm just venting. I don't really mean any of it. It's the crow talking. I just need to eat some crow, instead of it eating me." I laughed and she turned around without a smile on her face.

"Van, you need sleep. This whole insomnia thing is getting out of control," she said, while inspecting my cuts.

"Insomnia or its journal?"

Shaillie's brow furrowed. "Its journal? Insomnia is not writing the journal."

"Sometimes I wonder. It's as if it's writing itself. I feel like a conduit."

"From what?" She ran her wet hands through my hair.

"I don't know. I wish it were the cosmos. It's got to be the subconscious. What else is there guiding behavior?" I said.

"The conscious mind if you get some therapy. You're such a candidate for it, but you can't see the forest for the trees."

"I want to see beyond the forest. Therapy will kill that possibility."

"Just try it. It's about honing your internal vision. You'll see better. That's what it's all about."

Before I could reply, Shaillie jumped in, exasperation in her eyes. "Van, look you need to get to the bottom of this thing. It's taking over your life. Our life. We're treading dangerous waters. I can feel it."

"Shailie, I'm not quite sure what's happening, but I'm under some sort of spell. Pages and pages pouring out of me when I can't sleep. Like some hidden spirit that's been lingering unheeded for so long is now howling in the middle of the night. Abstract visions and twisted dreams are pouring onto the page. It's almost a religious feeling."

Shaillie shook her head.

"I feel as though I'm gaining some sort of unity within, but it needs more. It wants to run."

"Just let me read it. It could solve all our problems."

"I can't. It can't be read until it's done."

"You really still haven't glanced at it?"

"Not at all."

"Can't you remember some of it?"

"No. I fall back to sleep when it's done and then it's as if it happened to someone else."

"When will it be done?"

"I don't know. All I know…"

Shaillie put a finger over my mouth. "Let's stop." She rarely ended conversations. She would seek resolution until we had laryngitis, but I could tell from her tone and her eyes that she meant it. I gave her a kiss on the cheek, walked over to our CD player, and pressed play. A copy of *La Boheme* had already been in there. We listened to Puccini, watched the Cubs post-game, and didn't talk the rest of the night.

A few mornings after the crow incident, I was staring at my head in the mirror. The cuts were dry and clean. They were already healing, none of them having been too deep, but I did notice something else that seemed abnormal.

Shaillie was getting ready for work. She had made her lunch, put a mystery novel in her bag, and pulled her cell phone off the charger. We didn't immediately revisit that night. We were usually good about moving on from tension.

Usually.

"Sweetie, I think I have meningoencephalitis," I said with a straight-face.

"What is that? A big head?"

"Yes, and swollen meninges, too."

Shaillie smiled and took a sip of her coffee. "Ok, I'll humor you. What are meninges? Brain tissue or something?"

"Brain membrane."

"Insane in the membrane, like the song."

"Seriously, I think my cerebrum and cranium are swelling up. Maybe from the insomnia or the crow. Look at my head. It's getting

16

bigger, puffy and all soft from the swelling. Feel it. It's full of flowing fluids."

Shaillie laughed and stroked my head softly with her fingertips first and then her palms. "You're fine, besides a few bumps and scratches from the crow. The Muhammad Ali Crow did a job on you, but you'll be fine."

"The Joe Frazier crow."

"Oh, yeah, the Joe Frazier crow from Istanbul."

"Fine, don't take it seriously," I said.

"Van, there's nothing wrong with your skull. The problem is inside your skull."

"It looks bigger to me, that's all."

Shaillie shook her head. She put her coffee down and went over to the computer while I followed. She googled meningoencephalitis. We both read the definition.

"Dr. Arakalian, your diagnosis is ridiculous. The brain and meninges swell. Not your skull. You can't see the swelling."

"Ok, then it's something else. I just used the wrong term. I didn't go to medical school, Shaillie."

"I think the crow has pecked you over the edge. And you know what, the offbeat Armenian thing is no longer cute. It's getting tiresome."

"Shaillie, listen to me. The lack of sleep could be pumping more fluid between my skin and skull. I can feel it, pulsating, you know, like when you sprain an ankle and the blood is rushing to the area. Maybe I have some internal contusions from the crow. I mean I look in the mirror and feel like some cheaply concocted alien in a bad B movie."

"Van, it's not your head, it's your feet."

"Not that again. I know what I feel."

"Did you wake up last night?"

"Yes. The usual time."

"Did you write?"

"Of course."

"Do you want to marry me, Van?"

I hesitated for what I perceived to be a nanosecond. Much too long.

"That's enough of an answer," she concluded.

"I didn't answer. You gave me no time."

"I gave you enough."

"Not enough to answer. I couldn't even move my lips to form a syllable."

"Because you were thinking, hesitating. You shouldn't need any time."

"Of course, one needs time to hear, process, respond."

Shaillie just shook her head. She took a final blast of coffee, grabbed her bag, travel mug already filled with coffee and headed out the door for work.

"Shaillie, listen to my idea first, before you leave."

She turned around quickly, sharply. "I'm tired of your ideas. What is this one about? How you don't want to marry me? How you're supposedly transliterating your damn subconscious. How you want to travel Europe like careless college grads? That's a one-time period in life. You never get it back, Van. Never!"

I repeated her phrase *transliterating the subconscious* in my head. I liked that and wanted to write it down somewhere, but first I wanted to clarify my European plans. I wanted to remind her again of the practical side of the idea, but she cut me off.

She looked me sharply in the eye, silencing me. I was surprised to see tears forming in her eyes.

"Van, I need a good sob before work and I don't need you around to do it. Meningoencephalitis! My God!"

I didn't want to be there for the sob, didn't want to see the first tears Shaillie would shed over this crisis that was completely my own concoction. As if sensing this, Shaillie turned and walked down the front steps towards the driveway, leaving without drama and with melancholic dignity.

I closed the door and thought about how I was still in love with her, just as much as when our love was young and new back in college so many years ago. I wasn't sure why I was letting this concoction swell beyond its necessary proportions. Everything seemed to be taking on an existence of its own momentum. I just couldn't seem to get out of my own way.

This time it seemed that we weren't going to recover so smoothly. Shaillie was not the type of woman to cry easily. She cried for a reason. A die had been cast. Things were unraveling rapidly. I could feel a vague, internal cadence seeking crescendo, seeking audibility, getting too loud to ignore. We are so afraid of the internal crystal ball. Try to run from it, dance around it, look the other way, smash it to pieces, but it's impervious. An unbreakable Humpty Dumpty. It secretly rests in the entrails, nerves, floats along in the blood, along the contours of our thoughts, demanding to be seen when the lazy lag of the mind's eye finally accepts the finish line that could have been crossed so long ago.

The seeds were deeply sown long ago, prior to the actual unraveling. The roots grew strong and potently lethal. So many links and dominoes. Spirituality, another woman, insomnia, the mysterious,

Surrealist-inspired journal, road rage, turning thirty, self-absorption, gray omens, materialism-rex, resisting the sacred and sophomoric twenties, wide-windows of childhood, paternal echoes, starter homes, end homes and everything in between cascading upon consciousness in simultaneous alacrity...

Shaillie knew me better than anyone. Her Arctic feet theory might have had subconscious weight to it. To myself, I admitted the possibility. But these were the elusive, slippery prisms of the subconscious. It was all vague speculation, as precise as a whim. A fisherman casting his line into the deep sea. The world below *see* level so wildly unknown.

This much I did know. The puzzle piece had to be connected with the lack of sleep and its accompanying explosion of words done in the dark hours before dawn. For over three months I'd been religiously and cathartically piling up pages of oblique expressions and confessions, none of which I could accurately describe because I steadfastly refused to read a single word. The process itself was amazingly, if not absurdly, consistent. I usually slept for a few hours and arose shortly before or after three o'clock. I didn't need an alarm. The insomnia was chronologically reliable.

My sleeplessness began a few months back during a spate of frequent dreaming. The dreams seemed loosely connected in story and character. Shaillie was there, my father, the regulars at my new bar job, university friends, an art history professor, and various shadowy figures I almost recognized. Disguised members of memory I surmised. A few nights into this chimerical trend, I sat down at the computer and began writing. The dreams were so potent, so fantastically real, that I just followed their path into words. This wasn't dream analysis. This was dream transcription. All apologies to iconic Freudian logic, but analysis seemed like labyrinthine madness. The real merry pranksters of our hidden internal terrains clearly operated so far beyond rhyme and reason. Any attempt to truly connect the hallucinatory dots seemed like pure tomfoolery. So I chose to respect the pranksters and all their Houdini-meets-Fellini, subterranean-screenplays. Once the dream was reverently exhausted into words, the hazy plot propelled itself forward. I was in a creative trance. I simply peered into the manuscript in my mind and unraveled one of the thousands of scenes imploring exposure. The words flowed with no need to monitor direction. They, too, seemed to have their own momentum and plans. Within two weeks the dreams started to decrease in frequency, but the story had taken hold. I'd awaken and read the last few lines of the previous night's output and I was off. I felt like a conduit between varying levels of consciousness twirling within each other. The real moments of my life began to fade into a manipulated hallucination that dominated my nights into unplanned story lines. Plots that I hadn't lived, but had started living themselves out on the page. Until the page and reality began to seem eerily similar. Eerily surreal.

While it took nearly a decade long gestation period, I believed the immaculate conception of the automatic writing occurred the day I met Shaillie. A day I remember as vividly as yesterday. It was a few weeks into my freshman year in college. I was very unsure of what I was going to study, very unsure of my present, let alone my future—prototypical freshman confusion. However, despite the clear aimlessness, I wasn't indifferent. I just didn't know in which direction to be different. So I decided to engage in a little of everything and be open to all potential roads. I took courses in science, literature, economics, and art, offerings to both cerebral hemispheres trying to summon direction. Much to my surprise, my anxious mind gravitated to the Modern Art History class. I didn't know a damn thing about art, modern or otherwise. I couldn't draw or paint at all, but the fates and psyche sometimes brew a supra-logical potion that can transcend the expected. It wasn't long before I was introduced to Picasso, Braque, Cubism, and my future fiancée, more or less at the same time.

I always arrived at class early, taking a seat in the front row. I only did that in art class. Every other class evolved into a mere distraction to the wonders of those who could create. I wanted to absorb as much as I could about these artists and art movements I'd known so little about. The professor always sat at the rear of the room with a laptop on her desk ready for a narrated Power Point presentation. The lights were dim. A slide of Picasso's *Les Demoiselles d'Avignon* was on the screen just in front of me. Students were filing in while I stared at the five jagged and pointed nude women in Picasso's painting. I took in the crimson left edge, the rich blue in the middle, the sad plaintive faces of three women, and most strikingly, the odd, grotesque faces of the two other women. I tried to absorb the painting, take in the creativity and the energy without quick and obvious analysis. I noticed some fruit, maybe grapes and apples   below the women. A jab at the sterility and dryness of a still life. Of the still life of most of us, perhaps. A possible reference to Eve or the fruits of prostitutes' loins sadly being offered. I let the thoughts rattle and bounce in my head. The distorted and disturbing faces of two of the women began to dominate my gaze. Look beyond that, I thought.

The professor began her lecture, which would be followed by a discussion. I remember that particular lecture better than any of the others. She did a quick review of how the 19th century art movements sowed the seeds of change. Impressionism had initiated the artist's desire to have more control and power of their work. The nascent emergence of the artist finally wresting control over the object being painted. Impressionists did just what their name claimed. The name, in fact, was derisively given by a critic who thought the works hadn't been completed. They were sketches or *impressions* to be finished later. For the first time visible brush strokes could be seen. Artists were capturing the effects of light in color, leaving the colors in an unmixed intensity. Now, the viewer could mix the colors with his or her own eye. The artist and the viewer were now in it together. Reality was being questioned for the first time in Western art. The emphasis was now on the subjective rather than the objective. All along for centuries, for millennia, artists were saluted for their ability to reproduce nature like a photograph. But, of course, photography had arrived for that. Louis Daguerre had unwittingly hastened the arrival of modern art. Monet and Renoir loosened the restrictive seams. Artists were no longer technicians, but true creators. Van Gogh took it further, putting the passion of the artist into his painting like no one else had before him. Munch followed Van Gogh. His *Scream* unleashed the primal agony of modern life into art. The straitjacket was undone. Retinal art, all the art that had innocuously aimed to please our eyes, was rapidly fading into an ancient form.

Outside the art world in 1882 Nietzsche pronounced that God was dead. More importantly, he issued his idea of Eternal Recurrence. There were no other worlds, but ours. No detours to heaven or hell. Humans determined their own salvation or damnation. Existentialism was in its fiery toddler stage while Freud was assembling his notions of the subconscious, which would influence 20th century art more than anything else. Art, philosophy, psychology, and Marxist political theory, all of which were simultaneously seizing power from the divine, from celestial proclamations, and announcing that anything was possible. Anything was imaginable when one looked with new vision. Everything was simmering, implosion lurking around every corner. Jungian synchrony was a marching band heading down Main Street with a thumping, revolutionary drumbeat.

The 19th century led to the Matisse and the Fauvists using colors in unprecedented richness to express emotional and psychic pain. Expressionists seized the baton from Van Gogh and Munch. It was all about artists imposing themselves upon the object. It was all about the artist's state of mind. Then, along came Picasso and Braque.

She stopped her lecture at that point, instructing us to look closely at *Les Demoiselles d'Avignon*. She never directly explained the paintings. She'd describe movements, history, overarching changes in art, interconnecting them all into a rhythmic web, but particular paintings were put up for us to observe, to arrive at our own conclusions. Nevertheless, her lectures certainly had the energized air of seduction.

After the allotted silence, she said Picasso's *Demoiselles* was completed in 1907. It wasn't really Cubism, but it thrust open the Cubist door. It brought in tribal art since Picasso loved African art, the masks in particular. I looked again at the two women with grotesque faces. They no longer seemed so grotesque. They still seemed distorted, but became more pleasing and acceptable the longer I looked.

She replaced Picasso's forerunner to Cubism with Braque's *Harbor in Normandy*. She told the class this painting was done in 1909 and was early Cubism. Again silence in order to observe. The boats, sails, and sea were disjointed polygons realigned. It seemed like a puzzle with each piece clearly delineated. Reality cut up and slotted back together. The lighthouses in the background were intact and whole, providing the chaotic rush of the rest of the painting some moorings.

Back to Picasso. The professor announced *Standing Woman*, which was done in 1911-1912. She called it "Cubism unbound." I stared at the geometric shapes converging on each other. Triangles, rectangles, and occasional semicircles merged into the general shape of a human. Beige and black fading in and out upon each other. It seemed like a twisted and contorted collection of shapes and planes that somehow coalesced into a woman.

The professor broke the silence. By now, she explained, art had completely broken its ties with tradition. Reality was no longer given subjective nuances like the Impressionists did, or bold, aggressive strokes like the Expressionists. Visual realism had been slain. Concept art was in, being conceived within the collective unconscious. Objects had been shattered by Picasso and Braque. Then, they reassembled the pieces into a completely new form, into multiple realities. Cubism sought to see reality in ways that life could never perceive it. Art was now trying to elevate reality and transcend its shortcomings and also the fallacies and glaring ineptitudes of religion. She quoted Braque. "Senses deform, and the spirit forms."

The professor showed more Picassos and Braques and then other Cubists—Marcel Duchamp, Fernand Leger and Juan Gris. She paused for a long time at Duchamp's 1912 painting, *Nude Descending a Staircase*. I stared at the nearly robotic figure in motion. You could both see and feel the descent. A rush of stationary motion.

Suddenly, I felt something fall on my right leg. My eyes swung down and to the right, in the same direction as the nude descending the staircase. I looked over. A large, oversized black bag had fallen onto my right leg, sliding down and landing next to my foot. "Excuse me," I heard. I looked up at the painting for a moment, blinked, and then looked over towards the direction of the voice. It was a female classmate whom I'd never met. I smiled, implying it was no problem. She smiled back.

Instant attraction.

I stared at her foolishly like I had been doing to the paintings. She smiled again and motioned with her head towards the Duchamp. I nodded and returned to the *Nude* and the narrating voice from behind.

"While Picasso and Braque were the bridge to the great movement of Cubism, Duchamp was the link to Dada, the movement that turned everything inside-out and severed the hinges from any known doors. Duchamp's *Bicycle Wheel* of 1913 was the first readymade. Art was now questioning everything, especially itself. With his 1917 exhibition, *The Fountain*, an upside down urinal as art, anything was truly and absurdly possible. When he put a goatee on the *Mona Lisa* in his work, *L.H.O.O.Q.*, the past was irrevocably interred. Let us not forget the comedy of Duchamp either. He was interested in intellectual and abstruse topics like the fourth dimension, but he was also a prankster as shown by the urinal. Though it was seen as a profound statement on the state of art and humanity, and has endured to become an integral part of art history, it may have been just a joke to him. The title of *L.H.O.O.Q.* translates to something lewd and bawdy. Duchamp was both serious artist and class clown."

The professor walked to the front of the class, just a few feet from me. The lights were still dim and she cast a shadowy and mysterious presence before addressing us. "Next class ladies and gentlemen will be on Dada, which carried forth Duchamp's humor, but with a lot more danger to it. Then we will visit the world of Andre Breton and Surrealism. Don't expect humor there. Breton was quite serious in his belief that automatic art and writing would translate and decode the subconscious and therefore the internal universe that befuddles us all. Read the next unit and see if you can decode his nirvanic attempts at mining the magnetic fields of buried thoughts." She walked to the back of the class and turned the lights on. My mind always felt as if it had been purged and reordered into a new dynamic. It usually took some time to re-center myself, but I rushed the process in order to reach down and pick up the black case that was still lying on the floor next to my foot. I handed it to the woman next to me. Our hands briefly touched as the small handle was passed between us.

"Sorry, I distracted you. I know how much you were engrossed by these paintings," she said.

"Not a problem at all," I replied, recognizing that she had noticed me, much to my surprise.

23

"So, are you an artist?" she asked.

I shook my head, disappointed and embarrassed that I wasn't. "No, but very fascinated by artists. I can see that you're an artist." My eyes went down to the black case that initiated our conversation.

"Trying," she said, modestly.

"Can I see your work?" I asked.

She hesitated. "Nothing's finished. They're just, ahh, impressions right now." She smiled, shyly.

"Don't worry. I have no doubt that I'll be impressed. I've always revered creativity and even more so since this class began. A lot more now."

She began to unzip the case, stopping halfway. "I can't show my unfinished paintings to someone without knowing his name."

"I'm Van."

"Nice to meet you, Van. I'm Shaillie."

We were inseparable from that point on. I fell into Shaillie's life more than she fell into mine. I hadn't made many friends at the university. Kind of stuck to myself and the art history texts during the first few weeks. Shaillie had quickly made a circle of friends from her art classes. They were all artists of one sort or another. Mostly painters, but also sculptors, poets, film students, would-be novelists. Out of a strong, but vague urge to be creative and the pressing need to fit into Shaillie's world, I soon chose photography as my art form. It was a safe and obvious choice. At the time I thought I was inspired by my studies of Man Ray in the modern art class, but looking back, it was more likely I adopted photography and clung to it simply as an attempt at an identity.

Nevertheless, not wholly aware of my path's insincerity, I took photography very seriously at that time. I read everything I could about Emmanuel Radnitzky. I spent hours and hours in the dark room, applying what I'd learned about creative photography as well as my new knowledge of art history. It was all very derivative, but I was young and derivations were unavoidably essential and exciting. Moreover, would it ever be possible for some creation not to be derivative on some level or another? Everything new was just a step past the accumulation of old. I would half-develop shots, seek blurred images, abstractions, create Cubist-style collages, manipulate text into the picture like Braque's *papier collé*, all of it fueled by the belief in the subconscious as the sovereign puppeteer.

24

After graduation, Shaillie and I did our six-month European jaunt like good bohemians on the pose. I made an attempt to stay in Europe, transform the pose into a form of truth, but Shaillie dismissed it as a dead-end, immature notion. My resistance wasn't strong. I convinced myself that she was right. Things settled rather quickly into a moneyed and secure route. A mature path. The status-quo chasm was wide and deep with sides of swiftly falling beach sand flowing into a magnetic valley. Climbing out would have been a Sisyphean task.

Shaillie got an MFA at the Museum of Fine Arts School in Boston. She continued to paint and had a few shows in the area, but when she landed a job as an assistant curator at a small, contemporary art museum, the desire to paint faded. She became more concerned with acquisitions and management of art, rather than creating it. She was a Sunday painter for a stretch, before complete abandonment. Within a few years of graduating, her paints, easel, sketchpads, all her art supplies began their descent into the basement. *Nude Descending a Staircase.* Once in a while, I'd flip through her sketches, especially the beautiful, energized abstracts that I'd seen the day we'd met. For a while I'd try and coax the muse out of her, but she'd say she'd lost the urge. Starter homes were whispering nearby.

I spent a few aimless and neutral years bartending after graduation and taking some non-matriculated graduate classes in photography. I only had one foot in the creative waters. Through Shaillie's museum, I had a few shows and sold some photos, but I couldn't shake the reality that photography was a disguise for me. Truth perpetually rises like the sun, just without the reliable timetable. Photography was something I consciously chose rather than it choosing me. An artist should be called from within, rather than making a cerebrally-based decision. I would leave that for the bankers.

Once I gave up photography, I was no longer a bartender pursuing an art. I was just a bartender. I stayed that way until a family gathering changed things. An uncle asked Shaillie what she was doing for work. She described her job at the museum. He then turned to me. At this point, my father jumped in as if he'd been waiting for the opportunity. "Well, Van here is a bartender. Four years of studying and he's making martinis for a living." He let out a loud laugh. My uncle seemed embarrassed that he'd asked the question. Shaillie said that I was transitioning from photography right now. Bartending was just temporary. "Maybe, it's not," I said.

"Well then, Van, why don't you fix me a martini, nice and dry son," the old man said. He looked over at my uncle. "He makes a good

25

one. Lots of practice." My uncle shook his head. Much to my dismay, I obediently went and made the martini. I wish I hadn't.

Soon after, I got a *real job*. The job everyone around you wants you to get. I remember going to work on the subway my first day. Nice new suit, leather bag, ready for the world. I remember thinking about how I'd summarily dismissed photography. I didn't look back at that with real regret, but the internal howl, the void within that urges one into the arts was never dismissed. It couldn't be. It just lay dormant, repressed within like everyone else who toes the line. Not until years later, bartending again, did the repression finally lose the battle. The void wills itself into expression. The journal I would fill during those sleepless nights had to be its return...

My father had a contact at Boston Common Financial, a huge mutual fund-based bank. I went through the motions of an interview and got the job. For the next six years I continued going through the motions, day after day after interminable day. My first day in the cubicle and the dreaded ironies settled into my thoughts, giggling and mocking. Inspired by Cubism and Surrealism, you major in art history and take up photography, only to end up in a cubicle shuffling numbers on a screen. Perfect. Later, when I switched allegiances from the Red Sox to the Cubs along with Nomar, the assassins of irony returned. Yes, it was linguistic irony, a mere foolish coincidence, but I took the Surrealist approach. Coincidences can have supreme significance. Never dismiss them. Of Cubs, cubicles, and Cubism.

Casting aside my growing love and hate for all things ironic, I had a job to do. I started at level 18, entry-level fund supervisor. By the time insomnia invaded and seized my nights, I was at level 11, fund group D leader. I had climbed seven rungs *down* and I was making very solid, mediocre money. It was all very stable and secure. Shaillie and I were well on our way to the comforts of middle class; home ownership,two-week vacations in the Caribbean, seven HBOs, new furniture sets, sprinklers, grass clippings, IRAs...We were agglomerating all the numbing comforts and securities one could want in the United States of Accumulation and I couldn't have been more miserable.

Life in the cubicle was a fractured and severed existence. Disconnected. Each subway ride in the morning felt like a trip into a Kafka novel. I couldn't shed the utter meaninglessness of every moment of everyday. I'd enter the enormous BCF building and attempt to find comfort in seeing the thousands around me that were in the same boat. Fifty-five floors of cubicles. It was like a house of mirrors. Who was I to complain when everyone around me was dutifully marching to the same droning and draining beat? I stuck it out for six years with that self-

26

manipulative credo. Day after mindless day I moved X number of dollars into Y location, shifting X number of shares of company Z that sold product Y into retirement option A, splitting fund X that seized company W into funds X and Y, which turned X dollars into more Y products. Variables everywhere, but not actually going anywhere.

When I finally quit and returned to bartending, it was a step backwards to most. I quit just months after my father had succumbed to cancer, so there would be no laughter from him. None at all. To the living around me, it was ridiculous. I heard a lot of words from a lot of lemmings. "Van, what about the money, benefits, dignity, 401K, retirement, vacation pay…" But I knew one thing. It was an exit from perpetual mediocrity. It might have been a step down and foolish on most barometers, but it felt like emancipation. I was off the plateau, no longer luggage on the carousel. At least, that's how I philosophized it to myself. If nothing else, I'd rid myself of that bizarre fusion of feeling simultaneously anxious and anesthetized. On my last day of work, a 401K concussed colleague in an adjoining cubicle took offense at my departure. He told me about an article he'd just read, an obituary actually, about a hundred-and-one-year-old man. The man had worked for the LA Transit System cleaning buses for seventy-two years, quitting the day after his one hundredth birthday. He'd missed only one day of work in seventy two years; the day of his wife's funeral. My colleague passed on the story looking down at me, his head peering out of his cubicle into mine, as I removed the few possessions I was taking with me.

"He made it seventy-two years and you could only make it six. Getting married in a few months to boot. Very selfish, Van."

I didn't respond. Just filled up my bag with some pictures and a stash of novels that I'd kept in my drawers to read when managers were at meetings. But my cubicle-mate wasn't done.

He snarled at me, "Van, you're so full of arrogant shit if you think you've found an exit. Wake up! You're just taking off one straitjacket to put on another. You'll see. You'll be back. There's no exit."

Shaillie knew my days at Boston Common Financial were coming to an end. She saw my inevitable departure evolving during those six years. Yet, the day I told her that it was actually happening, she seemed taken aback.

"Tell me again why you are quitting, Van?"

"I'm done Shaillie. You knew I could never continue this. I knew it. The time has come."

"But we're so close to a decent down payment and we're getting married so soon, Van. The timing is very bad and disconcerting."

27

"I'm done. I can't do it. I prefer not to."

"You prefer not to?"

"Yes, I prefer not to."

"So what now, Bartleby?"

"Back to bartending."

"You're kidding me, right?"

"No."

"The timing is what kills me, Van."

I nodded knowing she was not only referring to our upcoming wedding, but also my father's passing. I chose not to respond. She chose not to pursue the paternal angle at that time.

"And benefits? Retirement? Vacation? The pay cut? What do you have to say about all that?"

"That's easy. Fuck'em." I laughed. Shaillie didn't.

"And when I become a mother and can't work for a while? Fuck that, too?"

"No, no, I'm sorry. I didn't mean to be so harsh. We've got plenty of money now. Sell the stock options, we've got savings, the goddamn 401K can be liquidated. Anyway, let's not think about all this logistical crap right now. It's that stuff that I'm trying to leave. Six years in a cubicle has got me a bit angry and claustrophobic. I'm just venting."

"And our child? How does our child deal with your venting?"

"Shaillie, slow the hell down. You're not even pregnant. You're too pragmatic. Let's not talk about hypothetical babies. You're jumping way into the future. Relax."

"And you're regressing into the past."

"Sweetheart, it's temporary. Don't worry, bartending is just a transition. It's not the end of the equation."

"What's next then? Please tell me the plan."

"I don't know. I'll go back to school. Get a Masters in art history. Teach or something. We could always travel."

"Van, we're not backpacking across Europe anymore."

"We should, just this time with all our possessions in our backpacks. We've saved plenty of money. We'll invest half and take off with the other half. When we're done, we'll still be fine. Shaillie, we can step off the conveyor belt for a little while and redefine things."

Shaillie shook her head. She took a deep breath with her eyes closed. When the pause was over, she demanded, "Will you take Europe out of your head. I'm not going."

"Did you really get turned on by watching me go to work like a robot everyday? Did you really enjoy fucking me because of the 401K and all the benefits? You've been fucking a robotic retirement plant. Is that a turn on?"

28

Shaillie half-laughed, half-snickered and then her mien morphed into a look of rumination. She went to the wine rack and pulled out a bottle of red wine. "How about French, my Europhile fiancé?"

"Sure."

She poured each of us a glass.

"To answer your question, Van. I always enjoy making love to you, good benefit plans or not."

"I'm glad to hear that."

"Maybe, it's you who doesn't enjoy fucking yourself."

I paused for a moment. "I'll have to think about that one."

She continued, "Besides being very disconcerting, the bartending thing also makes me a little jealous."

"Didn't we agree to an open marriage? What was it, one affair a year?"

"No, I think it was one for you and three for me because men are so pathetically and easily satisfied by whoever is put before them. The odds aren't as good for me."

"I'll take it."

Shaillie rolled her eyes. "That was a one-time thing, my dear. Won't happen again."

I nodded as wanton images from a night not so long ago flashed across my mind.

"You know I have to concede that there's something attractive about all of your impulsiveness, a kind of edgy *Armenianness* to it, but that doesn't make me happy. This seems like devolution so close to the wedding. It really does worry me."

"You have nothing to worry about, my love. It's all part of evolution, our evolution. The detours make it interesting," I said, not all that convincingly.

I raised my glass of Beaujolais, anyway. She did the same, slowly, with the pace of reluctance. I smiled and Shaillie tried to. "You'll see, sweetheart, we'll be fine. We'll be better, in fact."

I promised Shaillie the bar would not be a dive, full of down-and-out-Bukowski types. I found a fairly posh French restaurant in downtown Boston, where the bar regulars were mostly an aging post-work crowd. These were the drunks who cut their drinking chops back in the seventies, during the heyday of the happy hour when drinking and driving was not such an issue. Chez Lucienne's cast of dipsomaniacs was efficient. They got their daily saturation done not long after sunset, so they could return home to their suburban spouses and kids under a scotch or vodka halo. It was an easy five-hour shift for me. I was usually done by ten o'clock, not common in the world of bartending.

The regulars had been coming to Lucienne's for decades. I found them quite unique compared to the bar worlds I had previously tended. About a dozen or so would be there daily. This particular sodden lot of regulars was largely educated, astute and well-read. The spectres of Harvard and MIT hovered nearby. The banter was often intellectual, literary, and political. The alcohol frequently oiled the conversational wheels into the salacious, but even this had a touch of sophistication to it. The post-Berlin Wall leftists, now philosophical orphans, had to go somewhere, having been so quickly and thoroughly abandoned by their alternate dream. The unquestioned leader manqué of this literate lot was Seamus Rourke, who was known as Bishop. Unlike most of the others, Bishop seemingly had no real job, nor a family waiting for him after the alcohol.

The restaurant had a courtyard in front of it that led to the bar. A statue of Thomas Paine, *Common Sense* in hand, stood in the courtyard. It was a basement bar, which customers had to pass by in order to get into the restaurant. There was a small TV in one corner, but it was often off and the lighting was dim. Newcomers weren't welcomed with open arms. Spillover from the restaurant tended to go to the nearby tables rather than to the barstools. Almost everyone who sat at the bar was a long-time regular.

Usually, when I arrived for my evening shift, the bar was quiet, save for Bishop and one of his protégés. He used the mid-afternoon quietude at the bar to edit and discuss the manuscripts. This particular day Bishop was at the bar with his most favored pupil, Derek Koles. Bishop and Koles were starkly different visually. Bishop was in his early sixties, dressed in a blue and white seersucker suit, white shirt and bowtie. Meanwhile, Koles was the picture of the young artist. Disheveled, wavy hair, three or four day beard, long sideburns, wearing jeans and worn out, faded dress shirt. A small notebook and a pen peeked out of his shirt pocket. Koles's manuscript was on the bar in a giant pile of pages. Bishop had a red pen in his hand, gripping it tightly like a dagger.

Bishop believed he was creating a new literary and art movement. Koles would spearhead this new brigade of artists. As Bishop would say, "A long overdue vanguard of the arts like the days of early 20th century Paris where movements sprang up daily trying to shake the foundations and rattle the cages of the tired bourgeoisie." Bishop boastfully claimed literature had gone soft and tepid since those days, save for the brief Beat moments in the fifties. Bishop rarely talked.

Rather, he proclaimed, announced, hollered, and howled as if perpetually on stage, lectern in front, microphone on.

On this day Bishop was trying to get Koles to change his approach in his second novel. Koles had already had one published by small presses in France and America. Last I'd heard, the manuscript had grown to seven hundred pages. I was impressed by its sheer magnitude.

"Young Derek, you must get over the fear of the first person in your novel. Only the **I** cuts like a sword into the skin of the truth. Literature needs the first person more than ever before. It's the most beautiful of manipulations. The great antidote to loneliness. The third person needs cremation. Let it rest in peace."

Koles shook his head. "Then it becomes me. Everyone links it all to the writer. I went through that with the first novel. It's fiction and I want nothing to do with it. I am not fiction."

"Of course, you are. This is fiction right now!" Bishop laughed, which turned into a cough. He then took a drag from the lit cigarette resting in an ashtray. "Relent and edit the whole damn beautiful thing from third person to glorious first and I'll show it to my agent friend. We need to get it out there. Time is not on our side."

"It still needs work."

"Make the switch and it'll write itself."

"Why don't we try second person?" Koles asked.

"McInerney redux? We'll be skewered for literary theft."

"So, he monopolized a whole grammatical person."

"It's played out, my fictional friend. It was a one-time gambit. You've already ripped him off with the drumming metaphor to describe your anti-hero's migraine pain. Made me think of the Bolivian marching soldiers thumping through his narrator's cocaine-addled head. Clear, literary robbery."

"Everybody rips everyone off. It's a tribute to him."

"All you have to do is put in one of those disclaimers stating this is a work of fiction and any connection to real people and so forth and so on down the de facto road of prevarications."

"Sorry, Bishop, that makes it even truer. Christ, I remember reading *Look Homeward Angel* and Wolfe had that bullshit, literary dragnet intro. It was laughable. Everyone knew Eugene Gant was Thomas Wolfe."

"Not wholly true, but regardless, I didn't care. Once it's on the page, it's fiction. Gant has his own identity."

"You would have cared if you had been in Wolfe's circle of friends. Ashville castigated him."

"He shouldn't have hid behind the third person. He wrote it first person and Perkins changed it in the edit. That's cowardice. One must vault headfirst into the waters of words, absolute faith in Madam Art with your pants down like Henry Miller."

"A tribute to Miller? Talk about played out, Bishop. Very unoriginal."

Bishop shook his head and furrowed his brow. "*Tropic of Cancer* needs to be written again and again before it will permeate the collective. There can never be enough *Tropic* scions. Never enough *Rosy Crucifixions*! The trick is to make the madness your own, not a copy."

"I disagree," Koles said, taking a sip of wine. Bishop followed suit. They were both drinking white wine, Sancerre. The day-bartender had left them a bottle on the bar, chilling in a silver cooler, as he usually did. I topped off each of their glasses with the last remnants of the bottle. While they bantered back and forth, I ate my staff meal while setting up for my shift. But mostly I was listening to their literary tête-à-tête.

"These are Lilliputian complaints. You aren't seeing the big picture, Derek."

"The bottom line is that I refuse to be linked to my narrator. I'll get more grief than relief from this book. I want distance."

Bishop disagreed. "You need proximity. You need to lick the loins of your characters, not stand afar."

Koles sighed and he cracked his knuckles, then his neck. Loud pops from his bones.

"You're too uptight, Senator Koles."

"Look, Bishop, the book is full of cocaine, prostitutes, transvestites, existential madness. I don't want it all labeled as me."

Bishop looked at me with a frown that evolved into a big smile. "Goddamn cream puff he's become." He turned back to Koles. "Get some damn balls, stare into your wife's eyes, ex-wife's eyes, estranged, whatever she is and tell her and the world it's fiction! It's the imagination. Tell them you've escaped the slow, tic-tock of the clockwork pendulum."

"I'll never get her back if it's the first person. It's too perverse." Koles took a big gulp of wine, ran his hands through his thick, light brown hair.

"Perverse? You've written every man. We're all wanton, libido-driven, lab rats. Literature lets all it out into the open. It's nothing new. You've just channeled it into creation."

"Whatever, never mind her, Bishop."

"Let her go, Derek, or run back to her. This middle ground is quicksand. I vote for moving on, evolution. You've concocted some cockeyed image of what you never had and let it possess your thoughts."

"Bishop, leave it alone. I know what I'm doing. I'll take writing advice, not marital advice from you."

32

Bishop sighed. "You have no need to fear lewd and crude labels. You, you're a tart, my fictional friend. Harmlessly perverse. The mother goose of perversions."

"Ok, I get the point." Koles gripped his jaw, rubbing and squeezing the area around his mouth. The thinker neurotic.

"Rewrite it. Revamp it with the harrumph of the I! Remember, you couldn't write a non-fictional account of yourself even if you truly wanted to. It all gets convoluted in the transposition. The subconscious intervenes. Screaming ancestors buried in our mitochondrial madness all equivocate so-called truth. Truth doesn't exist. It's play-do." Koles and I both laughed. Bishop took a long drag on his cigarette and then put it out.

"Ole Lake Van here knows truth, Armenian style. Ethnic honesty behind our bar, Derek."

"Get Bishop a good, truthful shot of booze, Van." He covered his face with his open hands for a few seconds and then started massaging his entire face.

"You ok, Derek?" I asked.

"Fine, just tired, you know." His voice muffled by his hands.

I turned to Bishop, "Another glass of Sancerre?"

"It's dusk. Time for the switch. Time for Lady Amber."

Koles wouldn't let go. Hands now interlocked on the bar, he said to me, "You know, Van, the goddamn truth of the truth is my manuscript is my psyche guillotined. It's my own little personal revolution of the selves lived and unlived. Just took my damn presiding mother psyche and sliced her over and over like a big chunk of Gruyère, cut her down into characters screaming to get out of me like hundreds of butterflies reborn from a taxidermist album all at once."

Bishop smiled. He loved this Derek Koles, the Koles that shed his sullen cape and cowl and expressed his self, alive and poetic. "Koles has talent, Van. Resurrected butterflies aligned purely. That's great poesy, Koles. The guillotine as poet severing the psyche's straitjacket. It's ole angel midnight that begs us for something more, birthing of selves in an escape from the mind's eternal claustrophobia. The reign of terror turned into beatitude."

I gave Bishop his drink.

"Careful not to turn completely into a caricature, Bishop," Koles admonished.

"The best form to assume, my boys. Now, Monsieur Koles take your internal French revolution the hell out of here and carve those selves and butterflies like a holiday turkey into first person candor. A great big homage to Henry Miller. Your *Tropic of Boston*." Bishop laughed with phlegm rising from his cigarette scarred and charred throat.

He took a bar napkin and hacked the residue of forty years of smoking into it. Then he lit a Camel unfiltered.

Koles collected his seven hundred-page manuscript from the bar. He patted the sides of the mass of pages, straightening them like a giant deck of cards. The edges were curved and frayed. I noticed Bishop's red pen all over the manuscript. Koles stuffed the draft into a book filled backpack. He hoisted the weighty bag of words onto his shoulder while I poured Rourke another of his amber specials. This was Mount Gay rum on the rocks in a red wine glass with a splash of tonic, a lemon twist and a lime wedge. I watched Koles pass the statue of Thomas Paine and disappear into the throng of pedestrians walking and loitering in Boston Common. Bishop took a healthy gulp from his drink. I could only speculate as to how many glasses of white wine he'd already gone through.

"Van, our friend Koles has talent, but it's all being consumed by his failed marriage. He'll get there, though. The first person will bring his characters and his pen to life. He's afraid of his own talent right now. Of where it might take him internally. He captured whispers from the void in the first book. Now, he needs to draw out the howls of trapped ancestors within. True artists, Van, bring out the lurking ancient in modern costumes, cause cataclysm, shiver the static present and then move it forward. Society is a Ferris wheel until true art gives it roller coaster momentum. Koles can do that."

"You talk as if he's Picasso," I said.

"Good comparison, my Armenian deacon. He needs the Bateau-Lavoir and the Lapin Agile. He needs to explode. His potential is Picassoesque. Real art, not this manicured landscape, Japanese tea garden novel world we live in. He will leave all the academic writers in his wake. He knows what he needs to do. The MFA novel must end to propel literary evolution."

"That's a lot of weight on his shoulders, Bishop."

"Greatness needs gravity," Bishop said. He took a sip from his drink, seemingly pondering what he just said and then continued, "Van, you see him now. He's anxious, nervous. He's still tiptoeing along the periphery, hiding behind a dishonest manuscript. My red dagger can only salvage so much."

"Maybe, he should go to Paris and settle his marriage. Then he could…"

"Then he could be free to pursue his truth. That's all we have at the end."

I hadn't had many conversations with Rourke to this point. He'd inquired about my Armenian history a few times, specifically my family's connection to the Genocide and once suggested I write a historical novel of my grandfather's life. He was most impressed by grandfather.

"Setrag Arakalian, great name." Rourke repeated it many times. "I love the multi-syllabic Armenian words. Guttural beatitude." Rourke exaggerated his lingering, Irish brogue. "It's got that Gaelic chutzpah to it. Van, you ought to write his novel. It's got all the elements of art and story. I even made notes on it."

Rourke reached into his leather satchel. He always had lots of papers with him and he was surprisingly organized. I thought his satchel would be full of scattered, unorganized papers, notes on cocktail napkins, the chaos of the artist gone to drink. Though Rourke was quite surprisingly left brain organized like an accountant. He pulled out a small notebook with my name on it.

"Let's talk about you now, Van," Bishop said and he began to read from the notebook.

"Little village by mystical Lake Van with ghosts and shadows of Noah's Ark mythically hovering on nearby Mt. Ararat...Family slaughtered...Setrag's grandfather crucified to church door...Father slain after valiantly fighting with kitchen utensils...Setrag hides under thousands of corpses and avoids the puncturing confirmation of death by bayonet. Escapes orphanage upon news of child starvation plan and flees to Russia and works on a White Russian farm before Bolsheviks win civil war. Works on collectivized farm believing in Lenin and Trotsky...Escapes firing squad...Wanders Europe...Arrives in America via Cuba...Marries and drives canteen truck to armories during war...Runs a numbers business on the side...Goes to track daily and has an inside deal with an Armenian trainer...Conflict with son who resents father's gambling...grandson and grandfather form deep and true connection...paternal dysfunction...unity in the family universal skipping generations."

"It's not all true, Bishop. There was no firing squad and the inference to my father is..."

Bishop cut me off, "Sure it's true. It's all true. Once it's on the page it's truth. The highest truth of all. Fiction is more real than reality, my good Lake Van."

I didn't say anything for a while. I pondered Rourke's notes on my grandfather, his notion of "paternal dysfunction," and referring to me as a body of water.

"Look, Van, if you don't want to do anything with it, I might be able to put together a deal to sell the idea to one of the independent

35

studios I work with. I could get you a good little booty as the treatment's co-writer. Not to mention the posterity and eternity that Madam Art would bring your grandfather."

"My grandfather could care less about posterity. He's never seen a film in his life. Not one single movie. He'd laugh at the word posterity if he knew what it meant. 'When you're dead, you're dead,' he'd simply say."

Rourke jotted down what I had just said and then replied, "Of course, there's no heaven after what he witnessed. Well, Van, we'll see. You think about it. Maybe you'll want some posterity and eternity someday."

I began counting tips.

"Think about it, my friend. You're no bartender. I see through the disguise. You've got art in your blood."

I stopped counting. "Why would you say that?"

"It's there plain as day. Doesn't need to be explained. Just remember one thing, Van."

I nodded for him to continue.

"Keep death in your back pocket. It's the driving source of all greatness."

It didn't take me long to hear Rourke's autobiography. Alcohol and loneliness can fuse fast and hard into a muse that won't relent.

My own autobiography at that moment was about to detour in what would seem one endless night, but a night can never be a night. It has to be the culmination of years of soft voices, wants, echoes, failed remedies—all the dreams and dramas soldered into their final act. The subconscious finally hollering long coded messages.

"Yeah, I pissed away a lot of money. Big money. Millions, my Armenian friend. Lost my wife when I lost my money. Marriage and money so goddamned knotted together. Everything got obstreperous. Do you understand me, Van? Obstreperous!"

"I understand the word."

"Do you understand me beyond the word?"

"I really can't say, Bishop. Sometimes, I think I do. Sometimes not."

"Don't think so much, Van."

"Can't help it. Damn neurons keep firing signals." Bishop laughed and took a gulp of Lady Amber.

"Van, you know what that ole Graves said?" Bishop looked at me and I shrugged.

36

"There's no money in poetry, but then there's no poetry in money, either. Words to live by. I pissed the bills away. The noise got so damn loud I couldn't think above the rattling din."

"Obstreperous, right, Bishop?"

"Now you're getting it, my good Lake Van. Armenians have ancestral senses."

I smiled, choosing not to inquire about what he meant by that.

"I've never left her, though. I'll never leave art, Van. Money will always equivocate. Women come and go, everything does. However, she is eternity. We must defend her. We must defend infinity, Van. Louis Aragon wrote that long ago. He started it and Koles will continue it. God save the queen, Deacon Arakalian!" Bishop yelped in a throaty, phlegmy Gaelic tone while reaching for his glass. He took a large gulp of watered-down rum. It was only Rourke, myself, and a few waitresses occasionally coming to the service bar. He raised his glass and looked around for a partner to toast. With no other alternative, he looked to me and held his glass up. He drank and then glanced unsuccessfully at his watch. He pulled his wrist closer to his eyes, squinting and straining now.

"9:15," I offered.

"Time to change congregations, Van."

"Perhaps, you ought to try home. Save yourself for the next sermon."

He nodded, then shook his head slowly.

"You're getting married, right?"

"Yes."

"Yes, Van. Yes, you are."

He drank again. A little stream slid down his chin. He didn't notice. The rivulet of watery Barbados rum twisted and turned its way down his neck, across his Adam's apple, settling into the collar of his white shirt.

"Van, you know I produced several Louis Malle films, right?"

"I heard a little bit about it," I said, cleaning up and getting ready to close. I could sense Rourke was not done though he didn't need my attention for his verbosity to wander new lands.

"All of them lost money. Art can be such a divine whore. A beautiful Persian rug laid out across a bottomless, infernal pit. But I still love her, Van. All heaven and hell of her."

Bishop sighed and took a gulp of rum. I could tell he was ready to recollect.

"So much over so long. So many events."

He was moving his head rhythmically, slowly back and forth, looking down below his barstool. He looked up, but not directly at me.

"Poetry and booze, Van, perpetually married. Siamese monsters of mad, beguiling beauty launched from the guts of drunken nights and disemboweled verse. I lost millions honoring *Art for Art's sake*. The lyrical damsel is in distress. I've had too many Native American Manhattan sales. Too many to remember. My great failure in the material world is my lonely success in the arts. The true damn whore is the American dollar. She has fucked me time and time again, but I'll get the last laugh on the materialists. I will kiss infinity and she will return the kiss, Van. She will, you'll see. All the blunders will become beautiful in eternity." Bishop's voice trailed off and he closed his eyes.

I pretended not to notice and continued breaking down the bar; putting fruit in overnight containers, washing supplies, restocking beer and wine.

I heard ice rattling in Bishop's glass. Ever resilient in his libationary battles, he was loudly slurping the rest of his drink before returning to his rhetorical journeys.

I kept telling her we had aesthetic honor. I kept her a couple of extra years on that one since her core was creative. God, I must have lost fifteen million over the years. Hell, I've given so much to friends. My friends are all in Vermont. Old socialists never die, they just fade to the woods of Vermont.

I asked him why he never went with them.

"'Cause, Van, I'm a true individualist and a pure communist and the two are hard to reconcile. A cannibalistic catch 22. I contradict myself, so be it. A great 20th century conundrum that I choose not to analyze when it's much simpler to get drunk. Now get me another Amber and get both my ex-wives one wherever they are. While you're at it, take care of the guys they're fucking right now. Seamus Rourke is not a hostile man. He buys drinks for the men screwing his past. I'm an Irish man from Cork who believes in peace. Now, put some damn rum in this pathetic drink! I said splash of tonic, not splash of Mount Gay. You're mixing it up, ole son of Ararat."

I took his drink and added a drop of rum and another healthy blast of tonic. He was quite drunk, but I'd seen worse. He was in control. I liked Bishop and enjoyed his disjointed ramblings. There was never any small talk with Bishop. It was always big and bloated talk.

"Here, take a look at the list of films my company's working on."

He took a sip of his drink while I looked at this A-list of Hollywood films. I didn't question it. I saw no point in that.

"Now that's a better drink. Armenians know how to drink. You know what you should do. You've got fifty years to educate America. Get yourself over to Armenia, lie down in the soil of your grandfather's past and take in his life osmotically from Madre Earth. Breathe in, absorb the geochronology of his past and tell his tale. I'll put it to film. We'll make a good little take on that. The Armenian community will fund the whole thing. Armenians are like Jews. They know how to get things done. While we're at it, we'll get that damn, uptight literary phenom Koles over to Europe, too. I've got a vineyard over there, just north of Lisbon. It's magical land. Beautiful, end-of-the-Old-World Portugal with coastlines and vistas that would have turned Adam Smith into a beatnik. Seize your youth, boys, before time seizes you."

Rourke and I had often spoken of our mutual admiration for Portugal. He got up and stumbled over to the free food that was still on the buffet table from four hours ago. He filled a plate with dry, cold bacon-wrapped scallops and chicken wings.

"I thought you weren't supposed to eat that stuff, Bishop" Rourke had told me that he'd had triple bypass surgery six months ago. He'd almost died and claimed some Irish angel saved him. "Ole angel midnight intervened." This angel was the muse for his last mission in life—the rambunctious new art movement with Koles's literature as the vanguard, but it would be more than that. It would merge all the arts. When he was drunk, he'd cajole me to join the literary brigade.

"I said that before the Amber freedom liberated me into peace. I'm drunk now. Can't you see that! I'll eat whatever the fuck I want. What's the worst that can happen, death? Death is our best friend. It hath not a hold over my life. I hath the hold over death, old-souled Armenian boy. You of all people should not play self-righteous bourgeois on me. You, my friend, hath death in your blood and suffering rippling in your veins from poetic ancestors past. One can't run from past lives, which is why you should pen your grandfather's great and tragic tale. Let his brilliant illiteracy breathe out words before you lose your great icon."

"Bishop, I just thought you shouldn't eat such greasy food a few months removed from bypass surgery."

"Triple bypass, Van. Triple fucking bypass. They re-routed my heart. You know, they bludgeon you. A sophisticated sledgehammer cracking your ribs open like a lobster tail. Split you right open so your heart's pounding right out in the open. Felt like a locomotive had gone through me. Felt like losing your soulmate. I awoke dead and lay dead for months in that bed recalling my whole existence, my youth, my errors, my old socialist friends withering in vain in Vermont communes, my failed marriages, my entire nada." Bishop sighed, gulped some of his rum and then lit a cigarette.

"Van, the body needs youth. Ponce de Leon was no fool. He knew the meaning of existence. The meaning of life is youth. No cigarette or greasy food will do me in whilst I cultivate a new artistic

39

vanguard, a new beauty, a new blissful tragedy on the hidden American soul. This country begs for an altering muse and Koles and my other scattered lonely heroes penning their dawns in oblivion will give me what no strict diet will."

For some reason I always approached his melodramatic soliloquies and spontaneous poesy with logic. Only after, alone, pensive and reflective, could I realize the irrational or sublime never meets geometric proof. It was the irrational whose only proof was deep and covert in our entrails. Unspeakable. The same home the leap of faith takes for the pious against all possible vestiges of empirical realness. All the great and absurd monuments against aloneness.

"Bishop, I just heard you say the other day to Pavel Humphreys that you were ready to quit the booze and smokes. Cleanse the system. Live clean and sober."

"The only way to cleanse the system, Deacon Arakalian, is to turn off the modern world. No films, newspapers, TVs, computers. Total suspension. Find a bungalow on the shores of Guam or some similar lost island of the Pacific and read the literature of the 17th century, Defoe or Bacon, sit under a Joshua Tree in the Mojave and listen to Mozart. Recline on the Lisbon coast and listen to the waves of Magellan and Henry the Navigator crashing the mystical, Portuguese coast."

I wanted to remind Bishop of the contradiction of his film production company, but caught my logic before it dribbled out of my mouth like an overfed infant.

"Or, Deacon, there's one other way."

"What's that?" I asked.

"The fine art of a woman's body. The truest art of all. *Les Demoiselles d'Avignon* in the flesh."

Bishop had a knack for synchrony. I thought back to the art class with Shaillie while Bishop let out a smoke-laden, emphysemic harrumph of a laugh, lifted his glass, and toasted alone.

"To the great shining jewel of woman divine!"

Adding to Shaillie's red flags about her future husband was my behavior behind the wheel. Driving had become anxiously primal. I rarely lost my temper, but recently amidst all the changes driving had suddenly turned me inside out, resulting in very aberrant behavior. Road rage began to trigger instantly. Prior to the beginning of my insomnia, I had rarely lost it unless truly and justifiably provoked by another driver. Losing it only meant some profanity and minor yelling. However, since insomnia, road rage was growing out of control. The worst incident was just a few weeks before the crow attack. Someone was driving very slowly and methodically in front of me, constantly stopping for pedestrians, yellow lights, or cars trying to merge.

"Van, calm down. You're gripping the stick-shift like you're hanging from a cliff."

"What a fuckin' prick that guy is, Shaillie. Goddamn fuckin' prick."

"He's just slow. Let it go, Van. Think about something else."

"Jesus Christ. What the fuck are you doing?" I screamed through the windshield at the driver. "Shaillie, can you believe this shit? He's stopping for someone nearing a crosswalk. Never mind the cars behind him, he's got to stop for the guy half a football field away just so he can get credit. Just to get a wave. Citizen Samaritan. So pathetic! What a goddamn dutiful robot. He stops for some stranger on the road, but probably beats his wife and ignores his kids."

"Van, please."

"It's just really sick. Perverse. If he wanted to do a good deed, he should be a goddamn missionary in Africa. It's so dishonest. Sheer hypocrisy."

"Van, please. You scare me when you get road rage. You are losing control."

"It isn't road rage. Not a bit. It's exhaustion from being stuck behind some arrogant bastard who thinks he's helping the world by slowing down. It's dishonest generosity. It's obscene if you'd see it through my perception."

"Van, your perception is a mess. It has nothing to do with a guy being polite to pedestrians. What is so wrong with that?"

I ignored Shaillie's pleas for rational thought. I just kept riding the perpetrator's ass. Shaillie tried to snap me out of it by changing the subject. She inquired about Chez Lucienne and even asked about Bishop and Koles's novel, which she never did, in a futile attempt to distract me. Nothing worked. I told her my anger was not misplaced. I told Shaillie that this guy would be eaten alive in Europe. In Italy they'd hit him from behind so he'd move his ass. Europeans drive and try to get to their next destination without attempting to be Mother Teresa for everyone on foot. My voice got louder and completely directed at the driver in front of me, not Shaillie.

"Italians would eat you up, you soft, spiritless church-going doughboy. They'd peel you apart piece by piece like a ripe artichoke exposing your bullshit core. Have an espresso for Christ's sake! Let the damn blood flow. Drive you fuckin' bastard. Drive! We're here to go, man. Here to drive!"

"Jesus, Van, you're spitting and drooling. You are out of control. Calm down!"

After yet another pedestrian had been given the red carpet to cross, the guy slowed down at the first sight of a yellow even though he easily could have gone through it. It didn't even turn red until he was fully stopped. I could have gone through too, but no, he stopped and I almost slammed into his bumper. I began ranting again about his straitjacket approach to life and how Romans would hang him out to dry like a pig's femur aging into prosciutto. My blood was wildly pumping from aorta to artery to capillary and my lungs straining to maintain oxygen for my mercurial blood flow and yapping mad mouth.

"I wish we were on bikes. It'd be like *Breaking Away* when the Italians race by the country-boy greaser, kick him and push him out of their way."

I was still right behind him. He pulled to a stop coming out of a rotary despite the law giving him the right of way. Again, he had to be polite to strangers when it was beyond the realm of necessity. So wholly disingenuous according to my road rage philosophy. Balless Gomer Pyle waited until a string of seemingly fifty cars had gone by. A red state, Fourth-of-July parade could have passed through.

I squeezed the steering wheel, leaned on the horn and slammed the dashboard hollering all the while. Shaillie gave up. She opened the door and walked through the rotary traffic to the circular patch of grass away from me. Her exit had no effect. I barely noticed.

I roared a primordial scream, grinding my teeth and pulling on the steering wheel. I wanted to rip it out of the dash and pound the boob in front of me to death. Death by steering wheel. My seams of societal sanity were fraying and severing quickly. Years and years that had galvanized the textured nexus of pain into one pure, white-hot moment. One moment that would harvest so much so deeply sown.

Finally out of the rotary, I followed the asshole until he pulled into a strip mall in front of a video store. We both got out. A fighter I'm not, but the undone seams had momentarily created a new persona.

I immediately accosted him. "Excuse me, I've got to ask you a question, sir." I felt sweat dripping down my temples—my body seeking relief from my heart turned battering ram and the thundering flow of its Daytona 500 blood. The tightly wound core spinning the whispering past into liberation misdirected.

"What is your problem?" he asked. He was bit older than me, maybe mid-thirties, balding, short, slightly rotund, and wearing a suit and a wedding band.

"My problem? I, I just have to know how people like you go through life. How the fuck can you be so fucking slow, waiting for everyone and everything to pass you by before you go. I mean you see yellow and you stop. Fine. I lived with that. I cursed you, but I contained the rage to myself."

"You're a fucking mess, pal. Even your girlfriend knows that. Go find her before she realizes what a psychopath you are." I saw him glance at my ring finger. "She'll never marry you."

"Just hear me out, hero."

"You're out of your mind. Look at you."

"Look at yourself, you're a fucking lie. I mean the crosswalk. Do you have to let every fucking person cross when they're miles away. You're just obnoxiously nice, desperate for a wave or nod of approval from a stranger. Is your life that fucking empty that you need a nod from an anonymous nobody to feel content?"

He paused for a moment, shaking his head. He reminded me of Shaillie, who had been doing a lot of head shaking at my recent behavior. "Who the hell let you out of the nuthouse? You are..."

"And then the damn rotary. What in God's name were you thinking? How many cars went by before you moved your sorry, sad, suburban ass. Fifty or sixty when you should have gone before all of them. Do you know the fucking law? You go and they stop. You go and they stop! Wake up!"

"You aren't nuts. You're a fucking lunatic asshole! You need an institution."

"Just answer the question!" I howled.

"I'm going to punch your lights out if you don't get the fuck away from me."

I smiled. "I'd crush you. Now, just answer the question!"

"Fuck you!" he screamed, right hand fingers curled into a fist.

"Do you relieve some guilt by allowing every fuck to go while you sit on your ass? What about the people behind you? Think about them. All you have to do is go. You go and everyone wins, asshole!" I screamed and all my muscles convulsed around every one of my bones. He now had a look of fear, fully comprehending the capacity of my madness. His anger had subsided into the look of a trepid, wary foot soldier caught in a minefield.

"You still haven't answered!!" I yelled into his white-flag eyes.

"Pal, you've really lost it. Get some help," he said nervously. Then he turned and walked away, heading to the video store.

"Answer the question. Answer my fucking question!"

He took out his cell phone and was dialing while entering the store. He stopped halfway through the door and turned to me, "Here's your answer. FUCK YOU!!! You're a sick, SICK FUCK!!!"

I watched him disappear into the store. I took a couple of steps towards following him when I saw my reflection in a tinted car window to my right. I didn't recognize myself. I shut my eyes and pressed my face into my open hands. I massaged my face as hard as I could, pressing and stretching the skin around my eyes and mouth. I returned to my car, put the seat back as far as it would go and lay supine for a long, long time.

When I got home, Shaillie was in bed. I quietly went into the bedroom and took a book I'd been reading from the nightstand. I apologized to Shaillie, but she didn't answer. I knew she was awake but didn't want to talk to me. I was embarrassed. All the rage was gone and I looked back at the incident with deep shame. It seemed as if my life had started to belong to someone else. Someone else was driving. Someone else was screaming irrational reverences at wildly caffeinated Italian drivers.

I went into the kitchen to get a glass of wine. I saw a piece of paper on the kitchen table. It was a list of therapists with their phone numbers. She must have just compiled it. There was no note asking me to call one or talking about what had just happened. Just a list of therapists. Words weren't necessary anymore. I folded the list of therapists and put it in the back of my book. It was an appropriate place for them since the book I was reading was by a psychiatrist. Bishop had given me the book one night. He said it had been his bible since his early twenties. "Some light beach reading, my good Armenian," Bishop had said as he handed me Viktor Frankl's *Man's Search for Meaning*. I had read the book quickly the first night I got it. I was now on my third read.

Frankl's story was amazing and I was drawn to his ideas. He was a Holocaust survivor of Auschwitz, but his wife and both parents were killed by the Nazis. Despite that horror, he'd continued his work in psychology and neurology after the war and founded a third school of psychotherapy that wasn't direct lineage to Freud or Adler. Frankl didn't believe neurosis was all sexual or based on childhood woes and bad parenting. He thought our problems were often that our lives were off-target in terms of meaning. We led meaningless lives and his existential analysis would help patients regain meaning. He believed in a *will to meaning* rather than Nietzsche's *will to power*. He predicted that the middle and upper classes would soon turn every issue into a childhood source because of Freud. It was an easy escape, a new kind of religion. Frankl thought people and therapists would avoid or unconsciously manipulate existential dread, the fundamental lack of meaning in life

44

into a cycle of blame. I wasn't sure he directly predicted our pharmacologically mad society, but I didn't think he'd be surprised. I was sure if he watched American television today and saw that every other commercial was advertising a different kind of pill to deal with life that he would be aghast at how much more misaligned we'd become.

So he thought we needed to confront our existential dread head on, not redirect it or dilute it pharmaceutically. He called this existential analysis or Logotherapy. I believed what I was doing now was a form of Logotherapy. I was shifting meaning back into life and things would smooth out eventually. Road rage was residual neurosis from years ago, but it would fade in time. So would the insomnia once I was done with the heart of the therapy—the writing.

However, before I started writing to pass the sleepless hours, neurosis was acute. I often spent many of these hours in the bathroom. Shaillie would be asleep. She always slept through my sleeplessness, barely rustling in the sheets during my rise and return. I'd stare deeply into the image in the mirror. Passing the middle-of-the-night boredom with excessive self-consciousness. Shamelessly staring into the image. Straight into the eyes of self-absorption. I'd pacify the guilt by telling myself we're all egoists. It's the one thing that binds all six and a half billion of us. The Buddhists have expertly deluded themselves.

During these mirror sessions, I'd often think of Kundera's *The Unbearable Lightness of Being*. The main character Agnes and her husband were discussing faces. The troubled Agnes denied the truth put forth by her face. It was a lie. A mask. She said if there were no mirrors in the world until we turned forty and we saw our face for the first time at this age in a mirror, we'd have no idea whose face we were staring at. Our insides, our internal faces, have no connection to the face we present the world. A great and pure truth expressing the enormity of the chasm between the world and the self.

I'd stare at this face attached to the bones and sinew of truth for long periods of time. I'd examine it in unrepentant vanity and slowly slip out of myself, seeing the face as some mad abstract mask. Tonight, I looked at the brown eyes and thought of my father's brown eyes and how it seemed that I'd never really looked into his eyes. I wondered if our eyes were similar beyond being brown. If they were indistinguishable without the benefit of a face making it obvious, but that I would never know. I looked more deeply at the eyes in the mirror and saw little, tiny births of mortality slowly crawling away from the corners of my eyes. The infant crow's-feet were so slight that it took intense staring to really see them. Yet, they were there. Little did I know that an actual crow would...I squinted and the crow's-feet elongated and found depth within the crevices of furrowed skin. A hint of a future ancient face emerged in the present. I loathed the look of the future. The wrinkles bursting forth from the corners of the eyes were sad, defeated youth lost to a gone era. I'd always aimed for an Eastern reverence for the aged and experienced, but American cultural obsession had slain me. I just didn't know it until the early days of insomnia. I'd often ridicule youth as overrated and foolish in its self-indulgence. I'd resisted its attraction when other friends were pulled under its immortal, seductive call. Felt reassured when the alluring *mindfield* of youth exploded underfoot. Now, with this face attached to my bones before me, I felt billowing waves of anxiety at being in some future netherworld with youth and all its eternal possibilities fading into the wake of oblivion.

Leaving the eyes, I'd attack the harbingers of middle age and all its limitations exposing themselves in my hair. I had the typical turn-of-the-millennium haircut. The sides of my head were shaved close. The top was cut short, slightly up in front like a million other haircuts of today. I had noticed a few gray hairs before, but I'd more or less ignored them by reassuring myself that balding hadn't set in or fooling myself that they were blond deviants of my dark brown hair. But upon closer examination, there was no doubt that they were gray.

I counted the grays meticulously. There were exactly ten that I could see. Who knew how many other signs of aging, signs of the impending end lay beneath my skull in follicles ready to emerge and laugh at the transience of youth and life for that matter. Amazingly, nine of the ten soldiers of antiquity were on the right side, which led me to believe that this was a cerebral conspiracy. I'd avoided all the right brain rhythms of creativity, philosophy, and art in order to hibernate in the cubicle of the left brain tapping keys and watching meaningless numbers of others' fortunes roll across the sad mechanical screen. All in pursuit of material comfort and the unexamined life. All detours from truths rather than headfirst dives into essence.

I had abandoned art and creativity, left it behind as college life, as a four-year pursuit to satiate immature yearning. No time for humanism. Materialism was God. Maturity meant consumption, seizing the bull market by the horns, demarcating as many square feet of the earth as your own and marrying your girlfriend and...and...and...

Except now I couldn't sleep.

I searched through Shaillie's feminine bath products and found some moisturizer. I rubbed a dab between my palms. *"A dab will do ya,"* I recalled Nicholson saying in *Cuckoo's Nest* right before the doctors blasted him with thousands of volts. Electroshock didn't sound so bad at that moment. Jumpstart the mind into new directions, an instant derangement of the senses. I massaged the dab gently into my face feeling the skull beneath my forehead, the ocular, cheek and mandible bones beneath the skin, flesh, and blood of my face. I put some extra cream on my fingertips and carefully caressed the crow's-feet trying to keep them in their gestation period for as long as possible. I then found some dainty scissors and cut out the grays despite knowing they'd be back soon. I must have spent another hour in the mockery of myself while an internal *coup d'état* played itself out. It would foment and rise regardless of conscious efforts, but I wanted time to stand still while I danced along the surface one slow waltz at a time. Truth is an eternal eclipse. Can't ever look it in the eye too quickly, lest you go blind.

Shaillie had infinite patience with me. I reminded myself that I could never hurt her. That I should never hurt her. Things had calmed down a bit after the crow incident and the road rage. We continued our spherical conversations along their usual pattern. So many patterns to be relived and redone over and over again in a mockery to novelty. However, one particular night was an aberration. It did have precedence a few years back when Shaillie had invited another woman into our bed. I had thought that was a momentary leap from the treadmill. A wild moment of whimsy that got the better of Shaillie. She was an artist, preternatural at her core, and occasionally the reality within fought through the layers of protective armor. The core, at times, demanded oxygen. Demanded life.

We were in bed, touching and kissing and chatting. When Shaillie suddenly pulled away. "Van, you know what? I think I know why you can't sleep."

"Do tell."

"Maybe you just want a final taste before you marry."

"A final taste of what?"

"Of another woman."

I laughed. "Further proof that existentialism gets no respect these days, my dear. A man can't question meaning without being accused of wanting to get laid."

"I'm just offering an alternative. Maybe, your angst is a lot simpler than all that existential theory, no disrespect to the eminent Viktor Frankl. Maybe, just maybe, all your anxiety is due to the notion of sleeping with one woman for the rest of your life. Just simple masculine wedding fears. I know it's not easy carrying that thing around all day."

"How would you know?"

"It's a hypothesis based on years and years of male idiocy and deviance."

"Ok, that's a tough one to refute." I conceded.

"You want to hear my idea?"

"I'm waiting. It sounds like it will be interesting."

"Why don't you go to Providence and get laid with Bishop and all those train-wreck friends of yours?"

I couldn't have been more surprised. I was expecting more talk of the list of therapists that still rested in the back of Frankl's book, nary a number dialed. "That's not what I expected. You're kidding, of course."

"No, not at all."

"Yes, you are. This is one of those litmus test questions. One of those questions where it's like branches and leaves laid out across a huge pit. Answer it wrong and you fall into the dark hole."

"No litmus test. I want you to be with another woman before you commit to me. My present to you."

I shook my head. "But after that night with Rina, we decided the swinger thing was not us."

"This isn't a swinger thing. Not a *ménage à trois*. It's an old-fashioned bachelor party festivity. No big deal."

"You want me to be with a whore? I just want to confirm that there's no miscommunication."

"None."

"Irony?"

"No."

"Sarcasm?"

"No."

"Double *entendre*?"

"No."

"Triple?"

"Enough! Have some fun, but there's one rule."

"I knew it. Ok, what? The whore has to be male?"

"Please, that would be worse. The rule is, no penetration, Van Arakalian. I said laid, but I didn't mean it completely. So, I guess yes, there was some semantic gamesmanship."

"You're incredible. Asking me to be with a woman."

"A full body massage with a cathartic happy ending. As long as you don't enter another woman and it's before the marriage, I'm fine. Maybe a little dance with perversity will snap you out of this Armenian madness. Maybe, you'll even sleep through the night after a night of wildness."

"My ancestors and I are fully entitled to our madness," I said. "It's well-earned."

48

A couple of nights later I was at work thinking about Shaillie's unexpected offer when Koles came in. His normally long, unkempt hair was shorn nearly to the scalp.

"What the hell did you do?" I immediately asked.

"Shaved. Shaved my skull."

"What the hell setting is that?"

"One."

"Christ, are you going for the concentration camp look?" I asked, thinking of it as some strange homage to Frankl.

"Needed a change. Any kind. Should have gone totally bald, but I didn't have the balls. Maybe next time."

"I need one, too. Change that is, not a shaved head." I confessed, surprising myself.

"How so?"

I rarely shared much with my bar universe. I preferred to be a quiet, nondescript planet with the mad satellites spinning around me. I felt if I truly stepped into their whirl, I'd never return. But things were changing in the universe.

"I just haven't been sleeping lately. I've got a bout of insomnia and Shaillie thinks it's because I'm getting cold feet about the wedding."

"Are you?"

"I don't think so."

"Don't," Koles advised. "I haven't been the same since my marriage ended. I'm going to make amends, though. I'll fix things. I just need to figure out what went wrong."

I was about to ask him more about his ex-wife, but Koles quickly jumped in before I could get the words out. "I'll have a beer. Doesn't matter what kind." He sat down at the seat closest to the waitress station where he always sat. He had told me this way only one person at most could sit next to him. Koles said he enjoyed the voices of conversation at a bar, but wasn't particularly interested in being an active participant. He did, however, plan to steal many of the words in a crime of literary theft.

Chez Lucienne had no draft beer and only three kinds of bottled beer. It was a bar of hard alcohol and wine. I pulled a bottle of Heineken from the refrigerator. At that point Bishop walked in. He put his heavy leather satchel on a table near the bar. It landed with a thud. He exchanged salutations with a few of the regulars sitting on the other side of the bar. Long-time regulars who'd been coming in since the 70s. Drinkers from the generation that respected and accepted booze as a way through life, functional inebriation to get the head to the pillow each

49

night and survive another day. "The days when alcohol had a certain nobility," as my father once articulated it.

"My good deacons Koles and Arakalian," Bishop stated, giving each of us our own individual nod. He sat next to Koles and was clearly already well on his way to getting distance from what he would consider the dismal truth of sobriety.

"Where you coming from Bishop?" I asked.

"My parish is far and wide, Van. I was just christening a Cambridge diocese. I saw a young lady reading Nietzsche at the bar. An attractive woman reading Nietzsche. I can't think of anything sexier than that and where else besides the glorious People's Republic of Cambridge."

Bishop noticed a *New York Times* on the bar and picked it up. He pulled out the arts section and got lost in it. Koles took a big gulp of his beer while I poured Bishop his evening usual, knowing it was dusk and he was well beyond his wine-soaked afternoon.

He put the paper down and looked over at Koles.

"Why aren't you home going over our edits?"

"No flow today, Bishop. I aborted early."

"Poets wait for inspiration. Poetic novelists can't afford the time."

Koles took a sip of his Heineken and looked away. Bishop winked at me. "Alright then, that's when it's time to turn to the elixirs. We'll drink until those internal oases flourish again." Bishop looked over at Koles's beer and grabbed the bottle. "But this will get you nowhere fast. It's a lazy alcohol."

Koles seemed uninterested in literary talk. He snatched his beer back and poured the rest into the pilsner glass. I gave Bishop his drink. He raised it to toast with Koles, who obliged, though with a touch of apathy. "To tomorrow, when the words will flow with divine confluence." Koles managed a smile and their glasses touched.

Bishop took a long look at Koles. I could see that his white-wine mind was finally realizing Koles's new haircut. "What's with the Buddhist monk look?"

"I had time to kill. There weren't any words to kill the day."

"It's got a curt nobility," Bishop concluded.

"There's a good name," I said. "Kurt Nobility."

"Beautiful, my good Armenian. Use it for your novel. Kurt Nobility goes to the land of Ararat and climbs the great mountain to stand where Noah's Arc landed." Bishop again winked at me as if he were one up on my own thoughts.

"Kurt Nobility is far from an Armenian name."

50

"Van, those years in finance infected you with disease of logic. Kurt Nobility is half Armenian or he's, how do you say it in your tongue, an *odad*?"

"Yes, *odad*," I answered, very surprised at Bishop's knowledge of Armenian vocabulary.

"An *odad* obsessed with the first nation to declare itself Christian, the first nation to suffer modern genocide. An *odad* obsessed with an ancient people surviving under centuries of distress. Van, art is not about finite possibilities."

I smiled. "Well, I'll take note of your ideas when I sit down to write the great Armenian novel." For some reason I was determined to keep the text of insomnia unknown while Bishop seemed to know all the while I was up to something. He seemed to have moments of clairvoyance even with alcohol permeating his every pore.

"Van, all Armenians are artists. The sooner you realize it, the better. Why else would you be tending bar for the lost and forlorn folks of Chez Lucienne? It's part of your path."

I smiled and shook my head as if his notion were absurd. "You see right through me, Bishop," I said, attempting a facetious tone.

Bishop nodded slyly and turned toward Koles. "Now, young Derek, this haircut amuses me, but you've sought the wrong solution. You need a different kind of change."

"And that is?" Koles asked.

"The altar of alcoholic excess can only take you so far. It's as limiting as religion. You need another indulgence." Rourke sipped his drink, easing into the rum after all the white wine.

Koles looked at Rourke, awaiting the inevitable advice.

"My newly crowned Buddhist, it's quite simple. You need the honesty of pussy. My cock has more or less retired, but you and Van should be seeking truth like voracious omnivores.
Writers need to exorcise their cocks."

"I'm not a writer and I'm getting married soon," I said, quickly and defensively. I thought of Shaillie's suggestion—she and Bishop ironically on the same prurient page. I never thought that would happen, but she would find some link in the synchronous chain of events.

"Bishop, just cut the bullshit," Koles said.

"Are you turning on us, Koles? Venturing to the Oscar Wilde side? You wouldn't have to do time for it like Oscar, though. Hell, nowadays you'll win an Oscar."

Koles shook his head. "I can see my balls will be broken all night long."

51

"Only until those balls are actually broken. Why would you not want the taste of a woman?" Bishop asked, "If you want a man, that's fine. You just need some carnal taste, that's all."

Koles smirked at Bishop and then downed his beer. "Another beer please, Van."

"You can't stay loyal to her forever. The papers have been signed. It's over, right?"

"I know, Bishop. I know about the papers. I just don't have the energy or desire to meet someone and start something up. I'm not over her yet. It's that simple, ok. I'm putting those energies into the book. All for art and art for all."

"Don't manipulate Madam Art. Art shan't be a beard. You need to shave more than your head."

"Whatever," Koles said, trying to get out of the conversation.

"Besides, who said anything about starting something up. I'm talking about sex, not love. I'm talking about fucking, not making love."

Koles smiled. "Fine, show me the woman that will fuck me with no strings attached."

"Gentlemen, I took a break from afternoon Mass and went to the movies. The Brattle Theatre was showing *Last Tango in Paris* today. As potent today as it was thirty years ago. Have you seen it?"

Before we could answer, Bishop continued. Dialogue with him didn't necessarily need anyone besides himself.

"A *coup d'theatre* if there's ever been one. Gentlemen, while I was watching Brando's emotional strip show, I decided ole Koles here needs some Maria Schneider to snap him out of his rut, artistically and otherwise."

"Who wouldn't want Maria Schneider?" I said, taking some heat off of Koles.

"Van's getting cold feet," Koles said, gladly shifting the focus.

"No, not true. Just my fiancée's theory."

"Your finance theory?" Bishop asked.

"Fi-an-cée."

"Ahh, yes. The fiancée. It's not a coincidence that the words are so similar. Leave it to the French. So, your feet are getting chilled, my Armenian nomad."

"No, Bishop, it's just a rumor. No more chilly than the norm."

"The norm? No such thing. Women know exactly what's going on. A woman's senses, no matter how irrationally they may express them, are usually dead on, bull's-eyes to the psyche. They know us better than we know ourselves."

"I'm just going through some jitters, some minor regrets, whatever. Never mind."

"So, it's both of you who need the trip." Just then Bishop's eyes wandered to a nearby table. Two women were chatting. He seemed to be looking at one of them. When she said something about "Cork, Ireland" he had his call to duty.

Bishop got up from his stool. He rubbed Koles's head and turned to me, "Deacon Koles needs some rupture to align his bipolar thoughts. Shift his tectonic plates beneath the cerebral fault lines. He needs cataclysm like Brando in *Tango*. He needs no words with a woman, just primal grunting. No names, here. No names," Bishop said, attempting Brando's voice, "No words, just grunts."

Relinquishing the Brando moment, Bishop asked me what the nearby ladies were drinking. When I told him Sancerre, he had me pour them a round. With that he took his drink from the bar and maneuvered his garrulous madness to the two women. With Bishop departed, Koles immediately took out the little notebook from his shirt pocket. I had never seen him without one, yet I'd also never seen him write in it. As if I were suddenly an apparition, Koles started writing with barely a pause. His flow seemed to have suddenly returned. Over Koles's tensed shoulder I could see and hear Seamus Rourke work his grizzled, vexing sixty year old charm on the middle aged women. I wondered if Koles was simply recording the conversation.

"Ladies, allow me to introduce myself properly," Bishop said, conjuring his affected Irish brogue.

The one who had mentioned Cork seemed quite interested in Rourke. Her eyes were transfixed on him. Tonight he had on a silk ascot, instead of his usual bowtie, and an ivory white suit, a somewhat more masculine Truman Capote. She maintained an energetic and ingratiating smile while he settled in. She began to say something, but Bishop cut her off before she got the first word out.

"My dear, I'm a native of Cork, land of soothing beer, poet drunkards, and mirage-like green prairie hills. Did I hear my dear homeland mentioned?"

"Yes," said the interested one. The other woman seemed instantly annoyed.

Bishop continued, "A kindred soul, perhaps."

"Sort of," she answered.

Bishop took her hand and kissed it softly. "Consider me enchanted, my fair lady of Cork. One look in your eyes and a man ceases to consider the meaninglessness and absurdity of life as the prevailing forces of history. Everyday with you would be Bloomsday. Everyday an equinox."

"A pleasure to meet you," she said, shyly smiling.

The other woman's eyes rolled so much that they nearly disappeared into her forehead. She let out an audible sigh. Bishop ignored this while he still held the smitten one's hand. He kissed it again. "The pleasure is truly and eminently mine. The name is Seamus Rourke, but feel free to call me Bishop."

"Caroline Bonell. So, are you involved in the church?" She asked in an incredulous tone.

"Absolutely. I am a devout pagan and druid for all things created. A pious follower of the three letter God, Art, and a regular in the church of barroom theology. Welcome to the congregation of Chez Lucienne."

The other lady responded, "What a load of shit." Neither of them paid any attention to her.

"I welcome you to tonight's Mass, Caroline the Great."

"I'm honored to attend your service."

I brought the glasses of Sancerre to the table. Bishop and Caroline were chatting and giggling as if they'd met long ago. I took Caroline's empty glass. The other lady finished what was left of her wine and I gave them new glasses. "This is on Bishop. Cheers," I said. Rourke raised his Amber special and toasted, "Ladies, to the North and South Poles and everything in between. It's a beautiful world right now."

They all toasted, even the reluctant member of the triad. When their glasses returned to the table, Bishop said, "The pleasure and humility is truly all mine, my fair Irish lass." He extended his hand again. She put her hand in his and he pulled it to his mouth, turned her wrist downward, and softly kissed the back of her hand again. She giggled, surprisingly enthralled with Bishop's eccentric, flamboyant style of courting. He turned to the other lady and did the same, albeit a bit more tentatively and dispassionately. She smiled, now seemingly more amused and less aghast.

Meanwhile, Koles took a break from the barfly notebook novel and said, "There will only be one Bishop."

"Here, here," I said, pulling out my coffee mug of white wine and taking a big gulp while Koles drank from his beer.

"So, Derek, what do you think of Bishop's idea?" I asked.

"Depends. Where and when?"

"Providence and tonight."

"What's the deal?"

"Let's go. It's that simple."

"A brothel?" he asked.

"More or less, I guess. One of those massage parlors, I presume. You see them advertised in the *Boston Phoenix* all the time."

Koles looked down at his little notebook, seeming to read for a moment. After a few moments, he looked up. "Maybe, I should. Maybe, I'm taking this chastity and loyalty thing too far."

"Loyalty to whom?"

"Yvette."

"But, Derek, you're..."

"I know I am, but I don't feel that way. It was a sham. I'm going to get her back." He closed the notebook and put back in his shirt pocket, but held the top of it before pulling it back out and returning it to the bar. "Paying for sex isn't cheating, right?"

"No, not at all," I responded, not agreeing with what I had said. But how could one cheat on an ex-wife?

"And Shaillie?"

"I'll tell her it's my bachelor party." I didn't want to reveal that she actually suggested the road trip.

"You know, Van, I tried the promiscuous life after I got back from Paris, but it was awful. I mean I had momentary highs, but then I got lonelier than an old, dying dog. The day after each fling a profound darkness permeated my body and mind. A miserable, miserable loneliness set in. I ached for my ex. I know it's pathetic, but I can tell you, right?"

"Sure, I'm the bartender," I said, laughing.

"Bartender-regular confidentiality, right?"

"Of course. Maybe paying for it will give you a boost. All the cards on the table from the get go. No lies or deception."

"I don't know," Koles said.

"Is it a moral thing?"

"Moral about what?" he seemed surprised by the question.

"Prostitution. Some people might think it's immoral to be with a whore."

"Van, this isn't the bible belt."

"Ok, so?"

"I told you why already. You don't have to agree with it. I'll stay loyal to her if I want to and I don't give a shit if people laugh." Koles took a gulp of beer and looked away.

"No problem, Derek. Think about it and let me know. It's still early." I looked at my watch. It was 7 o'clock. "We've got a few hours before last call." Koles nodded and returned to the notebook.

I walked down to the other end of the bar to take care of the others. I was very intrigued by the proposed escapade by my ultra-liberated fiancée and then uncannily and serendipitously seconded by Bishop. I had to go now. There must have been some starry destiny to it if it was being offered on two wholly divergent fronts. Shaillie's chaos

55

theories confirmed. Maybe the taste of another woman would redirect the mad current drifting me away from familiar shores. Maybe the guilt would do it. After all, I was no picaresque anti-hero. This had to be an aberrant and temporary detour. Or alternatively, it could push me over the edge running and flailing with energized immediacy for that new direction. Maybe the aberration was the reality and the entire self, a priori, had been the real masquerade...

At the other end of the bar, I poured another glass of wine for Lionel Stewart and his fiancée, Rachel Holton. Both Lionel and Rachel had been through their share of bottles and marriages. Their wedding was on standby until the paperwork on their most recent divorces came through. This would be his third and her second. Odds around the bar were that they would soon hit an aggregate seven soon after they were married.

I met them both at Boston Common Financial. They had upper-level management jobs. Rachel was at a higher rung than Lionel, but they both had glass-walled offices rather than cubicles. I had met Rachel in the BCF cafeteria. We were drinking coffee and she invited me out for drinks at Chez Lucienne's with some other cubicle rats. While at Chez Lucienne's, I met the owner and on a whim asked him if he needed a bartender. I left my name and number and he called me a week later. I quit BCF right after I hung up the phone without informing Shaillie.

Jack Dunhardt sat at the corner seat facing Lionel and Rachel. Jack was an old-school liberal and proud of it. He would preach the virtues of his "Roosevelt" liberalism to anyone who would listen. He was quite open about his mission "to return the word liberal back to its original luster, rather than the tarnished, dirty word it's become. Got to give the Republicans credit. They are master manipulators. True, diehard Machiavellians. Damn good at getting elected and damn scary once elected."

Seizing any opportunity, he would go through his endless litany of modern liberalism's successes. He usually started with the 19th amendment then proceeded into FDR's achievements of the forty-hour work week, overtime pay, minimum wage, social security, then onto civil rights, education reform, and tax cuts "for those who should get it, not for the upper two percent. All positive change in America is a result of liberal thought. All delays in positive change are the result of conservative thought." He usually concluded with, "What the hell is so wrong with a Great Society? Shouldn't we all want a Great Society? Should we pursue a bad society instead?"

As had become commonplace, they were chatting about the war in Iraq. Jack usually focused on what he called the true lure of the war, oil, but Rachel liked to believe that Bush's intentions were actually noble, no matter how hopeless and misguided. He truly wanted to remake the Middle East into a region of democracy and capitalism. When Jack accused Republicans of being master manipulators, Rachel disagreed. "Jack, I really think Bush is a like a little boy. He's very naïve, as evidenced by his born-again state of mind. He simply wants to outdo his father. It's Psychoanalysis 101."

Lionel was probably the closest thing to a red state member that Chez Lucienne had. He was a centrist at heart. A Clintonian, neo-Democrat.

"I don't think so, honey. He's got that cowboy mentality, but I think it's more complex than that. I think hubris that infects all leaders got the best of him. If he had just stayed in Afghanistan, focused on democracy there, without thinning out his troops, he could have ensured a hell of a legacy."

"Bullshit," Jack said, rolling his eyes.

"No, Jack, it's true. He had justification to go into Kabul. He had it made if he stayed there. He would have appeased the hawks by avoiding Chamberlain appeasement and the doves would have gone along because the Taliban was guilty. It was justified aggression after 9/11. That's what Clinton would have done. He could have built a democracy in Afghanistan, affected positive change, and had enough troops to go after the real culprit."

"Who? Saddam Hussein?" Jack quickly replied. "He got him already."

"You're going to be sarcastic rather than actually debate, right?"

"No, no. I thought that's why we invaded Iraq. Because of 9/11?

"Cut the shit, Jack."

"Oh right, it was Weapons of Mass Destruction? Oh no, they weren't there. Let's see what was it? Why did we actually invade?"

"I get your point. My point is if he had just stopped short of…"

"But honey," Rachel interjected, "that's where the paternal angle comes in. If his father hadn't stopped short of removing Hussein, then hubris may not have entered the arena."

"Perhaps," Lionel said, "but then we would have been in the mess of opening Pandora's Box in '91. It was doomed no matter which Bush."

Jack was shaking his head vigorously. "This isn't about Napoleonic hubris or Freudian paternal theories. The damn thing was a set up," Jack insisted.

"Jack, don't go conspiracy on us," Rachel pleaded.

"How many has he had tonight?" Lionel asked me.

"Not many," I responded, knowing any bartender worth his tip jar never revealed a regular's drink count.

"No, no. I don't go so far as to say 9/11 was planned. Oswald certainly didn't kill Kennedy and I'm sure Bush didn't order the planes into the towers. Though I do think 9/11 was a something the Republicans crudely leveraged for every drop of oil, pun intended. Cheney had his ticket and they punched it for every ride in *Texxonland*. They'd never admit it, but Cheney and the Halliburton-Bechtel suits knew the door was wide open and no one was checking IDs."

"Not so, Jack. You're too cynical," Rachel countered.

"And tell me one thing. Why couldn't he just go after bin Laden? To hell with Kabul. Just get the mastermind, but as long as the enemy is out there, the military budget can go through the trillion dollar roof and America can play emperor again trying to remake the world in its image. Democracy at gunpoint doesn't work. Well, maybe, just maybe, the world doesn't want our image. If I have to listen to King George compare Iraq to the Marshall Plan one more time, I'm moving to a deserted island. What a crime to history! Does he actually believe this shit or just getting the last laugh on all of us?"

"We may push the image too much, but if I were a woman over there, I'd want that image," Rachel said.

"It's not our job," Jack rebutted. "Where should I go, Van? Tahiti's trite now. How about Curacao or Macao?"

"Curacao sounds good," I said for no particular reason.

"Of course, a bartender would say that."

"You contradict yourself, Jack," Rachel continued. "Liberals cause change and conservatives sit on their fat, rich asses. You've said it over and over again. Now, you're advocating no change. You're turning conservative now. Are you flip-flopping?"

"Great thinkers change their mind. Nothing wrong with that, but I'm doing no such thing. We can direct change within our borders and influence the outside indirectly. We don't need to shove change down someone's throat with a gun. It never works anyway. Democracy through violence is a lie and on top of it all, the damn guy running the show didn't even get elected democratically. What a tragic farce!"

"Well, I disagree with you, but it is a bloody mess. I never thought we'd live through another Vietnam, but it looks like it's Saigon redux," Rachel said.

Jack added, "It could get worse. Much worse."

Rachel finished her glass of wine and looked at Lionel, who as if cued by Rachel, finished his wine.

I'd heard this conversation in one form or another before, but I hadn't recalled it ending with overtures of the apocalypse. Before the world ended, I wanted to refill the drinks and get back to Koles and plan our run to Providence. Jack was shaking his head with a cynical glare in his eyes. I'd start my queries elsewhere.

"So, another glass of Sauvignon?" I asked Lionel and Rachel.

Rachel looked quizzically at her fiancé. "No, I had my fill of wine and politics. We'll get no answers," he said.

"Welcome to reality, Lionel. No room for Pollyannas here," Jack said carefully placing his drink onto the napkin precisely within the ring mark left from the glass. He did this with NASA-like exactitude.

"Just the check, Van."

I immediately gave Lionel the check. He signed his name to it and added a five-dollar tip. Chez Lucienne was truly old school. Regulars paid their tab monthly by mail like an electric bill. Very little cash was exchanged. The only regular who didn't have a running tab was Bishop. Too many unpaid electric bills.

"So, Van, do you miss the bank?" Rachel asked as she got up to leave.

"Not really."

"At the risk of sounding like your mother, you're not going to stay here forever, are you?"

"You mean at the risk of sounding like my fiancée."

"Not a big difference," Rachel said with a grin.

"No, I'll be moving on."

"That's good because Chez Lucienne has maelstrom-type powers, Van. It looks harmless on the outside, but the seduction is understated."

"Except in the case of Bishop," Lionel added.

All of us turned towards Bishop. He was still spinning his bardic rhetoric with the ladies.

"Nothing understated there," Rachel concurred.

"I've noticed the vortex. I try to keep one foot on stable land," I lied.

"And one foot in quicksand," Jack parried. "It's more interesting that way, right? What other choice do we have, the suburbs? Ugh. To paraphrase New Hampshire, live free or suburbia."

Rachel ignored Jack and leaned towards my ear, whispering, "Van, just be careful of Bishop. He's no saint."

I nodded.

Lionel and Rachel said their goodbyes to Jack, who responded with something about *realpolitik*. Rachel leaned over and gave him a kiss on his lined and weathered cheek. "Such a sweet curmudgeon, Jack. Try and have a good weekend."

Just then the image of Jason Taux leapt into the forefront of my mind. Must have been the word curmudgeon. I hadn't thought of him in a while. He was my former cubicle neighbor who had chastised me as selfish for quitting BCF and told me about the bus cleaner who never missed a day in a century or so. The same Jason Taux who mocked my attempts at a new life and warned me that I was trading one straitjacket for another.

"Hey, do you guys know Jason Taux? He used to sit in the cubicle next to me."

"Sure," both of them said.

"Can you give him my best? He never liked me much, especially when I quit, but I always thought he was ok."

"That would be kind of tough," Rachel answered.

"Why's that?"

"He no longer works at BCF."

"You're kidding. He quit? He really lit into me for leaving and now..."

"He didn't quit, Van."

"What happened? Did he get fired?"

Rachel nodded.

"For what?"

"Sexual harassment," Lionel said.

I gave Koles a Heineken. He was no longer writing in the notebook. It was back in his shirt pocket, the metal spirals peeking out. He gestured thank you while his eyes and countenance expressed the gravity of solemn and ponderous thought. He needed Providence as much or more than I did. All we could offer him was the city of the same name. Though no one would ever accuse Derek of a cheerful disposition, I didn't recall him ever being this morose.

Just then Carl Shapiro walked in with his patented salutation.

"Hello, my merry band of reprobates," he said taking the seat vacated by Lionel Stewart. Shapiro was another regular, though an infrequent one of late.

"Carl, how are you?" I asked.

"Van, ok, yes, ok, Van."

"What'll it be?"

"A beer, please."

"Oh no," Jack gasped, "you're not drinking."

"I haven't had a drink in months. I'm ready."

Jack lit up a Lucky Strike, "Christ, you have one of those and I'm checking out early tonight."

"Jack, you make a big deal out of my drinking when nothing..."

"Carl, you're not drinking."

"Van, I'll take a Kronenburg."

"Van, don't give it to him. Our man from Havana has been sober since the Red Sox won the Series. He'll not ruin his skein here."

"I've had drinks elsewhere. I just don't drink here anymore because you guys live in the past. My past, in particular. I'll take France's finest beer, please. I'll pay cash, upfront."

Jack had a look of sincere consternation. Carl only came in from time to time and he'd never asked me for a drink before. He usually had a Coke and watched a game on the small, corner TV. I didn't know him well, but I'd heard a lot about him. The "our man in Havana" sobriquet originated because Carl was a big fan of the author Graham Greene. Ironically, but no surprisingly, Bishop dubbed him after his own, not Carl's favorite Greene novel. However, Carl's legend had nothing to do with British novelists or the Cuban capital.

Carl was a loyal Red Sox fan. He'd been following the Sox since 1948 when he saw his first game, a playoff game between the Sox and Indians. I remembered the year and game easily because my father had also attended that game and told me all about how the Sox best pitcher, Mel Parnell, was mysteriously not chosen to start. Manager Joe McCarthy inexplicably selected the mediocre Denny Galehouse and, of course, as the then thriving curse would have it, Galehouse got lit up and the Sox lost the game 8-3. My father's memory was still vivid in my mind...but as for Carl Shapiro, this was not about 1948. It was about 2004. My old man never got redemption for his fruitless years as a fan, but Carl did with a peculiar twist to it.

He was watching the game at the bar with the rest of the crew. Chez Lucienne's had made an exception to their anti-sports stance for this event. When the Red Sox finally erased eighty-six years of ignominy, Carl was both inebriated and ecstatic. He was drinking gin and tonics, his potable of choice. Shapiro's other passion besides the Sox was a Ukrainian woman named, Reisa Zehtov, whom Carl had been interested in for many years. Reisa hadn't cared much for baseball, but the Red Sox feverish run cajoled her in from the periphery like it had so many Bostonians. Carl had his opportunity. He made sure he sat next to Reisa for every game. He explained the game of baseball to her and the significance and torture of the curse to true Red Sox fans. Carl deluded himself into believing that Reisa's interest was not just in the game, but also him.

After Doug Mientkiewicz caught the final out of the World Series, like everyone else at Boston bars, the celebrations began. Carl thought the Red Sox ending their nearly century-long tragedy would be the right time to end the five-year phase of his unrequited love of Reisa. He and Reisa hugged and kissed on the cheek. Carl then asked Reisa for a kiss. A real kiss. She politely declined and not thinking much about it started hugging and kissing other jubilant fans.

Things finally settled down, but Carl hadn't. He drank more and more gin and tonics and was clearly not enjoying the moment for which he'd long been waiting. Finally, he sat down again next to Reisa. He took her hand and asked, "to kiss this instead." Then, he placed her hand on his exposed cock. Reisa screamed and instinctually hit Carl. However, this wasn't a slap. As Bishop said, "Eastern European women are as tough as gulags." Reisa had no use for an open fist. She hit Carl with a straight right hand that had the fury of Stalinist intentions. Poor Carl spun off his stool and fell flat on his back. The bar went totally silent except for David Ortiz's celebratory voice from the TV while Carl lay there with *it* hanging out for all to see.

Reisa left the bar and never returned. Carl took a long hiatus and then came in with much less frequency than befits a regular. He also never drank, at least at Chez Lucienne's, until this night when he asked for the Kronenburg.

"Look, I can have a beer, Jack. I'm not going to get drunk. I did my AA, higher power bullshit time. I can handle it. Contrary to American alcohol philosophy, one can drink a beer or two a few nights a week and not be an alcoholic. This is a French bar after all. It shouldn't be so damn puritanical and uptight."

"After your very American display of dipsomania here, I think you should reconsider," Jack countered.

"One drunken mistake. I loved Reisa and it got the better of me."

"Van Gogh offers an ear and you offer a penis."

"I didn't cut it off. Bad comparison. Christ, am I the only guy in the world to make a mistake? The punishment doesn't fit the crime. This is a bar. We're not saints, we're libertines and…"

"Profligates. I know, Carl, we all know."

"France's finest beer, please. Thank you very much, Van." Carl was determined.

I looked over at Jack. I didn't want to be the one to end someone's sobriety. I thought of asking Bishop, but he would have been an absurd arbiter of whether to drink or not. He probably would have responded with a verdict of Shakespearean proportions. I needed a simple yes or no.

"Van, he's a grown man, but it's a bartender's call. My advice would be to keep him off the gin. Something about those juniper berries is toxic to him."

"I just want a goddamn beer, Van."

I pulled a Kronenburg from the fridge, popped the top, and poured it into a tall pilsner glass.

"Cheers, Carl."

"*Merci beaucoup*, my good barkeep."

"*De rien*, Carl."

Carl took a long, slow, satisfying drink. "Brewers of fine beer since 1664. They know what they're doing after three and half centuries."

Jack closed his eyes and shook his head before responding, "Such a shitty beer. Wine from France, beer from America, Carl. You always get things ass backwards."

Carl ignored him and looked up at the Cubs game on the TV.

"Why is this on? How about the Sox?"

"Ole Van here is a nouveaux Cubs fan. He's following Nomar," Jack told him. I always put the Cubs games on and the regulars rarely complained. Aside from the Red Sox World Series run, Chez Lucienne considered itself above sports. The small, thirteen-inch TV was usually turned off. I was one of the few bartenders who had it on. Carl was the first one to ask for the Red Sox. "Yeah, you see Van likes the underdog. Breaking the curse was the worst thing that could have happened to him."

"Well, I wouldn't go that far," I said.

"Hmmm, that's pretty good. Very roguish thinking. I like it. Cubs haven't won since 1908. No better underdog than that. How's Nomar doing, Van?"

"He's off to a slow start, but he's healthy."

"So far. The hamstring could go at anytime. Talk about cursed, Van. He gets traded from the Sox the year they miraculously win the Holy Grail and winds up on a team that has been cursed longer."

I noticed Koles had taken out his notebook again. He must have been jotting down live moments for his novel. This was fertile ground and, apparently, he didn't trust his memory. Maybe he was breaking through the block he'd had today and didn't want to relinquish any momentum. I thought of telling him insomnia was the best cure for repressed language. Instead, I asked him if he had made up his mind about the trip to Providence. He didn't answer nor show any signs of registering what I'd asked. Koles seemed to have the capacity to completely tune out reality as purely and unselfconsciously as an Alzheimer's patient. After a few minutes, he finally looked up and suddenly back in tune said, "So, Van, this little road trip isn't going to screw things up with Shaillie, is it?"

"No, not at all. She's fine with it."

"You're going to tell her?" He stuck the notebook back into his pocket. I noticed the spirals peering out again like smoothed-over barbwire.

"Yes. She already knows. Her idea, in fact," I conceded.

Koles took a gulp of his beer. "You're kidding me."

"No." I didn't feel right telling Koles this, but the urge to confess has its own volition sometimes.

Koles looked distracted again, as if what I had said triggered a scene in the cinema of his thoughts. I didn't want details. I just wanted to get on the road and head to Providence for a night of deviance. I kept reassuring myself it would be a mild, tepid romp into debauchery. One I could handle and fiancée-endorsed for that matter. I viewed my last six years as lost years agglomerating the currency for future, external comforts. Deviation would help restore the spiritual decay. Deviation would give much needed definition. I needed to tell Shaillie that. Time to define, time for definition. The elimination of all decoys, internal or otherwise.

Meanwhile, Bishop continued his courtship. He was now alone with his woman of choice. I hadn't even noticed the friend leave. I'd often seen Rourke flirt, resurrecting what seemed to be a Don Juan youth. However, this time it seemed more real. Underneath the perpetual aesthetic circus that is Seamus Rourke, something real seemed to be percolating. What's more, this time the woman was reciprocating. That I hadn't seen before.

"My Corkian lass, some call me Bishop, some Cardinal, depends on the congregation. The crying lot at Chez Lucienne tends to the title Bishop. It's equal parts patronizing and deferential to me and religion. A good balance."

"I don't see how it's respectful to religion, but I prefer Bishop. It's more down to earth than Cardinal," Caroline said sarcastically.

"So, sweet Caroline, when were you last in Cork?"

"Oh, it's been five years now. I did a year there in exchange with another professor. I taught an American lit class. She taught Irish lit and we collaborated on an article about our experiences. I do miss my time there. Ireland is a special place. Magical, as you well know."

"The Irish land is imbued with the tragic and magic. Together they create the most curious and triumphant of blooms. The only place in the world that could have created Lord Joyce. I myself have never left Ireland, my dear. I'm physically here, but spiritually I remain in

Cork. A little leprechaun will always thump in my heart with Celtic murmurs while I howl into the vacuum of Materialism Americana."

Caroline smiled. "Though my friend seems to have disagreed, I love your company, Bishop."

"No one has ever viewed me with moderation. I'm proud to be loved or hated. Anything but mediocrity."

"How long have you been here in the vacuum?"

"Forty years, but I've never left Northwest Cork. Never left my life there. My life here has been that of a headless chicken. Let's drink to the directionless cock from Cork." Caroline laughed and toasted Bishop's salacious comedy.

"If you're trying to scare me off, it won't work Bishop Rourke. I'm on to your religion my dear. We've got something going here and you're testing me. I'll pass every one, so let's skip the exam and cut to the diploma, my lost cock."

Bishop laughed a hoarse and phlegmy cackle, lit an unfiltered Camel, and then sipped his Amber elixir. "Many come, but few arrive at Chez Lucienne. You, my dear Caroline, have arrived. I accept you to the aging melancholic womb that is Chez Lucienne."

"Bishop, 'tis not this womb I wish to enter. 'Tis this womb I wish to pull you out of," Caroline said, invoking her own Irish brogue.

"I'm happily sad in this womb. Why leave?"

"When was the last time you made love to a woman and not a bar?"

"Bar fucking is very easy. My eyes always close after it's over. I leave in the glory of thoughtlessness after carrying around too many thoughts all day. Thoughtlessness is a good state, a good goal, Caroline. Entire religions of the East are built upon that notion. It's about intoxication, not drunkenness."

"When was the last time you made love to a woman?" Caroline repeated.

Bishop ruminated for a bit before a wry smile arrived. "It's been a while, that's for sure. But that wouldn't do me anything good."

"Why not? A break from the bottle might do you a lot of good."

Bishop shook his head and skewed his mouth. "No good," he said in a rare two word response.

"Why not?"

"Just, no," still shaking his head.

"It will be wonderful, Bishop. It might be the start of something very wonderful between us. I will repair you, my broken Bishop."

"Reparations on the scale of the Marshall Plan cannot fix this broken Irishman. I am…"

Caroline put her index finger to Bishop's mouth. "Shhh, my Bishop, shhh." Her finger slid across his lips, then she turned her hand and slowly caressed Bishop's cheek with the back of her fingers. Bishop closed his eyes and Caroline put her lips to his and kissed him. They kissed for a few moments until Caroline pulled away.

"Still no good?" she cooed.

"Still no God."

"What?"

"Still no good, my sweet, but it's better than before."

"It can be much better."

"My dear, don't try…"

"Bishop Rourke, you can still have your congregation and your bottle. I'm asking you to bed, you foolish sixty-year old boy. You may continue your rum-soaked symphony to the cemetery gates. I just offer you an intermezzo, my dear. It may not go any further. I don't think that far ahead. Been too many times for that."

"You are a special, special woman. Instant karma is finally striking me positively."

"Bishop, you tapped into something long hidden in me. It doesn't want to stay reclusive anymore. No more. You must realize this is very aberrant behavior on my behalf."

"'Twas never dead, dear Caroline."

"No…yes, who knows, but let lonely dormant days be gone and to hell with the cemetery as well."

"I will not go to the cemetery, Caroline. I will be crushed to ash and thrown from the hills of Cork into the Irish air and land. There will be no underground prison leaving me to rot in Goddess-mother earth. I will be free unto death. A great and liberating warm and wind-blown death."

"Beatific death you will have. Now, let's leave death's front porch and go to my place. I have no expectations of anything. I just want to lie near you and feel you near me."

"That's all we can do, sweet Caroline. The gods don't shine eternal."

Caroline smiled and winked at Bishop, "I don't care at all, my dear. I accept you in all forms. Let me hold you tonight."

"Caroline, most women would have been done with me after a few of my turgid sentences. Those who stay, stay just to enjoy the bohemian sideshow. The spectacle of my drunken aging vaudeville. I rarely give encores, my dear. I'm usually a one-act play."

"Tonight, we aren't keeping track of the acts."

He put his left hand on her thigh and his right reached for her hand. She put her hand in his. I was watching this unfold while taking an

66

occasional glimpse at Koles fill up more pages of his notebook. I'd never seen Bishop connect so much with a woman. He was right. They usually stayed for a while to enjoy the spectacle of literate logorrhea, but Caroline was different. She seemed to be truly falling for Bishop.

Bishop said wryly, "I'm not so sure I'm up for this, Caroline."

Caroline laughed sympathetically. "I told you nothing matters. We'll just connect, my sweet. I need you as much as you need me. Nothing to fear, Bishop." Caroline leaned over and kissed Bishop softly on his cheek.

"It matters to me," Bishop replied. There was vulnerability in his voice. It had seeped through alcohol's armor. Caroline had gotten through. But she soon pulled back, afraid she would lose him.

"Ok, sweetheart, ok. I won't push you anymore," she said, defeated. Bishop seemed relieved that Caroline had relented. The verbosity was revived.

"Tomorrow night is for you my new love. Tonight, I have an obligation to youth, to Art. Tonight, we must trigger the muse in my protégé, the guy over there who's buried in his words as we speak. He's bursting with bop prosody that can't find its right channel. Tonight, the poetry will relearn how to howl and whisper simultaneously. It will become the lyrical novel that will become a film at Cannes. We will win the Palm D'or. It will take the French by the balls. After all, the only way to truly take the French is by their Gaulic balls!"

"Do what you have to do. Then tomorrow night is ours. I will cook a wonderful, lustful dinner for you. We'll eat on my balcony. You bring your favorite bottle of white and I will take care of the rest."

Caroline got up and slipped her business card into his chest pocket. She flattened her hand against his heartbeat and held it there for a bit. "You've got some life left in this dear old body, my Bishop." She kissed Rourke, a long, but dignified kiss. Then she ran her hand down to Bishop's crotch, leaving it there for a moment before whispering something in his ear.

Bishop laughed, but said nothing. I'd never seen him at a loss for words, but I'd also never seen a woman so eager to be with him. The ribald flirting seemed to be just veneer. Just games to a larger truth that were too hard and too quick to express right now.

Caroline kissed him one more time and then came over to pay me. Bishop yelled, "That's on my tab, Van. Don't you dare take a dime from her! You do and I'll send you on a one-way ticket back to your cubicle."

Caroline smiled and said to me, "Take care of him tonight."

"I will."

Carl stuck to his word. He had one Kronenburg, kept his other Kronenburg in his pants, and then was on his way. Jack followed shortly after. Bishop and Koles sat at the bar waiting for me to finish the clean up. Koles had finally agreed to go with us, though his enthusiasm was limited. He continued jotting down his barroom prose while Bishop was sipping his watered down rum and perusing some papers he'd taken from his satchel. As I left the bar, I looked back at them. I immediately noticed a hint of a smile on Bishop's face. It was permanently there. He probably wasn't conscious of it. "You two ok? Need anything else?" I asked. Koles didn't respond. Bishop nodded and simply said, "We're fine, Van." I told them I had to make a phone call and would be back in a moment. Then, we could leave.

I walked outside to the courtyard and sat down with my back resting on the hard marble base of Thomas Paine. I stared out at Boston Common. A large throng of people was walking en masse, but they weren't all together. They were divided into pairs and small groups. A movie had probably just finished at the theatre on Tremont Street or perhaps a play at the Wang. I watched the throng lose its strength as it splintered in factions going to the underground parking lot, the subway, bars for a drink, and other destinations unknown. It didn't take long for the hundred-person swarm to dissipate into scattered individuals and couples traversing the cement pathways of the Common. For the briefest of moments, I had the quick image of British soldiers practicing on the Common like they had done over two hundred years ago. Their formal and stiff red coats, perfectly pressed and starched, white straps crossing their chest in a perfect X. A group kneeling and a group standing, then firing on command. After firing, the standing soldiers would kneel and the kneeling would then stand. Everything in unison. The most foolish way to fight a scattered and disjointed enemy. No Common Sense.

I pressed the S button on my cell phone, scrolled a couple names down until Shaillie was highlighted. Before pressing the call button, last night came into my mind. Red Coats fully exited.

We were lying in bed naked. We had just made love and were smoking the remaining half of a hash/tobacco cigarette. We had smoked the first half before making love. As for our sex life, naked expression didn't lie. We were going through the motions. We both knew it, but we didn't discuss it. We should have. I think we were both enjoying the hash high more than our carnal activities.

Shaillie got up and put in a CD. She listened to one CD for months on end. Played it until every word was ingrained into her consciousness and beyond. Right now it was Marvin Gaye's *What's Going On*. How appropriate, she must have been thinking.

I took a big final hit on the joint. We didn't smoke much, but every time I saw Koles's friend, Gilworthy, I procured a good little supply and made it last for an occasional cannabis odyssey. I exhaled a large cloud between us.

I passed the joint to Shaillie. She eked out a semblance of a hit and put the empty, blackened roach in the ashtray on the nightstand. She reclined until she was supine, holding the smoke in for a long time and then slowly exhaling it toward the ceiling. I gazed at the gently ascending plume of smoke until its spiraling rise collapsed in upon itself.

"So, this is all about the void, huh?" Shaillie asked and then exhaled a sort of laugh. I didn't think she wanted me to answer. "It's all very Allen Ginsberg. Very Beat, Van, in more ways than one."

"Maybe so."

"So Beat my dear, but be careful of the void. It might not even exist."

Shaillie picked up the phone on the second ring. I explained to her that Bishop, Koles and I were going to Providence for a massage.

"Enjoy your bachelor party, Van."

"Sorry it's kind of last minute, but Bishop suggested and what the hell. We have no plans tomorrow, right? I'll probably be pretty exhausted."

"None at all."

"Are you ok with this, honey?"

"Absolutely," she said, a little too quickly.

"You sound a bit strange. A little bit too fine with it."

"Stop being so analytical. Stop being so cubicle, Van."

I laughed. "Ok, ok. I won't call you because you'll be sleeping. We'll be back late or early I should say."

"Of course. Be safe. Who's driving?"

"Koles. He hasn't been drinking," I lied.

"See you tomorrow. Have fun, indulge, and then we can get on with our life right?"

"Bye sweetie."

PART II
PROVIDENCE

After my shift, the three of us headed to Koles's apartment for a pit stop before going to Providence. Koles lived a few blocks from Harvard Square in the basement of an "Old Tory Row" mansion on the very posh Brattle Street. This was Tory Lane with giant, beautiful Victorians from the 18th century, originally homes of the colonists who sympathized with the British. The Loyalists or Tories who never fired a shot or castigated those Red Coats. They had a different sort of common sense, the sense of wealth. Koles's place was in a mansion just few houses down from the former home of Henry Wadsworth Longfellow. This street had, perhaps, the most expensive property in Massachusetts built on generations of old, blueblood money. Derek Koles lived in a room next to our narcotics connection and the reason for our visit, the ethereal Calvin Gilworthy. Bishop said he would need more than alcohol to make it into the vampire hours. Enter, Gilworthy.

I remember my surprise the first time I visited Koles and Gilworthy at the mansion. These two were the prototypical bohemian wanderers and wonderers searching their internal universes while living check-to-check. Yet their base of artistic operations was on the glorious road of old Yankee, status-quo wealth. Of course, there had to be a catch. Every king's house needs their share of servants. Koles and Gilworthy were neo-indentured servants. But 21st century servitude wasn't so bad—a big step up from sharecropping days. They each had their own bedroom in the basement and lived rent free. Along with two other guys, they shared a kitchen, bathroom and living area. As for the indentured part, the four guys took turns taking care of Oswald Geary. Oswald was an autistic man in his fifties who owned the house. In addition to autism, he also had MS and was incontinent. They had their hands full on their days of duty. Oswald's devoted wife had passed away and neither of his two trust-fund kids wanted to deal with their father's care, so they hired help. Gilworthy had explained to me that Oswald was high maintenance, but he was not impossible to deal with. The worst part was changing the diaper. Gilworthy described the excrement as "smelling as if he'd eaten pollution for dinner and it just got exponentially worse during digestion."

However, the rest was easy. Oswald liked to be read to and it didn't matter what. Gilworthy said he got a lot of reading done during his "work days," which was only about seven or eight days a month. And since the reading was oral, Gilworthy found it very beneficial to his writing. He told me, "The sounds of the written word are too often neglected." Koles rarely talked about Oswald, but Gilworthy filled in all the gaps. All things considered, they had a pretty good deal. They even had free meals since the house had a cook who fed the help as well. All they needed were part-time jobs for some spending money. Needless to say, 401K futures didn't exist, but neither did straitjacketed cubicles.

While Gilworthy's source of extra money was obvious, Koles earned his in a little more mainstream manner. He taught a couple of creative writing classes at Harvard Extension. He'd never taken a single creative writing class and like Bishop, he philosophically disagreed with their very existence. "Only in America," Koles had told me several times, "did these ridiculous Master's programs exist. Hemingway is crying in his grave. Writing shouldn't be taught. It should be pursued alone and lonely and only after the desolate excitement of travel. It's fraudulent, but I'll whore myself out. The money's too good for hypocrisy to get in the way. It's an irresistible sinecure." Teaching a class or two a week gave him more than enough money to get by and the needed time for his second novel.

"So, has Gil got anything for us?" Bishop asked.

"Gilworthy always has something for us. What's your flavor?"

"Vanilla, perhaps. Powdery vanilla. That'll sober up my rum-muddled liver. I'm going to leave my liver to Barbados, boys. I'll put that in my will. To the beautiful rum-producing island of Barbados, I leave my liver because it's been swimming in your rum for half-a-century. How's that for a bequeathal?"

"I'm sure Barbados would be honored," Koles rejoined. "Now, let's get our *Further* bus rolling."

"It'll require a little pick-me-up. Long trip for these old bones."

"To pick him up you mean?" Koles said, looking at Bishop's crotch.

"I been down so long, it looks up to me," Rourke sang. "Here's to you Richard Farina. I have your artistic scions ready to inherit your picaresque mantle. You'll live on beyond your early motorcycle exit."

"Richard Farina?" I asked Koles, while Bishop prattled on.

"60s writer, folk singer. Thomas Pynchon ilk," Koles said curtly, not wanting to interrupt Bishop. Koles seemed alternately amused and exhausted by Bishop's jester-genius schtick.

"You know, more sex will free you up. Koles, you need to exercise that sabre between your legs. It'll get that pen going. Just the thought of it had you going tonight at the bar. Don't think I didn't see that notebook open and the ink flowing tonight.

Koles nodded and said, "Dr. Bishop knows what ails creators."

"Yes, I have the prescription. You expatriate yourself again in Europe, stay off motorcycles and you'll fulfill the Farina destiny. Farina

71

never got unbound, but you will. Yes, sex and Europe will be your artistic enema. Send the slithery muse scampering through your fingertips racing to divinity. That's your God, my boy. The only God you'll ever have. It's got to be coddled, kindled, and sculpted. This little hedonist run will help fuel our own *belle époque*," Bishop finished in a French-accented flourish.

"Let's do some coke, gentlemen," Koles said, clearly trying to change the subject.

I hadn't done any coke since college. Shaillie and I never went beyond infrequent pot or hash sessions after we graduated. We both had agreed that harder stuff belonged to a different era. Tonight though, I would do whatever was presented me. This was a night to indulge, a night to break free."

Koles knocked on Gilworthy's door. We heard some papers shuffling and footsteps. He opened the door, wide-eyed, yet haggard at twenty-eight. His crow's-feet were already inching towards his temples, steadily burrowing crevices worthy of someone on the downward half of life's slope.

"Well, look what the alley cat dragged in. A trio of mad mice. Though, Van, you're a bit too sane for this lot."

"I'm taking a break from sanity," I said.

"Good for you. All work and no play makes Jack a dull boy," Gilworthy responded, massaging his Tutankhamunesque chin beard with his thumb and forefinger. He once told me that he had the beard for this very purpose, an excuse to do something with at least one of his hands. "You know, you guys are interrupting me. I'm in the midst of a scene."

"We've got a scene for you to live," Rourke said. "Time for a break from *Macronesia*, uber-auteur."

"How goes the film to end all films?" Koles asked.

"It'll never end. I will never get to the end and that's the beauty."

"You need some sun, Gilworthy," Koles advised. "You're looking pale."

"What do you think, Van? Am I wan, Van?"

"Most definitely. The complexion of a hermit."

"Blame it on the screenplay. It's very consumptive. Scenes keep begetting more scenes like the fornicating folks in Genesis. Besides, I don't like the daytime. People rushing around, shopping, traffic, lattes and all that to and from wage-slave stress. I only come out at night."

"Like a vampire," Koles said.

"Like an artist," Bishop began. "Don't worry about the sun, Nosferatu, you just keep working, but at some point, we need to get this

72

cinematic behemoth into production. We've got producers ready to get the cameras rolling. Don't fret about the end. It doesn't have to end. We'll call it *Macronesia—Part I.* We'll just serialize it, infinitely. When you move on to the next dimension, the next vanguard will take the baton. It will be the *La Sagrada Familia* of cinema."

"Long live Gaudi," Koles said.

"Bishop, I don't know about this whole exhibit you've planned. It all sounds too Greenwich Village-Lower East Side to me." Gilworthy wrinkled up his face to underscore his apparent disgust with anything Manhattan. "It's too communal and Warholian. Let the 60s rest in peace for goodness sake."

Bishop looked at Koles and me. "Tireless nihilism fuels the artist. Don't worry about Gilworthy, he'll be in the show. You too, Van."

"I have nothing to offer, Bishop. I'm the opposite of Gil."

He winked at me. "We'll see about that."

"I want *Macronesia* to be seen in its entirety, not in parts," Gilworthy said.

I wanted to broach the issue of logic, but Koles thankfully did it for me. I never felt comfortable posing logic around these guys.

"Gil, how long is the film right now?"

"I don't know. The screenplay is at about two thousand pages."

Koles gasped, "That's twenty fucking movies!"

"So?" Gilworthy replied disinterestedly.

"So you expect someone to make a forty-hour movie? What's more, you expect someone to watch this?"

"I don't care about logistics. You're boring me with all this rational thought and suit-and-tie logic. Can we talk about something else? Like, why you are here."

Bishop put an end to the film talk. "Rational discourse has no place here. Nihilist or not, Gil is a merry prankster at heart. Merry pranksters made an eternal film without any considerations of the box office."

Koles quickly rebutted, "Kesey and the Pranksters finished the film when the bus trip ended. It was long, but not eternal."

"Well, my film is going further than *further*," Gil said proudly.

"Infinitely further, right?" Koles added.

"Look, I don't anticipate Paramount to be calling. It's art house all the way. A new kind of art house, beyond Sundance," Gil said. "Anyway, I presume you came here for a little lift. I'll need it too, now that my rhythm has been derailed." He sat down at the computer, saved his work, and took out a key from a little drawer to the right of his computer. He reached across his desk to another small set of drawers.

73

Each one had its own keyhole. He put the key in the bottom drawer's hole, unlocked it, and pulled a small paper square out from the drawer. Gilworthy reached above his desk for a mirror that had a picture of Paris on it. It was an aerial view of the city. The Seine was clearly focused as the center of the picture. You could follow its wending watery swath through images of the great city.

"My two favorite rivers are the Charles and the Seine," I blurted out like a kid naming his favorite baseball players.

"We will honor the Seine for you tonight, Van," Gilworthy said. He carefully opened the paper, keeping its crease centered and then poured a rocky hill along the river in the mirror. Then Gilworthy reached into the same drawer, pulled out a razorblade, slid the thin cardboard protective sheath off, and started chopping the hills into dust.

"Hmmm, Lake Van loves the Seine and Charles," Bishop said in a tone suggesting he was considering his rivers of choice. "The Charles is very underrated, Van. I grant you that. We often overlook what's right under our noses."

"Hell of a view from Memorial Drive into the city. I love that walk when the film is driving me mad. It's a very soothing stroll," Gilworthy added.

I nodded in agreement.

"I prefer the oceans," Koles said.

"They're too much. Too overwhelming," I offered.

"Can't see the other side," Bishop pointed out.

"Yes, exactly. I like to see the other side," I said, nodding agreement.

"Don't we all, Van," Koles said, "but I also like the mystery. The ocean puts existence into perspective."

We were quiet for a bit watching Gilworthy pulverize the Seine into powder-white snow. Bishop's health dawned on me at this point. Youth can handle a misadventure from time to time. None of us had hit thirty, though I was weeks away. This could be too much for Bishop.

"Bishop, I really don't think you should do this stuff having just had a heart attack."

"Don't worry about me, Van. I'm all about moderation in my AARP years. I'll just do a little bit and chase it down with some good old-fashion coffee." Bishop pointed to a coffee maker. There was a half-filled pot on it. The red light was on. "How old is this brew, Gil?"

"Only an hour. I always have fresh coffee around. You should know that, Bishop."

Bishop took a mug from a milk crate that was below the coffee maker and poured himself a cup. While he drank his black coffee, we did several lines. I hadn't had the burning sensation in my nostrils in so long. I knew Shaillie would be upset about this part of the sybaritic night, but the compunction was fleeting. I felt my heart beating faster. Gilworthy told us that we'd done all he could spare and, besides, he was cutting down. "When I turn thirty, I'll end all drug use. I've already cut down. This is an aberration."

"Wise decision, Gil," Koles said, rolling his eyes at me. "Now, are you going to join us on a road trip?"

"Where is this three-ring circus headed?"

"South of the border," Koles cryptically told him.

"And west of the sun, I hope."

"We're going to Providence."

"Muscular therapy?"

"Total muscular therapy."

Gilworthy raised his right eyebrow while lowering the left. He began playing with his chin beard for a few moments and then asked, "Van, you too?"

"Yes."

"What's gotten in to you? You are certainly turning deviant on us. Too many sterile years playing the game, huh?"

"Maybe," I shrugged.

"I don't know how you did it fifty weeks a year for so many years. I would have imploded after a few weeks. I take my hat off to anyone who did a job like you. Remarkable dedication albeit very bizarre."

"Gilworthy, you wouldn't have lasted a day," Koles said.

"People have to pay the rent, you know. It's not that bizarre," I countered foolishly.

"No, they don't. They can just clean shit like Koles and me. Anyway, enough mundanity. What's the occasion?"

"Call it my bachelor party," I said.

"Well, then, I'm in. Let's send Van off in style."

Before we left, I took a quick piss in the hallway bathroom. While I was washing my hands, I vainly examined my crow's-feet to see if they were as severe as Gilworthy. They weren't, but they were clearly there. When I smiled excessively, they became an isosceles triangle of deep crevices blasting out into my temples. I could envision my face old and tired, fatigued from life. I let my jaw go slack and shook my head so that my jaw swung back and forth as if it were about to detach from my face. Shake up the neurons. The sensation of the swinging jaw felt oddly good. I'd never done that before. My face looked ridiculously rubber-like in the mirror. The coke was good, perhaps too good. Adrenalin was surging through my body with monsoon velocity. I liked it, but no more coke tonight, I told myself.

No more coke.

I was in the passenger seat, while Koles was driving. He said he'd only had a few beers earlier, which I confirmed. Gilworthy was in back with Bishop, who'd instantly fallen asleep despite a cup of coffee and a line, his prescription of moderation. Bishop's head was hanging down with his chin bouncing off his chest with every bump. Pieces of his silk argyle ascot were peeking out beneath his jowls. His eyes and face showed the effects of four-plus decades of world class boozing. His breathing was uneven. Each inhalation produced a gravelly sound like pebbles and dirt being crushed underfoot. More smoke had passed through Bishop's lungs than the exhaust system of a coal-burning locomotive. Physical scars rivaled the emotional incisions. He had a beard, sans mustache, and slick straight hair combed back and parted in the middle. An old, oily 1950s style hair gel kept it from falling forward while his head bobbed down to a ninety-degree angle.

Suddenly, it dawned on me that I had no idea what to do at this type of place. I was sure it couldn't have been all that complicated. Get naked and supine had to be the gist of it, but I thought I'd inquire.

"So, what's up with this place? How does it work?" I asked, upon which both Koles and Gilworthy immediately laughed.

"You know what I mean," I said. "I've never paid for services before."

"Never?" Gilworthy asked, seemingly in shock. "And you, Derek?"

"Just once in Amsterdam."

"Amsterdam is horrible. Not an iota of eroticism to it." Gil immediately critiqued.

"Yes, very robotic."

"These places in Providence are much better. Decent looking Asian women treating you well. Exotic and erotic."

"Hey, by the way, did you hear about that American general who advocated for prostitution?" Koles asked.

"Yeah, about the rape case of the young Japanese girl," Gilworthy said.

"He tells the press that the soldiers who raped this girl were just horrible and damn stupid. They where stupid because they could have just paid for sex in Japan to get off."

"What happened to him?" I asked.

"The military dumped him for the comments," Koles answered, "but he was just telling the truth."

76

"He's in the wrong profession for the truth," I said.

"But it's not really the truth," Gil interjected. "Prostitution can salve male anxiety, but rape taps into another part of the psyche. It's not an either-or proposition."

"Not about sex at that point," I said.

"Not about sex at all."

"Of course, but he got crucified for advocating prostitution, not ignorance of the psychology of rape," Koles corrected.

"True, and I concur with the general. I advocate it, too. Good, safe, protect yourself and the whores and it's good for society. You want to hear about my experience paying for pleasure in Asia?" Gil digressed.

Without waiting for an answer from either one of us, Gilworthy began telling his story with the steady murmur of Bishop's snoring in the background. I turned around to hear what I expected to be a lewd and entertaining anecdote.

"So, my friends, thin rafts and papier-mâché pyramids were everywhere in this particular experience. It was during my haze of traveling the world. Intrepid clarity of hazy, early- twenties youth. The greatest period of youth's potential. Twenty-four I was! What an age to be alive! Hanging on until the inevitable stampede. Hanging onto oblivion like a desperate lover…"

Gilworthy paused for a moment, seemingly reflecting on what had just been funneled out of his mind and into the air of conversation. He closed his eyes, then opened them wide. His eyeballs spun in a full rotation, several times as if he were exercising them. Optical aerobics stretching his vision. Giddy madness glinting from his eyes before the words returned.

"Yes, gentlemen, it was all about Eve, all about traveling, framing the right frame of mind, living the film before writing it and all that righteous and beautiful aesthetic bullshit. I had just finished a one-year stint teaching English at UFSM, the wonderful University of the Federated States of Micronesia on the island of Pohnpei, out in the great South Pacific. Or to be more geographically accurate, in the middle of nowhere. Micronesia, the perfect place, the perfect word, to begin the film. Everything is under the microscope and then it explodes in one's own Big Bang Theory. No intelligent design to speak of, just the instincts of the universe. I probably should end it there if I ever have an end. Full circle like a line of latitude, but it won't end. I hate ends. They're all loose and they all lose."

Koles interrupted imploring that Gil get over his phobia of the end, get the film done, and give it to Bishop for exposure. He balked at that and told us he didn't trust Bishop at all. Koles disagreed. I was on a different wavelength and decided to pursue it.

"Yeah, but Gil, I just don't get it," I said. "Call me pedestrian and conventional, but don't you fear having nothing when you get older?"

"What do you mean by having nothing?"

"Money, for starters."

"No."

"No, you don't worry?"

"No."

"Yeah, but wouldn't you want the film to be finished, so you might get some money and attention for your work."

"I don't think about it."

I was persistent. It must have been the coke. I rarely inquired about practical concerns with Koles and his lot of avant-garde friends. I knew it would make me feel like I was some suburban, SUV-driving parent whose cultural awareness peaked at seeing *Fiddler on the Roof*, but my DNA contained these genes. Starter house chromosomes were in me. One can't change their genome. Not completely. Delusion can only swim so far against the genetic tides.

I continued my middle class sermon, "But do you really want to live in that room and clean up this guy's shit for the rest of your life?" I asked, realizing I was playing Shaillie to Gilworthy's me. The theatre of the absurd in rotation—it's all theatre all the time.

"Van, go back to the cubicle, my friend."

"I'm just curious."

"I don't think about money and money doesn't think about me. Money and I made a deal long ago. We parted ways respectfully. As far as cleaning this guy's shit, no, I don't think I will do it forever because he'll die. Then, I might just be cleaning another asshole."

"Can we change the subject back to Gil's geisha girl?" Koles asked.

"Any more questions, Van?" Gil asked.

I shook my head.

"Don't worry, my friend. You can't molt all the layers at once. You can't *unbuild* Rome in a day. Fifty thousand a year for a long, slow, invisible lobotomy. The needle got in about two inches behind your eye and then you began pulling it out. It'll take some time."

"I get your point."

"Nice pun, Van. You know I should be the one questioning you."

"Yeah, yeah, I know. I should have moved to Micronesia long ago."

78

I often daydreamed about Gilworthy's Pacific life while I sat in my gray fabric cubicle watching purchase orders, performance analyses, and various data that ultimately meant nothing pile up on my computer. I'd lean back in my ergonomic chair that the company had ordered "to keep our spines straight and erect" as the level 11 supervisor said in a seminar one day. A seminar on how to maintain good posture while sitting for many hours. I remember the person running the seminar began with "Slouching is bad for you, bad for the company, and bad for the world economy. The giant wheels of global capitalism start with good posture and a healthy back. We're all Atlas in our own tiny way propping up the world economy. Ergo, we need to stay erect."

Yes, I'd lean back, hands clasped behind my neck, spine corporate-erect, rolling Gilworthy's life in my mind. He'd really hooked up with a great position in Micronesia. The little world map by my desk showed Micronesia was north of New Guinea and East of the Philippines. A little Google research showed me that Micronesia had some historical significance. It was part of the U.S. island-hopping campaign of World Ware II. It was a steppingstone to Japan and thus became American after the war. A protectorate or a territory or some vague, not quite a state nominative. It probably had an interestingly miscegenational culture of ancient island natives, Japanese, and Americans. The women had to be exotic and seductive. Women of Gauguin's Tahitian ilk. Gilworthy was certainly no stranger to exotic, international women. He had been teaching English at a private language school in Harvard Square and bedding many of his international students. Each course lasted a month at this international sexual circus masquerading as a language school. By week two of every term, he'd had his lover of the month. Gilworthy's sexual exploits read like a member list of the United Nations, but he tended to lean on the Asian side of the globe.

One woman finally upset the steady skein of monthly lovers. Her name was Lolikeni. She was from Micronesia and she got him the connection to this junior college on the island of Pohnpei. Lolikeni took care of all the paperwork and the school paid for Gilworthy's airfare and gave him housing in a romantic, artist-against-the-world, one-room thatch cottage on the beach. He made fifteen grand American a year teaching a few sections of English to native Micronesians. The money was more than enough to live on out there. He said it was paradise and the day he arrived, he was inspired to write his film. He had thought he'd be some tragic, youthful Malcolm Lowry and write his own lost *Volcano* novel, but the day he arrived he knew his story needed the visual, not just naked words. The exotic women, swaying wind whistling palm trees, rocky cliffs, thrashing, frothing seas, whispering zephyrs, footprints along the sand all *alchemized* to turn novel ideas into celluloid visions. The first several hours of his screenplay had no words. It was merely instruction for the camera to follow mysterious footprints all over the island.

He settled into his life with Lolikeni and spent one year on Micronesia before he left the island. They'd agreed from the beginning that it wouldn't be permanent. She stuck to their plan, but he recanted begging her to join him in his global travels and help him create his film. When she refused, he said he'd stay and make his film about Micronesia. She asked him to leave. She would never marry an American. Then one day soon after she was gone.

He got over the heartbreak by traveling the world and immersing himself in the film. He lived the screenplay, keeping the plot of the film chronologically close to his real life, but assured us every event was reality manipulated, twisted or completely concocted. "This was no *roman á clef* of film."

At that point, he thought he would finish the screenplay when his wanderlust waned and the motion of his life slowed, but it didn't. It wouldn't. His imagination continued the momentum. There was no end in sight.

With Bishop's snore providing the story's score, Gilworthy indulged with the Thai prostitute story. Koles and I settled in because Gilworthy's stories often resembled his screenplay in length.

"My Micronesian paradise had come to an end. I was grieving the loss of Lolikeni, but I was on the run, trotting the globe like any self-respecting artist in their blindly visionary youth. I hopped aboard a cargo plane in exchange for helping unload and reload. Got myself to Southeast Asia. I stayed in Bangkok for a few days and then travel north to the mountains of Thailand rather than the seaside resorts of Kosamoi or Phuket. I wanted to avoid all the tourists and get a real taste of Thailand. Maybe drink some snake blood or stumble onto a dead body or strange hippie commune like DiCaprio in *The Beach*. Loved that movie. Besides, I'd had beautiful blue waters to say good morning to everyday on Pohnpei, so it was time to go inland. Time for the mountains. A time for elevation. I thought after that I'd head into Cambodia or Laos or Vietnam or all of them or wherever the impulse guided. I figured the film would grow following the plight of the peoples in and out of my head as I ventured west from Micronesia and returned to the States and perhaps ending full circle back in Micronesia, but that would have been complicated because of the end of Lolikeni. God, I hate endings, but I love pure and sensual meaningful meaninglessness. The lure of the digression is magnetic. More natural and more honest than anything planned. Bishop's not the only one with a drunken stranglehold on truth. So, I'm in the mountains. I'd just purchased the most amazing dope I'd ever had. I'm stumbling around the incredibly green covered mountains of Northern Thailand. Lush land layered with tropical plants. I'd been hiking and smoking all day. It's getting dark and I find myself on some dirt road in the middle of nowhere. I eventually wander to a little town. Not a town, really, just a few stores and a tiny motel above a bar. Beautiful, vestigial civilization. So, I head into the bar for some beer and dinner. I'm sitting at a table by myself extraordinarily stoned on the sweet Thai stick, stoned on the itinerant madness my life was becoming. Now, I've always believed my film is part brilliance and part Marx Brothers absurdity, but the absurdity part starts taking over. I'm having a middle class panic attack just like our Van here was moments ago. Memories of my father mocking my life's plan, voices start screaming in my head. 'Avocation my ass, boy, you're into provocation, but you don't even know what you're provoking. Maybe you didn't get laid enough in adolescence. What else could it be? What's that damn billy-goat beard for anyway. That will only get screwed-up girls in bed. Normal does exist, if you give it half a fucking chance.' The old man is such a comic book dad of the Sergeant Fury mold. Don't worry, I'm getting to the good part. There has to be some prelude, some foreplay. So, I'm in this mini-state of panic, you know, half laughing, half ready to ball my eyes out when this beautiful Thai angel approaches me. Now, I'd been in Bangkok before where the whores swarm you like prairie locust. They pull up their skirts saying, 'lookie, lookie, no penis, just pussy, real woman, want real woman, no cockie, cockie, just pussy, pussy…' This one here, however, just sat at my table and said, 'buy me drink.' So I obliged her with a gin and tonic. We sat and chatted in her adorable broken English and I don't remember a damn thing we said nor how long we talked, but I do remember going upstairs into the motel holding her hand, getting a room without the slightest look from the owner. She must have worked for the motel. Maybe got a commission for every room she sold. We go into my room and she proceeded to fuck my brains out until they were spilled out all over the floor in liquid peace. It was unlike any sexual experience I'd ever had, real or imagined. I have such permanent visions of her against the wall, on top of me gently and rhythmically rotating me into ecstasy, on the floor, on the desk…"

Gilworthy paused and seemed to be silently observing his own memories. I imagined his memories and drew sketches in my head of this dark Thai nymph, a bamboo and thatch motel and rolling green hills…

"Passionate, intense sex for hours and hours. Movie-like sex as if we were in the peak of a great love affair and would not see each other for a long time. A great and wildly carnal goodbye of true, chemically connected lovers. Lovers that could never marry and survive the plateau of marriage. After sex, she drew a bath and bathed me, then we smoked and slept a little. Then we headed down to the bar for some food and Singha. Then back up for more sex and she was so goddamn beautiful with perfect sized breasts and nipples that I tongue-worshipped for hours and we fucked in every way possible for two days."

Koles was shaking his head. He interrupted Gil to tell him that marital sex doesn't always plateau. He said that he and Yvette used to have sex like that, but stopped mid-sentence and insisted Gil continue. That was the most intimate detail I'd ever heard Koles say about his marriage. One of the few details of any kind. Gil suggested he say more, but he refused. Gil resumed his narrative undeterred.

"I'm convinced I'll never fuck like that again. So, I'm ready to force myself to journey onward, otherwise I'll never want to leave and I'll marry this Thai whore. I tell myself I have to head into the mountains. New momentum. I ask her how much I owe her and she says twenty-five dollars. I couldn't believe she said that. I gave her one hundred and you know what she did, she started taking my pants off to blow me a thank you. I stopped her realizing I was no moral hero. My cock was dead and I had nothing left. I'd appeased my libido like an Aztec God having received fifty virgins. I looked forward to the serenity of a libido at ease, but felt such shame for this woman who was compelled to thank me that way. I felt so deeply sad, such raw melancholy for her that I gave her another fifty and we kissed goodbye. She was so happy with all the money I gave her, but I believed there was a look in her eyes that said what we did, what we had was different for her. Perhaps I projected it, but who's to know? I mean the sex with this woman was sacred, a religious experience. There had to be something more, but then it all collapsed. I became stricken with fear. A practical fear. Mortality. I started walking down the dirt road back toward the bus that got me out of Bangkok. I was the most content and satiated man alive. I start reliving the great sex scenes in my head to pass the time when I suddenly realized I hadn't worn a condom."

"You didn't think of that once during the two days?" Koles asked incredulously.

"Well, I did, I think, but I just didn't care. I was really high and kept smoking all the way through and she was so clean and unlike a whore. In the midst of it I must have just convinced myself that

82

everything would be fine. Testosterone can grant you temporary omnipotence. One time wouldn't catch me. So, on my walk out of this mad mountain paradise, I completely panicked. I started crying like a little kid thinking I threw my life away. My existential japes about life's lack of meaning turned my jokes inside out and began laughing at me. I told myself I'd head home and never mind this ridiculous film and anti-materialist, wandering-the-world Beatnik existence. I'd get a job, a teacher or something, put a smile on kids' faces. I'd find a loving woman, settle down, have dinner on Sundays with the family and have a kid and watch football. I'd just toe the line and join the middle class microcosm. To hell with putting a ripple in the universe, but all these plans still didn't relieve the deep anguish I had that lasted two days."

"As long as the experience itself," Koles said.

"Then what? What did you do?" I asked.

"I went to a hospital in Bangkok and got tested. Came out negative, which of course, didn't reflect my two days of last tango in Thailand, but I still got a bit of satisfaction. Figured I had at least several years to live at the minimum. Headed down to Kosamoi, swam, rested and ate well. My libido took shelter like a turtle in its shell. I kept telling myself I'd abandon the nomadic life and the film. The old Sergeant Fury father would be happy. But it didn't last long. Had no veritable legs. All the tourists around me photographing temporary exits from tension depressed me even more than my potentially quickened death. I got over it. Gave myself up to fate. I was back to normal—the ole sincerely fucked up me, ready to smoke and create my life away."

"I can't believe you didn't wear a condom," Koles reiterated.

"Shit happens. Don't be so self-righteous."

"Have you been tested since that one time?" I asked.

"Clean bill of health every time as well as a condom every time since then."

"You still think about her?"

"Yeah, I do. It wasn't just the sex. It was so erotic and loving. Wild, yes, but gentle, too. We slept together, arm in arm, body in body. Like I said, she bathed me and we laughed and kissed. I lusted for her, but Jesus Christ, I did love her on some level. There was so much energy between us. Lust or love, whatever you want to call it. I think any guy with a prostitute falls in love on some strange, perverse level for at least a moment."

Koles sighed, "That's not love."

We stopped for a bathroom break at a gas station about a half hour from our destination. Bishop was still sleeping soundly. Gilworthy and Koles went into the bathroom on the side of the station. I sat on a bench in front of the station. A steady flow of truck drivers and teenagers moved in and out of the door to my right. A giant square spun above. One side read, "OPEN 24 HOURS" in gargantuan red neon letters. The other side read, "GAS, SODA, CIGARETTES" in equally gargantuan green letters. On top of the sign I could see two crows perched. I had started becoming very aware and wary of crows for good reason. I would be acutely aware of their presence ever onward. I watched them surveying the area as the sign took them in slow revolutions. A perfect crow's nest with absolute visibility. They were about two feet apart. One of them occasionally glanced at the other who was keeping watch dutifully like a noble and worthy sentinel. Stereotype led me to believe the male was the ultra-focused sentry. Maybe crows had no use for clichés. I presumed they were lovers for life as Shaillie had claimed. When the sign turned so that their gaze was in my direction, I turned away. Last thing I needed was another angry crow on the assault.

Far above the sign, the three-quarter moon shone its pale and gentle lunar light. Every time I'd looked at the moon since I'd read Murakami's *Sputnik Sweetheart*, I thought of his metaphor for the moon as a lonely orphan in the night. Thousands of metaphors and descriptions come and go, but that one stuck. I remember telling Shaillie how poignant and intriguing I thought the orphan metaphor was. She smiled, considered it briefly, and said, "I don't see it at all. The moon is never alone. It's more like a happy child perpetually tugging at its mother's skirt."

I looked up at the starry night sky. I liked Shaillie's moon better than Murakami's, but certainly felt more connected to his view. Under the spinning red and green neon and lunar glow, I people-watched for a bit, stealing occasional, furtive glances at the revolving crows. Gilworthy and Koles seemed to be taking a long time. The coke must have worn off by now since my heart no longer pulsed at a rate more associated with fear. I didn't want any more substances in my body. I had a sudden surge of desire to go home. I looked in the car at Bishop's head hanging precariously on his right shoulder, rising and falling in rhythm with every snore. The moon suddenly didn't seem so alone. It looked directed and on course.

Something seemed to be going on that I didn't know about. This whole thing had to be a litmus test that women are notorious for presenting their guileless boyfriends. It must have been a trap. Shaillie wouldn't let me be with another woman, would she? She had never been duplicitous with me before. But I had never put her through so much as I had recently, so close to wedlock. Perhaps, I'd given her no choice, but to test me. I had to get to the bottom of this. I could truly feel the fragility of my relationship for the first time. The fragility that Shaillie must have been feeling for a while now. I could feel it in my ribs. My heart now seemed to be racing faster than it had with the coke a short time ago. Everything felt out of place. Discordant. Like a symphony playing along until suddenly the violinists are replaced with amateurs and screeching strings take over. I looked up at the moon. Maybe Murakami had it backwards. Maybe earth was the orphan.

I took out my cell phone and called home. I had to get to the bottom of this. Find some gravity. I could still turn back. I didn't need this massage. It was just a detour. A harmless bachelor party, right?

The phone rang several times and then the voice mail picked up.

"Hello, we're not in right now. Please leave a message for Shaillie or Van and we'll get back to you," Shaillie's mechanized voice said to me.

I hung up. My cell phone read 12:24. She must have been sleeping. Shaillie was a deep sleeper. She never heard me stumble out of bed during the insomniac exits or returns. Everything must be ok. She's not tricking me. It's just not her character. Shaillie's a straight-shooter. Go and indulge in this pre-marital vice. It's standard American rite of passage. I assured myself with all these cajoling thoughts hoping to calm the calamitous nerves jangling within.

"Van, you need to go?" I heard Gilworthy's voice. I looked to my left where I could see half his body sticking out from around the corner of the building.

"No. I'm all set."

"But do you need *to go*?" he asked, the one eye I could see winked at me. I stared at his face, split in two by the cement corner of the gas station. He was peeking around it as if he were on the lam avoiding capture. Perhaps, his whole life was about avoiding capture. The cement edge of the gas station perfectly bisected his face. Half his straight, freckled nose, one glassy eye with crow's-feet drawing attention, half his King Tut goatee, half a smiling mouth. Who was Calvin Gilworthy? Who was half of him?

"Van, you ok?"

"Yeah, I'm fine."

"So?"

"No, I'm ok. I'm just along for the ride," I said. I wasn't exactly sure why that came out.

"Huh?"

"No, thanks. I'm all set on all fronts."

Gilworthy's half-countenance turned perplexed and then disappeared. He must have brought some for the road. Gil always claimed to be running out of "stuff," then suddenly more would appear. A few minutes later we were back on the road. This time I sat in back with the ever-somnolent and snoring Bishop, who apparently had sleeping skills of a narcoleptic. Nothing seemed to disturb him. I was envious because I knew at some point I would need to sleep. Months and months of insomnia, of just getting about four hours of sleep a night were going to catch up on me. I usually slept just a few hours before and after waking up to write and the time I did actually sleep never felt deep and true. It was a kind of semi-conscious floating sensation as if I were watching myself sleeping rather than completely disappearing into the beautiful escape of sleep. Bishop, on the other hand, looked like he had been tranquilized so peacefully that he could have slept through an angry God's reign of fire and brimstone. I recalled a real Bishop or Deacon in my Armenian church had used the phrase "fire and brimstone" to describe how God had dealt with Sodom and Gomorrah. I reminded myself to check the sky above Providence when we arrived.

Koles continued driving and Gilworthy was now in the passenger seat. They were talking, or rather, Gilworthy was monologuing and Koles nodding from time to time. I decided after tonight's excess, I would start to take Shaillie's advice to heart. I sensed that after tonight's road trip there would be some cataclysm. It was time to address recent detours, to get Shaillie and me back on the same page. It was time to start sleeping regularly. Maybe, I'd even address some past issues with my father and get some equilibrium. Maybe, I did have a touch of denial...

Images of the old man fluttered in...Those last moments with the forced oxygen mask keeping him alive while he limply pawed at the mask trying futilely to remove it and talk to me as death stalked like a starving omnivore. A man once so large in aura and volume, an enormous presence in both anger and joy, now reduced to a wounded lamb. It was impossible to fathom...images multiplied with the mind's fraction-of-a-second velocity. The very alive old man screaming in the kitchen for misplaced utensils...calmly walking along the Charles River sharing his endless knowledge with me...raging at Boston sports failures with the ice-filled, vodka glass always arms reach away...eulogizing him with a Dylan Thomas poem...casket so close by...the mysterious phone calls in the middle of the night that drove my mother honestly paranoid…argument after argument with my mother…I could still hear the voices echoing inside my skull.

I stopped myself as I always did. The memories always teetered towards the negative with the old man. It was an improper way to remember the dead. Better not to remember at all if possible…

"Bishop, wake up," Gilworthy said, reaching back and nudging Bishop's shoulder, the one functioning as a bony pillow.

His head snapped upright, "Yeah, yes, I'm up," he mumbled. "We here?"

"Yes."

We pulled up to the whorehouse. Was it a whorehouse? I wasn't sure if these ladies performed all that a whore should perform. I really didn't know what the hell this place was all about, but every man must surely want to try it once. Instant gratification was a biological urge. Just one time without any effort at all. Everyone wanted one visit to Sodom and Gomorrah. I looked up at the sky and it was starry white against clear black. I turned my attention to the whorehouse, which didn't look anything like a whorehouse. A neighboring pawnshop did lend a tawdry air of sleaze and danger. The low-budget geishas resided in a dull, two-story, tan brick building that looked like it housed some small, nondescript businesses. The second floor had long rectangular windows with white Venetian blinds flipped down. Above the glass door a red neon sign lit up the thin letters S-P-A.

"Gentlemen, shall we absorb one more boost?" Gilworthy offered.

"You know this shit makes it hard to get it up," Koles said. "I'd hate to pay the hundred and walk out of there un-cleansed."

"You can always cleanse yourself later," Gilworthy said.

"I don't need to pay for that."

"You're paying for the image that will cleanse you again and again. You'll have something new with no strain on the imagination."

"Gil, you should think before you speak."

"Yeah, yeah, you're right, we want the whole meal, dessert included," Gil conceded. "We're not here for virtual orgasms."

Bishop interjected, "You boys put too much emphasis on dessert. It's a mirage. Nirvana quicksand. It's the process, the touch of the woman, skin on skin that renders a lasting peace. The essence of Tantric sensuality. Sex isn't about doing, it's about being. America has isolated sex into a five second experience."

"Thanks for the Kama Sutra lesson, but I'll take the five second dessert," Gil said.

"Ahhh, the anxious ignorance of youth. You trade seconds for hours of joy."

"Bishop's got a point," I said. "Sex has become another element of our ADD society. Fast and quick joy."

"Van's getting it. The quicker the sex, the more time you'll have to buy like good consumptive capitalists."

Koles looked back at us. "Not now," he said and got out of the car. Gilworthy now turned back to us, "Do you want a hit or not? Enough of this philosophical bullshit on sex. We're here to get laid. Isn't this Van's bachelor party?"

Gil winked at me and then packed a bowl with his stash of marijuana. He pulled out the little paper case of coke and sprinkled some on top of the marijuana. "A little yin and yang, gentlemen." Then he lit the bowl and inhaled deeply before passing it to me. I hesitated, but took a small hit, the hypocrisy not lost on me. Gil looked out at Koles and motioned to him to see if he wanted any. He turned away and Bishop passed as well. "This ole Irishman will pass out in the midst of a woman's touch if he keeps clouding his senses."

"Let's get a drink," I suggested. "I could use a drink."

"We don't have time for that. Don't be nervous, Van. You'll do fine. It's by the book sexuality," Koles said.

"Besides, it's already so late and we'll probably have to wait. Loneliness has a long list of clients," Gilworthy added just before taking another blast off his one-hitter.

An old Asian woman greeted us with a curt and cold hello, that is until she saw Bishop and instantly smiled. She began speaking Chinese or Korean or some Asian language to him. She looked Chinese to me, but I was no expert at deciphering the Asian face. Bishop returned the salutation in her language. He was always pulling intellectual tricks out of his pocket. Either that or a flask. She pointed to Koles and me and said something to which Bishop responded in a mix of her language and English. She responded with "Ok, ok, ok, sit, sit."

Bishop explained that it was Korean that they were speaking. He had learned his share of the language in Pusan, South Korea while doing a stint of teaching on a music fellowship between the two Asian "Domino" wars. It was during his musical years when he was writing and teaching operatic composition. Bishop had told me several times during extended Chez Lucienne evenings that his twenties and thirties were his opera years. He composed several operas during that era of his life until he left music for film and literature. I took those stories with a grain of salt, but his agility with the Korean language added some meat to his rhetorical bones.

We all took a seat in the cheap motel-type lobby. There were six brown chairs, a flimsy pine coffee table with an ashtray, and scattered *Newsweeks* and *Times* dating as far back as twelve years ago. A picture of Jesus was on one of the covers. I remembered reading that those two magazines always put Christ on a cover when news and sales were slow. It guaranteed a profitable week. A laundry room to the rear was exposed by an accordion-style, sliding wall. The old woman, who had spoken with Bishop, was busy folding white towels. She was talking to another woman, whom we couldn't see, in loud, rapid Korean while Bishop began an orientation. The rest had served him well. He looked alert, even a bit sober.

"Koles, you know the scene in general and Gilworthy, you've done yeoman share of reconnaissance into this world. So Van, this is mainly for you. You'll go to a room to wait for your lady. Strip down, but out of respect put a towel around yourself. Keep your wallet with you at all times. When she comes in, she'll make a bit of small talk, the slightest bit and ask you if you've been here before. Say yes. Then, she'll ask when and you say a long time ago, a year or something. If you say no, you'll get nothing but her hand. Saying yes and that you're with me, may get you oral sex or intercourse, but the latter is unlikely. That usually takes several visits to the same lady. Got to build up some trust. If you do somehow end up entering her, she'll give you a condom. For her hand or mouth, it's condom free. When you go to the bathing room, take your wallet. Mostly it shows that you know what you're doing and you're not a cop. If they have any doubts, they may just give you the massage, nothing else. Loose muscles, but blue balls. I know you are all about the icing on the cake, but enjoy the cake too. It might be all you get. Don't argue or protest. They're in charge. You have one hour and the old lady is very strict with the time, so don't push it. I repeat, if you don't finish, enjoy the intimacy and peace with a loving, beautiful woman. As I said, there's more to sex than coming. Read your Kama Sutra, don't mock it."

I heard some doors open and shut and a couple of Asian ladies walked by the lobby. The old lady squawked something loudly in Korean to them.

"Ok, ok, ok, ready, two, ready, two first," She said to us.

Bishop responded, "I've got to go first while I still have energy. I'll be asleep if I have to wait."

Gilworthy said, "Let Bishop go first with Koles. Van and I will follow."

Bishop started to say something about Gilworthy's film, but Koles interrupted, "Bishop, not now!"

"Carnal instincts calling, Derek. Good to hear. This place will get you going. All three of you. A relaxed yet energized vanguard." Koles gave Rourke a nudge toward the door and they followed the old lady.

I was hoping to read and enjoy some silence for a while, but Gil wouldn't have it. As soon as I picked up the Jesus magazine, he cut me off at the pass and began telling me how the film was taking over his life. He didn't like to admit it in front of Koles or Bishop, but he needed to get it off his chest. He said it was becoming an albatross that was beginning to crush his shoulders.

"Van, you know, between you and me, you guys are right about the damn film. It's become a beast, it's reaching Brobdingnagian proportions and its maker is feeling Lilliputian! I've got to slay it. It's running my life to the point of ruin."

I suggested that he just let it go and move on, but Gil didn't think it was so simple because he deeply feared the end. He didn't know what was next and if anything would be next. He thought when he finished it, his creative well might be dry and then life would be intolerable. He said the worst torture was to have the instinct to create, but no creativity. Gil also loathed the idea of presenting his work, selling it, and playing the game of getting attention.

"You have to play the game, Gil," I said with a shrug, glancing at the Jesus Christ *Newsweek*.

Gil disagreed, "The motivation is larger, eternal, a reason for breathing. An attempt at ultimate beauty."

"Well, instead it's suffocating you."

"I know, I know, but it's like a bad relationship. It's driving you mad, it's a struggle to get through a single day, but you still stay. You want to make it right."

"Anything but lonely."

"Anything but that. Shot nerves, can't think straight, screaming and yelling, drive me fucking crazy, but don't leave me alone. Just don't leave me with myself."

We both laughed.

"We'd rather be in hell with someone than in heaven alone," I said.

"I can't break up with my damn film. That's it. It's a very co-dependent relationship."

I started flipping pages of the magazine and Gilworthy started massaging his beard, pulling on it and then stroking it, but I could feel that he wasn't going to let go of this topic.

"Yeah, that's right, Van. It makes me think of a scene in the film about a guy I met in Vegas outside a casino."

Everything went back to the film for Gilworthy. He was so deep into the imagined reality of his eternal screenplay that he'd lost sight of the outside world.

"In Vegas you meet them all, but this guy gave me the saddest, most painful, most awful lonely story I'd ever heard. He wasn't much older than us. Mid-thirties when I was mid-twenties. I'll never forget his monologue or at least the monologue I remember and recorded in the screenplay. I probably injected my own shit into it, but that doesn't matter. Not a lick. He laid it all on the line to me. How many times do you meet people who tell you even a fraction of the truth? This cat poured it out in all its glorious agony and shame. A truth bomb that imploded in all directions internal. Christ, saddest story I'd ever heard. He's the subtle heart of my film. No, the aorta, damn heart is too much of a master prevaricator. He directs the blood of the plot, though there is no real plot."

Gilworthy paused and looked around the room, then continued, "So I'm sitting on a bench on the periphery of the strip. I could see the mountains melting in the heat of a Vegas summer night. It was twilight and the strip was just beginning to light up the night. Nature surrounding the fifty-five billion watts of the strip is really spectacular. The heat was well over a hundred and the sun was on its way down. It was oppressive, but the way I like it. I love heat. The sweat and swelter. It's honest. Why we subject ourselves to winters is deep neurosis. Everyone ought to live between the Tropics of Cancer and Capricorn. We're so foolish, Van. We can stay in situations that we hate when it's easily changeable. We're too addicted to our roots. We ought to have group therapy for all six and a half billion. The whole godforsaken planet on the couch. One giant satellite beaming therapy to the planet in Esperanto. But that's a dumb idea because only thirty or so people know that weird, artificial language. I love being in a place where you don't know the language. Everyone seems so much more interesting. Eccentric. Fascinating. Then when you know their language all they're talking about is the same nonsense anyone talks about. All a lot of bullshit everywhere, but once in a while there's a chestnut in the debris."

While Gilworthy was waxing digressive I realized my heart was pounding again. It had slowed down before, but now it suddenly seemed to have accelerated. I put my thumb on my pulse and began counting while Gilworthy was still talking. He stopped mid-sentence when he realized I wasn't listening.

"What the hell's the matter? Your heart?"

"I think the coke has affected my pulse. It's beating really fast. Why did you sprinkle it into the pipe?"

"It was just a dusting. It has to have worn off by now. Your heart is racing for another reason. Nervous about this thing here, right?"

"Maybe. Never done this before."

"You don't have to do anything. She does it all."

"I know."

"Nervous about your fiancée?"

"Maybe, I don't know. I think I'll give her a call."

"Not such a good idea. The ladies here might not enjoy your making a call. Let's smoke a little green with no jimmies," Gil suggested. "It'll relax you."

I didn't answer. I was mindlessly turning pages and wondering how Bishop and Koles were enjoying their ladies and the experience. I thought back to Bishop and the lovely Caroline who was taken in by his perverse charms tonight. He should have stayed back in Cambridge and continued his connection with an intelligent and attractive forty-something instead of going to a quasi-whorehouse with a crew of bohemian deviants less than half his age. I saw Bishop as a broken down auteur trying to film his imagination into the tragic nobility of a new youth. But perhaps all of this was just his escape from Caroline. Despite her dreamy and idyllic offers of romance on his terms, Bishop's years of failed marriages and severed friendships, all the accumulation of varying loss, might have made it implausible in his heart to accept Caroline's entreaties. Maybe, a whore was simply the most logical and painless choice for Bishop. Your cards were on the table and there were no vagaries or variables. A jack was a jack and there would be no sleight of hand. The relationship was pure in its communications, wants, and needs on both sides. The removal of mystery eliminated beauty, but also any chance of pain.

Thinking of vagaries, I began considering Bishop's call for a new vanguard, a symposium for his new art movement. I had always heard bits and pieces of this grand plan by Bishop, but never the specifics. I asked Gil what he knew. He explained that Bishop was pushing Koles to get the novel done. He had this jazz band that was writing a companion CD inspired by the novel and linking literature and music. He had an artist painting a series of works that he claimed would link the novel and Gil's film. There would be sculpture, poetry, conceptual art, throwback Duchampian readymades, operas and others that Gil didn't remember. It was an exhibition that aimed at "integrated chaos" according to Bishop. It was an homage to Surrealism's untapped potential for a true reality. Bishop saw himself as a modern day Breton. The whole thing would all be on display at the Planetarium.

"At the Museum of Science?" I asked.

"That's the plan," Gil said.

"And your script?"

"He wants *Macronesia* playing on the ceiling during the show."

"But that will take forever with your film being —"

"I might give him a scene or two, maybe not. Don't know if I'm ready or it's ready to expose. He told me he's also got some deal at the new ICA, but I have strong reservations about Bishop. The whole thing could just be in his head."

"Possibly, but I think there's some honesty there. He may be a lush, but he seems sincere. He's even offered Koles some gig in Portugal. A little winery where Koles can live for free, work a bit, and finish his book. I should go with him."

Gil was surprised to hear this. "And Shaillie? What about you two? Aren't you getting married in a few months?"

"Supposed to be."

"What! You're jeopardizing your relationship to be a lost soul roaming Europe at thirty?"

"Who said anything about that? I might just take some time to get away. Christ, I've been toiling in nothingness for six numbing years. Now, you of all people are going to give me a lecture on staying straight and narrow. Look at you. A cokehead writing a film that doesn't end. Please!"

Gil's eyes widened in surprise at my harsh reaction. "Yeah, touché baby, I know I ought to end the thing. I really should."

"Both habits actually."

"One might take care of the other. I'm just saying reading and dreaming about escape might be more exciting than the actual escape. You get caught up in it just like the other side does with retirement plans and BMWs. I know I'm contradicting myself, but so be it. This life isn't for everyone. Besides, Shaillie is priceless."

"Yes, yes she is," I said quietly.

Gil and I were chain-smoking and taking a break from banter. The old Chinese woman stepped out from behind the accordion wall the moment we each finished a cigarette and emptied the ashtray. She'd wipe it clean with a rag and give us an extended and affected smile. She

93

was missing a few teeth. Her large, round face looked like a jaundiced jack-o-lantern when she smiled. After one ashtray-emptying visit, I had the urge to stick a candle in her skull.

When she wasn't dumping out our cigarette butts, she was behind the accordion wall with her partner. Each time the old woman came out, I got a glimpse of the other lady, who looked enough like her to be a younger sister. They were busy chatting and folding a mountain of white towels. There was a motley concerto of shrill, piercing Korean, the aquatic swishing of a washer, and the droning spin of the dryer. It had a strangely soothing effect.

A man in a suit with a clean-cut, professional look came in. The old Korean woman greeted him with a heavily accented "Hallo." He asked how long the wait was. The older sister looked back at us and our cloud of smoke, then turned to the suit, "One hour and half. You wait?"

"I'll come back, thanks."

"You leave name?" She asked.

He hesitated, spun his eyes to the ceiling, and seemed to be making up a name. "Roger."

"Okay, Roger. Less than two hour. Maybe, one and half."

He nodded, smiled slightly and walked out. She wrote something down in a notebook that lay on a small desk. It seemed like she were the hostess at a restaurant taking down a dinner reservation. She was, more or less.

"She wants a starter house," I said after lighting another cigarette.

"What?"

"Shaillie wants to buy a starter house."

"So, what's the problem?" he asked.

"I'm not sure. Various things."

"Let me throw something at you, Van. This alternative life, artist life, bohemia, whatever you want to call it is not for everyone. I mean I could never have done the time you did in a cubicle, but not everyone can do what I'm doing. Taking care of Oswald Geary isn't a real job, except when I'm wiping his ass clean of feces. Smells and feels real then."

"No kidding. I'm not envying you."

"Of course, but just beware of new waters. Do you really want to leave Shaillie, Van? You can't have it both ways."

"I'm not leaving her. I never said that. Never even intimated."

"Yes, you did. You sure did. More than intimated."

94

"Look, Gil, I'm just at a crossroad here. I ignored the crossroad long ago and it's coming back to get me."

"What crossroad?"

I was getting antsy. Tired of waiting for Bishop and Koles to finish and not in the mood to take advice from Calvin Gilworthy on life decisions.

"Nothing, Gil. Nothing. It's a big step and it's lifelong. Nothing besides that."

"Van, I'll tell you this, ever since Lolikeni left me I've been screwed up. Having the right woman, the right partner is everything in this world. I'm just warning you to think twice before leaving that for something that seems better when read or viewed."

"I'll remember that."

I was feeling an acute sense of anomie as if at that moment I was living a plot concocted by someone else. It had to be the coke or the whorehouse or cheating on Shaillie. It was a lot of things. For the last hundred nights or so I'd always been writing the *Insomnia Journal,* but tonight I was living it.

We were silent. Cigarette smoke twirled hazily toward the ceiling. The Korean ladies opened and shut the dryer door. The soft, comforting spin of more white towels resumed. I focused on the repetitive drone of the spinning dryer. I took a deep breath. I didn't want the sound to stop. The Madam peeked out from behind the wall again.

"Everything ok? Problem, boys?"

"Everything's fine. How much longer?" Gilworthy asked.

She looked at her watch, said something to her partner in Korean and turned back to us, "Ten minute more. One hour not up. Good massage. Full relax. You enjoy, yes, you enjoy, but patient, *prease*. No *roud* talk."

We both nodded and smiled. We were quiet for a while and then Gilworthy ended it.

"You want the truth about my film?"

"Sure. Give me the truth, Gil."

"Truth is writing the film makes me sentient. Finishing it terrifies me. I'm afraid I'll turn numb which is what you must have felt in the cubicle. I know half the world can't eat and when I see movies about the plight of Africans I feel guilty as shit, but there's something terribly wrong in the land of plenty. Something is missing here. With all that we have we don't have what we want."

I didn't say anything, but I knew what he meant.

"But writing the film fills the void. It's the only way, the only time I truly feel conscious. Otherwise it's all assorted perceptions and notions."

95

"Sentience is beautiful. And now?"

"Now? Do I feel conscious?"

"Yeah, do you?"

"I'm conscious of being conscious."

"Long live Descartes," I said.

"I wish we could do better than Descartes."

Gil took a long drag off his cigarette, and blew several perfect smoke rings. I watched them lose their perfection, fade into hazy floating ovals before coming undone.

"Starter homes aren't sentient, are they Van?"

"No, Gil, they are definitely not."

"They are inverted sentience. They are…" Gil paused, his eyes rolled back in his head, then they fell quickly back into glaring at me. "By God, they are closed doors. Boarded up doors. Big giant wooden planks forming an X on the door." Gilworthy said, starting to laugh again.

"Yes, yes. You know, come to think of it, I want the starter house to have revolving doors like a hotel lobby."

"I like that, Van. A house with hotel-like, revolving doors. You feel like you're on vacation every time you go home."

We were both laughing hard now, lingering marijuana fumes catalyzing it all.

"Starter house is better than the big house though," I said.

"Better than a half-way house," Gilworthy collaborated.

"Yeah, hmmm, revolving doors. I'm going to pose that to Shaillie. That's not too foolish, Gil. It will change the whole dynamic, the whole feng shui jazz and rhythm."

The accordion wall suddenly squeaked as it slid open. An androgynous Korean head peered through, "Too *roud* boys. Keep down. Almost time. Five minute, ok? Turn radio on for you, ok?"

We both nodded and she closed the door. We heard the static of a radio and then it settled onto a song. It was Norman Greenbaum's "Spirit in the sky."

When I die, and they lay me to rest, I'm going to go to the place that's the best. Yes, got to have a friend in Jesus. So that when we die, he'll recommend us to the place that's best…

Gilworthy started tapping his thighs and rotating his head, grooving to the tune.

Never been a sinner, never sinned, we got a friend in Jesus. Set us up to the spirit in the sky, when we die and they lay us to rest, I'm going to go to the place that's the best, the place that's the best...

I held up the issue of the Jesus Christ *Newsweek*. Gilworthy started singing, "Alright. The place that's the best, that's we'll rest."

The Korean Madam came out and put her index finger to her mouth, "Shhh!" She disappeared and then returned moments later. "Two minute boy. Two minute. Two. Patient, *prease*." Her head nodded up and down several times as she held two fingers up. We both nodded in unison like good horny marionettes waiting for our female puppets. Our heads matched hers, bob for bob. After the puppet show ended, I was thinking about all the religious ironies—the Christ cover, notions of Sodom and Gomorrah, fire and brimstone, and then ole Norman Greenbaum who must have been a Jew like the man on the cover. Shaillie would have a fine time layering the ironies and conjecturing on the specific synchronies...I could easily imagine it, "Van, on your way to the whorehouse...and all these religious overtures. You have to see it for something other than random events..."

I felt a tap on my shoulder snapping me out of my head trip, "Van, you know what? I got some schadenfreude to snap you out of your starter house angst."

"At who's expense will it be?"

"Don't you just love that word. Smoothest German word I've ever heard. Schadenfreude, schadenfreude..." Gilworthy kept repeating, ignoring my question.

"Gil."

"Schadenfreude, schadenfreude..."

"Gil!"

"Yeah, Van, sorry. Hell of a word. Feels good off the tongue. Try it."

"No."

"Just try it. It's surprising that German has got such playful lilt to it. It always seems like such an angry language."

"Blame it on the Nazis."

"A kind of schadenfreude. Now say it."

"No."

"Van," Gil implored, childlike.

"Christ, you're liking a nagging wife. Fine, schadenfruede," I repeated it several times. I had to admit that he was right. "Yes, Gil, that is a good-feeling word. It's linguistically soothing." We both began repeating it.

The accordion wall unraveled. "What matter, boy? What it is? Why you speak German?" I looked over to see our Madam Korea peering through the halfway opened pine wall. She was all over us. The other lady, the partner, was peering over her shoulder at us, a white towel hanging from her hand, looking like a boxer's corner person.

"What matter, boy!"

"Sorry. Just having fun," Gilworthy answered.

"You keep secret? Speak German to keep secret? Who you work for?"

"No one," Gilworthy said. "Don't worry. We are not..."

"You sure, you not?"

"No, absolutely not. Honest."

"You tell truth?"

"Yes," Gilworthy reassured, almost pleading now. "I'm telling the truth, the whole truth and..."

"Why speak German?"

"It's the only German word I know besides, ahhh, Kindergarten and Gesundheit. It's not really German. I mean, it is German, but it's English, too."

"How can be *Engrish* and German? It two *ranguage*. Make nonsense." She was almost yelling in her shrill and piercing voice. If Bishop and Koles were in the midst of enjoying any sensuality, they were doomed to lose the rhythm they'd achieved.

"They are German words used in English. Don't worry. All good." Gilworthy looked over at me and mouthed, *What the hell*, with his brow firmly furrowed in disbelief while Seoul's version of Nurse Ratched was vigorously shaking her head with distrust emanating from every pore.

"We're not Nazis or in any secret group," I said.

"What you say?"

"Everything's fine," I tried.

She nodded slowly, now looking me squarely in the eye without blinking. When she finally blinked, she turned to Gil.

"I no trust you."

Gil turned his palms to the ceiling, eyes wide in disbelief, and raised his shoulders. "Me?"

She looked back at me, "You trust. Not him."

I smiled, "He ok," I said, realizing I had unintentionally excised the verb to be, Madam style.

"You sure?" she queried.

"Yes, it's all good. We won't cause any problems. I promise."

"All good?" she asked, still looking at me.

"Yes, it's all good. We'll keep it down. It's just that we've been waiting so long. We're sorry for any disturbances or confusion. We're a little anxious. We're very sorry."

"Two minute. That all. Two minute more. You no wait, you *reave* now."

"No, no. We're fine. We'll be patient."

"Two minute. No more German. *Engrish* only. *Engrish* or Korean," she giggled. "Or Korean," she repeated, enjoying her own joke and looking back at her partner, who giggled while covering her mouth. Madam Korea then slid the pine wall closed before opening it quickly and staring at Gilworthy. "No trust you. Keep eye on you," she said seriously. The wall then closed tightly.

"Jesus, what the hell did I do?" Gil whispered to me.

"It's got to be the goatee. You come across as either an artist or a criminal to most. Apparently, the latter to her."

"I don't know. She probably sees right through me. I wouldn't trust me if I were her. I mean I won't do anything, but I'm just not trustworthy."

"You're Gilworthy, not trustworthy."

Gil shook his head with a half-smile and tugged on his goatee. He looked truly offended and slighted, like a student rebuked by his favorite teacher.

"Gil, don't worry about it. You're too hard on yourself. I trust you, pal."

"I'm not," he shrugged, but was still clearly annoyed at not being trusted. He was really pulling hard at his whiskers. I was surprised that he was so offended. I thought about bringing up his side-business, but we had never discussed it before.

"That starter-house phobia is much ado about nothing, don't you think, Gil?"

"More or less. You need an existential detective to figure out why it's bothering you and I'm not in the mood. Maybe, we ought to step out and smoke some more to relax."

"I'm going to pass, Gil. My mind's been altered enough for the night."

"Not mine. It can never be altered enough."

"I got too high, too drunk, or too wired. Too something or other. Time to stabilize."

"Van, you got your Armenian neurons in an anarchic tither. Don't worry, though, we'll both be relaxed soon when these ladies work their erotic magic. We're both wound a bit tight, but it'll all untwine just fine. Thank God it's not Amsterdam and those robots. Goddamn government sponsored whores—worst thing to ever happen to prostitution. It's like communism. Everything gets grey, dull, and lifeless. God bless capitalism. Puts the pro back in prostitute."

Gil looked at his watch. "Soon, we'll be in there. It'll be so good. The first part will get you squeaky clean in sweet, sponge-bath fashion. Part two will relax your muscles supple and pliant so that orgasm can flush the structure fully, Reichian style. Part three, well, that's the crème-brulee. It'll dissipate the lurking demons for a later day."

"They never quite go away though."

"Can't ask for more than temporary utopia, Van. Let's not get greedy."

The Korean ladies came out and told us one more minute. Then they walked over in the direction that Bishop and Koles had gone. I assumed they were going to end the session.

"Van, I've got to tell you something before we go in. Before Koles gets back."

I nodded.

"Koles is the guy," he said.

"What guy?"

"The guy in Vegas."

I wasn't sure what he meant, but then I remembered his Vegas story from which we'd digressed long ago.

"What do you mean?"

"He's got troubles."

"I know. Don't we all? He's trying to get his ex-wife back and he's hurting."

"Just be careful of him. You've been hanging out with him a lot."

I shrugged. I didn't think it was a big deal.

"Look, Van. It's not my place to divulge the inner workings of another man's marriage, but it's not all what you hear from one party. Koles can be spiritually seductive. All his types can. Lure you in, the soil feels new, real. Bishop too, but Koles more. Soon, that soil is swampland, the newness old, and truth is upside down. Just pay heed, Van."

"What are you talking about, Gil?"

"Just watch out, Van. Next thing you know, it's not what you think it is."

"What the fuck, Gil!"

"I'm just a trespasser with these cats. I visit and then stay away. Avoid proximity with Koles."

"You live in the next room for Christ's sake."

"Not emotionally."

100

"Could you just stop the whole twilight-zone shit and be frank?"

"Frankly, I can't. Not my place. Just be a sentinel around them, him. Some people are like viruses—once they get in, they attack your immunity. Don't let your immunity down. Don't let Shaillie down," Gilworthy winked at me and then walked outside.

That was too much to swallow. Maybe he had a thing for Shaillie. That must be what he was getting at. But Koles? I didn't know what the hell to make of it. Koles seemed harmless. Tortured artist type, marriage gone wrong. Bishop was part genius, part clown. I knew that. I had them in proper distance. I wish the damn Asian girls would hurry up with Koles and Bishop. What the hell were they doing with them? One minute was long overdue. I heard the dryer beep loudly for what seemed a full minute. It was a loud piercing sound, but it only momentarily interrupted the carousel of my thoughts. It kept going back to Koles. What did I know about my new friend? Was he a friend? Friends made after undergraduate days were few and far between. Could you ever trust anyone you met after the age of twenty-two? I knew this much—he'd spent his early twenties back and forth between Paris and New York City, where he begrudgingly began an MFA in fiction at NYU. He did one year and quit to reside permanently in Paris teaching English and working on a novel. He knew Paris because he'd spent his junior year abroad during his undergraduate UC Santa Cruz days. He couldn't stand California. When I brought up some friends from college that took the California exit to begin a literary journal and to pursue artistic and leftist political endeavors, he mocked the efforts. I told him that I often wished I had taken flight with them. That I thought I'd be more settled now. He said it would have been a cliché to go to California. "A very tired escape," is how he described it. When I told him Paris wasn't the most original of choices, he took umbrage. He spoke of Paris like it was a person, like a lover. He dismissed San Francisco's artistic heritage as a fad, "like Kerouac and the Beats were. Bishop romanticizes them. Sometimes a naïve notion, my friend. Don't worry, there's still time for you. We'll get you back to Europe to stay, not just backpacking for a few months."

And then there was Yvette. He'd fallen madly in love with her. They married quickly and he got his novel published in France shortly after. It was all going so well. Then "it was like someone closed the curtain. The big thick burgundy curtain of an old theatre came across the stage. Act One with Yvette had ended. The stage crew had taken away the entire set and a new one was put in. And we could never get it right.

It was all taken away from me, Van. Everything changed. I tried to undo it, but never could." He'd mentioned something about getting carried away with the minor success of his first book, getting too absorbed in writing the second, and vaguely hinting that she had changed, but with no specifics. That was all Koles had told me.

The carousel suddenly stopped when I saw Koles and one of the Koreans coming from the other room. She left Koles in the waiting room and rushed back down the hall. A few moments later she returned with a frantic look in her eyes.

"Your friend *sreeping*! You need get him out. We need room, now!"

Gilworthy walked in before we could say anything. "What's up?" he innocently asked.

Koles said, "Looks like Bishop is passed out."

"Holy shit. Goddamn Bishop!"

"Gil, take it easy. He's old and tired."

"I'm just anxious. Been waiting too long."

"You no swear. No swear here. Help Mr. Bishop," the Madam said.

We walked to his room. The door was still closed. The old lady let us in and told us to take him to an extra room in back that had a bed. He could sleep while we had our turn. She certainly didn't want to lose our business. Bishop lay supine with a white towel covering his loins. His mouth hung open, a little drool edging down the left side of his chin, strange sounds rhythmically coming out. He looked sad and beaten, a tired gladiator of life and art. His usually neatly slicked-back hair spilled forth in different directions. It seemed as though he should be put into a casket, rather than a bed.

"Damn, poor guy looks terrible," Koles said with concern.

"He looks really out," Gil said.

"What are we going to do?" I asked.

"Wake him up. Then he can sleep for an hour in the waiting room or the car."

Koles tapped Bishop on the shoulder. Nothing. He pushed his shoulder gently again. Still nothing. He took the towel covering his loins and wiped the saliva dribbling down his chin and then put the towel back. Then he slapped his face gently. Bishop murmured something softly. Koles decided to upgrade his efforts. He grabbed Bishop's shoulders and shook him hard.

"Bishop, wake up!"

Bishop mumbled, groaned and churned out sounds like a dilapidated Oldsmobile trying to start up on a cold, January New

102

England morning. Some language became audible, but I had no idea what language it was. It sounded like fluent gibberish.

"*Rag-mhuinealachd, ahh, ughh, aimbeart analiaich, tarruing anail. Botramaid! Beaumadair. Snaidheadiar neo-chealgach!*" Bishop punctuated the linguistic gymnastics by vigorously shaking his head from side to side. Consequently, his flesh and lips swung freely off his facial bones and it made a kind of underwater gurgling noise.

"What the hell was that?" Gil asked.

"Gaelic, I think," Koles answered. "Might have been a passage from *Finnegan's Wake*. Sounded like it to me."

"I don't know what's crazier, what I just heard and saw or that you read Joyce's madness."

"Agghhhem," Bishop cleared his throat. "That's not Joyce, gentlemen, that's Bishop. That's from Seamus Rourke's youthful oeuvre of Gaelic poetry. Published in Cork, 1958." Bishop's eyes widened and he sat up, torso erect, like he'd just risen from the dead off the mortician's slab. As he'd risen, the towel slid off his loins and onto the floor.

"And, gentlemen, that there between my legs is not from my youthful oeuvre." We all laughed. "How about some goddamn trousers for the old Irish bard?"

Koles quickly grabbed Bishop's clothes and gave them to him. As he began dressing, he asked "Hmmm, is the show ready, boys? You've got all the artists in place. We're all set to shatter perceptions and conceptions."

"What?" Koles asked.

"The show. We ready for the opening?"

"Bishop, you're in Providence. You passed out after a massage. It's not the opening of the exhibit."

"Ohhh, hmmm," He sighed, looking around. He pressed his fingertips into his lined forehead and massaged himself momentarily, closing his eyes in the process. "Yes, another form of art, boys. The truest and greatest art form, but only a sprint. We're looking for a marathon," he said this while continuing the self-massage.

"Bishop, the hundred-meter dash is over. You've crossed the finish line."

"Not yet, Derek. It never finishes."

"Yeah, I mean with the hour massage."

It was quiet for a moment. We were just staring at Bishop, staring at the bedraggled barroom saint as he continued dressing himself. "Defending Infinity. Yes, Defending Infinity! That's what we'll call the exhibit. All hail Louis Aragon and his great unknown masterpiece."

Gilworthy responded, "Wonderful Bishop, but right now we need to get you the hell out of here."

Bishop finished dressing. He looked unkempt and disheveled, but he was functional, which was all that mattered at this time of the night in a massage parlor in Providence, Rhode Island.

As we walked out of the room, Bishop asked me, "Van, what was the name of your grandfather again?"

"Setrag Arakalian."

"Ole Joyce would've loved that name. You pen your grandfather's novel. Don't think, just pour it out, exhale it like a good Armenian Surrealist and we'll put it in the show. Pen it like Gorky painted *The Water of the Flowery Mill*. Write like a painter, Van. That'll get you more honesty than the revised and manicured outlines being published today."

I almost uttered that I was writing my own surrealist novel during the insomnia of recent months, but I swallowed the utterance just before it fled my tongue. I didn't know why I couldn't tell Bishop or his peripheral circle of artists what I was doing, but it demanded secrecy.

"Yes, we need an Armenian Genocide survivor in the show. What else can defend the infinite better than story of Setrag Arakalian? It'll balance the madness, Van."

"I'll see what I can do."

Bishop and Koles sat down in the waiting room, exactly where Gil and I had sat interminably before.

"You ok, Mr. Bishop? You ok?" the Korean Madam sincerely inquired while darting out from her laundry dune.

"Couldn't be better, Ji Yao. Your geisha did well. Took care of the old man from Cork." Bishop smiled and winked at her.

"Good, good." She looked at Gil and me. "Mr. Bishop rest while you go. Ok? Then all you *reave*. It *rate*. Ok? Ok?" We nodded.

"You *rose* twenty minute *awready*. One hour begin when Mr. Bishop finished. We behind schedule. You have only forty minute now, but same price. Understand? Same price."

Gilworthy was perturbed. "We'll pay for the extra time. I want one hour. I need one hour. I'm not sixteen."

"No, we on schedule. Others come. You *reave* in forty minute. We behind now. You on clock. Go. Begin now!" Madam said imperiously.

Two women came over. One was older and had much larger breasts. She took Gilworthy by the hand and led him away. My lady was young, petite and very pretty. She took my hand and led me to a room with a sliding door, framed in wood and filled in with translucent rice paper. She slid the door closed. I saw Gilworthy and his lady's silhouettes walking away from the other side of the rice paper.

At this point, my nerves catalyzed. I told myself to calm down, enjoy the forty minutes of attention and pleasure. Let everything dissipate. Shaillie's visage quickly appeared in my head. Little rhythms of sadness sauntered within, but I diverted them. Shaillie knew about this. It wasn't deceitful. A last romp prior to eternity, no big deal. Hell, men and women everywhere do it while married. Why couldn't I do it without guilt before marriage and with my fiancée supporting it? After this, I would recline into Shaillie and the dictated life. Until then, indulge.

"What your name?" the woman asked me.

"Van."

"What kind name is that?"

"Armenian."

She paused as we stood face to face.

"Nervous?"

"Not really. Maybe a little. I have not been here or any other place for a year. It's been a while." I remembered what Bishop had told me to say.

"I take away nervous," she promised.

"Please do. What is your name?"

"Hyun. Van, you take off clothes, put white towel round you. I prepare. Ok?"

"Ok."

I did as I was told. The room was a tranquilizing blend of soft mahoganies, light browns, and the shadowy off-white of rice paper. The gentle dripping peace of a small water fountain could be heard. The floor was a faux marble. There was a drain in the center of the room. A large rectangular padded table to my right. There were some supplies in one corner near a sink where Hyun was busy preparing. She squeezed some soap into a bucket and put the bucket into the deep sink under running water. When it was filled, she lifted the bucket out of the sink. I could see numerous tiny, but extraordinarily defined muscles rippling in her arms. She carried the heavy bucket towards me with ease, placing it at my feet. Hyun sat down on a small wooden stool and slowly turned my body so that she was behind me. She reached around me, slowly loosening the tightened white towel from around my waist. It slid down my legs and dropped near my ankles. She picked it up, placing it on a hook attached to the padded table.

"Relax, my Van. I take good care you." I nodded and could feel myself calming down as a result of Hyun's gentle voice and peaceful energy.

Hyun took the soapy warm sponge and softly scrubbed my back, buttocks, and legs all from behind while slowly caressing me with her free hand. Her fingertips barely touched me, but they invoked energized peace within my skin — simultaneously tranquilizing and stimulating.

"Turn 'round, Van."

She wrung the sponge out over the drain. Then soaked it again in the bucket of steaming, soapy water. She stepped in front of me and glided the sponge tenderly across my chest and shoulders. She stretched high to dab my face and forehead. I must have been a foot taller than her. She moved down to my stomach. I looked down and saw my limp cock hanging there. I was glad I didn't have a schoolboy erection ready to go at just being near this very sexy woman.

Hyun had on tiny, tight black spandex shorts and a white cotton halter-top. Her breasts were small, but seemingly very firm like the rest of her taut body. Her nipples pressed hard against the tight white top, the darkened circles showing through. The golden skin of her cleavage curved wonderfully above the white of her top. The more I looked at the slope of her breasts, the golden brown color so beautifully contrasted by the white top, the more my blood began to flow centrally.

School was in session.

She squeezed a freshly soaked sponge along my chest and shoulders so that the sudsy warm water ran down my stomach and arms. Water dripped from my fingertips. She dropped the sponge in the bucket and dipped her hands in the white foam floating on top of the water, rubbing them together to create lather. Hyun cupped my arm below the shoulder with both her hands and slowly moved them down to my wrist. She then lathered each individual finger. She repeated the process on my other arm.

"You enjoy?" she asked, smiling and looking at my aroused state.

"Very much. You are beautiful."

She smiled. I was no longer nervous and my arousal was anxiety free. I was relaxed, ready, in the moment.

She took the sponge again, squeezed soapy water onto my penis and down my legs. She washed my pelvis and legs, not touching any area with her fingers.

"Lie on table," she sensuously demanded, seemingly enjoying her control, as did I. "On stomach, Van."

She took the bucket, rinsed it free of soap and filled it with plain water. She poured it over my prostrate body and refilled it again. While the water ran, she put her fingertips along both side of my spine at its apex vertebra. She dug her fingers deeply into the tissue and muscle, before sliding them slowly down the spine, bifurcating to go across the

106

center of each buttock, straight down the middle of my hamstrings, over the calves, Achilles tendon, the soles of my feet, carrying an accumulating ball of tension in her fingers. It culminated at the middle toes of each foot, where she squeezed the toes firmly. After a few moments, she gave the middle toes a quick twist. They cracked simultaneously, the balls of tension instantly dissipating. She slowly and softly released her grip.

"Turn over, Van."

Hyun was in charge.

She turned the water off and poured the bucket slowly across my chest and down the rest of my supine body. She repeated the same fingertip centerline movement across my front forehead, down the cheeks, along the Adam's apple, across the sternum, veering around my penis and down my legs to the front sides of the middle toe.

She was precise and methodically erotic.

"Now , you can stand."

She dried me off with a clean white towel, spending extra time gently drying my loins.

"You feel clean?"

I nodded.

"Feel good?"

"Yes. It's obvious, isn't it?"

"Yes. It very obvious. It obvious a lot, my Van," she smiled. "We go to other room."

I liked the way she said, "my Van."

She gave me another clean towel. I momentarily thought of the old Korean ladies busily running the machines and folding towel after towel. I wrapped the towel around myself and followed Hyun across the dimly lit hall.

We went inside a brightly lit massage room. She placed a white sheet over the table. Traditional Oriental music played serenely in the background. I noticed a metal bar overhead that went from one end of the room to the other. It was directly above the table. Various plants were scattered along glass counters all around the room. I recognized Bonsais and wandering Jews. Hyun dimmed the lights and I lay prostrate as per her instructions.

Hyun had massaged my body into absolute repose. She had especially focused on my back, using her deft and powerful toes. Holding onto the metal bar above, she had not only walked on my back, but had dug her toes around each individual vertebra, pushing and twisting the tissue into infant-like softness. Once that was achieved, she would sharply, yet nimbly torque each vertebra until it popped loudly. With my backbone making sounds similar to the crack of a baseball on a bat, I wasn't sure I'd ever stand erect again, but at that moment a pure and innocent relaxation floated throughout my body. As if the musculature and spine had been a coil pressed down upon for decades and now that coil was finally released, returning to its original and uncompressed form—a natural and real state of being. My neck muscles seemed to be finally released from the vice-like grip of my shoulders. I could feel my shoulders hanging loosely off my collarbones. My arms seemed inches lower. How terribly tense and tight I had been. Years of existential stress over the anxiety of nullity had fled my body at Hyun's magical prodding. The drugs still circulating in my body were in balance. I wished I hadn't done any to affirm more purity of feeling, but the high was subtle and comfortable now unlike during the conversation with Gilworthy.

Hyun told me to turn over and sit up while she poured me a glass of water. "Drink all, Van. Body need water now." I drank a full glass of water and felt its cleansing effect traveling within my system, quenching liberated and thirsty muscles. As I drank, I wondered what Hyun would do next. I remembered that usually the first time was with just her hand. It went progressively further with every visit. Bishop had said, "Trust had to be built. We were building a relationship with the woman and all relationships climb stronger along the scaffolding of trust. Be it marriage, siblings, fathers and sons, or whores and their clients."

"Lie down, Van," Hyun whispered as she took the empty glass from my hand.

I thought she was going to start touching me intimately. Instead, her fingertips grazed across my open palms, wrists and inner arms. She was barely touching me, but the effect was tantalizing and deep. Tantric perhaps, causing a tender and erotic confluence within. During the massage my erection ended. I wasn't even conscious of the change. Hyun had focused on my muscles and bones and had relaxed my thoughts into a sleepy state. Her fingers' gentle touch along my arms began to bring it back to life. She moved her hands to my stomach and began caressing the air just above me with the back of her fingers. She was circulating energy from her hands to my body with millimeters between us. The feeling was stronger than the sensation of actual touch. My internal chemistry was now a wild merger of desire and tranquility.

She walked behind me and began massaging my head with increasing force. She was pushing down on my scalp and making small concentric rotations into my cranium with all ten fingertips. The repose

108

part of the formula began to recede. She began pulling on my neck. Her hands were incredibly strong for a body that couldn't have weighed more than one hundred pounds. She elongated my neck and gave it quick jerks to the right and left, cracking my neck in several places. My head rested in her cupped hands as if it had been decapitated. She laid it back on the table as I exhaled.

"You scare?"

"For a second."

"Now, how does feel?"

"Wonderful. My whole body is at ease and peace. I'm so relaxed."

"Good, my Van. Nice name and you nice person."

My eyes were shut and neck and shoulders felt melted down as if the muscles there had been frozen for decades. The taut art of social being finally released into comfortable essence.

Hyun was now on the opposite side by my feet. I was half erect. With all the ease in my being, thoughts turned coital. Of course. At the same time, Hyun began a new phase. She pushed my legs together tightly. Then she backed up from the table to the end of the room. There was only enough space for a few strides. Nevertheless, Hyun ran at the table like a gymnast beginning her routine on the balance beam. I raised my head to observe, eyes widened as she leapt onto the table. I instinctually closed my eyes and braced myself.

She landed softly. The table moved slightly, but I felt nothing. I opened my eyes. Her knees landed perfectly on either side of my hips in the tiny space of table that existed beyond my body. Her hands landed on either side of my chest. She was on all fours and all feline over me. We locked eyes. She smiled and we laughed like giddy lovers. Momentary and monetary concerns notwithstanding, we were lovers. For the next twenty minutes we would be engaged in the lustful form of love. A form that would require $60 plus tip.

"What you do for job?" she asked, now upright and her beautiful little Asian ass resting on my thighs. As she asked the question, she began to touch me softly. With one palm she caressed me. With the other, she used the back of her hand until I was aroused immediately.

"I'm a teacher," I lied.

"Really?" she said, momentarily stopping the motion of her hands.

"Yes."

"You teach me English."

"I would love to."

"My English not good."

"Your English is beautiful."

"You come see me again. Not one year. Soon."

"Yes. Very soon."

She ran her index finger across my lips slowly silently instructing me to be quiet. She put some cream on her hands and rubbed them together, moistening her palms. We were silent for about five minutes, except for my heavy breaths evolving into groans. Hyun began increasing the pace and the end was near. Very near...

"You happy, my Van?"

"Very, my Hyun."

"I like happy Van."

I laughed deeply and heartily. She was beyond real. Surreal.

"I get tissue," she said as she jumped off the table. She moved quickly like a cat, real enough to be aware of the time. She cleaned me and then motioned for me to get up. I could tell time was up. I got off the table and kissed her cheek as I stood up. She giggled and didn't seem to mind. There was a private bathroom in the room. She told me I could get dressed in there. She pointed to an envelope, next to a bonsai, kissed me on the cheek and left the room.

After I dressed, I put one hundred dollars in the envelope and left. I saw Koles and Bishop in the waiting area. They were both drinking coffee from white styrofoam cups. There were two other men waiting as well. Neither of them was the "Roger" who had popped in before. One was a nondescript forty-something. He had very little hair. What was left of his graying flaxen hair was parted barely an inch above his ear and stretched vainly across his virtually bald skull. I imagined his troubles on windy days. A polyester, dull, ill-fitted suit hung over his bony shoulders. His complexion had the pallor of a long time office worker. My complexion had I stayed in *cubicular* narcosis. The other guy was a burly working class type with his sleeves rolled up revealing tattooed, muscular forearms. His wrists were probably bigger than the other guy's legs. He had on a blue maintenance-worker uniform.

The skinny guy was smoking a cigarette. He was blowing perfect rings of smoke into the air like Gilworthy had. However, he one-upped Gil's efforts. After he created a ring, he was exhaling the remaining smoke in a thin stream right through the floating ring without touching the edge of the circle. Ring and then stream. He was really good at it. Ring and then stream. I could tell he'd had a lot of practice.

"Van!" Bishop said, jolting me from a mesmerized state. He gave me a curious look, took a sip of his coffee, and then raised his brows into nonverbal interrogative. I nodded with a smile. Koles nodded approval, too. I sat down. Five men all in the same place for the same reason. The library of the libido.

"Who next? Who come first, I forget," Madam Korea screeched into the quiet.

Blue collar said, "I was here first."

Office worker countered, "That's not true."

Blue collar repeated sternly while glaring at office worker, "I WAS HERE FIRST!"

Office worker said, "Ahhh, yes, upon second thought, I think he was." Law of the jungle prevailing.

"Ok, ok, come you with me," she ordered blue collar while office worker went back to his game of smoke rings. Blue collar followed Madam Korea out of the room. "Your turn soon," she said to office worker on her way out.

I saw Hyun down the hall greeting blue collar. She had the same smile she'd given me. I smiled at her trying to get her attention. She never looked at me.

I could hear the old lady knocking on a door. "Time up, time up," she said several times between knocks that clanged louder and louder. "Time up, time up!"

There was no sign of Gilworthy. Madam Korea was obviously yelling at him to finish his business. Maybe he was having trouble with all the narcotics floating in his system. I had some trouble and he'd done much more than I.

Bishop whispered to us, "He better not piss off Ji Yao or we'll never be back. I need this place. You guys are still in the game, still players. I'm well past that era. I get all I need from my Asian princesses once a month."

"That's bullshit Bishop," I said. "You had that nice Irish woman all over you tonight."

"It wouldn't have worked."

"She was pretty, intelligent and was all over you. What's your problem?"

"It wouldn't have worked, Van."

"Why not?"

"Let it go."

"Christ, I was attracted to her. I would have been all over her if I were single," I said. I had the urge for Bishop to marry this woman and live out the rest of his life peacefully in a healthy relationship. Stop drinking and finish with dignity and serenity. Transcend his alcohol and art narcotic.

"Van, my exiled Armenian boy, I've got other priorities. It's about art for me, not love. I get my love once a month here. It sustains me, but searching for and attempting to seize the infinite is my nectar."

"Can't fuck art, Bishop," Koles said.

"I fuck it everyday. Best lay I've ever had."

"What a load of shit," I said. I wanted to say more, get to the bottom of Bishop, of Seamus Rourke, but I was interrupted.

Madam Korea was yelling, "Time up now. Time up now. You finish. Ten minute *rate*. Time up!"

"What the fuck is going on?" Koles asked.

I heard Gilworthy's voice from a distance. "We aren't finished."

"You finish. You finish ten minute ago. You *rate*."

"We aren't finished!" Gil screamed.

"Open door! Time up! No pay for this!" Madam Korea was Red Army angry.

"Fine. Charge me!" Gilworthy was panting behind his howls.

Madam Korea started pounding on the door. She was incensed. She was hitting the door with two fists, wildly angry.

"I can't concentrate! Stop it! Shut up for a second!"

Madam Korea banged louder. "Jing la, OUT NOW!!" She screamed before switching to Korean, which was louder and shriller.

"Just wait, you old bitch!" Gilworthy screamed back.

More Korean.

"Don't listen to her," Gil pleaded, but everyone in the libido library was listening to the drama unfold. Rice paper walls made for great audibility.

"My boss. She my boss," Jing la said behind the door.

"I'll pay you extra. Please. I'm almost done."

"Oh lord," Bishop lamented. "Thus spoketh the almighty cock. We got troubles boys."

I heard scuffling and then the sound of the door opening. "You go back," Madam Korea commanded in a stern maternal tone before returning to the waiting room. "You turn," she demanded angrily to the office worker. He got up and started to follow her, but Gilworthy suddenly appeared. "Sit down!" he said to office worker who quickly formed a sheepish grin in the face of Gil's angry affront. Life was probably always one step ahead of this guy.

"Miss, I just need a few more minutes. I'll pay extra." Gilworthy politely proposed trying hard to keep his voice calm and restrained. His hair was a mess, goatee twisted at a weird angle, shirt half tucked in, and zipper down, as well as his pride.

"Time up!" she yelled. "Time up!!"

Bishop had seen enough. He spoke some Korean to the Madam, seemed very apologetic, and then turned to Gilworthy, "Listen, you sorry son of a bitch, we're leaving and you're leaving her alone. You get an hour. If you can't finish your business in time, that's you fault. We'll stop at a bathroom and you can finish on your own."

"I'm not done! I didn't get an hour because of you and your damn narcolepsy. I only got forty minutes. It's not my fault, it's yours!."

"Falling asleep late at night is not a symptom of narcolepsy. I was…"

"Bishop, stay out of it."

"It's time to go, Gil," Bishop insisted.

"Son of a bitch. I didn't get what I paid for."

"You're done, Gilworthy."

Madam Korea was wide-eyed and frantic. She was moving her feet in different directions, but not going anywhere specifically. Then she glared at office worker who had a deer-in- -headlights look even though this had nothing to do with him. Madam Korea grabbed him by his slender wrist and yanked him out of his chair. His painstakingly combed hair was jerked the opposite way and fell over the wrong ear, exposing his very bald head and leaving a long flap of thinning hair ridiculously hanging down the side of his neck. She led him to the back while he futilely tried to pull the hair back over his head with his one free hand.

"Fuck this place!" Gilworthy howled, stomping out the door as we followed.

I heard the door open as we were nearing the car. Madam Korea reappeared by herself. Bishop and I turned back.

"You no come back. EVER! You ban. You ban!!"

She tried to pull the door shut with force, but the pneumatic device above would only allow it to close slowly. She jerked it a couple of times, but it wouldn't go any faster. Frustrated and scowling, she waited for it to close. Just before it finally did, we heard her voice one more time.

"No come back. No more Bishop. No more Bishop friend! Bad people!"

Koles was driving again and Bishop was now in the passenger seat with classical music on the radio. Gilworthy was frantically doing one-hit blasts of coke. He offered it to me and I refused. He asked Koles and Bishop who similarly turned him down.

Bishop broke the silence. "What the fuck were you doing? For that matter, what the fuck are you doing now?"

"You're going to lecture me on addiction? You haven't been sober since when? The Vietnam War?"

"Not quite, but a good guess my eternal filmmaker. I haven't been sober since Dien Bien Phu, the French version of the war." Bishop let out one of his throaty, phlegmy laughs, but it was stilted and forced.

Gil turned to me, "The guy has triple bypass and he's still smoking unfiltered Camels despite doctor's orders to quit or die. And he's going to lecture me? Save it. It's very unbecoming for a fucking Bishop."

"Death becomes us all. I'm just accelerating the inevitable," Bishop trumpeted.

"Then, so am I, Lord Byron."

"You fucked up in there," Koles jumped in.

"Look, I was about to come and the damn fucking Chairwoman Mao comes barging in. Goddamn gang of one..."

"She's Korean, not Chinese," Bishop corrected.

"Whatever. I don't give a shit at this point. My sweet buxom lady was willing to extend the time. I was going to throw some extra money at her. Twice I was about to come and her knocking and shrill squawking chased it away."

"It's not all about the orgasm," Bishop reiterated.

"For me it is. For normal people it is," Gilworthy countered.

Koles said, "Shut the fuck up, Gilworthy. You're being a prick. Take responsibility for Christ's sake. You did too much crap before and that's why you couldn't finish."

"What are you guys suddenly the PTA?"

"PTA? What the hell..."

"You're getting all high and mighty, Koles. All moral on me. Look where we were."

"So what? There's still a protocol to follow. You can't make up your own rules in this kind of place. We could've ended up in a lot of trouble."

"Christ, I just wanted to come. Isn't that protocol in a whorehouse?"

There was some silence. Gilworthy was angry and wasn't going to let this go. His tension was thick and pervasive within the claustrophobic confines of the car. The atmosphere reminded me of childhood car rides throbbing with paternal ire and maternal confusion.

I had an urge to call Shaillie. I took out my cell phone, but it had no service. I was glad this bachelor romp was finished. I wanted to talk to her, convince her to go to Europe. Maybe repetition would make her take me seriously. There had to be a way to compromise. I knew I didn't have cold feet. It was just the spirit looking for novelty around a different corner. Healthy escape. Marriage could go hand in hand with

114

this. This traveling theatre was an aberration, not the norm. Shaillie was the norm.

I noticed Gilworthy's hands were aggressively intertwined, fingers formed into an intricate web. He broke the silence. "So you finished, right Van? Got your money's worth?" he asked plaintively.

"Yes, she was good."

"Damn it! I was so close. All this way only to get interrupted right on the edge of peace."

"It's a long way from Bangkok," I said.

"Don't remind me of that. What I wouldn't do for that angel right now." He refilled his one-hitter and did another blast up his right nostril. Then he muttered something to himself before turning articulate, "So, you liked it? You'd go again?"

"My girl was really sweet and sexy, but I'm one and done I think."

"Fuck, fuck, fuck!" Gilworthy shouted. He was really disjointed, plus he kept feeding his nostrils. It was starting to worry me. I could tell Koles and Bishop were tired of his game.

"You know, it's the last time I go to that place, too. For other reasons."

"No shit," Koles said. "It's the last time any of us go, thanks to you."

"It's a fucking joke, anyway. It's a bullshit whorehouse. Next time we go somewhere without a time limit. It's a half-ass, ham and egg operation."

"Ham and egg?" Koles repeated, laughing.

"Yeah, ham and fucking egg! You heard me right."

"Let it go," I suggested.

"Easy for you to say. You finished. You're satisfied."

"You never finish anything," Koles goaded. "You should be used to this shit."

"Oh, so now you're going to lecture me on the film."

Bishop interjected, "Leave it alone, Derek. Our Gil's film is the perfect visual for the show. Finishing is irrelevant. Art's greatest lie. You just get me some excerpts and we'll hit production mode soon enough."

"What about you and Yvette, Derek? You can't finish that even though she's finished. Pot and the kettle if I've ever seen it."

"Are you over Lolikeni?" Koles parried.

"Long ago. She wasn't the first to leave me nor probably the last."

"Gentlemen, shouldn't we..." I tried.

115

Gil interrupted me and continued, "You're living off the past. It's showing in your novel, stunting its growth. You're divorced, Derek. Wake up. It's over."

"Words, have no emotional worth, Gilworthy."

"What are you kidding? They ooze emotional worth. From the mouth of a writer," Gilworthy snickered.

"Big epiphany. Thanks a lot. She divorced me. I didn't divorce her and I haven't let go. Wow, you really fucking nailed that one. *Satori* after the whorehouse. I owe you one, Gil. I feel like a new man already. Instant therapy. Thank you, asshole."

Gilworthy turned to me, "I can't finish, Koles can't go forward, and you my friend, sit on the fence and have no idea what you're doing. You're like the whorehouse. All halfway, half ass. What a liar. Whining about the cubicle and this and that. Do something about it. Be creative for Christ's sake. What else is there? You've been a puppet far too long, Mr. Armenia. Start walking the damn walk."

I instinctively thought of telling Gilworthy to go fuck himself, but I realized, I knew, he was dead on. Strings were on my shoulders, wrists, ankles and the invisible puppeteer played my limp limbs like a finely tuned fiddle.

Bishop seized my silence, "Cut ole Van some slack. He's molting at his own pace."

Koles added, "Cut all of us some slack. You're being a prick to one and all because you didn't get your rocks off. Just unzip and finish the job, so we can be spared your bullshit."

I looked over at Gilworthy, daring him, though I certainly didn't want him to follow through right next to me.

"Bottom line is "Our new man in Havana" Gilworthy needs to take care of those rocks in his sock. Pull over, Derek," Bishop calmly instructed.

"What?"

"Pull over. He surely can't drop his knickers and do it in front of us. I'm all about libertine expression, but I don't want to witness it. It's the most personal thing in the world."

"Might be a bit too *Brokeback* for us," Koles said laughing. "Good point, Bishop."

"Ole Gil will get his orgasm and we'll all ride back harmoniously."

"I'm not fucking beating off on the side of the road," Gil railed with exasperation.

"Though it'd be a tempting sight, I don't think we need to risk Gil getting arrested with his dick in his hand."

Bishop, Koles and Gil continued their edgy, yet frolicsome banter as I tuned my thoughts elsewhere. I had growing and gnawing feeling something was awry at home. The post-orgasmic peace from Hyun was fading fast.

I sensed things would be different at home after this. Shaillie might not cushion the crash I sensed coming. The parachute would be removed. Free fall remained. Maybe, it was time to crash, time for rupture and revolution. Time to plot an escape immersing identity in a new language, a new culture, new scenery...

Gilworthy interrupted my abstract excursion with a push on my shoulder, "Van!"

"Yeah, Gil."

"You ok?"

"Huh?"

"You seem out of it."

"More like into it. I'm fine. Have you settled down?"

"I'm fine. Getting there anyway. You pissed at me?"

"No, not at all."

"I was trying to ask you about Kate. Remember her?"

"Yeah, the one at Nakiri's party. His girlfriend."

"No, Nakiri and her are friends. Nakiri's got a million girl slash friends and I don't think he sleeps with a single one of them. He's a real aloof, cool Japanese cat. A real Murakami type. No poseur."

Nakiri was a member of the ESL circle of teachers that I'd met through Gilworthy. ESL teachers seemed to be an odd coterie of itinerant and artistic folk. Most of them seemed unsure of their role in the grand scheme of existence—prototypical searchers perpetually wondering and wandering. No one is truly and purely sure of their role I presume, but they were overtly conscious of that nebulous state of mind. This particular member of the peripheral lot of teachers was strikingly handsome. As if put off by that, Nakiri had long spiked hair and numerous silver earrings. Gil was right. There was an air of detachment about him.

"So, he's not screwing any of those women?" I asked.

"No, I don't think so. He's just friends."

"Is he gay?"

"I don't think so."

"Nothing's simple anymore," I said. "I've got to get new friends."

"Me, too. But never mind that now, my point is that I've got a tremendous crush on Kate. I've had one for a while." Gil was speed-talking fueled by all the coke. He had an edgy look in his eyes. "Saw her

117

at a party a couple of nights ago. Van, she had on this wrap-around, low-cut dress that hugged her body so perfectly, so damn sexy. Can't get her out of my mind. Her ass is perfect, so is her voice. Drives me nuts, man!"

"I get the point."

"I think she's part Korean, Brazilian, Portuguese, maybe Japanese. Rapturous miscegenation."

"The more mixed, the better," Koles uttered from the front, turning briefly back and then returning his eyes to the road.

"I wrote her a poem," Gilworthy admitted abashedly. "Yes, a poem. Stayed up all night composing it."

"Jesus, Gil, you're pretty gone for her," I said.

He took his cell phone out and started dialing.

"Don't do it, Longfellow," Koles warned. Gilworthy ignored him.

"Gilly, you're halfway into oblivion. Now is not the time."

"I've always liked oblivion," he responded. "A fine place to be."

"Here's to oblivion, eternity, never-never land, and all the elusive Elysian illusions you want, but it's not the time or place to make a first time call to a woman you like. Ground yourself, Gil. You're too atmospheric," Koles admonished.

Gilworthy clicked his phone shut, "Mind your own damn business. I'm the one who got screwed, or rather didn't get screwed. What's your problem?"

"I'm just trying to help you out."

Gilworthy had the phone to his ear again and looked over at me, "No, he's not trying to help. He's just in one of his moods. Never know with people like Koles. His personality is as reliable as weather. Koles, you take your medicine, today?"

"Fuck you, Gil. Go 'head and fall on your face."

I had never seen Koles in this light. He was always rather quiet and arcane, playing the archetypal writer close to the vest. The general melancholy seemed apropos to the role. Tonight he seemed angrier and edgier.

"Atmospheric?" Gil said to no one in particular. "That's a compliment. Never want to be grounded. When I'm dead, sure, but until then I'll take puffy white clouds and rainbows."

"Our man Gil is at the end of the rainbow, desperate in loin, and one big pot of gold up his ass!" Koles laughed as did I.

Gilworthy scoffed, "I'm calling her, assholes."

While he was dialing again, I tapped him on the shoulder. "Bad timing, Gil. Really bad."

"Oblivion breeds confidence." He continued dialing.

"Good luck," Koles said, "but you're doomed."

"Hello, is Kate there? Hi, Kate, it's Calvin Gilworthy... Yeah, my first name's Calvin...I'm in the mood to use my first name...Anyway, are you sleeping?...Good, good....I'm sorry to call so late...Good, good...What's going on?...Is Nakiri around?...No, no, I didn't mean..."

He turned to me, "Christ, she went to get Nakiri." He was holding the phone tightly to his ear. His head was bobbing in anxious anticipation.

"Oh, he's out...well, well...Thanks, Kate....Ok...Have a good night...Sorry...Ok....Bye."

He hung up and closed the phone tightly. "Shit, I blew it."

"Call her back, Romeo," Koles chided.

"I wouldn't," I said.

Bishop cleared his throat and lit a Camel unfiltered, "You know, Calvin, Kate is a pipedream."

"Look Bishop, I'm going to stop you right now before you philosophize about art and existence and truth and nothingness. It's all wonderful in its proper time, but I don't need it at this moment. That time is not now. Right now, I just want Kate. It's that simple."

"Pull over Koles and let Calvin finish his failed whorehouse trick alone," Bishop sardonically instructed.

"No, I need the touch of a woman. I need..." Gilworthy stopped mid-sentence and gave Bishop the finger from behind his seat.

"You should aim internal to rid you of this external charade."

"Blah, blah, blah, you fuckin' drunken evangelist. You're a glorified Jim Bakker gone artsy."

Gilworthy dialed. "Hello Kate..."

"This is not a good idea," I said softly.

"Kate, I, ahh, actually was not calling for Nakiri. I mean I wouldn't mind talking to him, but I was actually, you know, calling to see if you guys or just you, actually, since he's not around. Even if he were around, I mean you. You know what I mean?...Good...Ok, so a few friends and I are heading into Cambridge. We could meet at River Gods. Have you been there?...Yeah, it's new place, a couple months. Right by the Charles, of course, cause of the name. Pretty good vibe there, kind of San Franciscoesque. You lived there, right?...Yeah, I spent some time there, you know, traveling...Yeah, the film's coming along. Not finished yet, of course, but...Yeah, I don't really want to finish...Oh yeah, you're right, of course, it's closed...Look at the time. Shit, it's after four. I totally lost track. How 'bout some coffee then if you're up for it. We could, ahhh, watch the sunrise or something at the actual river. What do you say?...Oh really, how'd you do that?...ahhh-

119

huh…yeah, wow…too bad…are you elongating it?…or maybe see a chiropractor…don't suppose you want me to massage it, he-he-he…just kidding…yeah, yup, I thought so…ok, ok…hope you feel better…ok, tell Nakiri I called and…"

Gilworthy closed the phone and his head descended as if his neck muscles had suddenly failed him. He was squeezing the cell like it was a rope that he was holding to prevent from falling off a mountain. "Fuck, fuck, I can't believe I did that. Shit, now I blew it."

"It's no big deal," I lied. "You sounded fine. She'll think it was sweet in hindsight."

"What the hell did you ask her to elongate?" Koles asked, relishing his role as instigator.

"Fuck you."

"Kind of a Freudian slip, don't you think?"

"Take it easy, Gilly. It really isn't such a big deal," I said.

"I'm totally gone for her. Have been for months and I broach intimacy with her for the first time while I'm high and blue-balled from a bad whore experience. I got to fix it. I'm gonna call her back and apologize."

"That's an incredibly bad idea," Koles said. "Really, really, stupid."

"Van, what do you think?" Gilworthy asked.

"I think two middle-of-the-night impromptu drunken calls are enough. I think you should call her tomorrow and apologize. It's a reason to call."

"I just have to apologize now and tell her I truly wanted to take her for a drink or a coffee to get to know her. I really want to get to know her. I don't care about touching her or getting laid. It isn't about that."

"Yes, you do. It's all about the pussy right now," Bishop said.

"No, Bishop. I want to be with her."

"May be true, but right now it's only pussy. Go home, masturbate and go to sleep. It's very simple, young Calvin."

He released his grip on the rope and pressed redial.

"Gilly, you might sever any chance with another call," I warned.

He ignored me. "Yeah, Kate, I just…sorry to…I'm sorry…no, I just want…I'm sorry…ok…I know it was…I'm sorry…" He closed the phone.

"What happened?" I asked.

"She said to stop calling and that this was getting obnoxious and pathetic."

Koles and I were laughing slightly until Koles asked, "Those exact words?"

"Pretty much."

I tried to console him. I told him it took courage to call, but my laughter undermined any honest attempts at sincerity. It reminded me of Shaillie when she was listening to my crow story at first. It was just too absurd and funny. However, it was easier for the spectators to see the comedy. Nothing was humorous to Gil right now. He was staring blankly ahead. I thought I saw a tear eke out of the corner of his eye.

"Christ, Gilly, what the hell's the matter with you? You're taking this too damn hard," I said.

"Is he crying?" Koles asked disgustedly while focusing on the image of Gilworthy in his rear view mirror.

A few more tears followed. Gilworthy wiped his eyes and stared ahead. I'm not sure he had heard us.

Bishop announced, "You go ahead and cry, Calvin Gilworthy. Nothing wrong with male tears. You got to let it out. Truth exits the eyes. We men store it away too much. Let it out and taste some catharsis. It needs to come out of some orifice. The eyes will suffice. Don't let your cohorts deter you."

Gilworthy wiped the few tears and gathered himself. Luckily, he wasn't weeping.

"What an asshole I am," he said. "A goddamn fool."

Gilworthy took out his pipe and packed it with moist green herb and sprinkled a little coke on top. Snowy grass. He lit it and sucked hard, dimples deepening on his cheeks, holding it down in his entrails to let the smoke invade as many membranes and cells as he could. Finally, he released a giant cloud in the car. It lingered in the short space above our heads like thick mountain fog. Koles opened his window and the fog was slowly sucked out of the car.

There was silence until Gilworthy said, "Don't leave Shaillie, Van. You don't know what you're doing. You end up like me. I'm obsessed with Kate, which might just be a surrogate for Lolikeni. Christ, I got to call someone else to get my mind off Kate. Man, I can't believe I blew it. God, who can I call?" Gilworthy began scrolling his cell index and mumbling inaudibly. His eyes were half closed. Soon his head started nodding slowly up and down. I leaned over and pushed his forehead back with one finger. He said something else before fading away that I couldn't understand. I took the cell phone from his hand and his head slowly lowered in half-consciousness until it rested between his knees.

We were nearing home. Gil was sleeping away his humiliation and loneliness. I called home, but there was no answer. Again.

121

Meanwhile, Bishop was into a monodrama about another artist/disciple of his.

"I'll tell you what we may have here. We may have a case of autohypnosis. It's clearly a subconscious uprising. The interred seeking light. In case of internal turmoil, hypnotic states can ensue in order to deal with it. I told her to keep it going. Don't analyze. Don't worry about sleep, just keep the momentum. All artistic expression is the pursuit of hypnotic sanctuary. That's what creativity does. You know that, Derek. It's a healthy tease and taste of utopia. Delusional, but good delusion. The artist loses time, boundary, earthly and bodily confines so that the spirit breathes. It's religious experience, right, Van?"

I didn't respond. I thought Bishop was musing about my insomniac writing.

He continued, "She thinks she's gone out of her mind. I tell her that's the beauty. It could also be past-life invasion. Who knows who leads the brigades of creativity from within? It's less about why and more about what."

Koles had been trying to get in a word and finally did, "It's sensible. She…"

"Sense has nothing to do with it. It's all part of historicity, the great energy of history propagating the kinetic present. Fornicating the moment. This is no Shirley MacLaine illusion. This is no invasion by outsiders, but by insiders. Ancestors streaming through the blood of your past. The umbilical cord is the most psychically misunderstood force of energy and madness. It's there that the past enters us and never strays. Selves melting and molding eternally."

Koles the protégé played along, "We're all Siamese, Bishop. I think you might be ready for the Vatican now."

"Pope Seamus Rourke. It sounds good. Sarcasm aside, I know you're getting it, Derek. It's all so incestuously interconnected we can't even begin to understand it. Need millennia perhaps, but our interconnected exhibition will unravel a layer, peel off some epidermis."

"First, Cardinal, then Pope. I forgot the pecking order."

Bishop began to laugh, but it quickly transformed into a rumbling cough. He opened the window and spit out what seemed a golf ball of sickly yellowish fluid—a gross and perverse exclamation point to his oratory.

Koles sighed.

"Van, you awake back there?"

"Yeah."

"We've got to do something."

"About what?" I asked.

"Everything."

"Hmmm, where to begin?"

Bishop didn't respond. He seemed instantly drained from his moments on the poetry pulpit. He was passing out again while Gilworthy was coming to. He lifted his head from between his knees. Meanwhile, Bishop's head propped itself between the side of the car and the headrest. The odd dissertation on the origins of art and ensuing gob of expectoration apparently had consumed his energy.

Gil shook his head trying to rid cobwebs. A funny noise from his mouth accompanied his pendulous face. He stopped and took a deep breath.

"A good little power nap. Now, did I really call Kate?"

"Yes," I said.

"Did I make an ass of myself?"

"More or less."

"More," Koles jabbed.

"At least, it's done. You can't do any worse unless you're seeking to inspire a restraining order," I said.

"That fucking bad? Jesus, I remember it, but it's all a bit hazy now."

"That's a surprise," Koles said sarcastically.

"What's the matter with you?" Gilworthy confronted Koles.

"I don't know. Post-whore depression," Koles said. "You know what I mean from your Thai experience."

"Mine was panic. I don't know if the whore has anything to do with your depression."

I saw Koles's face in the rearview mirror. He was about to say something and then held back. He ran his right hand slowly across his buzzed hair stopping at the top of his head where he massaged his skull for a few moments. His eyes spotted mine in the mirror. I flashed a quick smile. He was expressionless and then he looked away towards the road.

Gil grabbed his cell and started dialing.

"Not fucking again," I said.

"No, no. I'm calling this woman I met at a Thai restaurant in Harvard Square. She was nice, a bit older and not all that cute, but nice. Real sweet. I need to be with a woman tonight. Don't care if we have sex. Just want to be with a woman. Nothing wrong with that. It's physiological. Bangkok's not that far, Van."

"It's illogical," Koles baited.

These two had fraternal rivalry and sparring in their blood. This was the most time I'd spent with both of them. Usually it was Koles amidst others in a group and Gilworthy occasionally for a purchase. He rarely came in to Chez Lucienne. I'd seen him once, maybe twice, talking to Bishop about aesthetic matters. About what had now evolved into the Planetarium Exhibition.

"You're not going to cry again, are you?" Koles continued his best Cain to Gilworthy's Abel.

"Fuck you, Derek. Nobody here is talking to you."

Gilworthy started talking on the phone with the Thai woman. Amazingly it seemed to be going well. I stopped listening to his antics. His uninhibited and unrestrained loneliness was disturbing. This whole evening was dancing along cataclysm. Life itself was growing more and more disturbing. I closed my eyes and was on my way to some much needed sleep. I could feel fatigue deep within my muscles, inside the tissue and bones. A real, raw exhaustion drained of all adrenalin. A *tired* turned so true from months without an honest night's sleep. Maybe when I finally slept well, I'd realize none of this had happened. I still worked for the big bank. I hadn't traded the cubicle for some perverse merger of Cubism and Surrealism. I would be married soon without any complications and the old man was still alive. It would all be simple. Very simple...

"Hey, Van."

"Huh," I said, opening my eyes. "Where are we?" I instinctually asked, realizing Koles was talking to me. I could hear Bishop snoring and noticed Gilworthy's head was back between his knees.

"We've got about twenty minutes left."

"How long was I out?"

"Not long. Ten minutes or so."

I needed ten hours, maybe ten days. "So," I asked, "do you need me to drive? You need a break?"

"No, no, I'm ok. We're almost there. I made it this far, what's twenty more minutes."

"I feel like I was out for days and it was only ten minutes. I wish it had been days."

"Well, Rip Van Winkle, I know where you can sleep."

"So do I. My bed in twenty minutes."

"No, not there."

"Ok, clue me in."

"Let's get out of here."

"Where? What do you mean?"

"Let's go to Europe."

"When?"

"Tomorrow."

"What?"

124

"Today actually. Tonight we can take off on an evening flight."

So, I got my wish. Be careful what you...Koles explained his plan, his (ir)rationale. It was all about Yvette, of course. He had to go back and make one last stand for his marriage. The divorce had never sunk in. He was going to bring his manuscript with him. Toss it in the garbage right in front of her. Tell her that he's giving up writing to make the marriage work. He had told me he got too caught up in his minor success of the first novel. Bishop had wanted him to change narrative structures, go for the first person, true fiction and all that Henry Miller credibility. But Koles couldn't switch because he just wanted to quit. Writing is no life. He called it, "seditious and infectious. A disease of reforming reality for discontents. What the hell is that all about? What's the damn point whenever all that is around the creation unravels including the creator and reality never truly changes?" He would surrender his massive manuscript and put his energies into his relationship, a true reality. He compared himself to Humpty Dumpty and all the Bishop's men couldn't put him back together. Only Yvette could do that, he'd fully realized. Bishop thought the run to Providence would re-energize Koles's muse, but instead it had become a refugee to a plan uninvolved with any artistic aspirations.

Apparently, he had been planning this thoroughly and carefully for a while. He had set up a meeting with an English teacher friend of his, Aldenna Sinitrau. Apparently, she would be our financial ticket to Europe though I told Koles I was skeptical about this and didn't really need nor want the money.

I had met Sinitrau a few times at the bar. She had taught at the same English language school in Harvard Square as Gilworthy. Like many of those teachers at the Cambridge School of English, she was eccentric, well-traveled and firmly entrenched in society's periphery. Not quite on the outside looking in, but clearly not within the machinery of mainstream. She was an interesting and attractive woman. Her face was rather plain and ordinary, but it was elevated by the most beautiful hair I'd ever seen. It was long with an alluringly unique, fiery color—a shiny fusion of autumnal tawny colors. The color of her hair seemed to give her an aura of energy and radiance. She was enigmatic to most because she was the over-achieving, ambitious-type in high school. If I remember correctly, she was the captain of the field hockey team or tennis or both, had great grades, an athlete for a boyfriend, and was very popular.

She got into Harvard and studied philosophy. A chasm opened up and alternatives took hold. A secular Kierkegaardian leap. Nowhere to land after that...

125

After graduation she backpacked the world for a year. Sometimes with a friend, and sometimes alone. She claimed to have visited eighty-seven countries. Along the way, she took photos, kept a mountainous journal and studied furniture of the world. When she came back, she turned her parents' basement into a furniture-making studio and started to work. I remember the last time I saw her she was struggling and making almost nothing. She had cultivated a pot habit with some help from Gilworthy that had steadily grown along with her cultural and world-weary awareness. She got some contracts from the local nouveau-rich who wanted custom furniture that was unique, but it took her much longer to complete a piece than she had predicted. She always low-balled her estimates so that she ended up making about a dollar an hour.

I recalled her saying, "I'd be doing alright if this were the 17th century, which is where I belong anyway."

Koles would set up a meeting for us. He didn't tell me any details, but I knew something illegal was brewing. I had a feeling I couldn't say no to the European offer. The momentum, Bishop's historical forces, were too strong. I'd ask Shaillie to come with us. If she refused then I would get my wish to traipse around Europe and finish the text of *Insomnia*. Get it out of my system. Molt all the layers that had been skillfully and invisibly laid on until they're as thick as a rubber scuba suit. It was time to unzip the suit. Things were happening, stranger and riskier than a one-night run to Providence, but I convinced myself the only way out of it was to head fully into it. Somehow, I believed I wouldn't lose Shaillie in the process.

We arrived at Bishop's apartment. He was exhausted. It took us a while to wake him up. When we finally did, he looked at Koles and sleepily grumbled, "Make the switch to the *I*." He opened the door and got out without too much difficulty. Standing at the car door and peering in the window at us, he said, "Until next time." Bishop clenched his fist, shook it a bit, sort of winked with both eyes, and then headed up the front steps of his Cambridge building. Just as he reached the top step, he tripped, fell over the rail tumbling into a large bush. We all jumped out of the car. He was mumbling a mix of Gaelic and profanity. We pried him out of the shrub. He was scratched a little bit, but nothing too serious. We stood him up and he teetered a bit like the Tin Man. Koles centered him from the right, I did the same from the left. The pendulum eventually settled in the middle. Koles straightened his ascot and jacket lapels. "I'll be alright, boys, just a bit tired. You guys have youth. I only have its memory, but it'll take more than a shrub to bring the Bishop down."

He looked at me, "Van, you with us?"

"Yeah, Bishop I'm here."

"No, the vanguard, the exhibit. Setrag's grand and tragic story. The abstract turned into rubbery concrete. Surely you understand. Oh, it's all one pile of holy manure and infinite beauty."

"Yeah, Bishop, I'm in," I told him appeasingly. I'd seen Bishop in this state many times. I was always astounded at how articulately incoherent he was when he was all sheets to the wind, on the vertiginous verge of pass out and black out.

"You get it, Van. Armenians get it. Tragicomedy. That's what it all is. 'Tis all tragicomedy. Next time they open my heart, I'm going to tell them to give me a hyena's heart instead. I'll laugh all the way into infinity. You got my cigarettes, Koles?"

"Yeah, Bishop, I'll bring them upstairs with us. Let's go."

"Where's the woman from Cork?"

"She left her number for you at the bar," I said. I thought of Bishop drying out and settling into old age with this woman. Sitting on a porch together and reading novels. Sharing coffee with her. Writing an autobiography of his twisted life from the seat of sobriety and the peace of a good woman. The impossibility of it saddened me. The tragedy of tragicomedy shone darkly on Bishop's tenuous, alcohol-sodden grasp of existence.

"Where is she now?"

"I don't know."

"Let's call her."

"Oh Christ, what are you, Gilworthy now?" Koles said. "Listen, we're putting your ass to bed and you can call the Cork woman tomorrow. You should have called her tonight."

"She's not the Cork woman. She's the woman from Cork."

Koles nodded. "Fine. Sounds good. The woman from Cork it is." Koles was really rushing, trying to get rid of Bishop. If I knew nothing else, I knew Bishop stopped talking only when he decided to, not anyone else.

"Derek, question for you. You think this'll hurt my chances at the Vatican?"

"No, I won't tell them, Bishop."

The two of them reminded me of a young Bishop, a young Seamus Rourke, taking care of Richard Yates. The Revolutionary Road had contorted to this.

We each had an arm tucked under his shoulders. His body was going limp, but his mouth kept humming along. Gilworthy had gone

127

back into the car armed with his cell phone. Bishop lived on the second floor. We got him in and his wandering verbosity drifted into something about Randall Jarrell, Anne Sexton and Maclean's Hospital until the words became semi-linguistic and then full-bore snore while still in our arms. We finally put him into bed. Koles took off his shoes and coat. I removed the ascot and loosened his collar. Koles went into the bathroom and soaked a cotton ball in alcohol. He dabbed Bishop's facial cuts from the shrub with the antiseptic. Bishop was completely out—the only time he could be silent. We shut the lights and left.

"You know, we could head to Portugal after Paris. Maybe, Yvette will come with us. She and I could start over outside of the memories of Paris. A new life, a new marriage in a new place."

"Sounds good," I said. Koles was suddenly expressive.

"You bring Shaillie. The four of us will go ex-pat for a while. Cleanse our vision, shuffle the senses into a new orientation."

"I'd like that."

"Great. This will be a fantastic change. Yes. I can feel it happening."

Koles was nearly giddy. I was in the front now and he was grinning ear to ear. He'd been angry for most of the ride back, but his mood had swung. I pondered what Gil had said about medication, depression.

He interrupted my thoughts. "You have that great picture on your wall of you and Shaillie and backdrop of all those colorful skiffs moored in the Cascais Bay."

"Yes, I do. I was trying to convince Shaillie to drop it all and head to Cascais the other day."

"What'd she say?"

"Not a chance."

"She'll come around. It's all going to work out."

"Since when did you become the glass-half-full optimist?"

Koles turned to me and glared, "What's wrong with my being optimistic? You going to rain on that like everyone else? Like I do to myself!" His eyes were suddenly different, almost feral.

"Take it easy, Derek. Nothing wrong with being positive. I was…never mind. Keep positive."

He seemed to relax instantly with scary rapidity. "Just kidding, Van. Just not in the mood for rain."

"Me neither."

"Sunny days ahead, right?"

"Sure, Derek."

"Good, because I can't deal with anymore rain."

We were silent for a bit. Gil was chatting up the Thai waitress again, who still seemed receptive. I realized I was receptive to anything as well. Whatever Koles wanted to do, I would. I felt propelled by the actions happening outside rather than any analysis or rationale within. Koles went on to explain about Bishop's vineyard in the Dao region, just north of Lisbon. It was very simple and primitive. He said we could all work there, live close to the earth for a while, and get things in balance—no TV, internet or phones, just land, wine, food, books and friendship. He assured me Shaillie would come around. Even if she didn't come right away, she'd join us later. He knew she had the impulsive instinct of an artist that would claw its way to the surface. She'd pull her feet out of the muddy mundane for a while. Derek had it all worked out while Gilworthy was successful with his desperate courting. We dropped him off in Harvard Square where he would meet this woman for coffee. We headed to my place. I told Koles to meet with Sinitrau on his own. I didn't care what he was doing with her and could get by on whatever money I had. I just wanted to go. It was all happening very fast and I didn't want it to slow down. Not yet. Not for a while.

PART III
THE RIVER GAME

I tried Shaillie once more after we had dropped Bishop and Gilworthy off. Still no luck. I had an ominous vibe welling up within. I convinced myself to confront the reality of Shaillie pulling out. Perhaps, she'd had enough. Who could blame her? I'd had more than enough of myself. If she chose the exit, so be it. We would both head for exits. When I envisioned the future, I still saw it clearly. In Europe, free, traveling, creative, unlocking the safe and reading the dreamy output, alive for the first time in ages. Not a single monetary instinct conducting behavior. A dramatic, true change. Like a soldier who had been marching in perfect unison. One in a thousand-soldier-strong battalion marching ten across, one hundred deep. Not a step, blink or breath out of sync until suddenly one soldier drops his gun, turns out of the march, and runs until their legs can run no more. Yet, it is even worse for the molded civilian because, at least, the soldier has a purpose to their absolute conformism—the goal of the larger group. The uniformed civilian has no purpose other than the drumbeat of dollars and numbness disguised as stability. The drumbeat, eventually, gets too loud and infectious. The pure recognition of one's situation becomes a glaring vision, blindingly clear. The civilian can no longer see or hear anything, but the sights and sounds of escape.

Koles dropped me off at my apartment. I took out my keys and instantly recalled standing on the front porch a short time ago, blood dripping from crow-induced wounds, and Shaillie coming to my aid. Was it a few weeks ago? Or just a few nights ago? Or did it even happen? I felt my forehead and nose for the crow's damage. The scabs were gone. I looked into the window pane of the door at my faded reflection. The cuts were nearly gone, but there were remnants proving the crow and I existed. Time was eerily out of joint, confabulation reigning. For a moment it seemed as if I had just written about the crow attack in the journal and it hadn't actually happened. But my face was proof that it wasn't fiction.

This could all be a result of insomnia rather than its journal. Lack of sleep had potent ramifications. It could put one in an internal state of disarray. Just march onward I urged myself.

I put the key in the door. This time my hand was steady, but my heart was beating rapidly. I labored to take in enough oxygen to my lungs. I could appease my instincts, stay faithful to Shaillie, and she'd understand. We'd find a compromise. I'd go to a therapist after Europe,

130

talk about those alleged loose ends and unfinished communication with my father, lingering sadness and anger, all things associated with grief. Maybe it was a toxic mix. I was so tired. So very tired. Perhaps, my fatigue was manipulating every thought and idea.

I opened the door and walked into the bedroom quietly so as not to disturb her. The bed was empty and made. I called for Shaillie.

No answer.

I looked at my watch—six o'clock. I went into the living room and saw the light blinking from the answering machine. Must have been a message from Shaillie. I pressed play, but was mercilessly subjected to several of my own messages. The mechanized voice was worse than the voice in my head.

No message from Shaillie.

Certainly, she was not the stereotypical angry, jealous woman, but I had just been intimate with another woman. Shaillie was human. The surging, ominous vibe seemed hell bent on realizing itself. The litmus test hypothesis gained momentum. Of course! Everything was not as it seemed.

I hung up my coat in the entry hall closet and told myself to have my mind made up rather than be dictated by any new reality presenting itself. The decision should be internal, not coerced by externals. I tried brainwashing myself before picking up the phone to call Shaillie. It was time to explode the game into a million pieces. I wasn't going to pull the ripcord and land softly. I wanted to crash. It had to be a new life and *why* didn't matter at this point.

But where was Shaillie?

I went into the kitchen to check for a note. Nothing. Maybe she had gone out with girlfriends, stayed over and emailed me from wherever she was. Maybe she had an impromptu bachelorette party. That made sense. I checked my email. Nothing. I dialed her cell phone even though she was probably still sleeping. However, we hadn't spent a night apart in such a long time and with our recent turbulence, maybe she wouldn't be able to sleep normally. The call went to voice mail immediately just like each time I'd tried during the night. I left her a message telling her I was home.

I still had the feeling this wasn't happening. I wasn't in this room. Everything was in the rhythm of a dream. Surrealistic perceptions. I walked around the house looking for clues of any change. I noticed the bedroom closet door was ajar. Shaillie liked things closed and organized. I fully opened the door. The closet seemed more sparse than usual. Clothes were missing. I looked in the drawers and saw that a lot of her things were gone. I went to the hall storage closet. Two suitcases were missing.

Shaillie was gone.

All the self-induced brainwashing and preparation of thought couldn't outwit the body. My heart was racing faster. My breathing was becoming more erratic and knotted. I decided to check out the study to see if she had taken things beyond clothes. Household things of real value like artwork, photos. This would let me know if it were temporary or she'd completely given up on me. Before I walked into the room, I tried to gather myself. If her paintings were gone, reality would gain deeper clarity. For a fleeting moment, I questioned whether or not this was the clarity I wanted. Had my recent actions all been propelled by trying to drive Shaillie out of my life? It seemed preposterous on the surface. I wasn't in the right state of mind to dig below the surface layers. I went into the kitchen, poured myself a tall glass of spring water and drank it down in one gulp. The water felt so good inside, cleansing all the toxins from last night. I poured another glass and drank it down. I hadn't realized just how thirsty I was. I decided to make a pot of coffee. It was very likely I wouldn't sleep despite the exhaustion. I'd virtually lost the ability to sleep. I'd have caffeine ready to help me through the day. I took deep breaths through my nose, exhaled through my mouth. Concentrated just on the act of breathing. Yoga-style breathing that Shaillie had taught me. My breathing started to improve. My heart slowed down. I drank another glass of water. I hadn't eaten in a while and my stomach was empty. I could almost feel the water cascading down my throat, splashing through my intestines like water rushing through an underground tunnel. It was as if the water could make things right. Purify. A short, cleansing summer rain. I heard the first sounds of the coffee bubbling and gurgling through the filter and watched the blackened water begin its descent into the glass carafe. The sound was pacifying. Caffeine was on its way. I could feel the imminent fix.

Ready to confront Shaillie's true departure, I walked into the study. I scanned the room. No change was immediately noticeable. Shaillie's paintings from college and just after, still hung on the wall. Her bohemian artistic period on display. Her very own *blue period*. There was a photo I had taken on our European sojourn. It was a shot of Cabo do Roca, the western most point of Europe. The computer was on a desk that we had built together. It was solid, heavy oak and a simple style. A print of *The Liver is the Cock's Comb* hung above the computer. One wall was all books. Shelves and shelves of mostly novels, biographies of artists, and books on art. Nothing seemed to be missing. To my left was a wall that Shaillie had painted herself. A mural of three colors across the whole wall in horizontal stripes. The top was a bright red, which dripped into the second tier of blue. The blue line faded into the third and final color of orange. Shaillie had chosen the colors of the

132

Armenian flag. Between the first two colors as they ran together, there were surrealistic-abstract representations of nature, such as stars, clouds, trees, tornadoes, flowers, animals. All of them were subtle and it took time to recognize exactly what they were if one could at all. Between the lower two colors were melting renditions of the man-made world—cars, buildings, bridges, explosions, homes, televisions, books, and art. I thought it was a beautiful work that should have been on public display somewhere. It was a tragedy that it wasn't in a gallery or museum.

I concluded that Shaillie was probably taking a break to let me sort things out. Made sense. That was exactly what I needed to do. Despite the whispers intimating otherwise, I didn't want to lose her. I just needed to unravel for a bit. I wanted to talk to a woman about all of this. I wanted to talk to our friend, Derisa. She was one of the few friends of ours that originated from me. Derisa and I had met in college before I met Shaillie. She was the first woman in college that I fancied, but it didn't go anywhere. Derisa was a lesbian. I hit on her hard and she let me down softly during the first week of school. She was also an artist, but unlike Shaillie, she hadn't given up. We stayed close after school. She knew me well and knew Shaillie and me as a couple more than anyone else. I could do some unraveling and, maybe, even some laughing. She probably wouldn't approve of my irrational trip overseas, but she wouldn't judge and toss rational discourse at me. I knew she'd be awake now, so I could call. She always painted early in the morning and some mornings she worked as a docent at the Harvard's Fogg Art Museum. I remember Bishop sliding me the notice of a Surrealist exhibit at the Fogg at the same time he had given me Andre Breton's manifesto and a copy of Sinclair's *Babbitt*. He'd urged me to read those "two masterpieces of the 20th century."

I called Derisa. She didn't answer, but her machine picked up.

"Derisa, hi, it's Van. Listen, are you there? Pick up if you can. Please. I really need to talk to you. Hello. Hello. I know you're probably painting and don't want to be…"

I heard a click. "Ok. Ok. I'm here."

"Hey. Thank God."

"Thank me."

"Thank you, Derisa."

"Listen, Van, pretty bad timing."

"Really sorry, sweetie. I…"

"Well, I'm very busy with my work, don't want to lose the rhythm, you know, and I have to be at the Fogg at nine for a tour."

"What time is it?"

"Almost seven. What's the problem?"

133

"Oh, nothing. I just got back from a whorehouse, Shaillie's left me, and I've decided to fly to Europe later today. Other than that things are normal."

Derisa sighed. "Ok, that's pretty good I have to admit. Worthy of the early morning call. There goes my rhythm."

"Sorry."

"No, don't worry. Life is more important. So I knew you and Shaillie were having some issues lately, but I thought you'd get through it. I thought it was just pre-wedding jitters, nothing serious."

"It seems to have gotten serious. I think she's giving me some space to figure things out."

"And you're going to use that space to head to Europe today?"

"That seems to be the plan."

"It sounds like you're not making the plan."

"Well, actually..." I stopped myself before I included Koles in this. Besides, I believed something larger than Koles was involved in this. "Actually, I'm not sure who is making the plan."

"What does that mean?"

"I don't know, Derisa. Anyway, do you know where Shaillie is? That's the meaningful and concrete question of the moment."

"Van, I have an idea. Why don't you meet me at the Fogg after my tour? We can talk this thing out."

"What time?"

"I'll be done by eleven, maybe earlier, depending on the group."

"Maybe I'll show up for the tour. Take my mind off things. Surrealism right?"

"Yes, Dali, Magritte, Tanguy and all their painted subconscious."

"Perfect."

"How so?"

"See you soon, Derisa. Thanks."

I just had to kill a couple hours. I thought about a short nap, but adrenalin was pumping. I poured myself a cup of coffee. The first sip of the black coffee felt so good. I thought about calling Shaillie again, but this would have been five or so calls without reciprocation. I had to give her some space. Let her come to me. I knew exactly what I could do in the meantime. Something I'd neglected for too long. I poured the coffee into a travel mug. I went into the bathroom and washed my face with cold water, brushed my teeth, and tried to ignore what I saw in the mirror. It didn't matter. I put on a jacket, took the mug of coffee, and headed out to spend some long overdue time with my father...

I drove down Mt. Auburn Street, the main artery of this little Armenia. As I often did, I took the long way through Watertown. I liked to drive by the homes of my maternal ancestors. My grandfather had landed in Providence after escaping the Armenian Genocide. The murderously possessed Ottoman Turks so hell bent on the extinction of an entire race had failed, but in order to survive, millions of Armenians spread worldwide. One of the enclaves they settled in was Watertown, Fresno's east coast sibling. My grandfather was one of the many survivors who made it to the new country. He had survived on farms in Bolshevik Russia after the slaughter of parents, grandparents, two brothers, three sisters, and all the uncles, aunts and cousins in his village of Van, which is now the stolen land of Southern Turkey. One uncle had escaped in 1894 during the first phase of the systematic attempt to eliminate Armenians. It was that uncle that Setrag sought out when he left Russia during the civil war between the Reds and the Whites. Gambling and fighting his way through Tbilisi, Marseille, pre-Castro Havana, and finally into Providence for survival. How different his Providence was compared to my Providence last night…

I drove by my grandfather's first home, where he had settled with his cousin. This house was at the edge of the Watertown Mall. The giant yellow and blue of Best Buy comically loomed to the west, while the red glow of the enormous letters of Target hovered to the north side of the crumbling two-family house. I never stopped at this house. My grandfather told me he was never happy there, but it did get him going to a new life. I took the back roads past an Armenian Church, St. Stephens. I headed to Dexter and Fairfield Streets where my grandfather moved when he married my grandmother. My mother was born on the first floor. My grandmother's two brothers and their families lived on the second and third floors. I pulled over by the house. It would have made more sense to visit this house first, but I always liked to visit in the chronological order that my grandfather lived his life. In my mother's childhood home she had her parents, her brother, two uncles and aunts, and five cousins. I thought about my childhood home in neighboring Belmont, the alleged step-up in the social ladder. The home of oft-warring parents and the father who was often gone for work or in temporary exile due to the marital wars. Neighbors hidden by giant shrubs, huge trees, and walls. Neighbors we barely knew.

The great Abstract Expressionist, Arshile Gorky, lived across the street from my mother's first home. He lived there after his horrifying escape from the Genocide. Gorky had worked at the old Hood Rubber factory in Watertown at the same time as my grandmother had, but he quit in order to paint. He was roundly mocked by family and friends. Concrete currency was more vital to genocide survivors than abstract expressionism.

I drove back to Mt. Auburn Street and took a right. Among the many stores, churches, street lights and signs, two things caught my eye. The first was across the street from a church. There was a big white house with a sign in front that read, "OUR LADY'S RECTORY." This one always amused me. The second one I'd never seen before. In front of a car wash there was an advertisement in big black letters, "HAVE YOU CHECKED YOUR INTERIOR?" Precisely what I've been trying to do.

The cemetery was on the Cambridge/Watertown line, very close to the Charles River. As the river curved its way north toward Boston, I turned south toward the Cambridge Cemetery. I drove into the cemetery where many of those aunts, uncles, and cousins from my mother's childhood home were now buried. I pulled over near my father's tombstone. It was at the top of a small hill. His stone was surrounded with flowers and paraphernalia making it easily recognizable from a distance. My brother always kept it stocked with Red Sox or Patriot banners and flags. It looked ridiculous to me. When I got closer, I could see letters duct-taped to the stone. Letters from my brother. When I mocked the spectacle of a tombstone covered in missives and banners, my mother and Shaillie told me I was arrogant and judgmental. "Your brother can grieve anyway he wants. He's dealing with it his way," my mother would say. To which Shaillie would contribute, "Van, at least, he's grieving. Perhaps, he's ridiculing your process, the process of non-grieving." We'd volley opinions back and forth never finding common ground.

I walked up the slope toward the blowing banners and envelopes. I'd never once pulled a letter out to read, despite my brother's queries wondering whether I had read the letters and his insistence that it was ok to do so. I didn't think I could stomach a sentence.

I could count my visits to the grave on one hand since my father had passed several months ago. After the second or third time I saw no point in coming. My reactions were always the same. I would sit and look at the name on the stone, James Arakalian. I'd focus on the last name and think about how strange, how very surreal it was that this man was dead. He was much larger than his five-foot, nine-inch, one hundred eighty-five pound body. Some people's energy, their ch'i as Shaillie liked to call it, superseded their body. My father's ch'i was enormous, overwhelming at times. Even when I grew to be five inches taller and twenty-five pounds heavier than him, he always seemed so much larger than me. It had to be this energy. I guess my ch'i was all out of whack.

Perhaps this was why I had shed the cubicle like a snake molted its skin. Why I had detoured and digressed my existence so much. Displaced and diminished and craving nourishment—the nourishment of change, creativity and travel. Anything to get out of the claustrophobic spectacle of 21st century America Inc., where everything seemed to boil down to one question—to buy or not to buy? But Shaillie would mock this, "Such simple and dated analysis. Your philosophy died long ago. Van, this isn't the conformist 50s. Let it go. Your reasoning is half a century off." To which I'd counter it was even worse fifty years ago. But around and around it went in a dialectical vortex.

I stared at the tombstone. As usual, for a few moments I would think about how strange it was to see my name in death. It made me think of my own mortality. My limited time with so much to do. So much to see, feel, express, consider. Then, I'd think about the day of his death, the oxygen mask, omnipotent father reduced to such a meek state. But I didn't stay long in this scene. Thoughts would then sprint into the past and in one form or another to three episodes of my father and me. Always the same three. I rarely thought about them, except when I came to the stone. Here, they became the dictators of consciousness. Prior to my father's death, I never spent much time delving into these moments of my childhood, but after his death, and usually only at the tombstone, these specifics of the past dominated. My brain was a lemming at the cemetery. It was the same thing over and over again. Images of the past furiously raced by my mind's eye. I couldn't control their arrival, but I could direct their pace. So I'd let the cerebration take its course, but quickly. However, this time I'd slow it down. Let it play itself out in its entirety—the film version rather than the thirty-second commercial.

I usually stood while I was there, but this time I lay supine with my hands cupped behind my head facing the stone. I quickly got up and switched directions. I decided to lie with my head facing the other way, parallel to the right of my father. Still not content with my position, I moved over so that I was directly above my father's remains. The back of my head was about a foot in front of the stone. I rolled my eyes back and saw my father's first name, our last name, letters flapping in the breeze, Patriots Super Bowl Champion pennants. I closed my eyes to remove external distractions. Let the ch'i flow. I imagined I was nearly precisely in line with my father's corpse, just six-feet higher. I wondered how long it took to turn to dust. His body couldn't have gone through decomposition. I took a deep breath. I was exhausted and could fall asleep right now. I forced myself to stay awake. I shook my head and rubbed my face with both hands. The anecdotes kept demanding the cerebral screen. This time, in this position, I felt like I was watching someone else. As if I were truly watching a film of my past, but a character was playing myself. All the while on the precipice of a deep sleep. A very deep sleep…

Your family is at the beach in Maine. The old man and you swim together a lot. It starts there, a happy memory. Many peaceful moments in Maine with the grandparents around, the entire family. You always go out into the deep waters in his arms. You are no more than five, but the movie has been repeated often in your head. The memory is potent. You are out deep, seemingly miles from shore in your child-mind perception. Like almost every time, you tell the old man to go further. Always further. He tells you the continent of Europe is beyond the end of the horizon. A long way away. Other countries that speak different languages. Your eyes widen with curious awe and you implore him to go. He tells you it might take forever, but you still tell him to go. He laughs and you swim out a ways. You wave back to your mother who is frantically waving from the shore. You are smiling and laughing and fearless in the old man's arms. Nothing can happen to him. All fathers are superman until that first, inevitable kryptonite experience unveils reality. The sun is shining diamonds off the salt water. He is up to his neck now and he tells you Europe is just too far. Someday, we'll fly. Eyes on the horizon, you still push him to keep going. He laughs again. He has a big, hearty and happy laugh that emanates from the depths of his belly. He is very proud of his laugh. He never hesitates to point out how your mother squeaks out her laugh from the top of her throat like a hen. Then, suddenly, the old man goes under the water. You fly into the air, skinny five-year-old limbs flailing and slapping the cold Northeast saltwater, until you are under. The current is rolling you in underwater somersaults. It isn't a long time, but it feels as though you are in the middle of the ocean about to drown. Completely alone in the Atlantic, near Europe. Five and half feet of water feeling like the Mariana Trench. As the fear mounts wildly in your mind, the old man scoops you up. No more than thirty seconds had passed. You come up coughing out seemingly gallons of the briny water. He brings you to the shore. You feel you're outside your body watching the events of your own death unfold like an omniscient narrator presiding over a novel. Your mother is frantic, but the old man demands for her to stay calm. The old man seems a bit panic-stricken too, but he's trying to hide it. Yet, the eyes don't hide it well. You have never really seen fear in his eyes. You hear him asking if you're ok and your mother's screams and gasps, but you are still gagging on the water. You feel his mouth on your lips, blasting air into your tiny lungs. He is your oxygen mask. You can finally feel the air entering your lungs. You feel him pressing on your sternum. You're afraid he'll crush your sternum, but you can't stop him because you can't breathe. After several thrusts, you feel a stream, a river rushing up your throat and out of your mouth. You instinctually sit up. The old man pats your back trying to get out the remaining ocean in your throat and lungs. You feel your mother hugging you and your father asking again and again if you're ok. You feel relieved to be breathing, but still a bit stunned. You nod you're fine, but don't say anything. You hear the old man explain that a crab bit him, locked onto his toe, and he lost his balance and accidentally lost you. He apologizes over and over again. You start feeling better and tell him and your mother that you're fine. Your mother's tears quickly transform into venom aimed at the old man. She severely upbraids him. You think she's taking it too far since it was an accident. She demands we never go out deep again and that you wear a life preserver at all times, even in ankle deep water. She really reads him the riot act. You have a vague, illogical sense that she might have almost enjoyed the momentary power.

There are many memories of your orbit within the multiple separations of your parents' chaotic universe. The most indelible experience occurs when you are ten. Lawyers are retained. Dates have been set. The house is apparently a divisive issue in a looming divorce. Apparently, the old man wants the property and your mother refuses. It would go to court. Your father has set up a scheme, unbeknownst to you. You will be visiting his old classmate from Harvard, who also happens to be a lawyer. You are spending a couple weekends a month at the old man's apartment. When he picks you up for this particular weekend, you are told you are going to Arshan Torakian's house. "Just a friendly visit," the old man assures. It strikes you as somewhat strange because you only remember meeting Mr. Torakian once at a barbeque several years ago. The old man reassures you it's just a short visit to catch up with his old classmate. Then the two of you will see a movie.

Arshan Torakian has a nice house in a tony, white-washed suburb, very different from the little-Armenia world of Watertown. Before going to Arshan's house, the drama is demarcated by a scene at your house at pick-up time. It starts normally enough within the world of separated parents. They are exchanging small talk. Mother making sure everything is packed, telling you to have a good time. You have no idea what is going on, other than two homes exist instead of one. Just as your father turns the doorknob and opens the door to leave, your mother unravels—screaming and crying, gesticulating madly. Your father looks shocked, even scared. A worthy drama of soap opera proportions. You stand there having no idea what to do. You are frozen, but you remember one surprising element beyond the madness of parents turning into angry children. You remember that aside from the swimming-to-Europe event your mother rarely had the upper hand in rage. Usually it was the old man bitching up this or that in shows of power and subconscious thunder.

Finally, the old man grabs your hand and takes you out of the verbal furnace. Your mother never stops. You can hear her primal howls as you're driving away even after your father rolls up all the windows. The old man apologizes over and over again for your having witnessed the scene. He tries to explain the issues that he and your mother have. He lapses into his favorite monologue of the past—having to turn down a job offer in New York City.

He was going to rise out of his mid-level management job for company X. He'd been working there for too long. An Ivy League man can do better than halfway up the company ladder. He reminds you and himself that he's done alright. He traveled a bit and had a company car every three years. He was a decent "small-time big shot." A big, little shit who had enough people below him to make him feel important, but enough people above him to pull the big shot feeling away and remind him in essence he was a little shit. You remember this being the first time he uses profanity in front of you. He says he's going to treat you like an adult. His big, little shit status had allowed him to leave the two-family house of little Armenia and make the move to the higher caste suburb of Belmont. He was as solidly middle class as they come. Your mother didn't have to work. Your life was incredibly comfortable, but it was average, and average didn't befit an Ivy League graduate according to the old man.

"You know son," he says on that long ride over to Arshan's house, "I screwed up years ago when I didn't take that job in New York. Your mother wouldn't leave home. She had to be in or near Watertown. Always. I got stuck at regional manager and could never move up. I could be VP right now in another company, but instead it's status quo. At least, we own the house. Lot of value in that house, son. You'll understand someday. Not now, but someday. Things get complicated. Wish they were simple. Keep it simple, son. KISS principle. Keep it simple, son. Not stupid, but simple, son. Yes, that's my advice to you. So Arshan's going to talk to you a bit about the house then we'll go to the movies. What movie do you want to see? I don't want to leave you in the dark. You're old enough to know some truth. A little taste of adult complexity so it doesn't hit you all at once. We'll see a movie. Don't forget that. Yeah, there would be two houses now if I had taken that job,

140

though. I could've moved into the second house instead of a crummy apartment. And instead of the job in New York City, I'm stuck here in the same level for years. It's a dead end, son. I see colleagues I used to manage now in New York above me with summer homes and look at us. Manhattan was the place to go, but your mom is very small town. We could have done even better than Belmont if I had taken that job. We move to New York for a few years and I make a lot of money and then I would have left and started the worry bead business. That worry bead business was a good idea, son. Remember we scouted packaging together? Old World meets the New World. It has cachet. Style. And it's practical. God knows the New World worries more than the old one. Things used to be simple and now it's all messy. Doesn't make any sense, but it's true. I should still do it. Yeah, by now we'd live over with Jack and Sarkis and Aram and all the other successful Armenians up on the Hill or we could have lived in a nice town like Arshan's, but instead we're stuck. It's very provincial, son. Your mother is very provincial. Provincial means staying close to home, not wanting to see and experience the world. It's no insult, just different ways to live life. We're very different people. She's small time and likes it. That's fine, but it's not me, son. We're just different. Forget it, I'm just confusing you. Your mom held us back, pal. It's that simple. And now she wants to...ohhhh, hell, I am probably the lowest salaried Ivy League graduate there is. That's humiliating. There are reasons that we make mistakes, pal. I mean I've got a decent salary, can't complain too much, but it could have been so much more. You know before I had to turn down the New York job, I went to work with big balls. You know, pal, I had real big balls. Like the Jerry Lee Lewis song. I felt I could have gone all the way up to the top, near the top anyway. I had an "S" on my chest, but it all dissolved after turning down New York. The damn "S" stood for settled. Your mom is not ambitious enough. You're a mature kid, you can handle this, right? Good. Not going to New York hurt me and your mom and I don't think we ever recovered. You don't mind that I'm treating you like an adult. That's how I'm treating you. You're mature, right? But, anyway, we'll see a movie after we visit Arshan. What movie do you want to see? I still ought to try that bead idea, though. I should take a chance at it, don't you think, Van? You know it could still work. It's timeless. It's as old as the Armenians. Worry beads. We all got worries, don't we, kid?"

You know he's had a few cocktails when his speech is disjointed and unfocused. The car ride is also anything but straight. You don't say anything, though. He's driven drunk a lot and always berated your mother if she requested the keys. You have to buckle up and hope. You

141

wish you had those worry beads when the old man is drunk behind the wheel. Wish he'd followed up on the idea beyond just talking about it.

The old man conceived the idea from his mother. She used them all the time. It is just a string of beads that you hold. There is about two inches of space to move the beads back and forth. Apparently this was common in the old country. It was a kind of stationary pacing, giving your fingers something to do when neurons are in overdrive.

The old man would always say, "Christ, the pet rock was a hit. This can make it if the pet rock could. This has intrinsic value. You can get rid of your worries by moving the beads. I'll have all these different colors and package them nicely in a blue velvet jewelry-type case. Opens like a pearl necklace or diamonds. We get it out with some advertising in October and it's the Christmas hit for a year. All you need is a Christmas blitz and the six-month follow up and you've got a fortune. We could take that trip we've always talked about, driving across the country visiting minor league baseball stadiums or go to Europe. Long walks by European rivers. You'll know every river in the world, son. I'd have more time. I shouldn't have let your mother hold me back. The New York job would have given me the money for it. I don't want to take a loan. Armenians don't do loans. We use our own money. Debt is treacherous. We buy everything with cash. Anyway, what movie do you want to see?"

Your father's rambling monologue and erratic driving makes you nervous. You really don't process all the adult-world content. You make it over to Arshan's house with the old man's chorus of pet rocks and worry beads and New York and mid-level management and Smirnoff blues. You're just happy to arrive and be out of the car. You always hated car rides with your father. So trapped. Arshan has one of those houses of success hidden from the street. Big trees and shrubs in the front hiding the house in a natural shroud. The top of the house peers over the tree limbs and tall shrubs, strangely ominous. The labyrinthine driveway wends its way up to the top where a manicured yard emerges between the house and the arboreal shroud.

You know you would have been happier in the two-family of a previous generation with grandparents downstairs and aunts and uncles often around. Two adults around aren't enough. You and Shaillie both bemoan the avuncular death in the American family. The nuclear family leads to meltdowns...

You head into Arshan's house and exchange pleasantries. The old man and Arshan are laughing and backslapping. Arshan is not tall, but he has a tremendous girth and a large face with a goatee of flecked gray and black. He has big, swollen semi-circles under his eyes. They are so puffy that the fluid within seems ready to ooze out of his eye

142

sockets. Or, if pricked with a pin, they would burst and spray whatever blood and fluid is filling those swollen pouches beneath his eyes. He sticks his hand out to you. Your bony, undeveloped hand disappears into his sweaty, fleshy, giant-veined paw as he shakes your hand.

"Pretty good grip for a little guy," He lies as he squeezes the skin covered bones.

The old man says, "Son, Arshan's just going to fill you in on some things and then we'll go see a movie. What movie do you want to see?"

"What things?"

"Just some basic things. You'll see. No big deal. Think of a movie and we'll see whatever you want. Even R rated. Don't tell your mother, though."

You shrug and sense something is up. A movie is not on your mind as your father leaves the room.

You sit on the couch and Arshan begins another monologue. He seems to pick up where your old man left off. It's as if it was from a script. But Arshan ratchets it up a few notches. He gives you the "I'm going to treat you like an adult routine." You wish they wouldn't.

"I'm not going to pull any punches with you. You're a tough kid, your old man tells me. We don't need small talk, right. Everybody's busy. You want to have fun. I've got work to do. So we'll cut to the chase, ok? Your mother's never worked. Not one day and she's demanding the house from your father. She doesn't deserve this house. She keeps kicking your father out and he stays in motels and little apartments and she keeps the house without working. Meanwhile, your old man keeps working and paying the bills. Now is that fair?"

You shake your head not knowing whether you should agree and disagree.

"You understand I'm not trying to upset you, but what your mother is doing to your father is not fair. Your father bought that house. He's the real owner. Sure her name is on the papers, but it's his money. She can't just ask him to leave what he bought with his hard work. That's not fair."

You feel tears emerging. You want to defend her, but you don't. You feel like a coward. You hold it together, reverse the tear flow. Your nose is running as the emotions are desperate for an exit. Your breathing gets heavy and stunted in a Herculean effort to prevent sobbing.

He continues talking about the house and your deserving father. He asks you what your mother says about the old man behind his back. If she tries to make him look like the bad guy. He wants to know what her plan is.

143

Your head is bobbing from the effort to prevent tears. You want to punch this man in the face, but your fist feels as though it weighs a thousand pounds.

He pushes you for information about your mother's plans. Asks if any men come over to visit.

You want to say so much. Nothing comes out.

More words fill the air, "Unfair...house...justice...New York...held back..."

Then, you hear steps. Your father comes into the room and ends the disgrace. The old man tells Arshan to stop. Tells you to ignore what he said. He was out of line. You keep the tears dammed and feel great waves of humiliation. You vow not to sob, to be a man in front of these "men," to get out of your ten- year-old body, but your efforts to stop the sobs lead to strange, stifled wailing sounds from your throat. You are almost gagging.

The old man gets you some water. He looks real nervous. His face has that look of fear that you remember from the ocean incident. At the behest of the old man, you will never tell your mother.

You drink the water and calm down. Arshan half-heartedly apologizes and you look away. The "men" each have a scotch on the rocks. You remember the bottle of Johnnie Walker Black. You remember the sound of ice plopping in the glass and Arshan saying to the old man, "You always kill good scotch with ice. Put ice in JB, but not Walker Black."

You finally leave and head to that movie. The long promised bait of a movie. You get to the old theatre next to a seedy Chinese restaurant. You see the only movie playing — The Jerk. Years later you can only laugh at the irony and you wonder if the irony ever crossed the old man's mind at the time, but you never talk about that day.

Your mind fast-forwards to your father berating your maternal grandfather. Your grandfather calls him a liar during a dinner conversation. Pushes his buttons. The old man reminds him whose roof he is under. Tells him to back up his talk with examples. Your ninety-five year old grandfather who has just moved into the house starts trembling and says never mind. Your father pushes. You intervene in defense of your grandfather. You are twenty-one. You tell the old man to calm down. He tells you to shut your fucking mouth. Who asked you to get involved anyway? More words until you are standing toe to toe, fists clenched. You are towering over your father. Your hands feel like they will have the impact of sledgehammers, but at the same time they are

144

light and ready to be released. You think back to Arshan's house. This punch has been building for over a decade. Shaillie grabs your fists. Your mother steps between you and the old man. Again, you see fear in your old man's eyes. Fear of his no longer diminutive son staring down at him from five inches above. Fear of your tightened fist cocked and ready to crash down on the sagging flesh of his sixty-year-old face.

I felt something crawling on my face. I opened my eyes. I was staring at blades of grass pressed flat. I lifted my head up and felt my cheeks for the thing crawling on it. It was hard and small. I stuck my fingernail between it and my cheek. It crawled onto my finger. A ladybug. I flung it into the air and it flew away. I rolled over onto my butt and saw my father's tombstone, recognizing where I was. I sat up Indian style. My face was very sweaty and I could feel the depressions in my skin from the grass and ground. I wiped my face with my shirt. The sleep felt so good. I wanted more, but I knew I had to be somewhere. Something was happening today. Yes, I remembered. Shaillie was gone and I was heading to Europe.

Yes, my life was coming apart.

As soon as I returned home, I got on the computer and poured out the dreams and memories that I'd just had while lying six feet above my father's corpse. I recorded the events in a twisted form, fictionalized into more truth than reality's inherent shortcomings could possibly allow. Arshan got his due. Father's plan backfired. Automatic writing without regard for direction, surrendering to the impulse without manipulation. Shedding layers of distended consciousness. An hour and ten pages later I printed out the work. I opened the safe and looked at the last page in the pile to find the page number—554. I wrote 564 on the last page of the current crop of words and added it to the pile. I wanted a mountain of pages. A Vesuvius of eruptive prose. I realized the accumulation of words was all I cared about. Nothing else seemed to matter.

I had no official title. I decided to give it a title page. Something simple and accurate. I went back to the computer, wrote the title and printed it out, placing it on top of the tome. It was now *Insomnia Journal.*

I locked the safe and poured myself a glass of filtered water, drinking it down quickly. I refilled and drank another glass. My mouth was very dry. My head was starting to find its way through the cobwebs of last night's chemicals and alcohol. I would not drink today. Today was for clarity and action. I got my keys and headed out to see Derisa. It was almost time for her tour to start. Apt confluence.

I raced into Harvard Square driving along the Charles River and parked at Derisa's house. She lived near the Square in a loft-style apartment. No starter homes for Derisa. As I walked out of her driveway, I looked into her 2nd floor loft. I could see two of her cats lazily looking out a large bay window. Behind the cats I could see a large canvas of fantastical colors reminiscent of Jackson Pollock. Gorgeous and rhythmic chaos.

Derisa and Shaillie attended the Museum of Fine Arts School. They each received their MFAs there and graduated together. However, unlike Shaillie, Derisa continued painting with ambition. She didn't capitulate. Derisa loved Cambridge as much as Woody Allen loved Manhattan. She wanted all her paintings to take place in Cambridge and particularly Harvard Square. She found Harvard Square to be a "sensual and alchemical convergence of academics, eccentrics, intellectuals, communists, artists, street performers, bohemians, entrepreneurs, all classes, minds and ages co-existing. Mix in tourists and provincial locals and you have yourself a gloriously quirky mélange of humanity with the giant corporation of university education in the background. It's a painter's paradise."

Derisa had done a series of paintings trying to capture that mélange. One review described her style as neo-Fauvist. Her paintings were immediately striking and alive due to her choice of colors, but what I loved about her work was that she combined traditional technique with the vague dreaminess of abstract. Derisa would choose one subject matter and draw it realistically in a pre-impressionist style. The rest of the painting would drift into the surreal and the abstract. It was as if she took the great movements of art and put them all into one style. The result was not derivative, but original. Perhaps, Shaillie gave up painting in fear (or knowledge) of never being able to transcend the styles and movements she had admired.

Derisa had the Harvard Square series exhibited at the Fogg. Her greatest achievement so far. She was one of the rare artists who also functioned financially. She was actually happy to be alive. She celebrated existence on the canvas and in her life.

I stopped for an espresso at Starbucks. I had a double shot and crossed Harvard Yard. As I passed Widener Library I realized I hadn't thought about Shaillie's departure since I'd returned from the cemetery. For a moment, I thought maybe this whole thing was about getting out of the marriage. I looked down at my feet. "Shit, maybe, Shaillie was right all along," I said aloud, noticing a few students looking at me with curious eyes.

I got into the Fogg without paying. Derisa had left my name at the desk as she always did. I could see a semi-circle of people gathered in the center of the Fogg's courtyard area. Derisa was already into her introduction as I joined the group. She gave me a look of recognition, but never paused her lecture to the group of about fifteen people.

"With the horror of trench warfare and World War I, one million casualties at Verdun alone, it's no wonder that Dada's core was negation and nihilism. Dada wanted to consume itself and that it did, but Surrealism resurrected Dada's spirit and transformed it, evolved it into something more positive. The twenties were a more energized period, the inter-bellum illusion of peace providing hope. Some believed that the war to end all wars had done just that. Hitler was still just an art school drop-out at this point. Out of this era came Andre Breton and the Surrealists. Like Dada, it defied reason and all that was rational, but it was in the irrational that humanity's hopes and dreams could actually be found. Surrealists sought to join the conscious and unconscious, to join outer reality and inner reality into "an absolute reality, a surreality" to quote Breton. Breton wrote all of this in *The Surrealist Manifesto*. He seized on the theories of Freud, but didn't consider the subconscious as the malicious maestro of Freud's world. Rather, Breton and his cohorts believed all shades resided within, both yin and yang. It was the artists job to channel deep within their psyche and let the images and stories flow unfettered into their creativity, providing individual and ultimately societal catharsis. Surrealists sought to break free of the restraints and shackles of logic. The logical world had led to World War I. They proclaimed complete faith in the imagination, in the chaotic irrational inner world of their own psyche. Therefore, their biggest ally in creativity was their own dreams. Dreams were not pranks perpetrated by the mind, but clues to surreality's pathway. In their paintings you will see dreamy images extended and merged without any heeding to temporal concerns. The depths of one's mind should be plumbed and expressed without analysis. Leave the analysis for after the painting or writing was complete. This was what they called automatic art. Any questions before we begin the tour?"

I looked at others in the group. They seemed to be mostly tourists and a bit overwhelmed by Derisa's heavy art history introduction.

"Ok, then, feel free to ask anything as we go. Let's look at the first painting in the exhibit." Derisa pointed the way to the exhibition. The group walked that way and Derisa walked over to me. She gave me a kiss on the cheek. "Hi sweetheart," she whispered. I smiled. "Almost thirty years old, Van, and you're still shy."

"Just around sexy lesbian artists," I whispered.

She smiled and said, "I don't know what it is about men and lesbians, but the attention is the worst thing."

"Have you talked to Shaillie?" I asked.

Derisa nodded.

"Does she know I'm here?"

"Yes."

"So?" I said, arms open, gesticulating for an answer.

"She's not happy, Van."

"What does that mean?"

"We'll have to talk after the tour." I could see the group looking at a René Magritte painting and waiting for their expert.

"She's gone, isn't she?" I asked.

"Van, you really pushed her away."

"How gone?"

"Gone enough to want to cancel the wedding. She was really upset."

I nodded and closed my eyes. I wasn't very surprised to hear this. I was surprised at my reaction. I felt guilty at the sense of relief I instantly felt. Guilty at putting Shaillie through all this. Guilty at feeling what I knew was wrong to feel.

"Van, you shouldn't have gone to Providence. How could you not know that it was a test?"

"It seems obvious now."

"You failed the test."

"I'm realizing that."

"Look, I've got to get to the tour. We can have coffee after. She told me not to tell you this, but I'm going to. She's at her sister's place. Why don't you go see her. Maybe there's still hope."

"I'm not so sure about that."

"Van, you ok?"

"Yes, Derisa, I am."

"I'm not quite sure how you look, but it's not what I expected."

"I'll be fine. I'm going to make a phone call."

"Good idea. Good luck, sweetheart. I think you can still save your relationship."

Derisa went off to the Magritte painting and I exited the museum. I sat down on The Fogg's cement steps, took out my cell phone, scrolled to the name I was looking for and hit the green button.

"Hello," Derek Koles said.

"It's Van."

"You ready?" He immediately asked.

"I will be. What time's our flight?"

"Eight."

"I'll be at Logan at six. See you there. You got the tickets already?"

"No, but I'll have them now that you're officially in. See you at six. Don't forget your passport."

"See you tonight, Derek."

The die was certainly cast. I was systematically dismantling my life. I felt a perverse sense of elation at the adventurous madness of jetting off to Europe with no real goals, but I also felt as if a giant wrecking ball was suspended behind me waiting to be released for a direct hit. Erecting a building knowing it might soon crumble. The wrecking ball contained all the compunction I should have felt for my wayward behavior. For driving Shaillie away. I had asked her to marry me. I had made the commitment and was detouring from it. On all levels mundane I was wrong. It was cut and dry for the unbiased arbiter. However, rationalization was simultaneously being constructed. I had tried to get Shaillie to go with me and wanted her along for the ride. I had even given her the option of running with me after the wedding, but she resisted. Goddamn starter houses had permeated her every cell. She couldn't step off the conveyor belt so I had to leap off. I even had surges of anger at Shaillie. Angry at her pushing me into sterility, a life of mediocrity, an existence that celebrated nothing but the droning peace of material progress. Angry that I wasn't more like Koles or Gilworthy. Angry that she wasn't more like Derisa.

Further staving off the guilt and loss was the belief that I didn't really think Shaillie was gone. The chasm between us felt temporary. We were both angry at each other, but it would dissolve with time. I'd go and take care of my exit. It wouldn't last. Just enough time to cleanse perception, seek visions. Edify and enrich. Reciprocity for those straitjacket years. Most of all, finish the homage to Surrealism. I was convinced that finishing it would lead to a new path. I'd get the bohemian rush out of my system and then Shaillie would be there when I returned. Then again, all of that could just be fabrication to soften the blow I'd just received.

149

I got my car from Derisa's. I had time to kill before meeting Koles. I decided to take a walk along the Charles River outside Central Square. I parked two blocks away across the street from a diner. It was just what I needed. Hot coffee, eggs, toast, potatoes. The thought of it jarred recognition of how hungry I was.

I sat at the counter. It was fairly crowded for early in the morning. Sleepy faces everywhere, many buried in newspapers or eating their full plates of breakfast. I could hear the sounds of the griddle sizzling with bacon and eggs, but mostly I heard the couple next to me. They were engaged in a loud, boisterous tête-à-tête, but I ignored them for the moment. I saw a stray sports page and opened to the scoreboard section. Cubs beat the Padres, 5-4. I checked how Nomar had fared. He had two hits and an RBI. I read the brief blurb about the game. "Garciaparra hits game-winning homerun in the ninth." Breakfast was going to taste better.

"What can I get you?" A waitress asked me in a gruff, no-nonsense tone.

She hadn't given me a menu. I looked at the paper placemat in front of me. It wasn't a menu.

"No menus, kid. Just tell me what you want and we'll make it for you. Breakfast food, you know, eggs, pancakes, waffles. Whatever you want at reasonable prices. We're thinking green like good Cambridge-folk. Why would you need a menu?"

"I don't."

"Good. Fire away."

"Eggs, toast, bacon, coffee."

"Scrambled?"

"Fried. Sunny side up."

"White, wheat, or rye?"

"Wheat."

"Cream and sugar?"

"Black."

"Hash browns?"

"Sure."

"See, wasn't that easy?"

"Who needs menus?" I said, smiling.

She winked at me, "You're a quick learner, sunshine." She returned with a pot of steaming coffee and poured me a cup. I took a sip of the coffee. It tasted so good. I was addicted to coffee, drinking it steadily from the time I woke up until dinner. Four, five, six cups a day. No matter what state of mind I was in, no matter how miserable I felt, I always looked forward to waking up. I needed to appease the screaming need for caffeine in my blood. It always gave me a reason to get out of

150

bed. Perhaps, my insomnia was tied to the excess caffeine flowing in my blood. I had tried cutting down at Shaillie's request, but did a poor job of it. Thinking back to my effort, I might have just been strangely reluctant to lose the insomnia. I was getting institutionalized by it.

Once I had finished half a cup of coffee, I felt a sort of equilibrium being restored to my system. I could focus better now. I was tired and burnt out from the late night festivities, but the coffee gave an ephemeral rush. The cemetery nap and caffeine both helped to diminish the excesses of the hedonistic Providence evening. My focus was now forced into the vociferous duo to my right. The woman was rotund and red-faced. The man was skinny and pale. They were Laurel-and-Hardy-like.

"Marley, shut up," the man said softly.

"You're pathetic," she shot back.

"So are you, which is why we hang out together."

"I don't hang out with you. I let you hang out with me. You always come over and you know how busy I am running my own business. Did you know my floral arrangements got written up in the paper last week?"

"I know, I know. You've told me a million times. A little townie paper. Big deal. And you knew the editor from high school."

"Don't rain on my parade."

"What parade? The one in your head?"

"You know how many people I have working for me? That includes your sorry ass."

"You got no life like me, Marley. The difference is I admit it. You're in denial."

"I rather be in denial than thinking like you. Besides, I have a life."

"You think you do."

"By the way, who was the whore?"

"Huh?"

"Sitting in your car the other day when you came by for a delivery. Who was the whore?"

"My neighbor. She lives across the hall. I would have invited her in, but I'm embarrassed by you."

"Peter, please, I can only upgrade you. Are you screwing her?"

"No. She lives in my building and we were running errands."

"You're a disaster. Why don't you screw her?"

"Shut up, Marley."

"You should get your vegetarian bones on a woman, or maybe a man. Whichever, it would do your ghostly complexion some good. Time to come out of the closet, Peter."

"Marley, stop taking your miserable self out on me. I don't know why I put up with this."

"Because you have absolutely nothing else to do. Abuse is better than nothing."

"Sad, but true," he said looking over at me. "Better than nothing, I guess."

I nodded and smiled. The waitress came by and refilled their coffees. She looked over at me and said, "You know these guys love each other. They're like a couple of fifth graders at recess, just a little more perverse and profane."

"Marley and me? Please," Peter said.

"A woman can't have sex with a gay skeleton."

The waitress laughed. "Marley, you're terrible. Lighten up on him once in a while."

"Yeah," Peter agreed. "Lighten up on me, huh? I'm tired of taking your shit."

"So, Peter, what's up?" The waitress asked.

"Nothing."

"I heard you bought another condo."

"Yeah, I'm closing soon. Doing all the paperwork bullshit."

"What are you doing for work?"

"Part-time at Trader Joe's. Just to get out and socialize."

"You work there to be with vegetables. The guy loves vegetables. He works in produce. Talks to the damn broccoli more than people," Marley told the waitress.

"How many condos do you own now, Peter?" the waitress asked, ignoring Marley.

"Three."

"No shit. You're a damn real estate mogul."

"Yeah, sure," he laughed. "They're just little places, but I'm doing ok. I get pretty good rent. Just have to take care of them, but it's easy stuff." He turned to Marley. "That's what I was doing with my friend. The so-called whore. Going to buy some plumbing supplies."

"She *is* a whore. I've seen her around," Marley said.

"Yeah, sure, according to you. She's actually a nice lady."

"So, you're making a good living. Good for you," the waitress said sincerely.

"Yeah, it's ok, but I'm bored. I'm so damn bored I take abuse from Marley."

"You're making a good living because of the money you inherited. Had nothing to do with you. At least, I've worked for my living," Marley snapped.

The waitress came to Peter's defense. "Marley, he could have pissed the money away. Instead he invested it in property. Best investment out there. I'm impressed, Peter."

"Carol, since when did you decide to kiss Peter's ass?" Marley asked the waitress.

"Just trying to balance this scale a little."

Peter looked over at me. "You think she loves me?"

"Possibly. Lot of emotion in her words," I replied.

"Please, I have better taste and can do better than pale, anorexic vegetarians," Marley said to me. "Anyway, I need to make a call." She took out her cell phone and went outside.

"So, you've got a lot of time to do what you want," I said.

"Which is?"

"I don't know. I said what you want, not what I want."

"I don't want to do anything."

"Well, what do you do besides working part-time? How do you spend the rest of your time?"

"I sleep 'til about seven. Make some deliveries for Marley a few days a week. Work a few hours on building maintenance. About ten hours at Trader Joe's. The rest of the time I stare at the walls."

"Come on."

"I'm serious. I spend a lot of time wall staring."

"Why don't you do something?"

"Like what?"

"Travel."

"Why? What's the point?"

"You can see the world. Change your scenery. Do I need to explain travel?"

"Then I'd just end up wall staring after a two-week diversion."

"Travel for a month."

"A month's diversion. I don't see the point. Besides, I don't have the energy. And Marley's afraid to fly."

"Maybe you ought to travel with someone else."

"Who?"

"I don't know. What about taking a class?"

"In what?"

"What are you interested in?"

"Nothing. Do they have classes in nothing? If they do, I'm already taking it everyday of my life."

I laughed. He didn't.

"Take a class on existentialism. That's about nothing, philosophically speaking."

"What?"

"Nothing. How 'bout history?"

"No interest."

"I don't know what to tell you."

"I don't either."

"How about reading?"

"Don't like to. Can't focus long enough to read a whole book."

"Read a short story."

He shook his head. "What else?"

"Volunteer work?"

"In what?"

"I don't know. Homeless people."

"I don't truly care about them. I hope the best for them, but I'm not going to help them."

"Painting?"

"Like pictures?"

"Yeah, take a class in it and then paint."

"No interest."

"Photography?"

"Of what, the walls?"

"Whatever."

"No interest."

"A pet?"

"No interest."

"Masturbation?" I said, surprising myself.

"Yeah, yeah, sure sure. Boring, too. No interest anymore."

"When you lose interest in that, that's trouble." I said.

The waitress brought my food. I was looking forward to eating and not talking to this existentialist. This apathetic existentialist. He made Camus and Sartre look whimsical and blissful. This guy was absolute zero personified. Though the fact that he seemed completely resigned to his fate without hostile protest made him strangely likeable.

"Let's go, you waste," Marley said upon returning. She looked at me. "So you get what I mean now after talking to him? Did he mention walls?"

I smiled. She was kind of likeable too. They had their routine down and it got them through the day.

"Who's buying?" Peter said to Marley.

"Why don't you be a gentleman for a change?"

"I will, when there's a lady around."

"I bet you are with the whore," Marley said and paid the bill. "Come on, let's see if you can make it another day without putting a gun to your head."

154

Peter looked at me, head tilted and a shy, what-can-I-do mien. "Nice talking to you."

"Yeah, good luck," I said.

"Yeah, you too. Maybe I should take a class. I might do that." His expression said he wouldn't.

Marley interjected as usual, "You should, just so you'll have something to talk about. You are so boring. Take a class. Do something, lifeless one."

On that note they walked out the door.

The waitress came over to me and refilled my coffee. "More or less the same schtick every morning. Don't take them seriously."

After the Godot-style conversation, I needed a break from humanity so I headed over to the Charles River. Rivers had always been a source of tranquility. I have great and peaceful memories of long walks along the Charles with my old man. The old man had a wide and varied range of knowledge, but geography was a particular area of expertise. We would walk along the Charles and I would quiz him on rivers of the world. I would name the river and he'd name the location. When I was young, I'd have an atlas in hand, but after a while the quizzing had taught me many of the rivers. We would take turns going back and forth. We called it "the river game." I always lost, but it would take a fairly obscure river to get me out, such as the Yenisei in Siberia, the Purus in the Peruvian Andes, or the Zambezi in Africa. My father was always relaxed and tranquil when we walked by the Charles. Harvard was nearby. He was very proud of graduating Harvard as the first generation son of immigrant Armenian Genocide survivors—no small feat. That pride seemed to fill him with peace whenever he was nearby Harvard. It made him forget about not taking the New York job or never following through with the worry bead idea. Harvard stadium was also filled with memories of the many football games he'd attended over the years. Our Charles River walks invariably included him reminiscing about Harvard's most famous "victory" over Yale. "Yes, son, we beat those damn Eli's 29 to 29. When you're down by three touchdowns with two minutes to go in The Game, a tie is a crushing win." It was during these long conversations amidst the soothing flow of the river and ivy tranquility that the old man was most at peace.

It was also during those walks that the cemetery episodes seemed a part of a macabre imagination. I deeply enjoyed my old man's company, his enthusiasm for life, the tension-free air outside the manic and mercurial household. It spurred my future interest in rivers. While Shaillie had a hobby of ornithology, I had potamology.

During times of stress, I often looked to the Charles for pacific energy. Any river for that matter was a reliable source of serenity. It was quite Pavlovian. It started with the old man and expanded when I'd read Mark Twain's *Life on the Mississippi*. Twain wrote about his days as a riverboat pilot and celebrated the romantic glory of the Mississippi River. It was then that I began to research and observe rivers as a hobby. I would take the interest beyond my father's superficial knowledge. I would poeticize my interest, add depth to the wonder, and even concoct an elaborate and romantic rationale as to why rivers were greater than any other body of water.

Rivers were more accessible than oceans and seas, which were just too big and overwhelming. You could see the other side of a river and not be stuck across from the unknown. Less mystery in this aspect, but more stability. Lakes and ponds were too still and lifeless while rivers gave one a visual rhythm, a steadiness in their constant flow. Yet they could also be emotional and unpredictable with raging twists and sudden turns. The same river can be wild in one place and tranquil in another. They are powerful, yet alluringly and seductively gentle. And rivers are so interconnected with the land. They are born on mountain tops from where they descend and flow into great cities, forests, valleys and ancient rock and soil until emptying into a lake, sea or ocean. Numerous tributaries spread and connect their waters far and wide. From headwaters to deltas, rivers are the umbilical cord of Mother Earth and an antidote to loneliness.

The Charles was certainly no Mississippi, but it had power and dignity. It was regal like its royal namesake. It snaked its way through Greater Boston quite narrowly at times. One could almost leap from one bank to the other at certain points. As it wended its way through Watertown and then past Harvard and MIT in Cambridge, it finally hit Boston where its flow widened dramatically. Universities lined the two major roads built along its edge. At its very end, the Museum of Science rested over the mouth of the Charles before it disappeared into Boston Harbor and the Atlantic Ocean.

I walked along the BU Bridge watching the sun at its mid-morning perch above the Boston skyline. I needed more sleep, but didn't want to at that moment. I couldn't sleep now. Insomniacs crave and loathe sleep simultaneously. I wanted a few hours awake and alone. I needed another perspective. One that doesn't comes from the confusion of conversation, but arises from the fertility of silence.

I stared at the Charles. There was a good flow heading into Boston Harbor. I crossed the street to the other side of the bridge facing

Boston; going with the flow for a change. There was a wonderful morning light and downtown looked beautiful and pristine from this vantage point. Boston to my right and Cambridge to my left. Boston's own version of the left and right bank. The division was similar to that of Paris—business, enterprise, capitalism on the right, artistic creativity, radical thought, introspective searchers to the left. The river separated and connected the dual energies. I could see MIT along the edge of the left bank highlighted by the dome. Harvard was nestled in behind it. The gilded spire of an old campus church rising high above. BU was nearby. Harvard was also on the right bank, but it was the business school, perfectly fitting the Parisian split. Cars were speeding down Storrow Drive into the city. The day was in full swing. Humanity was flowing along with the river. Between the banks, sailboats dotted the widening river as it neared the city. Skulls carrying university crew teams sped beneath me in the wake of motorboats with coaches barking out motivational words. There was an actual race going on. The rat race on the road and the Ivy athletes racing on the river.

Soon, I'd be in Paris standing on a bridge over the Seine. It made sense. I was feeling good. Peaceful energy. I'd bring *Insomnia Journal* and finish it in Paris. What better place to complete an homage to Surrealism than its actual birthplace? I'd gather Bretonian momentum and muse while beginning with the Charles and ending with the Seine. A very sane conclusion. The calming and seductive power of two great urban rivers and the mountain of words that emanated from subconscious terrain. Internal and external rivers seeking a natural flow, tempting and offering symmetry and meaning.

I walked off the bridge back to the left bank. I lay down on the grass at the edge of the riverbank. The double shot of caffeine peaked and ebbed quickly. The adrenalin of oncoming cataclysm was wearing off. I wasn't sure I could hold off a nap. I had to at least rest my eyes and mind by the river. I had time. About seven hours to kill before leaving for the Seine. Packing would be quick—just one bag of essentials. Lying down, staring at the diamonds flittering on the river's surface, I tried to let my racing mind slow down to the level of my somnolent body. There was a clear misalignment between the mind and the body. The former kept bouncing thoughts and ideas back and forth with the rapidity of Chinese ping-pong players. The latter simply implored for sleep.

Just when the Charles started tranquilizing my mind to another possible nap, I saw an old friend ride by on her bike. Actually, not really a friend, but an old lover. A lover of both Shaillie and mine. Our simultaneous one-night lover, Rina.

Rina was on her bike riding across the BU Bridge about to take a left towards Harvard Square. I waved and knew she had seen me, but there was no response other than a tiny pause while we briefly caught eyes. She kept on going. I yelled her name, but she wouldn't look back. It was as if that night had never happened.

I blame John Updike for the ménage-à-trois. Or rather I credit him depending upon how I looked back on the perversity. We were in bed not long ago. Chronology has become a blurry concept, but I believe it was shortly before my father passed away. Shaillie always went back to the loss of my father as the inception of our disarray, but at that sleepy moment by the Charles, it dawned on me that perhaps all the tumult of recent times had its origin with our invitation to Rina to join us in bed. The bawdy experience with Rina might have been the first domino that fell outside Shaillie's chaos theory radar. Perhaps, red-state moralists actually had a point...

The plan was conceived just after we had made love one night. Our sex life had hit a plateau. It had become functional and utilitarian. Orgasms had lost their potency. It seemed like we were doing it just to finish. Lying in bed after another episode of virtual passion, I was reading one of Updike's Rabbit books. I believe it was *Rabbit Redux*. Shaillie asked me what was going on in the story as she was wont to do. She loved to stop me in the middle of a book and ask for a plot update. I enjoyed sharing this with her and never found it interruptive. I described the scene with some detail. I can't remember exactly what it was, but it was a sex scene, of course. I believe Rabbit had slept with a neighbor's wife. I read a few passages to Shaillie. Then I went back to the book while Shaillie rested her head on my shoulder. After a few more pages of Rabbit Angstrom's angst, Shaillie and I began confronting our sexual plateau. It was her idea to experiment as a way to reinvigorate things. Or, at least, she was the one who first voiced the idea.

Shaillie found the woman. It turned out the whole *Rabbit Redux* moment hadn't prompted a truly spontaneous suggestion from Shaillie. I had just given her the right moment to camouflage a thoughtful idea as a whimsy. She admitted that she'd been thinking of it for some time as a way to inject some energy into our sex life. Shaillie had had a few lesbian experiences before we met, so it wouldn't be all new to her. More than two people, though, would be new ground for her and me. She thought we'd share something wild together and it would catapult new life and energy into our sexuality. She'd even talked about it with Derisa, who was very much in favor of it and also a willing participant.

Shaillie thought it best to get a stranger. She went online to the Boston Phoenix website and found a posting form a woman that she thought was safe for us:

Asian, 20s, looking for sensuality and temporary
connections, nothing meaningful, nothing too kinky,
no S & M.

She spoke with Shaillie on the phone prior to coming over, but Shaillie wouldn't reveal anything to me. Keep some mystery, she told me. She wanted the night to be extremely erotic for her and me. She thought it would be our little flight from the norm. "An exit from your cubicle, Van. A little fantasy for you and me." The caveat was that it was a one-time thing, but she also told me to relax and be free with it. "No hesitation and no jealousy from either of us. We do it once, but, we do it right."

The night Rina came over we shared a bottle of wine and listened to Leonard Cohen, who always put Shaillie in the mood. The only thing I knew about Rina was that she was a grad student in theatre at BU and from her emailed photos, she was beautiful. Seeing her confirmed it. After some small talk, she broached the notion that this was both a risqué and risky endeavor. "I just want to stress, I'm doing this to relieve stress, so to speak."

"Yes, let's stress no stress," Shaillie said.

"You know, it's just that I don't want a relationship now," Rina continued in her direct and unabashed manner, "I just want to appease my needs without hurting anyone or anyone falling in love. I just can't deal with celibacy or a relationship. Every fling I have gets so complicated and dramatic. Guys always want more from a woman who doesn't. Guess it's the challenge. So I figure this is the safest way."

We both agreed.

"Of course, no one's going to fall in love, right?" Rina asked.

"This isn't about love. We've got some, ahh, monogamy blues. Purely carnal for us, right Van?" Shaillie queried, looking at me, as did Rina. I could feel the gazes gaining intensity, the four eyes focusing their vision like one giant female eye. I looked over at each pair, back and forth a few times. The eyes were so direct and virtually free of blinking, like four bright flashlights aimed at me in a dark room.

I furrowed my brow.

"Well," Rina said.

"What?" I asked.

"No worries, right? I don't want a love triangle, just a sexual one. It'll help me study. I need erotic satisfaction, but no relationship headaches. It's hard to get one without the other."

I nodded. "Of course," I tried to sound matter-of-fact, but I was more or less in shock that this was happening. It had happened before to me, but never outside of my head.

"Van, answer the woman," Shaillie insisted.

"What?"

"You never answered my question," Rina said.

"No worries, Rina," I said.

Rina looked over at Shaillie.

"No one's falling in love. No worries at all," Shaillie assured. Everyone apparently had no worries.

"What if you fall for her?" I asked Shaillie, trying to take the heat off of me.

"She is beautiful, but that's not going to happen. This is what it is." Shaillie calmly said with a smile for Rina.

I nodded in agreement. She certainly was beautiful. Part of my nervousness was also that I was completely turned on.

Rina added, "You know, I also want everything out and done before my final relationship. I think it will help. I think our experiment will be good for future monogamy."

"We think it will help us, too," Shaillie said.

"Shall we? I have a paper to write tonight," Rina said, smiling.

Shaillie laughed. I let out some air disguised as laughter. I followed the ladies into the bedroom. Shaillie lit some pre-arranged candles and I sat down in a chair by the bed.

"Van, just go with me. Everything is all set."

I was so impressed with Shaillie's calm and confidence. It was so unreal that I thought the whole thing would suddenly stop and the practical joke would be unveiled. Someone would scream, "April Fools!" and the scenery would melt into miles of sun-scorched desert. But it didn't. It wasn't a mirage. It was really happening. Shaillie changed the CD from Leonard Cohen to Miles Davis—*Bitches Brew*.

Shaillie undressed Rina while both of them stood in front of me. Rina was a little shorter than Shaillie. She had jet black, silken Asian hair, cut above her slender shoulders. The ends were curved forward and upward, a natural frame for her lovely, sensual face. Shaillie started kissing Rina gently on her full and tantalizing lips. Rina kissed her back, but clearly Shaillie was directing the flow of everything. In conversation, Rina was in charge. In the bedroom she became soft and submissive. The energy in the room was electric. The energy of two beautiful women getting ready to experiment on each other's bodies. The energy of new sexuality, of the unknown, of fearless taboo and lewd adventure. The energy of an instant erection. Shaillie nibbled on Rina's lips, then slid slowly down her neck, staying longer just below the chin as Rina arched her head back and breathed deeply with pleasured heaviness.

I, the voyeur, took a deep breath.

Rina seemed to truly enjoy Shaillie's role of control. Shaillie unbuttoned Rina's blouse and slipped it slowly off her shoulders, letting it fall down her arms to the floor. Shaillie put her fingers under Rina's bra straps and slowly sliding her hands down Rina's alluring cleavage and under her bra.

"Van, undo her bra for me," Shaillie whispered as the two women kissed again.

My heart was thumping in my throat.

I made my way behind Rina while they were kissing passionately. I unhooked the clasps, the back of my fingers touching Rina's skin. It immediately hit me that it had been the first time I had touched another woman's skin since I'd met Shaillie over a decade ago.

Shaillie ran the back of her hands across Rina's golden breasts, back and forth across the small, dark nipples, barely touching them as they hardened quickly. Rina now took Shaillie's clothes off. All of them, while Rina still had her short skirt and high heels on. She began touching, caressing, sweetly teasing Shaillie everywhere. Shaillie whispered to me to undress and be free. Rina slid her skirt off and stepped out of her shoes as I took my clothes off.

The women got into bed together. Shaillie immediately went down on Rina. She paused and looked up at me. For a moment I realized that my soon-to-be wife was between another woman's legs, face deep in pussy, while I stood naked and watching. We were in a Henry Miller novel or an erotic film. I felt like a method actor in character and never wanted to get out.

Rina reached out and began massaging my penis before putting it in her mouth. At that moment my penis was no penis. It was all cock and the pussies were cunts. Cunts and cocks and we all loved it, free of propriety and pretenses. A happy cock and merry cunts. The cock was in the cunt house. Rina sucked me so perfectly while groaning beginning to come from Shaillie's tongue. It didn't take long before my orgasm blasted through my body, rippling within every muscle and tissue from head to toe. It was the orgasm to end all orgasms, satisfaction so thorough I thought I'd never need another one.

That is, until minutes later when both ladies got on top of me and...

I felt the heat of the sun warming the left side of my face as I lay on my side. When I opened my eyes, I was looking at the BU Bridge exactly where Rina had been riding her bike. I stared for a bit at the bridge trying to register reality. I was immediately struck with doubt about seeing her. I couldn't tell if my memory of that night with Rina was from a dream while napping, or if I'd simply been thinking about it before falling to sleep. Was Rina's biking across the bridge part of the dream? Was everything a dream? Paramnesia struck again, but deciphering what was real and what was dream seemed irrelevant. Recently, everything seemed to be hovering around the imaginary anyway...   I looked at my watch. I'd slept for a few hours. Along with the cemetery sleep, it was the most I'd slept in one day in a long time. It was time to go home and pack. Europe was calling.

I immediately cleaned up upon arriving home. I filled the sink with steaming hot water and draped a towel over my head. I leaned over the vapors, creating a makeshift steam room. When the water had gone tepid, I drained the sink. I looked in the medicine chest for some of Shaillie's fancy facial soap. Nothing. She'd taken it all. I grabbed a bar of soap from the shower and washed my face, rinsing it with icy cold water. I brushed my teeth, rinsed for an extra long time with Listerine, enjoying the harsh stinging effect on my gums and tongue. Then I took a long shower.

I put on a pair of jeans, a decent shirt, and a sport jacket as my traveling attire. I put my only other pair of jeans, two shirts, some underwear, socks and a small bag of toiletries in my backpack. The same backpack that I'd used in Europe with Shaillie.

I half-expected an angry call from Shaillie. Reproach for my actions would have almost been a relief. I needed some of her anger. But there was nothing. Just silence. Shaillie was better than that, always taking the high road.

I walked into the study. I had almost forgotten the most important thing, *Insomnia Journal*. I spun the dial of the safe and pulled out all the pages. All those pages that I refused to read. The dreamy transcription that I'd elevated into hyperbolic significance. Raised it high in divinely soaked delusions; a personal and glorious internal revolution. The great and noble mystery that lay tucked away in the cerebral cinema of escape. Fantastic tragedies and comedies beseeching the present to be unlocked as if there were some Svengali, some Oz figure, some holy fire-breathing dragon-lady turning on the cameras and choosing whichever tantalizing story to erupt upon one's all so unbelievable universe. A thick burgundy velvet curtain opening to a theatre of the bizarre. Orchestras and carnivals and honeymoons and nightmares all mingling in one mad tea party. Tiny gods hiding in the crevices of my head plotting secret symphonies and pronouncing the unpronounced characters, words, visions, actions and inactions wrapped within generations of family. Noblesse oblige. Catch 22. Linguistic anarchy…

I decided to take a modicum of responsibility for my actions by calling my mother to let her know I'd be gone.

"Ma, it's Van."

"Van, what's going on? I've been trying to reach you, but your cell phone is off. What's going on with you and Shaillie?" She said in a panicky voice.

"Everything is fine."

"Please. I'm your mother. I know when something's up."

I shouldn't have called. "We're having some problems, but..."

"I'm coming over. She called me and told me you're going to Europe and the marriage is off. I'm coming over to talk some sense into you and get to the bottom of this."

"Where is she?" I asked.

"She didn't say, but she did say that you're running off to Europe and your writing some strange book and she's not marrying you and on and on. What are you doing to your life and since when did you want to be a writer?"

"Ma, calm down. I'm going to Europe for a trip. I don't know if the marriage is off, but I just need to get away. I wanted Shaillie to come, but..."

"She said you are moving to Europe indefinitely. What has gotten into you? Why all these changes? What exactly are you running from, Van?"

"I'm running to something, not from. Never mind. You're making too much of this."

"Van, Shaillie was hysterical! I'm not making too much of this. What have you done?"

I was very surprised to hear that about Shaillie. She was always in control and composed.

"I need to get away for a while. I wanted Shaillie to come, but she didn't want to. So, I'm going anyway. It's that simple."

"It's not that simple! Get away? What does that mean? Get away from what? Quitting your job. Leaving your fiancée. Oh my God, Van.

We need to get to the bottom of this. Why did you quit your job? Let's start there."

"It was a shitty job, Ma. I don't want to get into it and we've already talked about it ad nauseam."

"I'm sorry to say this, Van, but you've become very selfish lately. What do you expect from a job? Your grandfather drove a canteen and sold sandwiches and coffee. And now you're above working in a nice comfortable office downtown with a good salary and..."

I cut her off before she said the word *benefits*. I couldn't bear to hear that. "I know, I know. I'm making a big mistake and everything was on its way to a good life. We were building a nice nest egg and now the shell is broken and the yolk is running everywhere and I'm not half the man grandpa is. I know all that."

My mother sighed heavily. "The yolk what? What does all that mean?"

"Ma, you don't understand."

"Ever since dad died..."

"Jesus, Ma, don't go there. I'm tired of clichés. I'm just taking a trip for a change. A person is allowed a detour once in a while. This is my detour. I'm sorry if it's causing everyone problems. But Shaillie has to compromise too, and she's not. I'll call you next week."

"Van, I'm coming down to talk to you. You've lost all common sense. Wait for me."

I thought of the statue outside Chez Lucienne's and then told my mother, "No one will be here."

"Let's talk about the past, Van. I know there are some things you hold against me and your father. Let's stop pretending and get to the core of the problem. It's ok to talk about it."

"I hold nothing against you or him. This isn't about childhood. Everyone would like it to be, but it's not. Can't everyone just get over childhood? Not every answer is there. It's so damn trite, Ma!" I noticed I was yelling.

"Van, I know it was up and down and could have been more stable, but you can't blame..."

"I'm not blaming anyone. I just told you that. You're missing the point."

"Do you blame yourself?" she asked.

"For what?" I said incredulously.

"For the separations."

"Ma, you've been listening to Shaillie and Dr. Phil too much. Listen, it's larger than that, ok."

"What's larger?"

164

"I've got to go," I said. What an absolute mistake I'd made by calling her. I understood her concern, but it was too late. There was no turning back at this stage.

"What is it, Van? Just tell me. Tell your mother. Please."

"Ma, not everything has an answer. At least, not an easy one."

"What's that supposed to mean? Everything is so vague with you. "

"I don't think it requires an explanation. I'm feeling pretty damn clear. Sorry, but I have to go."

"Van, just relax. This is too much, too fast. Let me ask you this. Is there another woman?"

"No. I'm not dad. I've got to go. It's just a vacation. That's all."

"A vacation?" she shrieked. "Van, that's absurd. The timing is…"

"I'll call you from Europe in a week. Everything is going to be fine, Ma. I'm doing what needs to be done. Check on Shaillie for me, please. Don't worry. Love you. Really, it's all going to be fine in one way or another. I've got to go. Bye."

She was saying something as I hung up the phone.

I searched the house for a box that could hold nearly six hundred pages. It was almost as long as Koles's giant manuscript whose magnitude I'd always envied. Using some string from the storage closet, I tied the pages together vertically and horizontally. This wasn't enough protection. The pages would get too ruffled and frayed in my backpack. I thought about taking just the flash drive that I'd saved it on, but I wanted the pages. I need to see and feel them. I took some aluminum foil from the kitchen, unfurled a long strip of it on the table and wrapped the pages securely in several layers. I tucked the giant silver rectangle into my backpack. Next, I went to the bookshelf and took out a couple of novels that I'd been planning to read. One novel was by Vikram Seth and the other by Haruki Murakami. I purposely chose foreign authors. I stuffed the books in the remaining space in the backpack and slid my arms through the loops. I was out the door and didn't look back.

I stopped at Uncommon Grounds for a cup of coffee. I knew the owners, Krikor and Ani. They were long-time friends of my father. The old man loved this café because the food was so good and many of his friends hung out there. It reminded him of old times when he said, "life was slower and easier."

I left my bag out front so they wouldn't ask questions.

"Van, how are you?" Ani asked.

"Fine. How are you guys?"

"No complaints," Ani said. Krikor gave me a wave from the kitchen. "You look tired, Van. You ok?"

"I'll be fine after a coffee. Large black to go, Ani."

"Where you headed?" I could see Ani's eye peering beyond me. I turned back and noticed my backpack was very visible. "Yeah, ahh, Europe actually." I didn't want to say that, but no lie came to mind in time.

"You're not taking much."

"Just essentials."

"Where's Shaillie? She's going with you, right?"

"Yeah, of course." The lie came this time. I wanted this conversation to be short.

"That's nice," Krikor shouted from the kitchen. "We should get away, Ani."

"Sure, Krikor. Just need to iron a few details like three kids and a seven-day-a-week business."

"Well, we ought to do something," he said while whisking a giant silver bowl of eggs.

"We don't have Van's life, honey. He's doing things differently." Ani seemed clairvoyant.

"Which part of Europe?" Krikor said, sticking his head out of the opening where servers picked up orders.

"Paris."

"Well, you guys are pretty cool, jetting off to Paris so close to the wedding. A premature honeymoon, huh, Van?" Ani said, winking at me.

"Just a five-day trip. Anyway, I've got to run." I was desperate to get out of here. This was another mistake. It was time to get away from all that I knew.

"You know, Van, if you don't mind me saying this, your father would have loved a trip like this. I mean with you. He told me just before he passed that you guys were planning a trip to Armenia together."

"We talked about it. Made vague plans, but..."

"Yeah, I know. I miss him, Van. Always livened up the place. James had a great spirit."

I nodded. "That's true. Well, I've got to go. I don't want to miss the plane. Shaillie might leave without me," I joked.

"No, Van, Shaillie would never do that."

"No, she wouldn't," I agreed. "See you guys soon."

"Bon voyage," Krikor yelled as I headed out the door.

I got on the 71 bus heading into Harvard Square. For a moment I felt a surge of panic that my mother would go to the airport and try to stop me. Or Shaillie. Shit, I didn't want the drama. I also felt a tremendous desire to be walking by the Seine alone. I didn't want to

166

analyze the need. Just fulfill it. Neither Shaillie nor my mother knew what flight or airline. And I don't think I'd said which city in Europe. No, they wouldn't go. Shaillie wouldn't. Armenian mothers, on the other hand, were capable of anything when it came to their sons. Hopefully, I'd get on that plane without any theatre.

After quickly finishing the coffee, I stopped for a quick lunch at a small diner on Church Street in Harvard Square. It was no frills—a counter with spinning vinyl stools springing up from the floor like giant mushrooms, a few booths, and a menu with choices like BLTs, burgers, sandwiches and soups for lunch. I sat on one of the stools observing the cook slash his spatula into a large piece of lard, slicing off a white mass of fat, and slapping it on the griddle. It sizzled instantly and the cook started plopping egg after egg into the sizzle. Good ole fashioned, dam-the-arteries American food. This was Lee's Diner and it had a 1950s vibe to it. It was instant nostalgia. It had been around so long that the old man and I used to eat breakfast here after many of our river walks.

I ordered a turkey sandwich, chips, big deli pickle, and another cup of coffee. I was going to ride caffeine until I sat on the plane. The food came quickly. As I took my first bite into the sandwich, I felt hands grabbing the back of my shoulders and squeezing my trapezius muscles. A knee went into my spine and pushed my lower back forward. I snapped into good posture. Who the hell could this be, I wondered, gulping down the unchewed bite of my sandwich.

"Straighten up and relax, Van. You'd think after last night you'd be as loose as change. Not me, of course, but you should be."

"The stress returns too quickly, my friend," I responded, knowing instantly who it was.

"It shouldn't. Blame it on modernity."

"That's as good a crutch as any, Gil."

He finally let go of my shoulders. I felt a moment of muscular relief. My trapeziuses were like old coiled springs ready to snap. Gil's brief squeezing uncoiled the springs. My shoulders lowered and neck relaxed. Twelve hours removed from the erotic massage and I was as tight as a virgin again. Gil sat down next to me at the counter. I always thought Gil looked much older than his twenty-eight years, but I had never seen him in the morning light. Certainly, last night didn't help matters, but he looked more like forty-eight to me. His blond hair was dramatically receding and thinning on top. The King Tut beard was graying. Deep laugh lines and splintering crow's-feet forming. Perhaps, he was just exhausted, but that wouldn't account for the wrinkles and hair loss. His aging process seemed to have been accelerated.

"Did you sleep?" I asked.

"Almost nothing."

Gilworthy ordered breakfast. Two eggs, bacon, potatoes, toast, coffee—the works. I saw the cook slice another chunk of lard for the griddle.

"Van, I haven't had one of these breakfasts in ages. Grew up on them as a kid. My mother used to cook a big breakfast everyday. How 'bout you? You grow up with the big, indulgent American breakfast?"

"On weekends, but my old man usually did breakfast."

"Not in my house. Had the stereotype 50s household in the 80s."

"Me, too. The breakfast thing was aberration. Besides, my mother had to clean the mess the old man made."

The waitress poured Gilworthy a cup of coffee and refilled mine. Gilworthy popped open two little creamers and poured a lot of sugar into his coffee. I thought back to Gil's desperation and tears last night. I grinned at him and he seemed to know what I was thinking.

"Don't go there, Van. Please."

"I wasn't, Gil."

Gil seemed suddenly sheepish. He was focusing on stirring his coffee.

"Really, Gil it's cool. It wasn't..."

"Look I know I made a fool of myself. Don't we all sometimes? It's ok to be human once in a while, right? Gil said, still staring at his coffee as the spoon went round and round.

"Sure, Gil. It's fine, really."

"Thanks, Van." Gil said quietly, finally putting the spoon down and sipping his coffee.

"So, did you meet up with the Thai waitress after all?" I asked, attempting to lighten him up.

He nodded.

"Wow, at four in the morning no less. That's a miracle for a first date. She must be really into you. What happened?"

Gil put his coffee down and all his embarrassment seemed to have vanished.

"Van, my God, she's amazing. We met for coffee, talked, a little innocent kissing by the river at sunrise. It was perfect. I'm going to see her again. I really liked talking to her. It was so easy. Fuck the sex. I realize all I want is companionship."

I nodded unconvincingly.

"Honestly, companionship first, sex after. We're getting to know each other. I want to know her well, be friends first. Add sex after. Every woman I've ever been with, Van, started out with sex and then we got to know each other. None of them ever worked. Pretty damn good data to work with."

"That's quite a switch from last night."

168

"Yeah, last night was, I don't know. Last night was a watershed moment. Epiphanic even. I cut through a lot of bullshit I'd layered around me. Melted a lot of armor. I'm going to finish the film…"

"No way!"

"It's time to let go. I'll give it to Bishop, let him get production going on whatever part he chooses and move on to something else. Focus on building a life with Wiranya."

"All good, Gil. I'm shocked, but impressed."

"It's time, Van. Time to make changes."

"Yes, Gil. You're right."

"Van, I'm changing skins. Last night changed me, man. Goddamn drugs and booze. Damn Thai massages. I'm done. I'm all done. I had the best time with this woman. I laid my cards on the table with her. Not everything because that would have scared anyone off, but she listened. She's the real deal, Van. The energy between us was all confluence. You know what I mean?"

"Yes, Gil. I do."

"I'm going to marry this woman."

My eyes widened. "Gil, wow! You're really leaping ahead."

"Van, I'm a new man. I'm done with all artificial stimulants. I'm really going to finish the film, quit drugs. To hell with Macronesia and its infinite path. It's time to accept things as finite."

"But, Gil, last night…"

Gilworthy furrowed his brow, clearly annoyed at me. "Yeah, yeah, I know, Van. I can't change overnight. Right?"

"Sure, Gil, yeah, you can. Change doesn't have a time requirement."

Gilworthy took a big sip of coffee as the waitress put a plate of food in front of him.

"Enjoy," she said, curtly and without a smile.

"Of course, one needs time, but this evolution has been simmering inside for a while, Van. I just didn't realize it. Last night simply brought it all together." Gil broke the yolks of his eggs, methodically smothering the running yellow all over the white of the eggs. He took a bite of the eggs, then added salt, and consumed both eggs in seconds.

Gil continued, "Confluence, Van. It all came together. Koles was mocking me, but I knew something was out there, something was pulling me. I could feel an altered flow in the universe. We can all have a Jesus-moment sometimes, right? Last night was my night. I thought it was Kate, but it wasn't. It was this beautiful Thai woman. It was Wiranya. Can you believe it, Van? I get a Thai massage from a Korean and meet a Thai woman right after. How's that for irony?"

169

"Damn good irony."

"Van, she's a doll. Works as a waitress during the day and is studying Public Policy at night at UMass. She wants to return to Thailand and work in health care there. And you know what, Van? You know what the most amazing thing is? You won't believe this."

"What?"

"You can't tell anybody, especially not her. Don't let her know that you know."

"Ok, ok, Gil, just tell me."

"She's a virgin, Van. A virgin from Bangkok."

I shook my head. "Gil, you're going to be her first. Are you ready for that? Or better yet, is she ready for that?"

"I am. I'll be her first and she'll be my last. We can't have sex until marriage."

"She told you that already?"

"Yes, she doesn't believe in premarital sex."

"Does she know how many women you've slept with?"

"More or less. She's got an open mind. Van, everything changed last night, this morning whenever it was…we talked for hours. It was…forget it. Words are an injustice." While talking, Gilworthy was eating ravenously, chasing everything down with big gulps of coffee.

"Is the feeling mutual?" I asked.

He put his thumb up, chewing quickly.

"Slow down, Gil. No rush." He kept his thumb raised until he swallowed and responded.

"We kissed. She said she doesn't kiss until at least five dates. She's kissed only one other guy in her life. Listen, Van, don't leave Shaillie. My whole life has been about displacement and being alone. When you find your other half, it changes everything."

"I'll remember that, Gil." Considering Gil's tears and behavior last night, his saccharine Hallmark advice wasn't out of character. But prior to last night, I'd always seen him as the loner artist, wild filmmaker out to remake the world one eon at a time. I'd never thought he was just another lonely, lonely man.

"The cliché is true, Van. Words to live by."

I ate my sandwich while Gil finished his breakfast. He continued going on and on about his new Thai love and finding truth about himself. He said he was going to quit taking care of Oswald Geary. He was going to get a real job, sell real estate or something, work on the film on the side, get things in proper perspective and on and on he went. I tuned him out after a while and kept reminding myself of one thing. It was time for me to leave. I put twenty dollars down on the counter, wished him luck, and told him breakfast was on me. Gilworthy

170

apologized for babbling on too much about himself. I told him that I was very happy for him and as I headed for the door, he tried to say something to me, but I interrupted him and said, *"Vaia con dios, Calvin."* Then, I left Lee's Diner.

I walked up Church Street passing the cinema. A reissue of Jack Nicholson's *The Passenger* was playing. Synchrony struck again. I had seen it once, a long time ago. I remembered Nicholson's character steals the identity of a dead man in order to start a new life in Europe. There he meets Maria Schneider. I had rented the movie after seeing *Last Tango in Paris* because I'd fallen hard for Maria Schneider. I stood under the marquee thinking various thoughts—how Bishop loved *Last Tango*, the bath scene where Brando sponge bathes Schneider's beautiful naked body, and the coincidence of *The Passenger's* plot to my escape. Gil was right. It's all about confluence.

"Would you like a ticket, sir?" I heard a voice say jarring me out of reverie.

"Huh?"

"The Passenger starts in two minutes," a man behind the window said.

"How long is the movie?"

"119 minutes," he replied quickly.

I probably had enough time, but it would be cutting it close.

"No, I'll pass. Got a plane to catch," I confessed unnecessarily.

"Where you headed?"

"Europe."

He smiled. "Same place as the guy in the movie. Drops everything and starts over in Europe."

I walked away towards Mass Ave. and the T station. I could hear movie-ticket man shout, "Have a good trip," but I didn't turn back.

I took the subway to the airport and arrived about a half hour ahead of schedule. I checked my cell for messages and saw one. Perhaps, it was Koles. I was hoping everything went well with Sinitrau and they didn't get into trouble. From what I knew of Aldenna Sinitrau, trouble was a distinct possibility.

It wasn't Koles. It was my mother.

"Van, I stopped by the house. Where are you? I'm at Uncommon Grounds. Ani said you were going to Paris with Shaillie. What's going on? This is crazy. Shaillie told me you were going alone and so did you. Now, I hear you two are going. I tried calling Shaillie, but she's not answering. I'm very confused. Call me, please."

I deleted the message. There was no point in trying to explain my plan to my mother. We would be speaking different languages.

I realized that I'd forgotten about one thing—money. I went to an ATM and withdrew as much as I could, six hundred dollars. I had credit cards to cover me for a while. I would deal with all of that later. What I really wanted to do was give Shaillie everything except what I absolutely needed. I'd find some cheap room somewhere, give some English lessons when needed, and just survive within an entirely new momentum that didn't include money. One might say it was too idealistic, but I felt it wasn't idealistic enough. It was still compromising.

I sat down at the entrance of Terminal E where all the international flights departed. I wished I could speed up time. I called Koles on his cell, but it went straight to voicemail. His phone was off. I left a message telling him to call me right away and let me know what was going on.

I took a deep breath and closed my eyes. More sleep would have been beneficial, but my mind was racing again. The energy of the airport, of escape and change, was too much while thoughts were seesawing to and from euphoria and dysphoria with bipolar velocity. I couldn't find a middle ground. This was the right thing to do. This wasn't a colossal error for which I'd pay the price for a long time to come. My head felt like a figure skater in the middle of those wildly fast corkscrew twirls. My nerve endings seemed to be making mad dashes at my skin as if my spinal cord had become an enormous Fourth of July sparkler.

I went to the bathroom. I looked in the mirror and noticed the dark half moons hanging heavily under my eyes. The few hours of sleep at the cemetery and by the river had helped, but I needed bear-like hibernation at this point. The drugs and booze and freakish location probably negated those hours of any true benefit. I was working on several months of steady insomnia whose mental impact had to be significant. Sleep was one of the three necessities of existence. I was trying to survive while missing thirty-three percent of life's absolute needs.

Above the dark circles, things didn't improve much. My eyes were glassy and bloodshot. Squiggly little streams of blood mapped the whites of my eyes. I rubbed my eyes with the back of my hands and ran my index fingers across the dark circles as if I could wipe them away. While doing so, I noticed my right hand was shaking. I opened up my bag and took out the bathroom stuff I'd packed in a little black shaving bag given by Shaillie on our first Christmas living together. I'd used it on every trip since. I took out some eye drops and squeezed out a couple into each eye. I closed my eyes hard, pressing the lids as tightly together as possible. I rubbed the closed lids with my fingertips and massaged them thinking this would spread the benefits of the medicine. Untrue tears edged out of the corners of each eye.

With my eyes still closed, I looked at the silver black kaleidoscope glittering in the cinema behind my lids. I had a sudden urge to find a dictionary and look up the words insomnia and subconscious. I wanted to see the precise meanings given by whoever gives meaning. I splashed cold water onto my face. It made me feel a little better. A little calmer. The anarchy in my head seemed a bit more regulated.

I went into a bookstore and found a Webster's Dictionary. I looked at the first few pages to see who was in charge of meaning. Anne H. Soukhanov was the Senior Editor. Howard Webber was the publisher. There were others though. Any good conspiracy has others.

Insomnia: Chronic inability to sleep: Sleeplessness.

No help there. No insight. I glided down to nearby words.

Insouciant: Cheerfully nonchalant.

I liked that word. I wanted to be that word.

Insolvent: Unable to meet debts or discharge liabilities: Bankrupt. One who is insolvent.

I thought of an elementary school-style spelling exercise. Insomnia has removed the insouciant-state of one's mind and may leave one insolvent down the road.

Why hadn't Koles called?

I jumped to the letter S.

Subconscious: Occurring without conscious perception on the part of the individual. Not wholly conscious.

Thanks, Anne H. Soukhanov.

I sat down waiting for Koles. Where the hell was he? It was getting late. We needed to check in. I felt a little twitching in my face above the right side of the mouth. It felt like a spasm. Maybe, I was developing a facial tick at this precise moment that would last the rest of my life. Jesus, was I living the script of a Woody Allen film? If that happened, everything else, all this unbearable lightness of being bullshit would slide into oblivion and I'd just want to erase the tick in order to find peace. Of course, if the tick ever got eradicated, I'd be right back in the unbearable lightness of being bullshit vortex.

The twitch wouldn't go away. There was no history of ticks in my family, at least from grandfather on down. Maybe it was Bell's Palsy. I went back to the bookstore. On the way I stopped at a mirror to see this tick. I couldn't see anything, but I clearly felt it. Something was twitching internally. It wasn't my imagination. I felt it between my nose and mouth. I believe Bell's Palsy leaves its victim temporarily disfigured.

173

I went back to Anne Soukhanov for answers.

Bell's Palsy: [After Sir Charles Bell (1774-1842)] A suddenly occurring unilateral facial paralysis of unknown etiology, presumed to be caused by virally induced swelling of the seventh nerve.

Everything seemed to be related to seven. Great, it occurred suddenly and had no known origin. Complete mercy of the Gods. No wonder religion persists. My cell phone rang. It was Koles.

"You got seven hundred bucks on you?" he asked.

"No."

"Where are you?"

"In the bookstore at the airport."

"Get over to Lufthansa. I'm in line to get boarding passes. You have to be here."

"I'll be right there."

Koles looked at my one bag. "Good. You're traveling light like me. We're going to be moving around a bit."

"Why's that? I thought we were going straight to Paris."

"Milan first, my friend."

Koles seemed upbeat, unusually happy.

"What for?"

"We're going to meet a friend of mine. It'll help us with finances. He's got a job for us."

I asked Koles if this came out of his meeting with Sinitrau this morning. He told me Sinitrau was a lost cause. She had devised a plan to steal money from one of her furniture clients. Something about learning the combination to a private safe, but this would require weeks to pull off. Moreover, Koles said he didn't have thievery in his blood. So he'd come up with a plan B.

I immediately told him, "I am not interested in making any money and why did you ask me about the seven hundred dollars?"

"For an investment with this Italian friend."

"I'm not investing in anything. This trip isn't about investments for me. If anything, it's divestment."

"It's fast money. We can triple it quickly. I don't know all the details, but it's got legs. This guy's in the game. He knows business, money. We don't know it. We just need it."

"Derek, I've been earning and saving for years now. I'm not going to Europe to get involved in schemes for money. You go 'head and do it. If you need some money, I'll give you some, but I want no involvement. Pay me back whenever you can."

174

"Thanks, Van. I need money. I know you don't or you don't care about it, but I haven't been toeing the line like you. I've got very little. Babysitting Oswald wasn't exactly a windfall. I'll be damned if I'm returning to Yvette with nothing. My financial ineptitude was part of our problem. I'm not playing down-and-out artist anymore. Yvette's done with that."

I nodded, "We're here for different reasons," I said. "Very different."

"Then, you just come for the ride. We fly into Milan and then my friend will drive us to Paris."

I thought of Bishop lamenting how money and marriage were so sadly interwoven together. I thought of Bishop calling the dollar the true whore of whores.

After getting our tickets and seat assignments, we walked to the gate and sat down. Koles got a coffee and I got a liter of spring water. I wanted to cleanse my system. I thought about drinking nothing but water for twenty-four hours. Start the European experience with ablution.

A family of four sat down across from us. The father had a little girl in a frontal backpack. She was sleeping. Her head slowly slipped to the side, so that it was hanging uncomfortably. The father cupped her small head in his large hands and leaned it against his chest. He slid down in his seat in order to make his chest less vertical, creating a makeshift bed for his daughter. The baby's head now rested comfortably. She looked peaceful and beautiful. The mother was playing cards with the older child, a boy, who seemed about five years old. I didn't recognize the game. I think the boy was making it up as they went along. He never lost a hand. They played on a magazine on the mother's lap. The father was reading now and the baby was hidden behind the newspaper. He was reading the sports page, but occasionally poking his head out from behind the paper and laughing at what was clearly a spontaneously conceived card game by his son. He laughed heartily as his wife lost every hand and pretended that she was really losing.

"Do you want to hear plan B?" Koles asked.

I didn't say anything. I was still watching the family. "Van."

"Van!" Koles yelled, nudging my shoulder.

"Yeah, hmmm, what?"

"Plan B."

"Go ahead."

"I'm thinking of how I can survive in Paris. You know, I might need time to get Yvette back. She may need time to change her mind. Might not be an instant fix. Can't rebuild Rome in a day. I may have to prove myself, but it will happen. I feel it deep inside. In the meantime, I'm not going to edit my book. Screw Bishop. I'm done with it. Third

175

person and that's it. I left it at his house. He can do what he wants with it, but I'm done. If I have to wait out Yvette, I'm not going to write some forlorn ex-pat novel of loss and redemption along the quays of the Seine. I already did that. Once was enough."

I nodded, half listening to Koles, half observing the family.

"Everything is riding on this. Maybe, I should have called her, but she'd probably be nervous and tell me not to come. I think the surprise will be good. Anyway, you want to know plan B."

"Sure," I said continuing to watch the family across from us. The boy was playing cards with the father now and the mother was giving a bottle to the little girl. He still kept winning every hand and the father acted shocked at every loss.

"It's all about sandals, Van."

"Scandals?"

"No, sandals. One word for you, Van." Koles leaned over and whispered, "Sandals."

"Don't you mean, "plastic?"

"New generation, Van. Times are a-changin'."

"To footwear?" I asked, still watching the family.

Koles laughed. "Yes, my friend, footwear."

Koles then began a discourse on the sandals plan. I didn't listen to the beginning. Beginnings essentially mean nothing anyway. It's just after the beginning that the wheels spin some form of veritable significance. As I didn't listen, I thought about not knowing anything in life before it happens. Having no practice, no rehearsals. It had to be an ancient theme in art. Kundera, I recalled, pontificated on it in one of his philosophical texts disguised as novels. No practice. No rehearsal. Just dive into everything. How utterly beautiful it was that we had no file for life. That we simply didn't know anything until it was presented. There was real beauty in not knowing. I had no idea what would happen in Europe, no idea who I'd meet on this plane. Life had an intoxicating and self-effacing beauty to it that I wanted to see and feel and live, activating all the senses into new realities while embracing the beauty of eternal unknowns.

I picked up Koles midstream.

"Wait 'til you meet Rennero Dellagni. He's got a touch of madness. He is all wound-up, wired, going non-stop. He's Bishop gone bourgeois to the core. He's got this vibrato Beat energy of its pure early days. He's hard to characterize because he's all contradiction. You'll see him in action. I don't need to prejudice you. Bottom line, he's worth the price of admission. A money-hungry, whore-loving, travel monster. He's been everywhere and the beauty of it is he hasn't got one single artistic bone in his body. He lives life for the sake of living, not for the sake of creativity. It's honest. Simultaneously, he's a neurotic case study desperate for therapy, but I hope he doesn't go. If he gets centered, all the fun will be gone. Centered, at- peace folk are so fucking boring."

Koles took a deep breath.

"There's no point in being in the center, right, Van?"

"Mediocrity is in the center," I said, wondering if I missed the whole sandals plan.

"Nothing eternal comes out of the center," Koles added.

Koles still wanted me to take part in his plan. I humored him and let him give me some details. First, he gave me a little background on Rennero and then went into the sandals plan. He and Rennero had met in Europe and were good friends back in his ex-pat days. Rennero visited Koles and Yvette every couple of months in Paris. He always had a new girlfriend with him and always bitched about his job. When Yvette and Koles lived their stint in America, Rennero visited every year. He loved America and would do anything for a green card.

Rennero's last job had been for an Italian company in Dubai. He went to Dubai for a six-month training and got fired after two weeks. While this was a bit briefer than usual, Rennero could never hold a job. He usually blamed the end of a job on his boss being gay and hitting on him too much or the boss's incompetence and jealousy over Rennero's production. Another target of Rennero's frustration was the entire Italian system, which was "bogged down in the bullshit of bureaucracy."

About a month after his most recent failure in Dubai, he told Koles he was going to sue the company for wrongful termination. He believed he could get something like two hundred thousand Euros if he won. He would take the money and represent his own line in a sandal company. This time he'd be his own boss. All he had to do was deal with a distributor and the buyers. He'd be the glorious middle man, who does little work and makes big money.

After turning down Sinitrau's theft idea, Koles called Rennero to check on the lawsuit and let him know he was on his way to Europe. Rennero said they had settled out of court for one hundred and fifty thousand Euros. He wanted Koles to be his distributor in France because he spoke the language. Rennero said to fly into Milan and he'd drive us up to Paris. He was happy Koles was going to get a real job and make some money instead of wiping some old guy's ass in order to be a writer. Rennero never understood the concept of being an artist, of "making things up" as a job anyway. He always gave Koles a hard time about artists. Rennero was also a big believer in Yvette and Koles as a couple. He thought they had true love and the writing life got in the way. Koles was very happy to hear someone echo his hopes.

"So, Van, that is why we're going to Milan."

"At this point, Derek, I don't really care where we go. I just want to go."

I unzipped my backpack and made sure I had *Insomnia Journal* with me. For a moment I thought I'd left it at home. I reached into the bag, feeling under the clothes for the smooth surface of aluminum foil. It was there.

Meanwhile, Koles called Rennero and gave him our flight information. So Derek Koles would be a sandals salesman. I was shocked. Koles was originally going to Europe to recapture the muse and create a new novel. New art. New creativity. The great bohemian prophet of Bishop's drunken rhapsodies turned into a lovesick salesman. As for me I was just along for the ride. My own private detour with a surrealistic novel that would rest peacefully on a shelf someday. But Koles was a real writer. He'd had a novel published and other assorted poems and narrative pieces. He had a voice, an outlet to the world and access to his own and now he was going to sell sandals! I always viewed Koles as a true artist, an honest seeker of truth. One who purely swore to follow art for art's sake. Instead, he was switching allegiance to Willy Loman. For that matter, so was Gilworthy. Both were dropping all their aesthetic dreams for women while I was dropping the woman for aesthetic obsessions. Worlds (and words) were turning upside down.

"It's all set. He'll be there," Koles said.

I nodded, refocusing on the family across from us.

"Van, you've got to be prepared for the Rennero experience. His English is pretty good, but he's got a thick Italian accent and every other word out of his mouth is profanity. Just give it back to him. He likes to test people. Push them for a reaction, some sort of Dale Carnegie, Donald Trump bullshit."

"Which is why he keeps getting fired, I presume."

"Probably so. He's got a good heart underneath the excess, though. He's ok." Koles seemed to be convincing himself more than me.

"Derek, I'm surprised." I wasn't too interested in anything else to do with Rennero.

"What about?"

"I don't get it. You're switching gears all of a sudden in everything."

"Like returning to Yvette? It's always been about her."

"Well, yeah, that's fine. I'm pulling for you. I know you love her and I hope it works."

"Then what? Selling sandals is a problem?" I saw a sudden strange look in Koles's eyes. An angry glare at me as if he were backed into a corner and under attack.

"It's a strange departure. You know, Derek, I got to say it's a bit depressing."

"Why? 'Cause you're holding me up to some bullshit artistic standard?" His voice was louder, angrier.

"Not in the trite way you say it."

"It's bullshit. All of it. Fucking bullshit, Van. What the hell do you know about it? What do you know about anything?" he snarled, his mood instantly upside-down.

"Take it easy. What's up your ass all of a sudden?"

"Don't preach to me, Van," Koles said with teeth-grinding seriousness.

"What about Bishop? What about the show? I mean, a couple days ago. Was it a couple days? Maybe it was last night. Time is out of whack among other things," I said, staring into Koles's feral vision.

"You're out of line, Van."

"Out of line? What the hell does that mean?" I had no idea why he was angry all of a sudden. How well did I know Derek Koles?

"Fuck it all, Van. You made your bed, now don't be a pussy and be afraid to sleep in it. Come on, Armenians have bigger balls than the raisins you're starting to show."

I noticed the family stirring across from us.

"Sorry. We'll be quiet," I said to them. "I apologize."

The little boy's eyes were wide and he was staring at Koles, who seemed to take no notice. I'd seen Koles moody before, but it was usually soaked in passive-aggressive silence, not vengeance.

"Derek, keep your damn voice down," I reminded him in a loud whisper, but I could feel rage irreversibly flowing in his veins.

"All I'm saying, Derek, is that Bishop inspired you to go back to Europe and get a grip on your book. You agreed. Now you are going back to the soil of your first novel and you're going to sell sandals. It doesn't make sense. It's ridiculous."

He glared into my eyes and in a growling whisper said, "Don't push me, Van."

"Push you where, Derek?" His irrational anger was starting to piss me off. "Balls like raisins" stuck in my craw.

After some heavy silence Koles said, "Look, Van, call it a Rimbaud move. I'm giving up art to make money. He ran guns in Africa. Me, I'm a sandal rep. It's a different era." He laughed and the anger seemed to vanish as quickly as it came. He was suddenly talking calmly, "Rimbaud gets the edge by a landslide in romantic notions and

179

adventure. Guns are a lot edgier than flip-flops. Sometimes a great notion, my great friend. It's a long story. A big, giant short story. Leaving art to sell sandals." Koles laughed heartily. "It's been a long path to find my niche. Now, I've got it. I'm a sandal rep and that's why I'm on the planet. Call it open-toed wisdom."

I wasn't sure if I should laugh or call an institute for neurological study. "And that's it? Done with writing?" I asked incredulously.

"Who's to say anything at anytime anywhere?"

"I'm not sure how to respond to that."

"Look, Van, you want to know the truth? You want to know the tragicomic truth of Yvette and me?"

"Sure, Derek. Everyone seems to have the truth today. I saw Gil…"

"I don't want to talk about Gil," Koles said harshly.

"Fine. Tell me your truth."

He nodded and didn't say anything for a while. I sat quietly, too. I waited for him to begin, but he never did. We didn't talk again while waiting for the plane. I watched the family and I wasn't sure what Koles was watching or thinking.

We finally boarded the plane. We had two seats next to each other. He took the window seat and I took the aisle. I looked at the phone buried in the back of the seat in front of me and thought for a moment about calling Shaillie.

I didn't.

Consciousness was very brief on the flight. I remember ordering a glass of red wine and drinking it quickly. I remember seeing the family of four sitting on the other side of the plane about ten rows ahead of us, happy they were away from us. I remember putting my seat back and feeling myself slide down the slope of deep sleep. So deep that I didn't wake up until Koles nudged me and said, "Van, we're landing. We're in Milan."

PART IV
THE FORCES OF HISTORY

It took a long time to get through Customs. The line was interminable and the stereotype of the slow motion, apathetic Italian bureaucrat held its weight. It seemed like our Customs agent needed a break after checking every third passport or so. When it was finally our turn, I noticed the pale imprint of a wedding band on his ring finger. His dark, Mediterranean skin made the former presence of a ring all the more very obvious. Observing his flirtatious manner made me wonder if the ring was taken off while at work in an inept attempt to appear single.

Before realizing this, I had watched a group of four young, attractive British women in line ahead of us. Naturally, it took an inordinate amount of time to check their passports. Questions, chatter and smiles aplenty. Couldn't say I blamed him if he, in fact, had been truly single. A pretty woman was probably the only adrenal jolt he received all day at his numbing job of checking passport after passport in the dimly lit, dull-gray coloring of Immigration. He was stuck in a tiny booth while every one was in international motion. Milan evoked images of a hip, swank crowd, *haute couture*, and epicurean sophistication. His life did not.

When we finally made it, Koles went first. Agent Italian smirked at Koles. He stood up and craned his neck to look out of the sliding glass window. He seemed to be checking Koles's shoes. He sat back down and asked Koles his purpose in Italy. Koles told him he was here to travel Europe, starting in Milan. He asked Koles a few more standard questions and then motioned for him to pass through. Next, I gave him my passport and he observed my previous European stamps from the trip with Shaillie before the borders had disappeared. We had stamps from at least a dozen countries.

"You return to Europe?" he asked in a heavy accent.

"Yes," I said looking at the invisible ring. I had an immediate and surprisingly intense contempt for him. His infidelity bothered me. Or, was it his foolish and pathetic attempt to hide his marriage? He all but had the ring on. Didn't he recognize the tan line? Perhaps, I was simply bothered by my actions last night, or my runaway escapist actions right now, or the echoes of my own anesthetic cubicle job. Agent Italian most likely became a convenient projection deflecting anger and past frustrations from its true target, but who can follow the twisting convolutions of the origins of raw emotions? Psychology was so sadly lost in mazes.

"What for?" he asked, following my vision down to his left hand.

I was all set to say "travel," sustain a few more standard questions—the length of stay, my job in America, and so on and then be on way. However, travel didn't come out. Instead, I blurted the first word that came to my mind like it was a Rorschach test.

"Ontological reasons," I said pretentiously.

"Eh?" He muttered, clearly puzzled. "Onto-what reason?" He asked as he slid his ring finger between his right hand's thumb and index finger, spinning the ring that didn't exist. I laughed at this ridiculous action. He quickly shifted his attempt at spinning the invisible ring to massaging his left hand as if this had been his intention all along.

He glared at me. "Now, tell me again, what you say," he said, sternly.

"Ontological," I stubbornly repeated.

"No. No good answer. Explain this. Another reason." He was shaking his head, frustration forming in his expression.

"Ok," I responded. I shut my eyes and tried to erase my thoughts. Let the first word pop out again..."Edification. I'm here for personal edification." I said, surprising myself at expressing what I perceived to be the truth, more or less.

I saw Koles's head drop down into open palms as he stood waiting for me.

"What?" Agent man said, clearly disturbed.

"Edification," I repeated.

"*Edificazione?*"

"Sounds right."

He scrunched up his face in pure perplexity.

"That is new one. Never listen this reason."

I decided to ride out my Rorschach spontaneity. "It's the truth. I'm really here to edify as ridiculous as it sounds."

"What do you build?"

"Myself," I said, noticing Koles shaking his head, disgusted with my behavior.

"*Non fa senso*. You waste time. Play games with me?"

"No, I'm not playing games."

"Why do you come in Italy?"

I looked over at Koles. He mouthed the word, "please."

"Travel," I relented.

Agent Italian hesitated. Then he said, "I don't like you."

I nodded, expressing the acceptance of his dislike. I thought of saying *likewise*, but I cut the candor off at that point.

"You fortunate I no mood for this. No time now or I make you life very difficult. *Molto difficile, capisce!*" He stamped my passport with a loud bang as if the metal ink stamp were a judge's gavel. He was getting order in his court. Koles told me I was very lucky. He pointed behind me as we exited. A very attractive woman was right behind me. Agent man had his duties.

Koles chided me for playing around with a Customs agent. He said that Immigration is beyond the law. They could do whatever the hell they pleased, whenever the hell they wanted. He'd had some trouble with Yvette at U.S. Immigration early in their relationship before they were married and all of Yvette's papers were finalized. Koles told the female agent who was mistreating them at the Canadian border that she couldn't do whatever she wanted. They had rights and there were laws, he reminded her. She responded that if she so pleased she could strip-search his girlfriend "at her leisure and pleasure." Koles whispered to me, "Don't ever fuck with Customs. They hate their jobs and they'll take it out on you."

I reminded Koles that I was just telling the truth. What the hell was so bad about traveling for the purpose of edification? If someone told me that they were pursuing intellectual and spiritual enlightenment, I'd be impressed. Koles disagreed. "No, Van, you'd laugh."

He was probably right, but that is wrong.

Upon entering the arrivals section of the airport, Koles immediately spotted Rennero. He walked ahead of me to greet him. Rennero had wildly wavy hair that rose about six inches above his head. It was a disheveled heap of hair that diametrically contrasted Koles's nearly shorn skull. It didn't seem authentically messy, but rather intentionally done to look Milanese cool and youthful. He had a three-day beard and as he smiled, I noticed his teeth were grimy brown, the color of a polluted river. His accent was indeed thick and his voice was cigarette saturated.

"Goddamn *Americano* arrives in Milano. The son of bitch is here," he said laughing and then hugging Koles, giving him two kisses, Italian style.

He looked at me. "Yeah, Koles taught me some real good English. English as a second fucking language from *Signor autore.*"

"That's all you wanted to learn," Koles said.

"Bullshit, I was a serious student." He looked at me again. "Rennero Dellagni. *Un piacere.* A pleasure to meet you."

"Likewise. I'm Van." We shook hands. I was fairly well rested from the long transatlantic sleep, but I wasn't sure I had the energy to deal with this bombastic Italian.

"How was the flight, *testa di cazzo?*"

"Van slept the entire time. I got a few hours, some bad food. The usual. Can't complain."

I noticed all the anger in Koles's voice and eyes from back at Logan was gone as if it had never happened. A few images of an angry Koles at Chez Lucienne came to my mind. It always seemed to appear suddenly and without adequate cause, but it also seemed to disappear quickly.

"Let's get a café and we'll, how do you say, cut across the chase?"

"Cut to the chase," Koles corrected.

"Yes, *si, professore.* We'll cut to the chase and I'll tell you the plan."

We walked over to an airport café. There was a crowd of men drinking beer standing around a table, smoking and talking loudly in a British or Scottish accent. We all ordered espressos. Rennero lit a cigarette after drinking his café in one sip. "Once I heard you guys coming in, I called my *contatto* in Paris. We have a meeting this afternoon in Paris at four o'clock. That doesn't leave us many time, but we should make it."

"You always have to time things so tightly, *Cazzone*. You love pressure, stacking everything with no room for error," Koles said.

"Carpe diem. That's the way to live, right?"

"It's not carpe diem. It's pure neurosis. You're always in a rush. If you were sick in the hospital, you'd be in a rush to die. Just get whatever is at hand done, and move to the next thing. In this case, the afterlife. Let me in God, I'm here to check out this damn place. I've heard all about it. Let's see what you've got behind the clouds, *Dio*. Open the goddamn gates!"

"He won't let me in if I scream open the goddamn gates!" Rennero laughed loudly at this. "Doesn't matter though. I'm going the other way. I've got a spot in *inferno*. The devil's waiting for me. We got a deal already in place." He winked at me.

"The flames await you," Koles said.

"Us, *amico mio*. You've got a spot next to me. And you, Van, will you be joining us in hell?"

"Probably," I answered.

He looked at Koles. "But you're seeing it all wrong, *professore*. Maybe, I'd be in a rush to get better rather than die. Why'd you pick the direction of death?"

184

"Why not death? It's a legitimate direction. The only true one, guaranteed."

"Derek don't get all dark on us. Life is beautiful like the movie said." Rennero looked at me. "But I don't disagree with the *professore*. I'm neurotic. I like broken-ass Derek here because he's good contrast to me. He's pretty calm most of the time. Holds back too much though. A little *represso* for my taste, but he's got that edge like all artists. You know, I like artists. They're good sideshow for businessmen like me. It's like having the circus traveling around with you. So you are an artist? Are you a member of the circus?" Rennero asked. He spoke rapidly like he was in a rush to finish each sentence so he could quickly start the next.

"Not me," I answered, glancing at my backpack that I'd placed on the chair next to me.

"An artist, a businessman, and so what are you, Van?"

"What am I?" I asked back, surprised at the question. Certainly, it was second language phrasing, but I didn't think I'd ever been asked that except when it was about my ethnic background and Rennero wasn't asking this. I'd thought about it many times and presumed every one on the planet considered the question in the conversations we have in our heads. It's the eternal question, the ultimate quest. The secular holy grail of the individual. Thoughts were rolling heavy and weighty. Perhaps, it was being in Europe. I'd always had a delusional glorification of Europe, viewing it as above the pursuit of money, more philosophical, the birthplace of existentialism, Sartre, enlightenment, renaissance, café life, Picasso, Surrealism...

"What are you? You know, what do you do?" Rennero asked again, snapping me out of my Euro-daze.

I hesitated. "Hmm, tough question. I'll get back to you on that."

Koles said while laughing, "Van is here for edification."

"*Edificazione*? What the hell do you want to edify," Rennero asked incredulously. "Are you a builder? Engineer? What do you build?"

I wished I had said travel back at Customs. Koles was right. It isn't something you articulate, but I tried. "I'm going to read, take in culture, study philosophy for a while." I felt foolish for saying it. I should have gone with the Italian translation, something actually concrete.

Rennero laughed and looked at Koles. "Yeah, he's in the circus, too." Then he turned back to me. "Did you have a job before you decided to find enlightenment?"

"Not really," I said, grinning.

"You had to do something."

"Sure, I did something. I was a bartender."

"An artist, a businessman, and a bartender. Ok, now we're getting somewhere."

"The cook, the thief, his wife, and her lover," Koles said.

"What?" Rennero asked, looking confused.

"Doesn't matter."

"I only understand him half the time. It's better that way," Rennero said to me. "Ok, my artist-clowns, let's blow job this place."

Koles shook his head. "Nice malaprop, huh, Van? Speaking of blow jobs, how are the transvestite whores treating you these days?"

"Best blow job you'll ever have," Rennero proclaimed proudly.

"Have you ever truly examined your sexuality? It might be the source of all your problems," Koles goaded.

Rennero and he clearly had good friendship. They could give and take with no restraint.

"You'd never know it was a man unless you went down on him. I only took the blow job. I have no issue with it anyway. You're the homophobia fool. It freaks you out because you might be gay. Come on, *autore*, it's the millennium third. We should be over the gay thing by now. Besides, I thought all you writers and artists were gay anyway."

Koles was shaking his head, looking at me. "Can you believe this guy? Got a blow job from a drag queen and is damn proud of it. Thinks he's evolved because of it."

"Like I said, best blow job ever. Of course it was *cazzone*. It's logical. Who knows dick better than a guy? You think we can eat pussy better than lesbians? It's obvious, you broken-ass. You're just afraid you might turn gay if you get one."

"As scintillating a study of human sexuality as this is, what do you say we just get out of here?" I offered. "Get on the road and get to Paris."

"Yeah, yes, we're done, Van. Lighten up," Koles said curtly. He then turned to Rennero, "How long is this meeting going to be?"

"An hour."

"Then what?" Koles asked.

"What do you mean?"

"Do you need anything else from me?"

"No. Hopefully the meeting goes good and then we can sit down and I explain your whole role in this, but it depends on the meeting."

"I'm sleeping in the back during the ride. I didn't get enough sleep on the plane. After the meeting, I'm going right to Yvette's. We'll make some money, but Yvette's my priority."

"Fine, broken-ass, but do me one favor."

"What?"

186

"Convince Yvette to fuck first and talk later. You need some release. You're tense."

"*Ficcate nel cuolo i tuoi consigli, va bene? Quando voglio il tuo aiuto, ti chiedero, stronzo!*" Koles said in what sounded like damn good Italian to me.

Rennero told me, "His Italian is terrible. Makes my English look like a Noble Laureate."

We weren't actually in Milan. The airport was in Malpensa, a good distance northwest of Milan. I had expected to see some of the city as we left the airport, but it was nowhere in sight. We were on our way to Paris via Switzerland. Koles laid out in the backseat of Rennero's Volvo. He wanted to be rested and fresh to meet with Yvette. I sat in the front. Rennero's cell phone was constantly ringing, he had a cigarette going every five minutes, and most of the time he steered by putting his knee against the base of the steering wheel. His hands were too occupied with the phone, cigarette, or stick shift. Obviously, I never understood his conversations on the phone, but emotions need no translation. Several of the calls were rather heated. He occasionally looked at me with exasperation as if I should have understood what was going on. A man to man, unspoken connection. I assumed it was his girlfriend on the phone giving him a hard time. Between calls and cigarettes, he cursed any driver that didn't let him pass. He drove within kissing distance of the car's bumper and then tore the driver up and down in Italian reminiscent of my road rage. During one of the fireworks, I asked Koles what was going on.

"You awake?"

"What do you think? With the phone and his screaming I'll never sleep."

"What's he saying?"

"Just swearing at the guy."

"Like what specifically?" I was curious.

Koles began translating. "Get off the fucking road Sunday driver. Fucking God. Dick face. What's so fucking hard about changing fucking lanes. You drive like you are in the damn Pope-mobile. Move to Switzerland, etcetera, etcetera."

"Where'd you learn Italian?" I asked.

"I'm more proficient with profanity than anything else because of Rennero, but I also had a little thing with an Italian woman before Yvette. Picked up a little of the language."

187

"English, French, and Italian. Not bad, Derek. You're very marketable."

He laughed. "You know the one thing about the Italian language is that it uses the word cock for fuck. Italians use cock for everything. Direct translations come out as 'What the cock are you doing? Why the cock don't you change lanes? What the cock do you want from me?' It's all about the penis in Italy. Sort of makes perverse Freudian sense with Italian mothers doting on sons with the passion of a paramour. The culture of *Mamissima.* My ex said Italian men never leave mama."

"Maybe not just Italians," I added.

As soon as Rennero finished castigating the driver in front of him and found some open road, his phone rang on cue. I looked at the speedometer. He was going two hundred and ten km/hr. He was nodding and occasionally starting to say something, but apparently was being interrupted.

We were driving along Lake Maggiore. Just beyond the lake you could see the onset of the Italian Alps. It was a majestic view. The enormous lake with a few islands scattered in the center, and the mighty Alps at the horizon. We each had our own mission. Hannibals crossing in a different direction...

Once we passed the long stretch of road along *Lago Maggiore,* we were into the Alps. The Swiss border was only fifty kilometers away. The road started twisting and turning as we began our ascent in the mountains. Rennero didn't seem to care about the treacherous roads. His kneecap controlled our fate. I could hear the voice at the other end of his cell phone. It was loud and angry. I turned around to ask Koles for another translation. Despite all the noise, he'd managed to fall asleep.

Rennero hung up. He relaxed his knee and gripped the wheel tightly with his hand, frustration emanating. He was shaking his head slowly, annoyed and exasperated. Again, his knee took over steering duties so he could open a new pack of Marlboro's. He disposed of the wrapping out his window and lit a cigarette while instant revulsion lit inside me.

"That's not necessary," I said.

"What?"

"Throwing out the cigarette wrapping."

"Oh shit, I didn't even realize it. Usually I don't do that, but my mind is all over the place."

"Still no point in doing that."

"Listen, Van, I've got much going on. That was my girlfriend and she's pissed off that I'm on this road trip. Plus, I'm waiting for a real big call from my lawyer to finalize a lot money going my way."

"Coming my way," I corrected.

188

"Whatever, coming, going my way, in my direction. Yeah, I've got a lot of shit on my mind. This new business, the money, my girlfriend breaking my balls. I can't take this much more. Can you believe she's pissed at me because I left on this trip without giving her enough notice? I get a call from Derek yesterday. I call her immediately and she gets mad, yells me for not telling her earlier. I told her I would have told her earlier, if I was Nostradamus!"

Rennero sucked so hard on his cigarette that his cheeks dimpled in dramatically as if the inhaled smoke were oxygen for his suffocating lungs.

"So, explain the logic, Van. I need to tell her something I don't know yet."

"No logic there," I said. "I don't think logic applies too much in a relationship, but it does apply to tossing paper out the window."

"Look. I'm fucking sorry, Van. Christ, you gonna break my fucking balls, too. That's great. Just what I need, the Green Party president next to me. You want me to turn around and search for the fucking wrapping? Is that what you want? I'll turn the fuck around and find the plastic."

"Never mind. Not a big deal."

Rennero was shaking his head again. He was mumbling something in Italian, under his breath. I looked forward to being alone by the Seine. There, I would be able to collect my thoughts. Relax. Begin something. Begin what could not be articulated.

"Are you married?" Rennero asked.

"No."

"Got a girlfriend?"

"Kind of."

"What's that mean? You are very vague. Vague Van."

"Maybe we broke up."

"You don't know?" Rennero asked, pushing for a definitive answer.

"It's kind of vague right now."

"Great. Nothing makes sense these days. No more black and white. What happened to clarity? *Mio Dio!*"

"You're right. I was just saying the other day how everything is indirect and ironic and..."

His cell phone interrupted me. He looked at the caller ID. "This better be good fucking news. I need to some good goddamn news, Van!"

His Italian took on an angry tone again. Bad news. He hung up and lit a cigarette, swerving a bit. We were on an incline heading into the Alps. The road wasn't as twisting as I had expected the Alpine roads to be. However, one slip off the edge and the drop would have been enough to turn edification into mortification.

"You want me to drive?" I asked.

"No, no. If I don't drive, what am I going to do?"

"Relax. Smoke and talk on the cell phone without the potential of killing all of us."

"No, no, *Americano*, don't know what is the word, fret, I can say instead of worry. Don't fret, right?"

I nodded.

"I need more vocabulary. If I don't drive, then there is time between smoking and calls. Well, I don't need that time. Too much thinking. I need distraction. The last thing I need now is time to think. I might actually understand my situation. And then what?"

I laughed. "Clarity."

"To hell with clarity."

"You were just bemoaning the lack of clarity," I reminded him, sensing logic was inappropriate just as I had said it.

"No, no. I just said it's gone. No moaning it. I actually hate clarity. There's no such thing. Every clarity I've ever had becomes unclear in time. Rather start with illusion. It's more comfortable. Clarity is how do you say, a cock tease, right? Time always fucks it up the ass. *Lucidita* hasn't got a chance in today's world. *In fatto*, clarity is a *mito*."

"A myth?"

"Yeah, that's it. It's a myth. *Che Mondo*, Van."

"Yeah, *che mondo, Italiano*."

"Don't you agree?"

"Sure, clarity is overrated. Unless, it's actual clarity. The clarity you're talking about isn't clarity. It's delusion from the very beginning."

"That's all I've ever met. Take Koles here. He thinks he has clarity about his woman."

"He might."

"He might not."

"True enough," I conceded.

"One month from now he might realize that the biggest mistake he ever made was coming to Paris to save his marriage."

"One month from now he might be so happy that he won her back."

"You're an optimist. I hope you're right. Italians are naturally cynical. There are only two reliable things in life. Mama and death." He laughed. "Everything else is a how do you say, a smoke dream?"

"Pipe dream."

"Yes, *certo*, pipe dream. *Un sogno irrealizzabile*. Makes no sense in Italian. Love idioms. American idioms make me laugh. You

190

see, *Americano*, Koles needs to embrace money. This writing life, the artist life, is a good period in youth, but has no sense. Money is real. Everyone wants money. Who wants art? Just a few bored rich people. Mama and money, *amico mio*."

We had just entered Switzerland. It was interesting to cross the border as if we were driving from one American state to another. There were some empty tollbooths where the border guards used to be. We sped right through. I remember Jack Dunhardt preaching about the end of the nation-state one night at Chez Lucienne. Borders and countries would soon be in the ashbin of history according to Dunhardt. A "world government" would be the next stage of human history. I could easily envision that. In the future hindsight might view nation-states as neurotic and anal attempts to control and over-organize the globe. A stage, much like the feudal era or the age of empires, on the march towards the end of government.

A sign for the Matterhorn, elevation 4,478 m, caught my eye, diffusing futuristic musing. I didn't know there was a real Matterhorn. I thought it was a fairy tale, something from Disney perhaps. Instinctively, I rolled down my window and stuck my head out to get a view of its peak. The wind was whipping my face so much that my eyes were watering profusely like someone in the midst of a profound sob. I kept at it though and saw the snowcapped top about fifteen thousand feet up—only half of Everest. Then I felt a strong tug on my shirt pulling me back in the car.

"What the *cazzo* are you doing?"

"Checking out the Swiss Alps. The Matterhorn."

"I thought you were trying to kill yourself."

I laughed. "No, Rennero. No clarity in suicide. Or possibly too much."

I rolled up the window and wiped my eyes and cheeks dry. I could hear Koles shuffling in the back, but he didn't wake up despite all the commotion.

"So, Rennero, did you read Koles's novel?" I asked.

"I tried to."

"Did you like it?"

"Hard to say. There wasn't really a story. I didn't get it. No ending. A big, lost circus of characters."

I smiled. "In a way it was."

191

"Book like that can't make money. You need a beginning, middle and end. Reminded of Fellini a little bit and I hate Fellini. What nonsense."

"It was a little offbeat."

"Koles needs money. We'll make some good money with the sandals. Work with figures and data, make charts. Study numbers. Real stuff. Life is not circus, Van. I make up stories to get laid, not for a job. Money is reality. Koles thought he could avoid money, but it always catches you. Yvette probably left him because he had no real paycheck."

"I think there's more to Koles and Yvette's problems than money."

"What is it then?"

"Don't know. He rarely talks about it."

"He gets mad easy. Koles got angry at me because I told him his book had no story. I asked him what the hell the characters were looking for. What was their mission? In other words what the hell was the damn book about. He wouldn't answer me for the longest time. Told me the work should speak alone. Compared it to abstract painting or something."

We were nearing Geneva. In the distance I could see water, probably Lake Geneva. I was looking forward to seeing water again. Not quite the same peaceful energy of rivers, but lakes would suffice. Being surrounded by mountains was claustrophobic. That visual combined with the audio of this Italian Andrew Carnegie on amphetamines was too much. I needed an antidote to Rennero. What the hell was Koles getting into with this guy anyway? Maybe there was some truth to Yvette wanting Koles to make more money. Maybe, this was all about a starter home, French style, but I couldn't convince myself of this. I knew very little about Yvette, other than her being a Ph.D. student in literature, philology, or something like that. I remember something about her painting or sculpting as well. I could see Koles with an academic or an artist, not someone pressuring him into making money. Not someone like Shaillie had become. I wanted to know more about Yvette, but Koles kept her and their relationship shrouded in mystery. I was curious to know more about her. Curious to meet this woman who owned Koles's heart.

Meanwhile, Rennero left nothing to mystery. He prattled on about how Europe was waking up from a long slumber. His half-baked analysis claimed Europeans were too interested in art and philosophy. It had held the economy back for so long, while America charged ahead in its unrepentant materialism. However, the Euro was a good start to a new century. "The continent finally realized fifteen currencies in a landmass the size of fucking Texas is too complicated." He said the Euro and the EU had put Europe back in the game now. No longer on the outside watching America and Japan share all the wealth. Europe's disappearing borders would galvanize and utilize the continent's resources and skills. Give it the economic size to compete with the United States. He had gone to Boston to study English because English would become the language of Europe. One language. One currency.

"Everyone needs sandals, right, Van? They're cheap and necessary. We'll sell them all over the world. Two billion Indian and Chinese ready to wear our sandals. The internet makes anything possible. Everything's possible in the 21st century. You in?"

"What?" I asked. I'd been half-listening, half-Alpine dreaming.

"Make some money. Distribute my sandals? You in America. Koles in France. I'll handle Italy. Then we hit the mother lode in Asia. I'm lining people up all over the globe. Got contacts in Korea, India, China. Europe and America will battle it out for a while, Van, but that's merely a transitional thing. China and India, Van. They're the future."

"I don't know. Money isn't an issue right now."

"Hell, Van, money's always an issue. This can be a quick score. Build it up, make it global, let the internet do the work. People just click and we collect. Click and collect. What a beautiful world we live in. See, I can be an American optimist. Then, we sell it to someone else for the big score. We make fast money, invest in real estate, live off the rent. We can retire and enjoy life. Retire young. Live the good life. Like the movie *Sexy Beast*. Did you see it?"

"No."

"Artsy film. Koles, of course, suggested it. I usually don't see those films."

Rennero's cell phone interrupted. He prayed aloud that it was his lawyer with good news. When he looked at the screen, he swore. He answered and immediately began arguing. Clearly, his girlfriend.

Meanwhile, we were now driving along the Southern shore of Lake Geneva. All the signs for the lake had its name in three languages—English, French and German. The Alps were still everywhere. They seemed eternal, infinite. This part was called the Savoy Alps. We'd passed the Bernese and Pennine Alps.

Rennero slammed his flip-top cell phone shut. He took a tissue from the center console and blew his nose furiously into it before coughing loudly a few times. He sounded old, well beyond his youthful age. The chain smoking must have been wreaking havoc on his system. After wiping his nose, he tapped a Marlboro out of the pack, grabbed it with his mouth, and lit it with the car lighter.

"Same old shit. I'm going to Paris. Nothing has changed. What does she expect that I'm going to turn around? Van, I'm not pussy-whipped like sleeping beauty back there," He said loud enough to get a rise out of Koles, but Koles was still out.

"What the hell has he been up to? He's exhausted."

I didn't answer. My mind immediately darted into imagery of Hyun. Imagery of her bathing me gently and sensually.

"So, what were we talking about before?"

Hyun was leaping onto me and then straddled across my hips, her hand maneuvering between my legs…

"Van!"

"Yeah, yeah. What?"

"*Sexy Beast*. We were talking about the film. Very artsy. Ben Kingsley is in it. You know, Gandhi. You'd like it…"

I wondered why he thought he knew that. He barely knew me and he already thought he did. We always think we know what someone else likes or dislikes.

"The beginning was great, but the rest of it was a whole lot of nonsense. It begins with two couples lying by a pool at their villa Spanish. Beautiful villa in Southern Spain with sun and quiet and good dinners and wine. Me, you, and Koles can get this. Have our wives and kids around. Sneak out once in a while for some whores and take it easy. *Una vita civilizzata* like it should be in the century twenty-first."

"What about time?"

"What about it? We'll have it."

"You'll go crazy with it."

"Not after I got a piece of the pie. I'll invest and learn how to enjoy time. Open up a business to kill the time I don't enjoy. You guys will do your circus stuff. Everyone wins."

"One step at a time."

"You don't get it. Villas in Spain are cheap. Nice big ones for seventy thousand, American dollars. You can't go wrong. You can spit into the Mediterranean from your balcony or dive into your pool. Good whores in Spain, but it's no Cuba where they greet you a minute from the airport. It's like Castro sends a welcoming party of communist pussy. They come and hug you, grab your balls thirty seconds after you arrive. The best fucking trip of my life. You don't even pay. You just take them out to dinner and fuck all night and say goodbye. They're clean, too. Good national health care in Cuba."

"A whore lover's paradise," I said with little interest in my tone.

"You don't like whores?" Rennero asked, incredulously.

"Not too much."

He sighed loudly. "Americans are so fucking uptight about whores and adultery. In Italy it's assumed you will cheat on your wife."

"I don't believe that."

194

"Because you think with American mind."

"The women assume this, too?" I asked.

"More or less. We don't have open discussions about it. It's not spoken."

"Unspoken."

"Yeah, it's unspoken," Rennero repeated. Despite his thick Italian accent, his English was excellent. He must have studied hard, knowing English and money were siblings.

"I don't believe it, Rennero."

"Different culture. You guys got lots of jobs and money. You're the, how do you say, juggernaut? Here we don't have jobs and dollars, but we got more time. Time for family, for kids. Time for whores. Time to cheat. All kinds of time to fuck. *Il tempo per scopare*." He looked over at me and smiled. "That's why American women don't know how to fuck. European women fuck like it's the meaning of life."

"I'm not so sure about that."

"Trust me."

His cell rang again at the usual interval.

We'd just left France and were now in Switzerland. I could see the outskirts of the city of Geneva. I took out a map of Europe from Rennero's glove compartment. Geneva was a little urban enclave at the southern tip of its eponymous lake. This part of Switzerland was surrounded by France. That's the beauty of Europe—countries, cultures and languages changing rapidly over tiny distances. Switzerland itself was a hodgepodge of languages and cultures in a size no larger than Massachusetts. It had only been a few hours, but we'd already been in three countries. I loved the variety and newness. America was so big. Long drives only broken up by giant gas stations or strip malls all looking the same. Most American cities had homogenized so much that they were now just expanded strip malls at this point. The same consumer feeding stations every hundred miles or so.

I could see a sign saying "The Republic and Canton of Geneva." A throwback to the city-state era, I presumed. I definitely needed a break from the world according to Rennero. My only hope was to feign sleep. One more gaze at the Alps and the Southwestern tip of Lake Geneva before I closed my eyes, leaving all views to the imagination. The masquerade of sleep quickly turned real while the imagination began its dreamy dictatorship.

As I drifted into sleep I could hear Rennero close the cell phone. A fading Italian-accented voice said, "Van, you awake. Van? Hey, Koles? Derek? Great. All alone. Now what? Shit! All alone. What the hell...Damn *Americani...Che Palle! Solo Io adesso...Che faccio io da solo?...Chiedero la mia ragazza...*"

Walking along the Seine. Finally free of sandals and prostitutes as the answers to existence. Koles is now with Yvette sorting out his future and past. Thoughts of my mother panicking and Shaillie deeply distraught…Doing what is necessary. Not everything is as it seems. Time and geography floating inversely and perversely along its own whimsical pursuits. Keep reminding myself the whole trip is necessary. Down in the quays walking, listening, watching, pure fulfillment of the senses. A street musician is playing at the edge of the Seine. Just his guitar, a small amp, and a good voice. I move closer to the musician. A few people forming a semi-circle around him. Music sounds familiar. I recognize the guy. His name is Brian Webb. Often saw him playing at the Harvard T stop as I made my way into Chez Lucienne for the evening shift. I join the semi-circle and listen to the song…

Shame, Shame, Shame

It's not about you now, It's not about you now

You can count the way in which you gave

But it's more about why you love and less about how

Oh it's more about why you love and less about how

So I got this story that plays in my head

Like a bird and a stone in my hand

But I've simplified myself to cause and effect now

Cause It's much too scary to say that maybe I just am

So I offer you only what I know of love

Though I confess what it is I think I forgot

I tend to remember more about what love is not

(but the truth remains still the same

it's not enough, but it's all I've got)

Everyone claps at the end of the song. There's some dialogue between the audience and him, all of it in French. I ask him if he's ever played in Cambridge. In French-accented broken English he says he's never been to England. I tell him I saw him play near Harvard University in the other Cambridge. He laughs. I tell him I know this song. I've heard it before. He shakes his head, still laughing. He tells me

196

its his song, an original. Mumbles something about cover songs and laughs again. He starts tuning his guitar and then begins another song while I walk away. I can tell the semi-circle people are talking about me. I turn around, look back, and everyone is quiet. After enough distance so that I can't hear Brian Webb's French clone or audience chatter, I see a large white tourist boat pass by. I think I recognize my brother on it, his hands filled with envelopes, licking and sealing them closed, one by one. I keep staring, but the boat pulls further and further away. I can't tell if it is him or not. I hear another musician playing by the Seine, this time a saxophone player. Some jazz. I can see the spires and gargoyles of Notre Dame in the distance. Just before it I see a coliseum. It looks like the famous Coliseum of Rome. I climb the stairs out of the quays, the saxophone fading away and enter the Coliseum. People are milling around, speaking English with Boston accents. Where the hell am I? Nobody stops me as I pass through a turnstile and enter through a portal. It's a stadium full of people. On the field, the football field, I see crimson uniforms and a large capital H on the helmets. The other team is in green. Harvard vs. Dartmouth. Borders have really melted, cities have merged. I tell myself it has to be a dream. I'm aware of the madness of this new reality, but it all feels so madly real. The geography in my mind is whatever the master puppeteer determines it to be. Capricious cartography. I walk the aisle between the seats. I instinctively look for the score, but there's no scoreboard to be found. Then I hear my name being called. I turn my head to the right, following the voice. It's Arshan Torakian. The lawyer. He calls me over again. There's an empty seat next to him. I sit there obediently, foolishly. "Enjoy the game, Van," he says, "it's just a game. Don't take it too seriously." He pauses and then adds, "Don't let it spread like...No, never mind. Look behind you, Van." He points to a section behind me. I look back and see a man waving at me. He looks like my father, but he isn't. Things aren't as they seem. I look again at Arshan, more closely. He's got the same face, the goatee, but he's a lot thinner. "Time cures everything, Van." I start massaging my face, rubbing it vigorously, stretching my skin. I open my eyes and look over at Arshan, but he's no longer there. "Van, you ok?" Shaillie asks. I smile, not surprised that she's right next to me. ..

I could hear Koles and Rennero's voices. I opened my eyes to countryside rolling by, small houses in the distance, a little town. I saw a sign for Paris, only fifty-five kilometers to go. It was another long and profound sleep with a dream as vivid as a poignant memory. Layered

197

and potent *dreamery*. I wanted to record this quickly, add it to *Insomnia Journal*, but I couldn't. My backpack was in the rear of the wagon. Rennero's cell phone rang again like an alarm that just wouldn't quit as I began having mildly paranoiac sensations. While French terrain raced past my vision at more than two miles a minute, I had a sense of detachment from the situation. Rennero and Koles seemed by-products of the imagination. Less real than the events and people of the dream I'd just exited. In fact, at this moment the events of the last twenty-four hours seemed more hallucinatory than real. More like something happening in my head. Something I would write about in the journal, events concocted during insomnia. Put it in the safe and then climb back to bed. But this time I'd be alone in the bed and there was no more safe.

I rolled the window down. Rennero asked me how I'd slept. I told him fine, but I was still half asleep. I rested my head near the window and let the wind whip into my face. Not quite as much as when I stuck my head out of the car, but good enough.

When we took the exit that led into Paris, Rennero asked Koles, "Are you going to call her?"

"No. Stop at a florist," a rested, but anxious Koles said.

"We have the meeting in ten minutes. Do you understand that this is not the circus? It's real. This is not a novel, not a goddamn *romanza*! It's about money."

"Shut the fuck up, Rennero."

"Just making us on the same page." Rennero laughed loudly. "How's that for a metaphor, huh? Perfect. *Che metaforo*, huh, writer man?"

"It's a pun," Koles said dismissively. "*Che stupido*. Now stop at a florist."

"Screw the flowers. I've got to park and we don't have time now. The meeting will be brief. We'll go after," Rennero said.

I was in the back now. We had stopped for a café and Rennero gave Koles some last minute information about the sandals sales plan and briefed him about prices and percentages in order to be ready for the meeting. Rennero found a parking spot on Champ-Élysées. I could see the Arch de Triumph. The first image in my head was of goose-stepping Nazis and Hitler, the failed artist, mockingly walking under the great monument with Parisians watching, each step must have felt like a rape of their beloved city.

"Besides, you need to change and clean up," Rennero told Koles.

"My mind isn't on this meeting, Rennero."

"Look, if you are going to have any future with Yvette, you need a job. You need money. You want to settle down and get your wife back, right? You can't do that in a cheap studio teaching and writing weird, unread novels for the rest of your fucking life."

"Fine. Let's do it. You're a pain in the ass, you know that."

"Of course, I do. You got a tie?"

Koles laughed, "Yeah, it's in my garment bag with my three-piece suit."

"Alright, king of bohemia, just look decent then. This is business, not finger painting."

"If you're going to be an asshole, I'm out."

"Ok, ok. I'm just breaking your balls. Take it easy."

"I'm doing you a favor here."

"Yeah, yeah, you're right. *Mi dispiace*. Sorry. I'm getting carried away."

"Yes, you are!" Koles seemed really pissed-off. "And shut the fuck up with the goddamn circus bullshit. Money this, money that. Who the hell is the American here?"

"I should be the American. You don't know how to handle your citizenship."

"Shut the hell up, ok. *Stai Zitto!*" There was rage in Koles's voice.

Rennero raised his eyebrows in surprise while looking back at me.

"Derek, calm down. Perhaps, we stop at the *farmacia*. Did you run out of pills?" Rennero lit a cigarette. He picked up his cell phone, opened it, put it back down. He turned back to me. "He's angry, huh? Always was a loose cannon. He's fine for a while and then the sky falls on him. I think it's a disorder. There's a name for it. You know what it's called, Van?"

I didn't answer. I could feel tension escaping Koles's pores floating heavily within the small enclosed atmosphere of the Volvo. Emotional gravity weighing us further down. The car seemed smaller. Three tense men in a small space. Each one with a woman lingering and hovering on various levels in their thoughts.

I needed to get out of this pressure cooker.

"Never mind. Ok, ok, maybe we need a beer. Yes, *ragazzi*, I feel a little stress now. We all need the touch of a woman to calm us down. The power of money is pushing our buttons. How about a peaceful beer?"

"Fine," Koles muttered. He was a million miles away from this endeavor.

199

We pulled over at a brasserie. I could see the Seine and the Eiffel Tower. We seemed to be in a very touristy part of the city. It didn't feel like the Paris of Breton, Stein, Picasso or Hemingway.

"Listen," I said halting Koles before entering the bar. "I need a break. I need to be alone for a while."

"What for, *amico*?" Rennero said, overhearing. "A beer will calm everything down. You'll see, Derek can change moods like a New York second."

"Minute. New York Minute, dumbass," Koles retorted with disgust and without taking his eyes off me.

"Whatever, *professore*, you get my point. Anyway, Van, what's the problem?"

Koles now turned to Rennero. "He doesn't have to explain. He just needs space. He's sick of your sorry ass. It's that simple. Does everything have to be diagrammed for you?"

"Fucking Americans. You're the only ones who can afford space!" Rennero lit a cigarette and walked away.

"Cultural differences," I said to Koles. I could sense and feel anger still emanating from his depths.

"No, he's just an asshole."

I laughed uneasily. "He's ok. I think he's harmless. A little tiring, but somewhat entertaining, actually." I wanted Koles to relax.

"He wears me down. Breaks me after a while. So you want to talk about it or you just want to go?"

"Let's meet later."

"Why don't you meet me at Yvette's in a couple hours? That will give me time to talk to her alone. I'll give you her address. She lives in the Latin Quarter near Notre Dame. It's a bit of a hike from here, but you could walk it in an hour. Or take the metro. You'll probably be on your own for directions though. Parisians can be downright nasty to Americans who don't speak their language. But there's no better city to walk and get lost."

"Perfect. It will give me some time. Is she near Jardins du Luxembourg?"

"Yes. Real close."

"It's four o'clock now," I said. "I'll be at Yvette's around seven. Is that enough time for you?"

"Plenty."

"What's going to happen to him?" I asked, pointing at Rennero who was in the brasserie.

"He'll probably head back to Milan tonight or get a hooker and crash at a hotel. I told him I need the time with Yvette, but don't worry. You can stay with us until you..." Derek paused. "What exactly are you going to do?" he asked, laughing at the notion that I'd come to Europe with no plan at all. Before I could answer, he said, "Oh, yeah, edification, of course."

"Of course," I repeated.

"Hey, Van, you know, I'm so nervous about Yvette. I can't lose her again."

"Derek, what really happened with..." I stopped myself, mid-question. It wasn't my business.

"I'll tell you someday, Van. I just need her back so badly. She's my world and it took me too long to realize that. I don't pray. I wouldn't know how and I'd feel like a fraud, but I'll get on my knees and sincerely try if that'll bring her back. I'll stop writing. Believe in God. Become a monk. Whatever it takes." He laughed, but seemed serious.

Being in Paris, so close to Yvette and his past, must have had a trenchant effect on him. His eyes radiated. He was all emotion, longing right now. His guard was down as he would soon face the reality of his mission.

"Whatever it takes, Van. I can feel her presence in Paris. I know she'll see our truth. She's my truth, my destiny. I know it sounds like juvenile, romance stuff, apropos of our maudlin Gilworthy, but it's just that simple, Van."

"Hurry up," Rennero yelled from a distant table on the patio. I saw two glasses of beer in front of him. Koles ignored him.

"What if she's not there?" I asked.

"I'll wait."

"I wish you luck, Derek."

"Thanks."

We hugged. I was turning to leave, when Koles said, "You miss Shaillie?"

I hesitated for a moment. "Yeah, I do."

"Call her. Let her know what's going on. It doesn't have to be over," Koles said.

"See you in a few hours, Derek."

Koles went into the bar with a change of clothes. I looked back at Rennero. He was waving goodbye, cigarette dangling between his fingers, cell phone pressed between his ear and right shoulder. His left hand rose above a sea of French people walking along Champs-Élyées. I waved back and headed on my urban sojourn for a river.

Though not nearly as numerous as Koles's, I had my own set of memories of Paris. It was all about Shaillie and me. Twenty-two year olds traipsing across Europe, hostels, backpacks, movement and newness the only currency worth a damn at that time. So in love. Rapturous love in its bloom. I vividly remember a photo of us in Paris at an English language theatre on Rue San Michelle. The two of us kissing intensely under a marquee for the film *Truly, Madly, Deeply*. It captured us at the peak of our love. Why didn't we frame that and put it on the wall? Why didn't we stay in Europe? Who said you have to return home? I wanted to stay. Drew out the plan in my head one sleepless night after Paris when we were in Prague. Pounced myself and the idea on Shaillie in the middle of the night. I couldn't wait. We'd teach English and learn languages. Find a way to live decently here. Extend the borders and timeframe of bohemia. Live the ex-pat life. The only life with a chance of honing and cleansing perception. Roots and birthplace were a conspiring trap, an existential conspiracy. We would emphasize *Being* above all else. Turn our backs on the *Nothingness* that awaited us. Play the game differently and avoid falling prey to the meltdown of the paved middle ground. I pleaded with Shaillie, "Let's tempt truth. Teach here and there. Words, photos, paint. Just keep going and experiencing life."

I conceded that my plan lacked any defined substance, any notions even slightly resembling logic. We had jobs waiting for us back home. Shaillie had grad school, too. But that didn't stop me. In fact, what it lacked was used as further support. I unraveled a long, mostly abstract litany in defense of what I perceived to be the alive and examined life.

She would have none of it. We would work toward that starter house paving our path into nest eggs and insensate comfort. Buy that house near so many identical others. Spend the rest of our lives umbilically tied to mother mortgage. We'd already seen the prototype-house a few years after Prague. The door perfectly placed in the center, two windows on each side, all symmetrical and tidy. So ordered and concrete it turned my stomach upside down. And now this trip was the offspring of its denial years ago. The offspring of years of posturing and posing. Repression finally finding its expression at heavy costs. I had forgotten about that conversation until just now. This was not something hatched after my father's death or in recent months. It had its source in Prague so long ago and was finally realizing itself now in Paris.

Nevertheless, all the cerebral detours and deviations unveiling themselves now didn't change my heart about us. It was the path I wanted altered, not Shaillie. Regret for jumping ship on Shaillie, actually losing her, was sinking in suddenly and quickly like a capsized ocean liner being swallowed by the deep sea. I thought back to that photo under the marquee. It was always about Shaillie. I couldn't excise so many years together so easily. I wanted her with me now, just like before. This was not nostalgia. The feelings were firmly sown within. Though a part of me wanted them to disappear, I knew they wouldn't. Emotions get triggered and race at their discretion and speed. They are the decision makers.

I continued picturing us kissing. We hadn't even seen the movie. I remember the moment the stranger finished taking our picture, we tossed our tickets, raced to our cheap hotel room and leapt into bed. Those were the days when we fucked rather than went through the motions of intercourse. I thought of her body and how I wanted to leap into bed with her right now. Feel her nakedness. Touch her everywhere, slowing down at her breasts. Touching her nipples, softly, slowly, until they hardened. I thought of how many times we'd made love. So many times over so many years. I thought about how she loved to have her breasts caressed and adored. I was only too willing to appease that desire. Shaillie reduced to soft sighs and deepening breaths. Everything gentle, sensual. My thoughts sprinted along our sexual patterns. Our sexual memories. Gentle and sensual becoming aggressive and raw. Fucking hard and wicked, slamming skin, ass, and grabbing onto whatever was within reach, legs spread, bodies slapping and scraping, awkward poetry, coming long and loud, and then deep sighs until collapsing onto the bed like a fallen tent, hanging onto the last few moments of the pure peace of purged thought.

I needed to deal with this daydream, needed some release. I looked for a bar, café, anywhere to find a restroom and privacy. I saw Notre Dame in the distance. No, couldn't do that. The pious atheist in me reconsidered. I thought about it. It would have been good homage to Dada, but I didn't have the Dada balls for that. I saw a brasserie a block away and rushed to it, went into the bathroom, locked the door, and finished my fantasy into cheap French toilet paper.

I wondered if Shaillie on some unknown level felt something. A psychic ripple, a whispery thrill in her loins, some hidden wave in the willowy flow of the collective subconscious.

Dreamy and chimerical notions aside, the wanton indulgence was calming. Temporarily soothed the anxiety resulting from my actions and thoughts. Yet, I sense the wrecking ball was still teasingly aligning its inevitable release. I was just buying time.

I looked in the mirror and decided I needed a shave. My beard hadn't grown in much, but the last shave was uneven. I'd missed patches of whiskers under my nose and chin, random whiskers along my neck had escaped the blade. I figured a clean shave would be an apt complement to my internal cleansing. I'd arrive at the Seine, sit down in the quays, cleaned internally and externally, and absorb the flowing peace of the magnificent Parisian river.

This bathroom would suffice. It had a lock. The place was quiet with minimal chance of interruption. Besides, we'd already become intimate. I'd go buy a razor and some shaving cream, come back to the bar and have a glass of wine or a beer. Then return to the bathroom hovel and put a razor to my face.

There was a little grocery store next door. It had only two aisles. There was a very short man behind the register and no sign of any customers. I immediately saw a carousel of guidebooks and picked out the smallest one. It had pictures, maps, and some brief descriptions of sites. I'd see some of Paris on the way to meeting Koles. I was hoping he and Yvette would be back together. I was looking forward to a reunion, something to celebrate. If not Shaillie's and mine, then another couple's. Vicarious pleasure, not schadenfreude.

I looked around the little store with the little man for shaving cream and a razor. When I couldn't find anything, I approached Little Man.

"*Excusez-moi*," I attempted.

"*Oui.*"

"*Parlez Ingles?*" I asked, summoning most of the seventh grade French left in my brain.

"*No-no*," He said, looking away. I remembered how surly and arrogant Parisians were when Shaillie and I had our jaunt through the city. Paris was far more enchanting than Parisians.

"*Oui* shaving cream?" I tried pathetically.

He shrugged his shoulders and shook his head, dumbfounded. I pretended to shave my face and rubbed and pointed to my beard, but he had stopped looking at me. He was reading *Le Parisien*. It was open to the front page. The headline was about Lance Armstrong. Just what he needed, more Americana.

"*Monsieur?*" I said loudly.

He pulled his eyes from the newspaper. I air-shaved again.

"*Oui, oui, oui*," he said with surprising and sudden merriness. Maybe I was wrong about Parisians.

He continued speaking as if I now understood French. He left the counter and *Le Parisien*, walking past me. I followed. He pointed to a set of shelves with cologne, hair products, and toiletries. Then he stretched his arm as high as it could go, which was up to my height. He was straining to point to the top shelf. I could see a couple of cans of shaving cream tucked behind other products.

"*Merci, merci beaucoup.*"

"*Du rien,*" he said, nodding and smiling as he walked back to his little home behind the counter. He now seemed like a nice chap.

The shelf had to be nine-feet high. I got on my toes, and reached as high as I could. The shaving cream was in the second row of items. So I had to nudge my hand through the tightly compacted first row. As I removed the can, the other hygiene items began shaking. I noticed the shelf was very unstable. I continued to gently ease out the can of shaving cream, but my wrist nudged the shelf. I saw it start to give way, as if I had pulled out the small rock that would trigger the avalanche. "Shit!" I instinctively dropped the can and reached for the falling shelf. I got my hand under it before it plummeted. However, a few items slipped off. As they fell, they bumped a few other items from below, knocking them off their shelves. Glass shattered and cans bounced and thumped off the floor. I looked down at broken glass, perfume puddles forming, rolling objects, while my right arm was fully extended. My hand was the only thing keeping the shelf from creating a complete disaster.

Welcome to Paris.

Little Man came running down the aisle from his perch behind the counter. He was screaming at me and the small mess. He was pointing and gesticulating madly. I had a fairly clear idea of what he was saying. The momentary merriness was all gone.

"I need help," I said desperately.

He kept screaming at me and motioning to let go. I shook my head. With my free hand still clutching the guidebook, I motioned down.

"It will fall," I said as calmly as possible. I could feel sweat accumulating at my temples. The shelf was getting heavier, my arm stiffening and tiring. I flung the guidebook away from the mess at my feet and now held the shelf Atlas-style.

He yelled even louder at me. He began pointing at the broken merchandise and counting out loud. I heard the word "Euros" over and over. He was tallying up what I owed.

I said, "I'm not paying for anything." Then I said more loudly, "The fucking shelf will fall, shithead!"

He turned and rushed towards the counter. I noticed that he was bow-legged. I remembered my grandmother telling me never to trust bow-legged people. His hurried walk seemed more like a waddle befitting an overweight duck. He began punching keys in his old-school register.

The strength in my arms was nearly spent. I tried to pull the shelf out to me so that I could balance it and lower it to the floor. I

205

figured I'd lose few items in the process, but not everything. However, only one end of the shelf was collapsing. The other side wouldn't come free. I had no choice. I eased the falling side down and placed it on top of the merchandise on the shelf below it, vainly hoping it would rest safely. My arms were now achingly tired. There was no way to save the shelf from falling without help and I wasn't getting any. I stepped back. Momentarily, the shelf rested on top of the items below it. Momentarily. Then, reality struck. The shelf swung down in one fell swoop like a broken arm on a clock. From three to six o'clock in seconds. Boom! At least one hundred items crashed to the floor. It sounded like a shooting range of glass bottles where each shooter was an expert marksman. More broken glass, giant puddles and rivulets of perfumes and colognes, creams oozing along the edges of the puddles.

I closed my eyes and took a deep breath. Not knowing what the hell to do now, I knelt down and began picking up the unbroken items. What a start in the glory of Paris! Bad perfume permeated my nostrils. I shook my head and started to laugh. What else could I do? My Parisian life had begun in absurdity. I wasn't sure what act this was in the crow-initiated theatre of my absurd.

I heard Little Man screaming and his feet scampering down the aisle. I looked up, trying to stop laughing. He looked like an irate penguin. When he saw me and my reaction, the screams grew louder. He was playing the role of mad Frenchman perfectly. He'd been cast well, howling and waving his Tyrannosaurus arms frantically. He motioned for me to stop. I kept hearing the same phrase over and over. "Shut up" or "Stop laughing" I presumed.

I continued picking up unbroken merchandise while he continued screaming the same phrase. Maybe, it was, "You fucking bastard!"

I stopped laughing and said, "I'll help. I'm sorry. It isn't funny. It was an accident. Though it was inevitable because..." I stopped myself.

Little Man had now gone completely crazy. He was running back and forth from the register punching in prices from the fallen items. I continued to clean, while he sprinted back and forth, screaming and tallying the Euros. Finally, he stopped and yelled out one figure over and over again.

"Fuck it!" I said out loudly. My heart was pounding. Did this happen because of my bathroom hedonism? A payback for Dionysian indulgence. Moral gods balancing the scales. Who's directing this play? I wanted to get the fuck out of there. I thought of running out the door, but changed my mind instantly. I got up. All hint of a smile and laughter was gone. I picked up a can of shaving cream, the guidebook and a razor from the floor and brought them to the counter. I placed them in front of Little Man on top of the photo of Lance Armstrong.

"I'll pay for these," I said sternly.

I saw the cost on the register. Now I understood his French.

"500 Euros! 500 Euros!!" he yelled over and over.

"You're insane. *Loco*," I said, wondering why the hell I blurted out Spanish. "I'm paying for these and that's it."

"500 Euros!" he repeated.

"I'm only paying for these."

"500 Euros!"

I pointed to the three items on his newspaper.

"500!" he screamed, pounding the counter with his fist.

"I'm paying for these and that's it!"

"500 Euros! 500 Euros! 500 Euros!"

I hesitated. We were like two six year olds, squabbling over toy ownership.

"Fuck you," I Screamed.

He repeated his mad mantra. I shook my head, not saying anything this time. He hurled more angry French at me, wildly pointing at the aisle where the avalanche had happened. I tried to remain calm, but I was starting to come unglued. Little Man was an ass. So he could understand, I changed my linguistic method from oral to gesture.

"Do you understand this?" I raised my hand and emphatically blasted my middle finger between his little eyes.

Those little eyes widened wildly. He marched out from behind the counter and attempted to get in my face, except his face was in my sternum. He continued screaming.

I decided that was enough. I didn't want the police to come because I assumed they'd believe him and book me as the ugly American. I'd be fucked, French-style. I turned around and started to leave. He kept screaming, but I didn't look back. I just wanted out. Suddenly, I felt my backpack getting pummeled with punches. Little Man was attacking like a crazed chimp pounding on my spine and shoulder blades. Before I could fully turn around, I felt a swift kick in my ass. I couldn't believe it.

I turned around and charged at Little Man. He instinctively backed up. I grabbed him by the collar and threw him behind his register. He fell in a heap to the floor. He was screaming and let out an "oomph" and an "owww" and other universal sounds of pain with a French accent. For a split second, I looked at the shaving cream, razor and guidebook and thought of grabbing them. Immediately, I rejected the notion and briskly walked out of the store. I was half a block away when I began to run. I heard Little Man's voice yelling on the street. I looked over my shoulder. He was standing outside the store. We caught eyes for a moment before I quickly turned at the first corner and was gone. I ran for as long as I could. Everyone was looking at me, but I kept running. I stopped in front of a black, wrought iron gate. I was panting like a dog. I couldn't remember the last time I had run like that.

I slumped to the ground and leaned against the black iron bars. My heart was pounding and my hands were trembling. Eventually, I caught my breath and calmed down. Then, the humor of it struck. It started with a grin, then a full, ear-to-ear smile, followed by loud and liberating laughter.

Once the laughter ceased, I looked around me. I looked at a sign posted on the gate, La Sorbonne. I continued sitting for a long, long time in front of Paris's version of Harvard.

I still had a couple of hours. So far, I had pleasured myself in the bathroom of a seedy restaurant, destroyed private property, and been attacked by a little Frenchman. I was off to a great start in Paris. Time to go to the Seine. Time for the river sane.

It was a short walk from Sorbonne. About four blocks. I descended the stairs and sat down in the quays with my back to the large cement wall. The river was dirty brown, hardly beautiful, but it had a grimy glory. I looked in each direction of the river. It wended its way through the city with frequent walking bridges connecting the left and right banks. So unlike the Charles, which was much wider at its urban incarnation and only had a few bridges connecting Cambridge and Boston.

I didn't see any tourist boats with my brother on it nor was the Roman Coliseum nearby with a Harvard-Dartmouth game. But the dream was very alive in my head. I unzipped my backpack and took out *Insomnia Journal*. I held it in my hands, enjoying the weight of nearly six hundred pages. I had put in a stash of blank white pages for this very moment. For the European end of the journal. Now, it wouldn't just be insomnia inspired. It would continue whenever I had the urge. I would *edify* the journal with as much writing as possible. Not just sleeping dreams now, but conscious dreams as well. I handwrote fast and automatic, true to the journal's inspiration, about my visit to the Seine today, the visit in my mind. Once that was put down, I recorded the ride with Rennero, the conversations, verbal sketches of the mad Italian, and Koles, culminating with the little Frenchman who tried to kick my ass, who *did* actually kick my ass. The journal was leaving dreams and

208

entering waking reality. I took faith in the instinct that propelled the words. The journal would be my ally in Paris.

I wanted thousands of pages, millions of words. It was as if a mountain of words had been walled within, cubed in for so long, forever in fact, and they were finally breaking out, demanding the light of articulation. I took some deep breaths and stared out at the Seine, mindlessly and peacefully watching the water flow. Twenty minutes passed in the soothing state. The resonant silence of the written word and the rhythmic flow of the river aligned into a tranquilizing elixir.

As soon as I climbed the steps leaving the quays below, I saw an outdoor stand with guidebooks. I was next to Notre Dame. I bought the smallest guidebook available and a bottle of water. I walked towards Notre Dame. I sat down on a bench in the big square in front of the church. People were milling about. Some were sitting on benches like me, others buying souvenirs, or eating a late afternoon snack. It was spring in Paris. People were happy. People seemed happy. My vision latched on to a family of four. Another family of four like the one in the airport. Again, parents and a son and daughter. The archetype. The children were playing some version of tag, running circles around their parents, who were holding hands and laughing at the children's game. Every once in a while one of the parents' free hands would reach out and touch their son or daughter. Each time one child got tagged, the other celebrated wildly. Eventually, the mother grabbed the daughter and the father grabbed the son and both children were laughing hysterically at what seemed to be the effect of tickling and the simple joy of the game of tag. I watched them until they made their way into Notre Dame.

I looked in the guidebook for something on Notre Dame. I wanted to know who built this haunting masterpiece of spires, towers and gargoyles. It was overwhelming—enough to make you want to believe in a God. Enough to make you fear God.

I learned that in the same spot as Notre Dame, the Romans had long ago built a temple to honor Jupiter. After that was razed, a Christian basilica was erected, followed by a Romanesque church, the Cathedral of St. Etienne. It was in 1163 that construction of Notre Dame actually began. The designer was a Bishop of Paris, Maurice de Sully. My mind promptly leapt into the imagery of the Bishop of Boston. The honorable Seamus Rourke. I missed Bishop. I wished I could pop into a brasserie and get a dose, a fix of Bishop. Listen to his lyrical logorrhea. Hear him trumpeting some new and hallowed madness, critiquing today's tepid art, deifying European culture or celebrating some divine concubine. I wondered if he and the lady from Cork had ever met up. I hoped so. As for the other bishop, Sully's Notre Dame took about one hundred and eighty years to complete. Notre Dame's history included: Crusaders praying before departure; pillaging during the French Revolution; the crowning of Napoleon; near-burning by the Communards of 1871; and Victor Hugo's fictional world of Quasimodo and Esmeralda. It was impressive to the eyes and historically monumental. Notre Dame was the ancient heart of Paris.

I knew if my old man had been here with me, we would have been discussing Notre Dame, the Crusades, Napoleon, the Paris Commune. His knowledge of history, like geography, was so vast. We would have been walking and talking along La Seine like we'd often walked along the Charles. Of course, the talk would have been more of lecture. Just then it struck me that Bishop was in some strange way, an ethereal, artistic version of my old man.

I considered going into Notre Dame, touring the interior, but I didn't want to be inside anything. The thought of being in the gothic church gave me claustrophobic sensations. I wanted to be outside. It was springtime in Paris, after all. One had to seize the outside world, not a dark, medieval church.

I searched the guidebook for something outside and fairly close by. I knew I wanted to be in Jardins du Luxembourg for sunset. I would do that after meeting Koles and Yvette. I would just touch base with them, hopefully stay at Yvette's. I needed a place to stay, about which I hadn't given any thought. Practical considerations weren't a priority. I had enough money, some resources, and irrational hopes. I wasn't the happiest man alive, but I knew I was onto something and avoiding a model T life even if just for a little while. I had the feeling that being alone in a new world would lead to something. Everyone's entitled to their own attempt at *Satori*. I sensed it coming too. I could feel something in my bones. It was as if I knew exactly what I was going to do, but my mind wasn't yet ready to articulate it. I just had to be patient until the visceral evolved itself intellectually. In the meantime I began feeling a shadowy hint of peace for the first time in ages. Maybe it was all the laughter inspired by my little enemy at the store. Maybe a good, hearty laugh from the depths of the intestines was all I needed. It had the therapeutic effect of a good sob. Perhaps, it was the intensity in the bathroom. Or being near the river…

I looked at a map in the book that had various sites listed. I was on Ile de la Cité, an island strangely located in the center of an urban river. The Seine bifurcated at Notre Dame, reconnecting at the other end of the island, just a few blocks down the road. This tiny island of Ile de la Cité was the actual birthplace of Paris. My eyes scanned the little map in my book. There was another neighboring island. It was the smaller of the two called Île Saint-Louis. I didn't recall seeing this island with Shaillie during our time here. It was a posh, quaint area, very residential.

Most of the houses were built in the 17th century. Marie Curie and Charles Baudelaire had lived there. Great alternative minds in the same small slice of Paris.

I decided to walk to Île Saint-Louis and check out the homes of Baudelaire and Curie. Both were great contrasts to Notre Dame. From God to its revolutionary offspring, art and science.

It was a short walk. I crossed one of the Seine's many bridges, Pont Saint-Louis, which connected the river's two islands. I first walked to Marie Curie's house, which overlooked the left bank. There was a plaque with her name and the dates she lived in this home. Two young men were standing in front of the house. They both had baseball caps on and sneakers and were speaking loudly, poster children of the American tourist. One had on a San Diego Padres cap and the other a San Francisco Giants cap. Three Americans in Paris visiting Marie Curie. A couple of times they looked back at me while I pretended to read my guidebook. San Diego asked me if I was American. I squinted as if I didn't understand. He asked again. I responded, "*Spagnolo*."

They resumed their conversation. The San Diego guy was telling San Francisco about his chemistry class in high school where he remembered learning about how Marie Curie had discovered radium and later died as result of overexposure to her discovery. San Diego said that radium was on the periodic table as Ra and that he had memorized the entire table and investigated the origins and histories of all the elements. He told San Francisco that he learned more in that class than any class he'd ever taken. San Francisco seemed surprised. San Diego told him he was completely in love with his teacher, Mrs. Nevin. "Oh man, I couldn't get her out of my mind. I would run home from school hoping my parents weren't home and my sister was out so I'd be free to relieve myself. Mrs. Nevin was all I thought about. Oh God, I was obsessed with her. I was failing other subjects just so I could study my ass off and get A's to impress her. I wanted to ask her to the prom."

San Francisco laughed hard. "Man, you are ridiculous."

"I was sixteen and if you had seen my teacher, you'd understand."

"Well, I had a male teacher for chemistry, Mr. Curtland. I didn't study at all. I had no interest in impressing Mr. Curtland, but I wish I had studied."

"Why's that?"

"Then I could have studied science and become a researcher or a doctor and now I'd have a job that matters. A job that makes a contribution instead of the one I have."

"You've got a good job," San Diego said.

"No, I have a comfortable job and I hate it."

211

"I can't see you as a scientist."

"If I had done things differently, you would be able to." San Francisco said.

"Go back to school."

San Francisco laughed. "It's too late for that. My cards have been dealt."

"Well, we can't go back, but if we could I'd go right back to Mrs. Nevin's class. It was a daily dose of blue balls, but she was amazing. She was all…"

American Pie comes to Paris. I'd had enough of listening to San Diego's blue period. I realized I didn't want to hear English anymore. I only wanted to hear French or any other foreign language. Anything, but English. The only way to escape the banal would be to surround myself with all things novel or unclear in the vague search for new myths and truths.

I headed to the other side of the island. I passed lots of small, swanky shops, cafés, bistros, brasseries, tiny grocery stores with variously colored fruits in stacked crates. Yellows, oranges, reds, purples, greens all caught my eye. They didn't have the artificial Windex-glean of American fruit. The colors and fruits seemed real, not genetically modified or transmogrified or whatever it is they do in those laboratories. The entire street had the smell of freshness, not chemicals. It was just detached enough from the city so that the massive haze from the exhaust of thousands and thousands of buses, scooters, and cars wasn't present as in Paris proper. How many cities had islands within the city? This was a unique little paradise in the middle of the historical Mecca of artistic pursuit. All the small stores on the immaculate, tree-lined street focused on particular items. Each one had their own personality. There were no super giant, omnivorous American-style stores selling everything anyone could ever want along an interminable aisle where consumption hunters could spend whole *daze* lost within the consumer safari.

The street was very quiet and peaceful. There were only a few cars, mostly BMWs and Mercedes. People were dressed well and walked with the air of wealth. The apartments had to be the homes of the Parisian Brahmins.

The island was so narrow and small that it took just three blocks to reach the other side. I stopped at a *boulangerie*. There were about forty different kinds of baguettes, all of which were seemingly fresh out of the oven. The little store was pristine and redolent. I inhaled deeply absorbing the intoxicating scents. After buying a baguette, I went to a wine store and purchased a half bottle of Bordeaux. The seller uncorked the bottle and provided me with a paper cup. No catastrophes in either store. I was getting the hang of Parisian existence. Things were looking up.

I walked along the other side of the river taking bites out of the warm baguette. The outside was crisp, the inside soft and steaming. Baudelaire's house was number sixty. I found the front of it, which was buried behind the scaffolding of construction workers who were refurbishing it. I remember visiting the homes of many writers. Shaillie definitely had a thing for the tortured writer. I presume most women did on some level. It must have triggered their maternal rescue-and-nurture instinct. Shaillie and I had visited the homes of Faulkner in New Orleans, Hemingway in Key West, Dante in Florence, Saramago in Lisbon, and Keats in Rome.

Baudelaire's house overlooked the right bank while Marie Curie's was on the left bank of the island. The set up was cerebrally proper—an island of intellectual balance. Standing before Baudelaire's house hidden behind iron bars and dirty mesh, I could barely see it. Yet, I liked being here. It wasn't about the visible.

I sat across the street on a short wall. I draped one leg over each side so I could view Baudelaire's house on my left and the Seine on my right. I thought of how I had been sitting by the Charles what seemed just moments ago. How long had I been toeing a new line of deviation? I could sense the line splintering and the deviation beginning to disintegrate. Somehow it would lead to a new integration—construction through destruction.

I looked up Baudelaire's house in the guidebook. "Perhaps the greatest French poet of the 19th century. He died of syphilis. He had been addicted to opium and hashish and died in his mother's arms, penniless, unrecognized, and largely unpublished."

I poured myself a glass of wine washing down the baguette with the tasty Bordeaux. I felt a moment of deep peace, a sense of integration. No irate little shopkeeper. No frantic Rennero. No anxious and desperate Koles. No cell phone ringing, cigarette smoke spiraling, car racing. No fiancée perturbed by my sudden dissent from the beaten path. No external chaos. Just the internal to deal with…

The moment was interrupted by a motorcycle loudly passing by on the left. The bike began hissing and moaning as the driver downshifted, grinding its gears until a loud gunshot-like sound exploded out of the muffler. The driver then glided about fifty feet ahead and came to a stop near a bench overlooking the Seine. He stood up and then stepped down harshly on the kickstand. The rusting black bike seemed like a WWII relic. The kickstand resisted. He jumped up into the air, caught the one-inch extrusion of the kickstand on the way down, and it released to the pavement. Then he pulled back on the bike, jerking it up a few inches and letting the kickstand do its job. Motorcycle man got off the bike, patted the torn leather seat like it was a horse and made his way to the bench. He had a black leather satchel hanging off his side, the strap slung across his body. He reached into his bag and pulled out a manuscript. Of course. I peered over my right shoulder to my backpack. I opened it and saw the giant stack of pages appeasing the paranoia.

Motorcycle man seemed too perfectly bedraggled with his worn and frayed jacket, disheveled hair, and mostly black clothing. He seemed to be playing the role of down-and-out artist as if he'd just stepped off the stage of La Boheme. I wondered if the manuscript was a great and authentic piece of literature, Bishop-style literature that would inspire a new movement, a new generation lost. Or if it were just the words of a fraud. He pulled a pen from his shirt pocket and began flipping through the manuscript. He often wrote or crossed something out. He pushed the pen aggressively against the page as if smearing ink rather than creating or changing language. Jackson Pollock editing. His free hand spent most of the time rubbing his head, even pulling on his hair as if he were physically going to pull the idea out of his skull. Sometimes there was a pause to stare out at the Seine, but then it was back to attacking the page with ink. Turning pages back and forth. Pen making contact. An array of editorial motion across the page. Must have been cross-outs, arrows, new words squeezed in between others. Pages turning. Hair pulling. Facial contractions and contortions. The massive collisions of revision.

For a moment I thought I might be witnessing the process of a great artist swirling in the internal heat of creation. Van Gogh in the solar flames of Arles. Lowry coming undone under a Mexican volcano. A benzedrine-fueled Kerouac in a squalid bowery flophouse, fingers furiously dancing along the typewriter keys, the legendary teletype scroll unraveling by the yard. Billie Holiday hitting the depths of a note in the smoky, late night darkness of a Manhattan jazz club. This man at this moment along the Seine in 21st century Paris. The great French novel coming into being before my eyes. He might be here for Baudelaire's presence looming over him as a towering muse, soaking in the post-mortem energy. Perhaps, he had fallen under the spell of *Les Fleurs du mal* and was now writing his own modern flowers. Or it was simply my imagination that had been unshackled and unbound. Perhaps, he knew nothing about Baudelaire or that the house was even here. Maybe it was genre fiction, a mystery or romance novel.

I heard footsteps behind me. A woman walked by my left shoulder, grazing my sleeve. When she passed the motorcycle, she reached out and slid her palm slowly across the leather seat. Then she turned her hand over so the backside ran back, ever so slowly, almost caressing the leather seat of the great French bohemian. She approached the artist-hero from behind the bench. He never looked at her. His pen was still jumping and darting all over the pages. She stopped behind him and began massaging his head. She ran her fingers across his scalp several times before stopping to press down on his skull. Pushing into his head, holding, and then releasing. Simultaneously, she was whispering something in his ear. He snapped something back, loudly. I couldn't make out the language. She put both her hands on his forehead, slid them down to his temples and rubbed in circular motion around them. He continued his editorial madness until the woman, his muse perhaps, pulled his head back and kissed him. She kissed him softly at first. He tried to pull his head free, but she pressed her mouth into his with tenacity. Her tongue launched into his mouth. His pen hand fell off the manuscript, his fingers unfurled slowly and the pen fell to the ground. He let the manuscript rest in his lap, and put his arms around the muse. They kissed and fondled and passionately devoured each other. I shook my head, merrily surprised. Now this was the Paris I imagined. When they finally stopped, the king of bohemia picked up his pen and returned to work with the same feral focus as before. Perhaps, even more. His muse had invigorated him into another terrain of consciousness and creationism. Meanwhile, she went back to massaging his head and neck, relaxing and fomenting his soul all at once. I poured another glass of wine. The bottle was empty and I had finished the bread. This was live theatre on an island in the Seine. I couldn't have asked for more.

Bohemian king finally closed the manuscript. He put the pen in a pocket of his leather satchel and held the manuscript, staring at it, squeezing it. As he stood up, I decided to walk by them to catch a glimpse of the manuscript. I wanted to see the title. I gulped down the remaining wine, left my cement wall perch and walked toward them. He now had the manuscript at his side. He walked towards the motorcycle. The woman got on first, sitting as far back on the seat as possible. As I was passing by, he was opening his satchel to place the manuscript in its resting place. I slowed to a near stop to see the title. I noticed him looking at me as my eyes glanced quickly at the cover. I saw titular words in big, bold, black ink. *Les Forces de l'Histoire*. He tucked the manuscript in his satchel and sped off on his antiquated motorcycle. Bishop's "historicity" was flowing along the Seine in the pen of this classic societal discontent. He was no scion of Baudelaire, though. From his title, he had to be the offspring of the Communards. The Paris Commune still breathing one hundred and thirty years later. Bishop was

215

wrong. They didn't all go to Vermont...Transatlantic coincidences and confluence gaining force as moments helplessly slip into history. This man should be seated at Chez Lucienne, manuscript on the bar, Bishop's red pen in motion, Marxian banter bouncing back and forth, alcohol in flow, a member of the vanguard...

I left Île Saint-Louis by crossing la Pont du Sully (recognizing the last name) and returning to the Parisian mainland of the left bank, the Cambridge side of Paris. No longer on the islands between the banks. They seemed like aberrant places, replete with libidinous Americans describing the daze of swollen balls and French intelligentsia attempting to articulate the flow of the future. The prurient and the Marxist.

I descended the stairs where an aging metal placard read, Quai de la Tournelle. I loved being down in the quays. Kind of an urban womb. The cement banks of the Seine were so different from the Charles's green grass banks. The Seine flowed right through the heart of Paris, the Parisian aorta, while the Charles drifted along the edge of Boston. I associated the Charles more with Cambridge than Boston. Certainly, the Charles couldn't compete with the Seine. It didn't have the grandeur, history, or the poetic divinity. Of course, that had much to do with the cities. Paris overwhelmed Boston. As a result, the Seine reduced the Charles to a lesser status. However, the Charles did have its own small, cozy nobility. It was no pauper. It was a prince or duke to the Seine's kingship.

I sat down with my back resting on the soot-darkened, gray brick wall that led from the quay back up to the streets of Paris. I found it interesting how Paris was built above the Seine as if it were the River Styx. It seemed fitting considering Parisians felt that their city was the center of the universe. Both Galileo and the Catholic Church had been wrong. The earth was not the center, nor was the sun. It was Paris. Everything in the system of Western civilization revolved around Paris. I found Parisians' notorious arrogance somewhat admirable. Paris was the capital among capitals. What other city could boast being a real life model of communism? Parisians took it out of the textbook and the classroom and actually attempted to apply it. So much had happened here—A victim of Nazism, the birthplace of Surrealism and countless other art movements, Cinéma-vérité, Existentialism and Sartre, the '68ers. Paris has been an experiment in possibilities both imagined and real unlike any other city in the world.

I looked out at the Seine. It was dark brown and murky, but the majesty didn't come from its color. I could see Notre Dame on the other side. People crossing the many black metal railed bridges across the river. Another tour boat slowly went across. I could hear a voice broadcasting from the boat while a few seagulls hovered above it. The sun was breaking through the all-day cloud cover, shining on the Seine's bleak brown surface.

The old man would have liked the title of the Motorcycle man's manuscript. If he'd been here with me and seen that, it would have sparked a conversation of history, though his vast knowledge was less about the forces of history and more a static awareness. What happened when and where. The ramifications. He knew dates and historical events with unflinching accuracy. Doubtlessly, he would have brought up 1066. "Always remember 1066, The Battle of Hastings. It changed the Western world forever." Of course, invariably we would go back to the river game. We'd usually warm up with the U.S. and then move international.

"New Orleans?"
"Mississippi."
"Kansas City?"
"Missouri."
"Boise?"
"Snake River."
"Portland?"
"Columbia."
"Lisbon?"
"Tagus."
"Marseilles?"
"Rhone."
"Hamburg?"
"Elbe."
"London?"
"Thames."
"Kinshasa?"
"The Congo."

And on and on it would go. I never remember stumping him.

I looked at my watch. I'd lost track of time. Two hours passed by so quickly just like it had during the peaceful walks along the Charles with the old man. I was late to meet Koles at Yvette's house, but I didn't feel like going at this moment. I figured they could use more time. They'd probably made up and were screwing passionately right now. I didn't want to interrupt that. God knows what had happened to Rennero. Now, with some separation from the Italian madman, I started to miss his perverse energy. The truly deranged were strangely intoxicating.

They attracted the normal into their perverse carnival. The normal needed the spectacle and vice versa.

It was time to break from the river. I felt something crystallizing within, but it was vague, shadowy. Anxiety, perhaps. A panic attack forming from disconnected roots. I couldn't decipher the flow of the internal. Time would take care of it. Something told me that being away from the river would allow it to manifest. Being by the river would stunt it, keep it asunder and impalpable. I looked in my guidebook and randomly opened the book to a page about Pére Lachaise:

"The greatest landmark of the 20th *arrondissement*. The resting place of Amedeo Modigliani, Jim Morrison, Edith Piaf, Marcel Proust, Colette, Oscar Wilde, Alice B. Toklas, and many more luminaries of the arts. Otherwise, the 20th *arrondissement* is a dreary melting pot prone to upheaval."

I had my next destination. It would be a long walk. I would have to traverse the fourth and eleventh *arrondissements* to reach Pére Lachaise. I decided to take the subway. I always liked to travel by subway in a new city. Best way to get a true taste for a city, feel its rhythm and pulse. One could role play as local denizen.

I got on the Metro at Boulevard Saint-Michel and exited at Gare du Nord. The station was sprawling and enormous, but for all its space, it was still bustling with crowded and crunched humanity like a giant elevator jammed tightly with faces pressed to its steel doors. I looked for a subway map on the wall while cutting an uneven swath through the French rush-hour crowd. The map was a labyrinth of colors and lines. Finally, I found the route to go from here to there. The route everyone has always been looking for. In order to transfer and get to Pére Lachaise, I had to descend five levels. Gare du Nord went into the depths of the earth unlike any place I'd ever seen. I'd never been five stories underground. It felt as if I had slid down an esophagus and landed in the bowels of the earth. It was dark, the air heavy and dank. The screeching roar of trains echoed throughout. Several graffiti-covered trains shot out of darkened portals, rusting wheels grinding to halt. Swallowed humanity moved about lost in newspapers or blankly staring after a day of cubicle anesthesia, Parisian style. Urban angst and anguish turned subterranean by nightmarish civil engineering. I started feeling discomposed and claustrophobic, wanting to ascend back to the streets of Paris immediately. Exhume myself from this tomb. People suddenly seemed to be moving at lightning speed. I was slowing down while most everything else seemed sped up. Society on amphetamines. It felt as if I were an extra in a Chaplin movie. I had to get out of there. People were bumping into me more often than seemed necessary. I closed my eyes and rubbed my face. An image of Koles flashed within my internal vision. An image of him rubbing his face as he had done so often at Chez Lucienne. Simultaneously I saw Bishop sitting at the bar with hundreds of his Amber specials lined up. He was drinking one after another. Koles's manuscript was the only thing on the bar besides the red wine glasses of Barbados rum. Koles let his hands drop from his face. He stared at his manuscript, almost catatonic, while Bishop kept drinking. The manuscript was piled high to the ceiling—hundreds of thousands of pages, millions of words. At the other end of the bar was Gilworthy, stroking his chin beard beneath a wry half-smile. He was watching the corner TV, which was showing the bar, live at that moment.

I heard another train emerge from blackness and screech loudly, coming to a slow halt. I heard the pneumatic hiss that preceded train doors opening. I opened my eyes. It was my train. I got on and found an opening in a corner. I looked at the map above a door. Five stops until the cemetery. For some ill-defined reason I wanted to cry. I held back what felt like an avalanche of tears mounting behind my eyes. I grabbed a hand rail and held on as the train began to move. I blinked rapidly many times trying to prevent making a fool of myself for the second time in Paris. I could see the headlines of *Le Parisien*—"American weeps like baby at Gare du Nord." Not the Warholian fifteen one would want. Desperately wanting to stay invisible from others helped me get composed. Necessity is the mother...

It seemed eternal, but the fifth stop came and I got off the train. Only one staircase and I saw an exit. I was back up and out from the infernal depths of Gare du Nord and back onto the open womb of Mother Earth.

I walked into the closest brasserie. I wanted something cold thinking it would clarify my senses. I waited at the counter. A few men were drinking cafés, smoking, and discussing something lazily. I ordered a beer. The men looked at me, said something in French, laughed, and then ignored me. The bartender brought me a bottle of Kronenburg, Carl Shapiro's beer of choice. I looked at the dirty glass he'd given me and then drank from the bottle, finishing quickly. Big giant swallows that felt so good. The men said something again and laughed. I turned to them, looked them in the eyes, and loudly said, *"Bon soir, monsieurs."* They seemed taken aback. I randomly chose one to ask where Pére Lachaise was. He pointed to the exit behind me, then to the right, repeating the same indecipherable French phrase several times, all the while still pointing to the right. I got the message. Who needs language? *"Merci, Monsieur."* He nodded and said, *"Du rien."* I left five Euros on the bar and headed out the door.

I took a right, walked a few blocks and there it was, Cimetiére du Pére Lachaise. I walked through two gray cement posts. Opened black, wrought iron gates were attached to the posts. I thought for a moment how I had just been in a man-made Hades in the depths of Paris. Now, I was walking into the earthly home of the dead. I sensed a cosmic puppeteer pulling the strings of a marionette.

Countless tombstones were before my eyes. The first one I recognized was Guillaume Apollinaire. I remember Bishop trumpeting Apollinaire several times at Chez Lucienne. "The first king of the avant-garde, Monsieur Apollinaire. Do not forget your lost king." Then he would wax drunkenly about Koles being on the verge of taking that baton from Apollinaire. I wondered how much Bishop's swollen orations had to do with my being here right now.

I looked at the great avant-garde poet's stone. As usual, I felt awkward at a cemetery, whether it was the tomb of Apollinaire or Arakalian. Death did not become me. After the eeriness of seeing my father's name, my name on a stone of death, I didn't know what to feel. Emotions seemed scattered, unruly. You stare at these engraved stones with a name and years of existence. Six feet below was the decomposed or decomposing corpse. There was no soul there. No spirit. Even if I believed in any form of religion, even if I didn't see religion as an absurdly wishful and dreamy form of hope, being at the cemetery served no purpose. The spirit was in heaven or hell for the believers. The cemetery contained nothing, but a monument. Yet, I felt compelled to be here. I wanted to walk and see the memorials of death.

I walked by many greats of the arts—Proust, Seurat, Edith Piaf, Balzac. I thought of *The Human Comedy*. There couldn't have been a better title of any novel. It was the title of every novel. There were very few people around, but I heard some sounds up ahead. I followed the noise after paying my respects to Moliére. Not surprisingly, it was at the grave of Jim Morrison. A few people were walking away from the famous tomb while a young man about college age sat cross-legged on the ground in front of Morrison's chipped and broken headstone. He was smoking a joint, had a fifth of Jack Daniels in his left hand, and a copy of the Morrison hagiography, *No One Here Gets Out Alive,* rested on his lap. His jeans were tattered youth. It was the perfect scene of poetic American youth on the run. He had a big backpack resting at his side. I clutched my backpack, feeling the shape of *Insomnia Journal* within, strangely needing the assurance of its existence.

He turned toward me as I approached.

"You want a drink for Jim?" he asked, serious in tone with no trace of sarcasm.

I smiled, "Sure."

He handed me his bottle of Jack. I took a sip and returned it.

"Thanks," I said.

He didn't say anything. I stood there looking at the stone. He kept puffing on the joint. I was surprised that he hadn't offered me a hit. I wondered how many youth like him had traveled to pay homage and see James Douglas Morrison since he died, July 3, 1971. Must have been thousands who made the pilgrimage, but I didn't think it was still common these days. This particular pilgrim just sat there, seemingly mesmerized by the stone, sipping on Jack and smoking his joint.

"Who you here to see?" he asked, without looking at me.

Good question. I wasn't sure what to say. I said the first person who came to mind.

"Oscar Wilde."

He nodded.

I was about to leave when he said, "Mr. Mojo might be risin'."

"Really?" I remembered the story of a friend of a college friend who had allegedly traveled to Africa looking for his idol, Jim Morrison. One of the Doors' songs contained a mysterious throw-in lyric about being in Africa. Some Morrisonologists believed he'd staged his own escape and never died. He just faded away to Africa to live in anonymity as a poet. I figured he would be referring to something in this vein, but I was off base.

"Yeah, the French want to get him out of here. Tired of Americans visiting, causing chaos. They want the remains moved to America."

"I'm paying my respects. No chaos here."

"Certainly not. Respectful respects. I think he ought to stay. He was really a poet more than a singer and this place is full of the great ghosts of poetry. I think he'd want to be here, not in America. Doesn't belong in America. That's why he left."

I nodded again. I didn't know what to say. I wasn't knowledgeable about The Doors beyond the myth of an African escape and a handful of songs.

"Thanks for the drink. Good luck."

"Good luck for what?" he asked, not looking at me.

"For whatever you are looking for." I said. He nodded ever so slightly. As I started to turn away, my eyes caught a glimpse of the Morrison biography resting in his hand. Everyone needs a bible.

Morrison's stone was tucked away, not easily accessible. After a few mistaken turns, I found my way back to the main road of the cemetery. I saw what looked like a guide to the cemetery. It had a listing of all the names of the famed deceased at Pére Lachaise. I found Oscar

Wilde's name and the number of his location. I made my way there if for no other reason than to turn my lie true.

Oscar Wilde had a brilliant headstone. It was a large white angel, positioned as if it were going to fly away. It was beautifully maintained, a clean and white stone. It was diametric to the decrepit and chipped Morrison headstone. I sat down opposite the angel to give my feet a rest. The fading warmth of Jack Daniels and a beer lingered in my blood. I took a deep breath. Exhaustion began to spread throughout my body. Adrenalin was gone and the reality of fatigue was freed. It had been lurking beneath the surges of adrenalin. Now it spread rapidly, saturating bones and muscles. I checked behind me. A mix of dirt and grass. I lay back using my backpack as a cushion for my head. I was ready for a rest. I didn't care that I would be late to meet Koles. I shut my eyes, but my breathing was very heavy. I began to sense the return of the anxiety that I felt in Gare du Nord. Fatigue and anxiety intermingled strangely. Opposites conjoining, conspiring. Teary sensations began to return as well. I thought I'd extinguished the urge before, but it was temporary repression. I couldn't shed the need to cry, but this wouldn't be an ordinary cry. I could feel that this would be an omnipotent weep. This would be years and years of tears. The dike was old, breaking down. The Berlin Wall crumbling all of a sudden. I had tyrannized my tears into hiding for too long. They burst through my futile defenses and started pouring down the sides of my face. I capitulated instantly. I let them flow, knowing I was as powerless as small prey locked into a tiger's jaws. The tears more than utilized their unrestricted freedom. Memories raced across my thoughts. Memories I hadn't thought of in ages. Related emotions I hadn't felt in ages. My face was soaked. I sat up, put my face in my hands and let the teary avalanche tumble into its necessary conclusion.

I didn't know how much time had passed when I heard a voice say, "You ok, man?" I realized I must have been sobbing loudly, making a spectacle of myself.

"Yes, I'm fine," I answered, wiping my face and eyes dry, attempting composure. I looked up. It was Morrison's descendent. "Thanks, yeah, I'm fine."

"You want another drink. Seems, you could use it."

I thought about it for a moment. "No, I'm good."

"A hit?" He reached out with the joint and lighter pressed between his thumb and index finger.

"No, no. All set. Thanks, though. Very kind of you."

He started walking away, but turned back and said, "Good luck."

"You too."

222

After he was out of sight, I put my head back down and closed my eyes. A few more tears leaked out and then I felt dry. I fell asleep instantly.

A nudge on my leg woke me up. It was dusk and night was quickly approaching. A Frenchman in a uniform was talking to me. Of course, I couldn't understand him, but I heard the word *fermé* many times. The word must have meant closed. I rubbed my eyes trying to expedite my mind out of the haze of repose. The man was patient, not angry. His uniform seemed to be that of a city worker or ground crew. It was a faded blue jump suit. A giant ring of keys hung from a leather tool belt around his waist. The tool belt was empty besides the keys on the right and a walkie-talkie hanging on the left side. He was pointing behind me. I turned my head following the direction of his index finger. I saw a gate, an exit. I looked at my watch. It was after eight. Obviously, he was trying to get me to leave. Can't sleep with the dead, I thought. They have to rest in peace. The great benefit of death. The living must pursue something.

I stood up. *"Oui, oui,"* I said. "I'm leaving." I was glad we couldn't communicate besides bare essentials. Language barriers cut out the bullshit.

He nodded and smiled. He was no angry store clerk, just a peaceful cemetery man. I stood up, putting my backpack over my shoulder.

"Au revoir," I said.

"Au revoir."

There was barely enough light to make my way out of Père Lachaise. The cemetery man followed about ten feet behind me. I exited necropolis through the same cement posts that I had entered. I saw the brasserie up ahead where I'd had a beer. As I headed to the Metro, I heard the sound of the black gate closing. I looked back and saw cemetery man with the ring of keys in his hand. He was locking up for the night. We waved goodbye to each other.

I got on the Metro and was on my way back to Gare du Nord, but everything felt differently on the return trip. I felt lighter. The great weep was monumental catharsis. Another form of the river game. Each individual tear must have contained an ocean of emotions and memories. I thought that I had let so much out while writing my surrealist dissertation during insomnia, but I had only let out words. Linguistic release. A thousand words couldn't rival the potency and honesty of a single tear. The purity of physiological release. Shaillie was partly right, after all. I had needed that cry for a long, long time. She thought it was six months coming. I thought it was more like twenty years in the making. No one could have thought Oscar Wilde would be involved. The importance of being earnest, indeed.

While Gare du Nord still felt like the bowels of Paris, it didn't have the haunting interred effect as before. It was more like a superficial scary movie with no visceral impact on the viewer. My plans were internally finalized during the trek to Yvette's apartment. She lived near the Jardins du Luxembourg, near arrondissement fourteen. I passed La Rotonde on the way and stopped in for a glass of wine in the café where the lost generation evolved their identity. I walked by the Les Deux Magots, where Sartre and De Beauviour romanced and sought philosophies true and eternal. I observed Parisians passing time with wine and chatter, still glad that I didn't understand a word. I people-watched peacefully, without depth. Just watched and listened, taking in the panorama of life without analysis or critique.

I arrived at Yvette's apartment on Rue Sommerand a little after nine, two hours late. A woman's voice came through the intercom in French, of course.

"*Bon soir*, Yvette. It's Van, Derek's friend."

"Hello, Van. Come on up." Yvette's English sounded impeccable and her accent was very sexy. I climbed three flights of stairs. The door was already open, but I knocked anyway. "Come in, Van," I heard from within the apartment. I walked in and Yvette stood up from the couch that she was sitting on. She was strikingly beautiful, a Eurasian fusion of blue eyes and ivory white skin with cascading black hair. Her beauty had an instantly arresting effect. I could see why Koles couldn't let go.

"Van, are you ok?" I heard her ask.

"Yes, sure," I said, gathering myself. "It's been a long day or two."

Her hand extended in order to shake mine. I obliged.

"Nice to meet you," she said.

"Likewise." I noticed her eyes looked a bit red, as if she hadn't slept well.

"You're quite late."

"Yeah, got the tourist itch. Got lost a bit. Kind of. Well, I'm here now. Where is Derek?"

"Would you like some coffee?"

"Sure. Yes, that would be nice, if it's no trouble."

"Not at all." Yvette went into the kitchen, which opened into the living room. The apartment was simple, almost Spartan. In one corner of the living room I saw two closed doors. The bathroom and a bedroom, I presumed. There was a balcony off the living room.

Yvette returned with a tray containing two espressos, two glasses of water and a plate of cookies.

"Let's sit on the balcony," she said, motioning with the tray.

We sat down and sipped our coffee. We made some small talk about my adventures in Paris. I told her about getting attacked in the store, observing the author of *The Forces of History*, a little panic attack in Gare du Nord, and hanging out at Pére Lachaise. I saw no need to share the Oscar Wilde moment, but it probably didn't matter. She didn't really seem to be listening. She was politely pretending to show interest, but I could tell she had something else on her mind.

"Where's Derek?" I asked again.

She hesitated, stirring her coffee slowly as I watched the spoon's many revolutions in the small cup. "He left," she finally said.

"Where to? Why?" I said, surprised.

"Well, it's a long story."

Clearly something had gone wrong. I didn't know this woman at all, so I didn't expect any details. I told her that if she felt like talking, I would be a good listener. When I said that, she smiled and asked if I were being sincere or polite. I reassured her it was sincerity. She seemed to relax at that moment.

"I don't even know you, but perhaps that's a good thing."

"Sure, like therapy," I said, sipping the espresso.

"Did you want sugar?"

"No, thanks. This is good."

"Well, Van, I don't know where to start. How about at the end?"

"You can start wherever you want."

"I don't know how much you know about Derek and me."

"Very little. Derek never said much. I just know he wanted to save the marriage. I know he loves you."

She paused, sipping her espresso. "Van, the end of the story is the end of Derek Koles and me. Clean and simple. Derek thought he could walk back into my life on his time." Her countenance abruptly became stern and severe. Perhaps, the beginning would have been a better place to start. Ease into things.

"He thought the past would just be forgotten and we could pick up the pieces. Such arrogance and hubris. I didn't need that from him. I told him it was over. Over meant forever. I never want to see him ever again. Isn't that clear enough, Van?" She was almost yelling.

I nodded. "Yes, very clear."

She took a deep breath and exhaled slowly. "Van, I'm sorry. I'm coming across as mad at you." She forced a smile into her expression. "I guess all men are indicted right now."

I laughed and she tried to.

"It's taken me so damn long to get over our relationship. I wouldn't let him manipulate me back in. You have no idea what I went through. No one ever knows anyone's relationship. We always assume we can judge other couples from a dinner or two. What a joke. Human nature I suppose."

"He must have been devastated. He was really hoping…"

She cut me off, "Derek Koles is devastated everyday of his life."

My eyes opened wide. "What do you mean?"

"Do you know your friend?"

"I thought I did, but maybe not. I mean, actually, I really don't know him that well to tell you the truth."

"How do you know him? How long may I ask?"

"I met him through some friends about a year ago, but mostly I know him through the bar I worked at. I was the bartender."

"Chez Lucienne?"

"Yes."

"You know Bishop?"

"Sure."

She shook her head. "So you know Derek on the basis of alcohol."

"I guess I don't know him too well."

"I better stop," Yvette said. "There's just so much, so many things have happened. I may never shut up if I start." She took a sip of her coffee.

I knew she wanted to talk and I wanted to listen. Though I'd just met Yvette, I had an immediate desire to help her feel better. She was very beautiful, but there was something else. Something very authentic about her. I felt as if I had known her before. She seemed like an old friend I hadn't seen in a long time. I felt something strangely familial in her presence.

"It's up to you, Yvette. Like I said, I'll listen, sincerely. Maybe it will help to get it out, to voice it."

She took a cookie and bit into it. It seemed as if she were still sorting things out in her head. She was dead on about how I truly didn't know Koles. Quiet, aloof all the time at the bar. Never said much. Played the role of detached writer, pained artist very well. During the trip I did learn that he was edgier than usual. The edge he had at Logan in front of the happy family. And his mood changed a lot when we were with Rennero and as we got closer to Paris.

"I haven't really told anyone the truth, Van."

She seemed so distraught. I could see it in her eyes. Things must have been really bad with Koles. What did he do to her?

"Did he ever tell you about his depression?"

"No."

"Did he ever tell you about the medication?"

"No."

"His mood changes? The hospitalizations? Suicide attempts?"

I didn't think I needed to answer at that point.

"How well do you know Derek Koles now? Van, he put me through hell. Depression is agony for the person who has it. I realize that all too well, but the spouse has it just as bad. Maybe worse. You know, people always ask me, why'd you guys get divorced. You two seemed like such a good couple. I hated when people said that. After all the failed relationships, we still think the appearance of a couple, its behavior over a couple of hours can determine its essence." She took a deep breath. "Do you know what you've started, Van? You're going to think I'm crazy sharing all this with you, but you must understand the timing."

"Feel free, Yvette. I will not judge you."

She looked me in the eye as if she were trying to gauge who this stranger was. Then she looked down at the street and began.

"When I'd tell people we got divorced because depression is a marriage killer, I got two reactions. A skeptical look and couched words that said, 'you didn't stand by your man. You didn't support him through his troubles. You jumped ship at the first sign of trouble.' Or, I'd get the 'didn't you see the signs before you got married?' I don't know which one makes me more frustrated. Yes, Derek was very sweet in the beginning. He held down the furies and demons for a while. Love is powerful, but it isn't all-powerful. That's your Hollywood myth and illusion of youth. He kept the depression in check for a while, but the monster returned over time."

"I'm so sorry, Yvette." I wasn't sure she heard me. She seemed to be in a trance, talking to herself.

"How could I stay? He would call me at work and tell me that I would find him dead when I returned. Do you know how many times I left work in panic thinking I'd find my husband had killed himself. When he wasn't threatening me with his life, he was blaming me for everything. He thought I was sleeping with every guy at work. Jealousy was out of control. I kept telling myself, this isn't Derek, this is depression. I tried to separate the two. That's what his therapist told me to do. It was the worst advice I ever received. It kept me in the nightmare even longer. I can't believe I listened to that. The depression is talking. No, Derek and the depression are the same. At what point is the person suffering from depression responsible for their actions?"

I didn't know what to say.

"A depressed person doesn't have the right to destroy those around him. I hate him, Van. I'm sorry to say that. I spent years giving him *carte blanche* because he was diagnosed with depression. Because he didn't have enough seratonin firing in his brain like me. Because he had some trauma in childhood. Because he was sick. His whole life his family handled him with kid gloves because people like Derek Koles manipulate and abuse their family. They can say the depression is responsible. It's not their fault. Well, I disagree. One day, I stopped. I'd had enough. He threatened me with his life and I told him, 'Derek, it's your life. Do whatever the hell you want.' I kicked him out and said go get some treatment. Balance yourself on your own. Then, I'll think about it. So what did he do? He started sleeping with my best friend."

I felt very bad for her. She'd been through hell. Koles had always talked about his writing getting in the way and that he didn't make enough money. He was completely detached from the reality of his relationship. A very disturbing denial.

"But that was actually the best thing that ever happened to me. I mean it was horrible at the time. I was losing a husband and then I lost a best friend, but his infidelity released me completely. I no longer had to feel guilty about not curing his depression. I think that's what drives those around the depressed. The need to cure because you feel responsible for it. But now I was leaving a cheater and that was manageable." Her voice had been very emotional, but now it was a little calmer.

"I'm glad you got out. He should never have come back."

"Yeah, it brought back some horrible memories, but I'll be fine. I'm a lot stronger now."

"Why did he come back? Why did he think you two had a chance?"

"In his own sick, perverse way he probably loves me. I've learned that there are all kinds of love. I just don't want his kind. I want healthy love. Functional love. I will accept nothing less. Being alone isn't bad at all compared to wrong love. I don't want to be afraid of everything I say or everything someone says to me. I definitely don't miss the eggshell life. I don't want to fix someone's childhood. It's impossible. I want real life back. Derek stole it from me and I let him for a while. But not anymore."

I couldn't believe that Koles had the delusional audacity to think he could get Yvette back.

228

"Van, if I were you, I'd stay away from him." I remembered Gilworthy saying the same thing.

"I'm not married to him."

She smiled. "I'm just saying don't get tangled up in his energy. He will lure you in and then drag you down his dark road. People like him prey on their closest relationships. You're just lucky you're not sleeping with him." She hesitated, then looked me in the eye. "You're not sleeping with him, are you?"

"No," I said, surprised at the question.

"Good. The ones who are sexually intimate get it the worst. It triggers the agony and the anger. The monster finds a target."

I looked away from Yvette's eyes briefly. I could see a man smoking a cigarette on an opposite balcony on the other side of Rue Sommerand.

"I think I've definitely said enough," I heard Yvette say. I turned to her. "Thank you, stranger. I really needed to get some of that out. All of this just happened and I had no idea it was coming."

"I understand."

She took a deep breath and exhaled slowly. We made eye contact and smiled at each other.

"Wow," she said.

"That's an understatement."

"Yes, it is."

She excused herself and went to the bathroom while I thought about all the things she had said.

When she returned, she looked a little more relaxed. Her eyes seemed to have a little more tranquility in them.

"And you, Van? Why are you here in Paris, may I ask?"

"You can ask anything you want."

"After I told you my life history, I guess it's ok to ask about you, right?"

"You only told me about your marital history, not your history."

"That's true, but enough about me. You never answered my question."

"It's not such an easy answer, but I think it's because I just needed to get some things out, too."

"Is it working?"

"Yes, I think so."

"I'm glad to hear that. So how long are you going to be in Paris?"

"For a while I suppose. I have a lot of reading to do."

"You came to Paris to read. Interesting." She smiled. "So no wife or girlfriend?"

I thought about telling her the whole Shaillie story, but caught myself, "A girlfriend until recently, but we broke up."

"I'm sorry to hear that."

"Yeah, me too. It just wasn't meant to be, but it took me a long time to realize that."

"One of these days we'll find the one that is."

"Until then I guess it's not so bad."

"No, it's not. Life offers more than true love."

"Definitely."

"So where are you staying?"

"I've got a hotel nearby, across from Jardins du Luxembourg," I lied.

"That's only a couple blocks from here."

"I'd better be going. You must be tired." I really didn't want to leave, but it seemed like the right thing to say.

"You can stay here if you want, Van. All I have is the couch in the living room, but it's not too bad."

"No, no. Thank you. That's really nice of you. I've got a place. Already paid for."

"Are you sure? It's no imposition."

I hesitated for a moment. Something told me to decline this beautiful and intelligent woman's invitation. Something directed me to spend the night on my own. She had just had an intense scene with her ex-husband and I had just runaway from a marriage. Even though I had the desire to get to know everything about her and share my story, tell her things that had been hidden within, I felt compelled by another direction. At least for now.

"Yvette, thank you. I really appreciate the offer. Maybe down the road because I think I'll be in Paris for a while."

"How long?"

"I really don't know, but longer than I thought."

"Anytime you need a place, Van, let me know. I just paint and study. I'm very boring."

"That sounds anything but boring to me. That's sounds like a good life."

"Of course, you came to Paris to read. How boring too."

I got my backpack on and walked towards the door. As I was leaving, the part of me that wanted to stay spoke.

"So, Yvette, maybe we could have some coffee together. I don't know anyone here and I'll need a break from reading."

"Sure, Van. I could always use a new friend, especially since you know more about me than most of my old friends."

I smiled. She wrote down her telephone number.

"Call or just stop in. I'm either here or at Sorbonne. You know where that is?"

"Yes, I do. I was already there today. Kind of."

She looked puzzled.

"I'll tell you over coffee."

"Good. So, I'll see you soon, then," Yvette said warmly.

"Yes, Yvette, see you soon."

She kissed me on both cheeks. I took a few steps down the stairs and then turned around. Yvette was still standing in the threshold.

"Yvette, would tomorrow be too soon for the coffee?"

She smiled and was silent for a few moments. Then she said, "Van, tomorrow would be perfect."

I arrived at the Jardins du Luxembourg. I knew exactly how to spend the time between now and seeing Yvette tomorrow. I wouldn't need a hotel or sleep. I'd slept enough, especially for a devoted insomniac. All I needed was a place to sit and some light. I found a bench with the best light and sat down. I unzipped my backpack and took out the entire tome of *Insomnia Journal*. I unwrapped it and held in my hands for a while and then placed it carefully on my lap. I randomly opened to a page and began reading...

I parked the car in front of our house. Unfastening the seatbelt, I noticed that the strap traversing my torso was frayed and cut as if someone had randomly run a razor blade across it...

ABOUT THE AUTHOR

Ken Janjigian is also the author of *Trapped Doors* (Pocol Press, 2005), a collection of novellas set in San Francisco. Mr. Janjigian was honored to be a guest speaker/reader at the *Jack Kerouac: Writers of the Next Generation* event in 2007. He lives in the Boston area with his wife and teaches English at Harvard University Extension and Northeastern University.

www.ingramcontent.com/pod-product-compliance
Lightning Source LLC
Chambersburg PA
CBHW051640260626
47170CB00004B/1255